Valentine

a D.V. Hent novel

Naughty Ink Press

Valentine

Naughty Ink Press

P.O. Box 1958

Sugar Land, TX

77487-1958

www.naughtyinkpress.com

ISBN 978-0-9842508-1-3

Acknowledgments

First and foremost, I would again like to bow my head and give My Lord and Savior honor for the multitude of blessing he has given me. Without His grace and mercy I am doomed and without His love I am lost. Please forgive me for the things I do and continue to lead me down the path of righteousness so that one day I may walk with you.

Secondly, a huge thank you goes out to my parents. I know it's hard having a son who writes such great novels...about sexual topics, but knowing that you're still in my corner means everything to me.

To my partner, who constantly challenges me and forces me to put out the best possible product, you are the absolute gem of *Naughty Ink Press*. I may be the flagship, but without you, I'd still be rusting in the dock. People often say things they don't mean, I only say the things I do: I love you to death.

To my friends who read *If You Don't Tell*, and also those who motivated me, helped me, and also harassed me about this book; you're enthusiasm warms my soul. You think it's great that you know a writer, but I think it's better knowing I have you to support me. From Mickie, who helped with the risqué, to Aneesha who helped with the story's direction, I appreciate it all. Even my editor, Pat, who charged me out the ying-yang, but helped me to see what I could not, I say thanks.

And lastly, to everyone else who bought the first book to just support me, as I move upwards, you'll always be there with me. This ride isn't an elevator, it's a starship and I'll bring as many of you with me as I possibly can on this journey. Love ya.

~DV

Chapter 1: *Introductions*

New York City

"Damn, baby, you keep fuckin' me like this, you might just see a grown-ass man cry."

She slowly licked the underside of my shaft, kissed me at the very tip of my manhood, and put just enough tongue on it to make me shiver like a wet damn dog.

"So, you'd cry for me, Antoine? I didn't think men like you cried for much."

She was right. Even though I'd only spent three days with this woman, I couldn't stop myself from acting like a goddamn fool whenever she was around me. *What the fuck is wrong with you, man? Show her why they call you the 'Rock Hound'.*

I'd come too far and I wasn't about to become a bitch now, not when I was so close. I was Antoine 'Rock Hound' Davis and it was time that she knew this, too.

"Perhaps *cry* is too strong a word. See, you got me wearing this damn blindfold and I'm not really feeling it right now because I can't see shit. But I do know that if my dick is anywhere near your mouth, you can't take what I say seriously."

She wrapped her hands around my dick like a singer with a microphone, and softly whispered into it, her warm breath making me shiver again.

"You mean like this?"

I cringed but there wasn't a damn thing I could do about it, she had me trapped. "Stop doing that shit! If you're just going to tease me, then you got to go."

"What are you willing to do for *me*?" she asked, before licking the tip a second time.

"What the hell do you mean, what else am I willing to do?"

I pulled against my arm and leg restraints. I was securely tied to both ends of the bed, helpless and vulnerable. "You think I would let some *other* chick do this shit?"

She laughed and I loved it when she did. "I think I've made you wait long enough. It's time for Daddy to cum," she whispered.

She made her way up to me and softly slid her clit across the tip of my nose before asking, "Can you smell it, baby?"

"I can smell it."

"Does it smell good to you?"

I loved the way both she and her pussy smelled. I didn't care if other men had been here before me; all that mattered was that she was with me now. "I wanna taste it. Can I taste it, Ma?"

"I want you to taste it, Daddy."

I could feel her heat above my face, calling me. I wanted nothing more than to grab her and press her against my face, but with the handcuffs still restraining me, it was a losing battle. I cursed her several times for doing this to me, but as soon as she pressed her clit against my lips, I ate greedily, lapping at her like a starving man.

She softly rocked her hips, sliding across my face; my tongue followed her every motion. Several times I pushed my tongue inside of her, but as I felt her clit growing against my tongue, I began to suck on it.

"Don't do that," she begged. "Not yet." But as she clamped her legs against the side of my head, I knew I was near and needed to finish her off.

I continued to suck on her until she yelled out my name and spilled her essence over my lips and inside my mouth.

When her body relaxed and stopped trembling, she stood up and quietly stepped off my bed.

"I know you not gone leave me hangin' like this, right?" I heard her moving around, but when she didn't answer, I tugged at the restraints again. "*Right?*" I yelled angrily.

"Don't get so mad, baby. I just had to get something." She straddled my thighs and I became a little more agitated when I felt her slide the condom on.

"What the fuck is this?"

"You know what? I don't have time for this shit. I'm gone." She climbed down again and walked away from the bed. I could hear her footsteps heading toward the door.

Still chained to the bed, I wasn't about to let her leave so somebody else could catch me like this. "Whoa, you need to just chill the fuck out. I just thought that since this was the third date and all—that we could get past this goddamn jacket thing."

"You know I can't do that."

Even though I couldn't see her, she sounded upset.

"Look, I said if anything like that ever happened that I'd take care of you, didn't I? Hell, I told you I'd take care of you after the first night, so why you trippin'? I got you, Ma. Whatever you want, I got you. Don't take that lightly."

I could hear walking back toward the bed where my erection was still waiting for her.

"The condom stays on."

"All right, but after this is all done, I really wanna talk to you."

Before I had a chance to say anything else, she grabbed hold of me and slid me inside of her. I gasped, trying to prepare myself for how good she felt, but she'd moved too quickly for me to prepare. As she rode me, her body grinding against me, her warmth permeating the condom, I tried desperately to stave off my orgasm—but I couldn't. We were only thirty seconds in and I could feel my body giving way. I hated how she did this to me, but I loved the way she did it.

I didn't know whether she saw my toes curling or because I allowed an extra 'fuck' to escape my mouth, but she quickly switched from grinding to riding. With our flesh slapping against each another, I felt more like I was in Madison Square receiving applause than in my bedroom getting my brains screwed out.

"Talk to me, Ma. Tell me you love this dick."

She dug her nails into my chest before reaching up and grabbing my throat. With one hand on my chest and the other firmly clutching the front of my neck, she began to squeeze.

"What—the—fuck—are you—doing?" I asked, barely able to get it out past her choking fingers.

"I'm almost there, baby. You got me there."

With her so close, I didn't want to say anything, but even in complete darkness, I was beginning to black out. "Get it—Ma. *Please*...fuckin' get it," I yelped, hoping that she got hers before I passed out.

"I love your dick, Daddy. I love it. You love this pussy, right?" she whispered, her smoky voice exactly what I needed to push me over the edge.

"Fuck you," I wheezed, her hand still tightly squeezing my neck. "*Fuck you*!"

"I'm coming, baby," she said, and that was all it took.

We both came, but that didn't stop me from cursing this woman and what she'd done to me. As soon as I began to relax, she pulled me out of her, removed the condom, and sucked up any remaining seed. As several shockwaves rippled through my body, a single tear began to form in my eye and I thanked God that I still had on a blindfold. Crying like a bitch wouldn't do anything for my image.

When she finished, she left me alone in the room. My neck hurt like hell and I wanted to choke the hell out of her ass, but I simply yelled, "Yo' ass better be coming back!"

With her gone, I was forced to listen to the sounds of my own breathing and inhale the wonderful scent that she'd left on my nose and tongue.

Damn, she even tastes like strawberries. *How the hell did I get so damn lucky?*

That woman was so fucking perfect that it hurt not to be around her. I'd just met her three days ago, through Angelica's service, and already I was ready to give up all this shit for her. Hell, I was afraid she was white for the first couple of days, but she always swore she wasn't; told me she was Creole. Shit, it wouldn't have even mattered. Creole, Italian, Irish—I didn't give a shit if she was all three; the things we'd done in the last few days, coupled with how fine she was, made me want to put a ring on her finger. Not really a wedding ring, shit, I was still 'Rock Hound', but definitely a promise ring.

She was light as hell and I knew I was gonna catch hell from my momma, but I got butterflies in my stomach as I thought about them meeting her. Her hazel eyes were so clear that I felt like I could see her soul and because she was also built like a sister, I really didn't give a damn what my family was gonna say. Truthfully, she was everything that I'd ever wanted in a wife: smart, sexy, well toned, and the pussy was so damn good she could keep my wallet.

This wasn't the first time I'd used Angelica's Escorting service, but she had certainly gone out of her way this time. Shit, for the grand an hour I was paying, the service should've *always* been this good.

There were two problems I had, though. The first was that she didn't know what I did, almost no one did, and if she found out, how long would she stick around? I mean, I made good money, but then traffickers always do.

From drugs to stolen cars, I could have anything shipped anywhere in the world, but for the last few months, I'd been trafficking kids. Goddamn *kids* from other countries were being shipped in to me and suddenly, I found myself up to my ass in Slovaks and Eastern Europeans. It made me sick to my stomach, but I just needed this last deal to pay out and I'd be set for life. I'd just have to eat another bottle of antacids for the next few days.

That brought me to my second problem: my *wife*. She didn't know what I did either, but I suspected she didn't care. We weren't together out of love, at least not anymore; we were together because we had to be. She was a well-known marriage guru and when we were married, I was legit. Now that I'm not as legal as I used to be, a divorce would be very bad for her lucrative business and even worse for me.

Shit, if it wasn't for her terrible business sense, buying all this shit that we don't need, flying all around the damn country trying to promote her fuckin' book, I wouldn't have even had to get on the hustle.

I had to take a deep breath to keep myself from thinking about how pissed she made me. I exhaled and once my wife was out of my head, I smiled.

That was the past and this fine strawberry tasting woman that just screwed my brains out was certainly my future.

"I'm back."

The sound of her sexy Southern drawl brought me out of my daydream and back to the present.

"What took you so long and when can I get these damn chains off? My shit is starting to hurt. It's not fun anymore." I tried to keep the bitchy whine out of my voice.

"I still have a surprise for you," she crooned.

"And what kind of surprise is it? You came, I came—you wouldn't happen to have a friend with you, would you? Because I think I can squeeze out one more if you brought a friend."

"I had to make a call, and it doesn't seem as if my friend will be coming."

"That sounds fucked up, but I still need to be untied. This shit is really starting to hurt my rotator cuff."

"You never answered my question," she asked as she stroked my flaccid dick and ran something extremely cold down the center of my chest.

She brought ice. This bitch is freak-y! I think I'm in love!

"And what question is that?"

"What are you willing to do for me?"

I pulled hard against my restraints, hoping that she would let me go. This was getting tiresome. "I answered that already, but if you want to know more, then fine. Look, I'm really digging you, Val."

"I'm digging you too, Antoine, but I need to know something. Would you *die* for me?" When she said the word die, she ran a fingernail down my chest, making me shiver.

"Die for you? Hell naw! I mean, I don't even know the real you. What's your *real* name? I know it can't be Valentine, right? That's just your trickin' name, right? I mean who the fuck names their kid after a holiday?" When she didn't answer, I stopped joking. She was obviously serious and wanted an answer, so I took in a deep breath and continued. "I mean look...I see a future for us. I know you don't wanna be an escort for the rest of your life and I wanna be able to take care of you. That's real shit."

Suddenly there was only silence in the room and her hands were still. "That's so sad to hear."

"What do you mean? Why is it sad to hear? It's still a future, right?" And that's when I began to smell something strange.

"You cookin'?"

"No," she replied. "Well, not really."

"Because I smell something funny? Do you smell smoke?"

"You know something? I do. See, baby, I had this gun in my hand and I was just going to shoot you; you know, make it quick, but I can't do that anymore. After the phone call I just made, my benefactor decided that you should suffer just a little bit more."

Benefactor? *Suffer*? What the hell was going on? If this was another game, like tying my ass up, I wasn't down with it. "What the fuck did you do?" I yelled, struggling to break free of the bonds she'd placed me in, but they wouldn't let up. "Val, let me go. This shit ain't funny."

"To answer your question, yes, my name is Valentine and the sad thing is that this is goodbye, Antoine. I'll always remember—your *tongue*."

She gently placed tape over my mouth as I flailed around my bed, trying to break free.

"It's time for me to go, but I just wanted you to know that your house is on fire. Maybe we can hook up next lifetime—if there is such a thing as reincarnation, but in this one, you shouldn't have crossed someone you know. Didn't you know selling kids was a *no-no*? Had I known about what you were really into, I would've poured gasoline on you myself, but I guess this will have to do."

I heard her heels clicking against the bedroom's wooden floor as she walked away from me, and then suddenly she stopped.

"Just so you know, you weren't that great of a fuck, *Rock Hound*. Maybe next time around, you'll get a bigger dick. And uh, your last ride was compliments of the soon to be widowed *Mrs. Davis*."

Fuck you! I wanted to scream out, but the tape was pressed so hard against my face that all she could hear was gurgling. I tried to push my tongue against the tape and scream for help, but it wasn't moving. I wriggled around my bed for what seemed like an eternity, but no matter how hard I fought, I knew this was about to be my tomb.

For the next few minutes, I panicked. I screamed, wrestled, cried, cursed, and fought against the handcuffs she'd put on my hands and feet—all the while feeling the steel dig deeper into my flesh. Even though I couldn't see the fire, I smelled the charred remains of my house and I could feel the heat from the flames moving closer to me. I fiercely pulled against my restraints one last time and I could hear the headboard cracking, but I was already too weak. I had inhaled too much smoke and the world was slowly darkening.

There wasn't a doubt in my mind now, I was going to die.

As I felt the unbearable heat from the flames closing in around me, the last thought going through my mind was a satisfying scene with me choking the life out of both my wife and that *fucking* Valentine.

Chapter 2: A Separate Life

Houston

Sassia

I turned the key in the lock and walked into my cool, quiet apartment. It felt good to finally be home. Even though I felt like a hot walking mess, instead of immediately taking a long, hot shower, I sat down on my plush leather sofa and turned the TV on to a random national news station.

After about fifteen minutes of political fluff and weather reporting, I finally saw it. A picture of the recently deceased Antoine Davis and the grieving Lynette Davis filled the screen. The reporter described Antoine's death as a ritual killing, most likely from the result of his past gang affiliations, but the tearful Mrs. Davis swore that that part of his life was behind him.

Damn, she is good. Damn if I wasn't better.

I smiled at the screen before standing up; pulling away the clothes I'd been wearing for the last two days and letting them fall to the floor. Ordinarily, I liked a clean apartment, but the payday for this job was the biggest I've ever had and I deserved a little time to celebrate.

As I walked toward the shower, my satellite phone, which I dubbed 'the hotline', began ringing.

"What the hell do you want now?" I mumbled. Because it was the hotline, I had to answer. I'd just gotten home, but there might be another job to do. I hoped it would be closer to home.

I picked up the phone and heard a series of beeps before I spoke. "What is it, CT?"

"One sec, okay—the line is secure. I just wanted to say that you did a good job, Val. You have them looking everywhere but where they're supposed to. How about I come over and we celebrate?"

"How's about you kiss my ass."

"I can do that, too."

I'd known CT since I'd gotten into the business—barely a year ago. I'd never actually met him, we'd met through a mutual acquaintance, but he was kind of like my agent. He'd get the CFT's, or contracts for termination, and he'd get them to me. In the year we'd known each other, I didn't have many notches under my belt, but I was still good at what I did. And getting better.

CT always swore I didn't get many contracts because of all the other professional killers he had under his umbrella. He always tried to make it seem like there were dozens under him, which I doubted, but I didn't care as long as I got a job every so often. Because he was always trying to get in my pants, I figured he'd still push the best scores in my direction, like the Davis job. It was almost too easy for the thirty-five thousand I stood to make.

"I'll tell you what. Give me your real name and I may let you have a taste."

"My real name is CT."

"No it's not, liar! I gave you that nickname! How can I ever be with someone who can't tell the truth?" I whined. One thing I did know about him was that he was a terrible liar. I'd given him the name CT because of all his off the wall conspiracy theories. Before that, he was just 'Dispatch'.

"Shit, you know I can't give that information out, so I don't know why you ask. It's called covering your ass. Your name ain't Valentine so I don't know why it's so important that you know mine."

"Because I like to know the names of the men I fuck."

"Is that what you told Antoine before you baked his ass? I don't get you. You'll screw a bad guy like Antoine Davis, a goddamn modern day slave trader, but not me?" He asked like a man who'd been snubbed before.

"What makes you think you're any less of a bad man than him? You arrange deaths. Doesn't that make you bad, too?"

"So what you're saying is, I have a chance?" He lowered his voice an octave, trying to be sexy.

I answered back just as seductively. "If you do get that chance, don't be mad if I have to kill you afterward."

"I'd risk it."

"You could try. Speaking of trying," I quickly changed the subject, "have you found the man I asked you to find?"

"Not yet, but I'll let you know when I do. He can't hide forever, especially not from me. Anyway, you know you owe me for this. I'll take my payment in the form of a massage...a *personal* hand massage."

"Good night, CT."

He laughed. "The second half of the payment is in your account. Have a good night...Valentine."

I hung up the hotline and stepped into the shower. Before I even turned on the faucet, I could hear the screams of pleasure emanating from the next apartment. With such thin walls, I listened to my next-door neighbors, Charlie and her fiancé Steve, screaming like banshees.

Hmmm, now that's some of what I really needed.

And I might just get it, but after two days on the bus traveling from New York City back to Houston, I needed this hot shower more than I needed a good lay—but not by much. Even though I hated how slow the bus lines were, for me, it was a matter of anonymity. Airports have too many cameras, too much security, and the last thing any professional killer needs is more exposure. With a baseball cap and a made up ID provided by CT, I bought bus tickets to eight different cities before I finally boarded the one to Houston.

As the water poured down over me, I teased my clit with my fingers while I thought about the last thing Antoine had said to me. I wondered if he had really wanted to take care of me or if was he just another Omar.

Omar.

Remembering him made my skin crawl, but it didn't matter now, he was dead. Both of them were and the world was better off for it. Because of what I'd been through, taking out people who deserved it seemed like justice, but it was a little harder with Antoine's last confession.

"Let me take care of you."

I shook it off and lathered my body, letting the hot water caress me. I'd heard that line many times before and I'd probably hear it a million times more. He loved what I gave him, they all did, and I'd be lying if I said I didn't enjoy any good fuck. Besides, letting him live would be breaking the first rule.

As I continued listening to my neighbors, I smirked. The way Steve was crying out her name I guessed that Charlie knew what a good lay could do, too. I was certainly going to have to make another trip next door sooner rather than later.

I stepped out of the shower feeling like a new woman, the smells of sex, smoke, and death down the drain. After flexing several times and admiring myself in the mirror, I stepped out of the bathroom to the sound of my personal phone's jazzy ringtone. Because it was almost midnight and I didn't have any friends besides the two screwing next door, I knew who it was.

"Hello?" I answered as innocently as I could.

"Sassia, don't give me that goddamn nice hello BS! Where the hell have you been? I've been calling your ass all week and you haven't been picking up. Most of your fan club is mad as hell that they have to go somewhere else. What excuse do you have now? Sick? Relative died? What? Tell me *something*!"

That was Lady Zara. She ran the most lucrative escort service on this side of the Mississippi. Because I was one of her best attractions, she'd always treated me like a beloved member of her family, but every now and then my other job would conflict with Lady Zara's. That's when I really became family—the type of family that catches the ass-whooping.

"Sorry, Lady Z, but I had some family business to take care of back home." That's all she was getting this time because I didn't feel like concocting another crazy ass story. She'd already heard so many.

"Look, Sassia, if you don't want to work here I have plenty of girls who would love to escort your clients."

"I'm sure they would too, but no one does it better than *me*, LZ. You know that as well as I do."

"Fine, but I'm not going through this shit again, you hear me? For the rest of this month, your commission is down to fifty percent and I don't wanna hear another word about it. Get your ass in early tomorrow. You have a lot of time to make up for!"

I knew she had to flex her muscles in front of the other girls because she didn't want to appear soft on me, but I wasn't about to lay down either. "Sixty percent."

"You're fired."

"Fine, dammit, fifty percent and I'll be in early tomorrow!" I had to start getting on her good side again. I didn't live extravagantly, but I needed my escort money for the cushy retirement I had planned. It was a good thing that I'd just finished that job for thirty-five grand.

I threw on some jogging shorts and a loose t-shirt, then sat down on my bed to read a few pages from *Sleeping with Strangers* before falling asleep on top of the covers.

My last thoughts before sleep took me were about the book's main character. That crazy Gideon, I need me a man like him. I cut off the light, closed my eyes and let my head rest on the pillows.

It was time to put Valentine back in her box; a few hours of sleep would help me do it. I was home now and here in Houston I was Sassia Santinos, *escort extraordinaire.*

"I will ask you again. Do you seek vengeance?"

"Who the hell are you? Are you the police? Get me the hell out of here, please!" I cried.

"The offer is only valid for five seconds. Do you seek vengeance for what was done to you?"

"Yes, dammit," I yelled desperately. "Get me the fuck outta here and I'll give you whatever you want!"

She stood up from the bed and began to walk away.

"You don't want vengeance, you want freedom. Sorry, Valentine, I don't do freedom, only vengeance."

"Don't leave me, dammit! If you don't let me go, they—they won't stop! They'll keep raping me until I'm dead! Please, help me god dammit!"

I screamed, choking so hard I woke myself up.

I jumped out of bed, knelt beside the mattress, and pulled the shiny black Beretta from under my pillow, wildly pointing it at the darkness. I didn't utter a word, just listened intently for creaking floorboards, whispering, or even an exhale. For several minutes I didn't move a muscle and aimed the gun at my bedroom doorway as my eyes adjusted. When I didn't hear anything, I turned on all the lights and walked around the apartment just to be sure.

I sighed and shook my head when I didn't find anything wrong; I peeked in all the places where I stashed weapons. Everything was as it should be, but that still didn't bring me any comfort.

"It was the damn dream again," I mumbled, returning to my bed. I didn't dare cut off a single light, though. If I hadn't been so agitated, I would've laughed. I mean, whoever heard of a professional killer who was afraid of the dark? But after what I'd gone through, it wasn't totally implausible.

I grew up in the heart of New Orleans' fourth ward. We had our gangs and rivalries against the other wards in the parish; murder was an almost daily occurrence and the city stayed dirty, but even still, there was no better place in the world. There was soul and passion in the fourth ward like no other place I'd ever been.

My mama was Creole, born and raised in the city. She always told me that she considered herself black, but her hair was as blond as any white lady I'd ever met. She'd always called me her little mixed blessing and according to her, everything good I got from her: my hazel eyes, light complexion—the beauty I'd traded on my whole life. For as long as I could remember, people tended to trust a pretty face like mine and I always banked on their naïveté.

She also said that the only good thing I got from my father, who was Guyanese, was my dark hair. He came by every so often to see me and give Mama a check, but as I grew older I stopped caring when he didn't show. Mama was different. Every day she would ramble on about how no good he was, until he died. He wasn't ever really around, so I didn't miss him much, but Mama cried for him every night.

My mama used to make a mean shrimp etoufee, but after my daddy died, she stopped cooking and grew a little colder and more distant each day. We didn't have many friends, so I just went to school and came home to her, but when she got sick, I didn't go to school at all anymore. The doctors said there wasn't anything medically wrong with her, but even I knew what a broken heart looked like. Daddy died when I was eleven, and Mama died shortly after I turned twelve. At that age I became a skinny orphan surrounded by the heartbeat of the French Quarter.

After her death, I became property of the state and I hated that. Everyone reminded me of how pretty I was, especially when I started filling out, but the only people that wanted me ended up being perverts. After the last man tried to touch me, I ran away for good. I lived in the streets and alleys for about a month, scraping together a living by helping an old lady sell fresh fruit and shrimp in the French Quarter. With the smell of shrimp always on her smock, she reminded me a lot of how my mama used to smell. I liked working with her, but one day she just stopped showing up and never came back. I was alone again, this time without anywhere to go and barely any change in my pocket. .

That's when I met Omar.

He was a light-skinned, round faced, overweight man who wasn't at all handsome—just another ordinary street hustler. I met him on a corner and was ready to wash his shiny dark blue Caprice Classic when he asked, "Hey, you wanna make some *real* money?"

I vehemently nodded and he opened the back door. "Get in, sugar."

His car was as nice inside as it was outside. The seats were covered with white fur and the whole dash board looked like it was made out of real wood. This man had money and he was asking me if I needed some? I grew suspicious. I was going to scratch his eyes out and run for my life if he wanted me to trick. I would never do that—not for anyone.

He saw the skeptical way I was looking at him and smiled. "It ain't what you think, kid. I'm not that kind of pervert. I need you to be a lookout for my...operation. You look like you need some food and I need some eyes on the street. Can you do that for me?"

He seemed like a nice guy, so I nodded again.

"What's your name?" When I didn't answer, he smiled again, this time showing all of his gold teeth. "Okay then, how old are you?"

"I'm twelve." I answered, barely moving my lips.

"How about I call you Twelve then?"

I shrugged. Didn't matter to me, just as long as he didn't try to touch me like those adoption perverts.

For almost six years, he called me Twelve. He asked me my name several times, but because my mama and I shared the same name, I never told him. I never wanted him to know her name because if he did, I might die of a broken heart like she did. During that time, I sold a few drugs and played lookout for Omar. He didn't pay me a lot, but he gave me enough to buy things I needed and he let me live with him in a rundown house in the middle of the fifth ward. After being in crappy foster homes and on the street, it seemed like a castle to me.

On my eighteenth birthday, everything changed between Omar and me. I'd cared about him for years, had come to depend on him for my very life, and even though I'd finally offered him my body out of gratitude, he'd never accepted. He always treated me with respect, which made me admire him even more. On my eighteenth birthday, I gave my virginity to Omar. It hurt like hell, he was a big man in every way, but I believed that I loved Omar more than I loved my own life. He knew that I would do anything for him, and I ended up doing everything for him, too. To make him happy, a little pain between my legs was nothing.

We had been together for almost a month and we'd just finished making love when he turned toward me and said, "Twelve, I gotta give you a different name. You can't be helping me run my shit with a name like that! Is there a name you want me to give you? Like maybe you can finally tell me the name you were born with?"

I was still sweating from the workout he'd given me and I rested my head on his hairy chest. Even though he was the only man I'd ever been with, I didn't care much for the sex. It was something I did to make him happy. I still loved him though, and if we were going to be together, then he should know. I smiled and told him.

"I don't really like that name for you. You're too good for such a plain name. How about I call you *Valentine*?"

"Why Valentine and not my *real* name?" I asked as I fondled him under the covers.

"Because yo' li'l pussy is so damn good that every time we get down, I wanna fall in love with the shit." I smiled at what sounded like a compliment, but he wasn't finished.

"Look...Valentine, I'm going to need you to do something for me."

"Anything, baby."

"I need you to help out the girls. They money ain't right and I might need you to drum in more business. The way I see it," he lifted one of my breasts to his lips and softly kissed the tip of my brown nipple, "you got this pretty-ass hair that's halfway down your back, these big-ass titties, and that nice ass you totin'. Oh yeah, you gone make Omar a lot of grip."

I felt uneasy about what I knew he was asking, but we loved each other. He wouldn't ask unless he really needed it, right? Besides, I'd lived with him for all these years and it was time for me to start pulling my weight.

"Whatever you need."

"Good, good." He picked up the phone off the nightstand and called his friend Cali. "Yo, Cal, get Honey, Temp, and Dixie asses up here. They're gonna show my new girl Valentine the ropes." After he hung up, he kissed me. "But them bitches ain't got nothin' on you. You will always be number one. You never forget that."

It took a while, but the name grew on me and for two years I honed my craft, which made Omar a very rich man. I made a living turning both men and women out. Local judges, politicians, and men who invested in Omar's illegal businesses were typically treated to a night with Val. After it was all done, I had the kind of power over them that even Omar couldn't dream of. I usually didn't think much of the power I yielded, but it seemed to make the sex more enjoyable when I did. Omar would always tell me that I had the GP, the *Golden Pussy* he called it. Because of the prestige I had, there would be regular feuds between me, Honey Sugarpot, Temptress Jones, and Dixie Wrecked. Due to my fair complexion and hazel eyes, they always called me the "white bitch' and in turn I'd call them what they were: old pussy.

Life was great for me until I met Boogie, then it got complicated. I didn't want to betray Omar, but love is a fickle thing and after the first time Boogie and I got together, I was whipped. In Omar's world, it didn't matter how many men I fucked for money, but for me to love another man meant I was betraying him. I'd signed my own death warrant by loving Charles 'Boogie' Jackson.

Chapter 3: Memories

New Orleans
5 Years Ago

Sassia

I didn't know how many times he'd struck me, but I could feel my bottom lip swelling more after each time Omar attacked. I didn't mind being punched in the belly, that would heal, but Omar was slowly working his way up my face.

For the first time in my life, I was truly afraid of the light-skinned, balding man that had practically raised me. As he twirled his gun around his finger like someone from a thirties gangster movie, he just shook his head at me as I lay sprawled on the bed we'd shared for so many years. He'd walked in with the cadre of men, loyal to him, all of them looking at me as if they knew. None of them spoke, but I knew what he wanted.

So this is how I'm going to die.

"Where the hell is my *shit*, Valentine?"

I wanted to cry, to show how remorseful I was for sneaking around behind his back, but my body wouldn't let me. I tried desperately to squeeze a tear down a cheek, but I couldn't. Perhaps it was biological, but I knew better. I'd seen too much while living with Omar to allow myself to be weak in front of anyone—even in the face of the man himself.

"I don't know who's got your money—or your blow, Omar. You know I ain't got the shit, so why are you fucking with me?" I pleaded, but I knew that once Omar had found me that he knew. Even though I could only speak out of one side of my swollen mouth, I still lied. Boogie was my boyfriend, swore he'd die for me, and even gotten *'Val'* tattooed inside a huge red heart on his neck. After what we'd shared, I wasn't about to sell him out—not even for Omar. Deep inside, I knew he was going to be waiting outside and he'd rescue me from my impending death.

"That's funny, Val, because I can't find Boogie anywhere. From what I hear, he ran off with my cash, my weed, and my blow... and that's after fucking my woman. But you wanna hear some *real* funny shit? I had heard you and Boogie were fucking weeks ago, but since you were always by my side, I didn't see how that shit was happening. I even heard someone was planning this little robbery, too. A little bug put something in my ear, but I knew my girl, Val, she wasn't about to betray me! Me! The man who gave her a fuckin' life—money—prestige—everything her ass didn't have when I got her off the streets!"

"Omar, listen, baby, I..." I tried to lie again, but Omar wasn't listening to anything I wanted to say.

He slapped me, this time his hand landing flat against my cheek, the stinging almost unbearable.

"Shut the fuck up, Val! I suspected you were fucking Boogie, but I didn't think you were stupid enough to fuck him and steal from me!" He laughed and the other men around him all cracked smiles. "It looks like you're the fucking scapegoat," he continued, "and he left you to take the blame." He laughed again as he looked at me with the same contempt I'd seen him look at others before me. Betrayal wasn't a new thing to Omar, but for the first time I had a firsthand account of what the others must have gone through before their end.

"Omar—baby...let me tell you what happened..."

"Fine, I'll let you explain. Get yo' ass in the car." He grabbed me by the hair and led me toward his new black Escalade with everyone following. As soon as he threw me in the back seat, he jumped in with me and snarled. "Now, fuckin' talk."

With every word that came from my mouth, Omar beat me repeatedly. I tried covering up, but he was too big and strong.

I knew I was biding time, but something must have gone wrong if Omar was onto me this fast. Boogie and I were supposed to meet up and run away.

Where was he? Why hadn't he saved me yet?

As I cried, he shouted over my pleas of mercy. "I bet you didn't know anything about that, did you?" As quick as a rattlesnake, he flung his arm at me and tightly wrapped his chubby, yellow fingers around my throat. "You bitch. You crossed me? Me? The man who gave you the world and turned you into the best pussy on this side of the Mississippi—and you had the nerve to cross me! Cross me and then you got double-crossed. Ain't karma a mothafucka?" Omar laughed, but there was no humor in it.

Chopper, who was Omar's driver and dark-skinned counterpart, laughed too.

I curled up in the back seat of his Escalade while they laughed and prayed that Boogie would be wherever he was taking me. I didn't pray often—hell, I never prayed, but since I knew that I was living my last few moments on Earth, it seemed like a good idea. As I huddled against the dark tinted window, tears collecting on the underside of my chin, I thought about jumping out and running for my life. Straining to see out of the window, I faced two major obstacles. The first was that we were going sixty-five miles an hour. The second was that we were crossing the mighty Mississippi River on the Lake Pontchartrain Causeway. In either case, I was a dead woman if I tried to escape.

But if I jump out as soon as we get across the bridge...

It was the last thought I had before a painful flash of light led to complete darkness. That goddamn Omar had thought of *everything.*

I woke up on a bed with no sheets.

I shivered because the room was so cold, but when I tried to move, I couldn't. When I opened my eyes to see where I was, I suddenly felt the blindfold pressing into my face. After a few minutes of struggling to see and move, I rested my head on the bed and in the distance I heard men talking. I couldn't distinguish the voices, but when one of them laughed loudly enough, I knew Chopper was around. Because all that fat-ass did was laugh, I knew his big man laugh better than I knew the sound of my own voice. Since my legs were free, I tried to use them as leverage to pull my hands out of what felt like handcuffs, but all I succeeded in doing was alerting the men that I had awakened.

One of the men walked along the right side of the bed and spoke.

"So you're finally awake. I was gonna fuck you while you were unconscious, but I decided I wanted you up. I wanted you to know whose dick you were lovin'."

"*Fuck you!*" I screamed. I didn't know his voice, but he'd already promised to rape me and there wasn't a damn thing I could do about it.

For what seemed like forever, I endured the types of torture than no one should endure. I was beaten, punished, violated, and barely allowed enough water to live. They wouldn't let me up and so I was forced to piss in the bed, but that didn't stop them from raping me. Only when I shit on myself did they take notice. I was beaten until I passed out and when I finally awoke, the smell was gone and whoever had cleaned me had removed my underwear as well. I desperately wanted to kill them all, but without anything to sustain me, I was living on air and borrowed time.

One by one, they continued molesting me, and several times I simply dry heaved until I blacked out. When I couldn't do that anymore I just endured the torture. On the occasions where I was lucid, I screamed as loud as I could, hoping that someone would hear me and save me, but they laughed at my attempts. If I knew Omar, no one would find me, no one would save me—certainly not Boogie, who had deserted me—betrayed me.

For several days I was repeatedly violated by men I did and didn't know. On more than one occasion, I'd wished I was dead, but death ignored me, watching and forcing me to endure more. I could taste the dried blood on my lips and I also felt it drying on the inside of my thighs.

Whenever a man would walk into the room I clenched my eyes and begged him to kill me. I'd even laugh at random ones and tell them how small their dicks were, but I wasn't greeted by death, simply more beatings. I knew Omar and I knew that this ritual wouldn't stop until I was dead, and maybe not even then. He wanted me dead all right, he just wanted to make me an example.

I was barely alive, clinging to life, when the angel of mercy finally came. I was asleep on the bed when I was awakened by a woman's voice.

"Are you with these men?"

I had lost my voice, mostly due to all the screaming and choking I'd endured, and it hurt to talk, but I managed to whisper, "No."

"Then, I offer you a chance for vengeance, do you accept?"

She spoke with an accent that I'd never heard before. After not having anything of substance to eat for the last few days, I thought I was dreaming, but when I realized how weak I was, I knew I was wide awake.

"Oh, thank God you found me! They were gonna kill me." When she didn't loosen the handcuffs, I spoke again. "Are you gonna get me outta here? If anyone comes in, they'll kill us both!"

"I will ask you again. Do you seek vengeance?" This time she seemed a lot less caring, almost angry.

"Who the hell *are* you? Are you the police? Get me the hell out of here, *please*!" I whispered while crying. Who the hell was she to keep me here after everything I'd been through? Couldn't she see what they had done to me?

"You have *five seconds*. Do you seek vengeance for what was done to you?"

"Yes, dammit," I screamed. "Get me the fuck outta here and I'll give you whatever you want!"

She stood up from the piss-stained bed and began to walk away.

"You don't want revenge, you want freedom. Sorry, I don't do freedom, only vengeance."

She wasn't an Angel of Mercy, she was the Angel of Vengeance; I was caught between newfound freedom and inevitable death.

"Don't leave me, dammit! If you don't let me go, they—they won't stop! They'll keep beating and raping me until I'm dead! Please, help me!" I screamed, my voice cracking and weak. Whether she let me go or not, I knew it was probably going to be the last time I cried anyway.

"Then do you want vengeance? Do you want them to pay for what they've done to you?" she shouted.

"Yes!" I tried to scream, but with my voice so hoarse, it was barely audible. "I want them all to pay, god dammit! I want them all dead! I want them all to die."

She walked over to the bed, unlocked the handcuffs, and pulled off my blindfold. It took a few minutes, but as my eyes adjusted, I saw a beautiful Middle Eastern woman standing over me. She couldn't have been much older than me; her eyes were the shape and color of almonds, her skin wasn't too much lighter than mine, and her hair was pulled back into a ponytail, but she still had the look of someone who was ready to kill me at a moment's notice. As she helped me sit up in the bed, I saw that in her right hand she carried a Glock.

My body hurt so badly that with every movement I wanted to cry out. For what seemed like an eternity, my arms had been tied above my head and my legs hurt from what those animals had done to me. I wanted to move—to stand, but I could barely blink without grimacing in pain.

"Get up, we must go."

"I can't move. It hurts so much."

She pointed the Glock at me. "You get up now or you die here."

I slowly stood up and pushed myself away from the bed, arms and legs tingling from lack of circulation. She threw a shirt and a pair of pants at me. With her Glock aimed squarely at my head, I dressed as fast as I could. As I did, the feeling in all of my extremities began to return and the realization of where I was began to settle in. I looked around and saw that Omar had hidden me inside one of his warehouses. I wasn't sure which one, but as we stepped out of the room, there were enough compartments to make a life-sized labyrinth. As I limped away from my torture chamber and down a narrow hallway filled with empty barrels, I noticed that no one was chasing us, shooting at us, or even talking, and quickly I learned why.

The mysterious lady brought me to a locked room and as I looked through the small window, I saw four men with bags over their heads, kneeling on the floor. As she pulled out a key and opened the door, several of the men stood up, but a quick kick to their midsection from her sent them all sprawling back to the concrete floor.

"What the fuck do you want?" The only man who was sitting in a chair yelled. Even through the fear, I knew that voice. It was Omar, his arms and legs were securely tied to a wooden chair.

When she didn't answer, one of the men on the floor began to cry.

"Shut the fuck up, 'Cal', and die like a goddamn *man*!" Omar shouted.

"I agree," said the mystery woman and shot Cal in the leg. Then she walked over to Omar and punched him in the face. "You don't talk."

With their hands bound behind their backs and cries of pain echoing through the room, I feared and loved the way this woman dominated these men, especially Omar.

I didn't know if any of these men had pissed in their pants, but the foul smell of urine permeated the room. Because of the last few days, I knew the scent well. I slowly looked around, hoping to find out where exactly the smell was coming from when I noticed several barrels of ether in the corner. This wasn't just any warehouse; it was where Omar processed his meth.

Suddenly this woman I'd begun to admire didn't seem so stable. Firing her gun with all this ether around wasn't the smartest thing to do. One bullet could turn the warehouse into a big Fourth of July fireworks display.

I turned and slowly began to work my way back toward the door when the mystery woman grabbed my elbow and led me to a chair a few feet away from the men. A million thoughts scattered through my mind, but the chattering ceased when she spoke.

"These are three of the men who treated you like the dog. When you were hungry, they laughed at you. When you were thirsty, they did not give you water, they spit in a cup and forced you to drink it. They raped you and when you asked for mercy, your pleas fell on deaf ears. There was no mercy for you. Not one of them stopped indulging their carnal efforts to violate you and they all left you to die a horrible death."

She walked over to me, reached inside of her green camouflage jacket, and pulled out a 9mm. After making sure the safety was off, she reached over my shoulder and placed it in my hand. "If you want, I will find the other guilty men, but these men have taken something that they did not deserve. Show them your wrath."

I dry heaved several more times, my throat raw and sore from screaming, as I recalled again what they had done to me. Regaining my composure, I looked at each hooded man. Now that I had the power, each one of them was a coward. Each one of them knew the name Omar had given to me, Valentine, but that hadn't stopped them from treating me the way they had. One pleaded for forgiveness, the others profusely apologizing and wanting to live, but this time *their* pleas fell on deaf ears. Without any remorse, I shot each one of my torturers in his groin. The noise inside the small room was deafening; I had forgotten momentarily about the chemicals. I just wanted to inflict pain—as much pain as I could, but not enough to kill them.

At least not yet.

As each man screamed, the feeling of the power that overwhelmed me was nearly orgasmic. For several brief moments, their cries faded and I stared at the gun—wondering why I'd never had the pleasure of firing one before.

When the men's shouting had returned, I realized what I'd done—then I quickly reminded myself of what they had done to me. They all deserved to die. I pointed the gun at one of the hoods and softly squeezed the trigger. It was so easy that I did it once more, putting several bullets in the second man's head.

I heard Cal whimpering and I knew it was him all along who said to me that, "Mercy was for the weak." I shot his kneecaps out and watched in joy as he fell to the ground and whimpered like the animal he was. As he gyrated against the floor, I walked over to him, stepped on each of his hands before I put a bullet in both of them.

The Angel of Vengeance smiled at how much satisfaction I received from torturing him and sat down atop one of the barrels of ether.

I allowed Cal to wriggle across the floor for a few more minutes, blood trails scraping across the concrete, before I gave him the mercy he never showed me. I pointed at his chest and emptied the clip.

Click. Click. Click.

I continued pulling the trigger even though not a single bullet fired. I looked over and saw Omar jump like a scared rabbit with each trigger pull, looking completely mortified with his blindfold on, now that Cal was reduced to a bloody mess.

He was the last one left. *Omar.* I began focusing my emptied gun on him, when my mystery Angel of Vengeance pulled a huge Desert Eagle out of the holster she had on her hip. She quickly pointed it at me even while she had her other gun focused on Omar's skull. "He is mine. You are free. Go. I will contact you when I have found the others."

I dropped my impotent gun on the ground and only then did I see the blood and pieces of skull and brain matter on my arms and shirt. I should've been repulsed, but I didn't care. Those men deserved exactly what they got.

"I just killed three men," I said dryly. "Where the hell am I supposed to go?"

"Val, is that you?" he asked, sounding as if he were about to cry. "I'm so sorry, Val, but you stole from me. If the shoe was on the other foot, you would've done the same damn thing! You know you would! Don't let her kill me, Val. Remember everything I did *for you*?"

I bent down and picked the gun up off the floor, even though the mysterious lady still had her gun on me. "Don't do it," she said solemnly. "He isn't worth the life of you."

I thought about what Omar said to me and what he meant. *Remember how I saved you! It's time to return the favor.*

I pressed the clip release and let the empty magazine fall into my hand. "Do you have anyone who might want to rape him first?"

She smiled. "Rule one—no attachments." Without even looking at Omar, she pointed the Desert Eagle at him and fired. Everything seemed to move in slow motion as I saw the bullets rip through Omar's skull and watched as he crumpled to the floor.

I felt nothing as I watched his blood join the pool of the others staining the concrete floor. I wasn't sure exactly how long I was staring at him, but the mysterious woman—my angel, took my 9mm and returned it to its hiding place. She holstered her guns inside her jacket and pulled out a lighter. I was still in a daze as she grabbed my arm and led me away from the massacre we'd just created.

"We need to go." As we left the room, she lit a fuse and I watched as a trail of fire ran toward the barrels of ether.

"Go where?" I asked as she pulled me away from the only life I'd ever known.

"You don't need to know until we get there, unless you want to stay here?"

With my heart beating so forcefully I could feel it banging against my chest, I still limped as fast as I could, trying to keep up with the woman who had just callously killed the mighty Omar. Thirty seconds later, we were outside the building. She took my hand and suddenly we were hurrying around corners and sprinting down streets. When we were finally done running, we were in front of a dilapidated yellow Chevy. She took all three guns and placed them inside a metal container in the trunk.

Just then an eruption lit up the dark New Orleans sky. Both of us instinctively ducked.

"We need to go!" I shouted hoarsely. I'd just killed three men and I didn't want to be caught here during the aftermath of an explosion at a meth factory. "And what the hell kind of getaway car is this? It's a piece of crap."

"This is rule number two. Never draw attention to yourself." She quickly ushered me in the passenger side of her car as she looked around.

Once she was in the driver's seat, I had more questions for her.

"How did you get all those men tied up like that by yourself?"

"Rule number three, Krav Maga is your best friend."

"What's Krav Maga? Is that a gun? What is it—a *drug* or something?"

She shook her head.

"Rule four—*shut up.*"

This woman had a rule for everything, but the only other time I've felt this kind of rush was right before I climaxed. I was hyper excited. She started the car and in a matter of minutes I was leaving the only city I'd ever known, my home. I wanted to miss NOLA, but as the adrenaline wore down, the pain between my thighs reminded me why I needed to leave. Still, I had one thing left to do. I had to find Boogie and make him pay for what he'd done to me. He was going to pay for leaving me to die.

Chapter 4: An Everyday Hero

Charlie

"Cadet *Charlie Briggs.*"

I couldn't help smiling as I walked across the stage after my name was called. Becoming a police officer wasn't nearly as hard as the Navy, but it wasn't easy either. Though I knew it was inevitable that I'd make it through, it was still an accomplishment I was damn proud of.

The graduation ceremony was held outside, near the actual station where I'd be working, and they couldn't have picked a better day for it. It was a little past ten and the sun had just made it over the horizon. With the sun came a modicum of warmth on what was an unseasonably cool spring day in Houston.

While I was sitting down, I had to blow on my hands to keep warm, but now that I was on the stage, nothing else seemed to matter. It could have snowed and I probably wouldn't have noticed. As I accepted my diploma, I waved to my father sitting in the front row, the both of us trying not to weep.

From the time I was born, everyone knew my father wanted a third son, which is why he named me Charlie, but I'd never seen him more proud of me. He wiped a single tear and when I looked away to keep myself from shedding a tear. I heard both my brothers screaming my name from somewhere else in the crowd.

My father wore his Philadelphia Fire Chief's uniform and my eldest brother had donned his own Philly PD uniform for this auspicious occasion. My younger brother, the only civilian in our family and the only one whose dark hair was long and untamed, wore a white shirt and tie—a complete contrast to the oil covered overalls I usually saw him in. To keep myself from crying, I kept my head up and looked directly at the Commissioner of the Houston Police Department. After shaking his hand, I received my diploma and shield and walked off the stage as a newly appointed civil servant.

When I sat back down and listened to the rest of the names called, I looked around at all the new graduates, street-worn officers, and gray-haired brass as I rubbed the fingerprints off my badge and thought about what this all meant. I was once again part of a family, something that seemed unachievable after my mother had passed.

Before the last names were called, I received a text from my fiancé that read: *Congrats.* I turned around and looked for him, but with all the faces directly behind me, it was impossible to spot him. I hoped he would stand up and wave, but that wasn't who Steven Briggs was. Truthfully, he was adamantly against me being a cop. With as much money as he made as a tax attorney, he wanted me home—probably barefoot and pregnant or at worst, back doing architectural engineering—but things had changed and that wasn't who I was anymore.

It was funny, though. Not laughable, but odd. As much as Steven didn't want me putting my life in harm's way, when I'd met him, I'd been considering leaving the military and he was a motivating factor for me to follow through. He was self-employed and his office, though not very big, sat between a bakery that made sexually themed cakes and a chiropractor who was older than my father. With me having just made the move to Houston and not having filed taxes since I graduated college, I needed his help. I thought he was sexy and cute and after our first meeting, he asked me for a date. I accepted. Within six months, he'd proposed to me. I said yes before he finished getting the words out.

Through the last three months, though, we've argued constantly. Since leaving the military, I still felt a strong sense of duty and when my mother died, I knew what I had to do. What Steven didn't understand—or didn't want to understand—was that I wasn't doing this solely for my father, but because even though I liked engineering, I wasn't happy. I was happiest when I was serving my country and protecting the people I loved. Now that I had a chance to do it on a local level and be home in time to do all the things we talked about, he still believed I was afraid to detach myself from my family. I loved Steven, but I couldn't be unhappy for him. I wouldn't be unhappy for him. I wasn't going to spend my life doing a job that was just okay.

That disagreement didn't stop us from making up last night, however. I trembled as I reminisced, remembering his tongue..

I looked at the phone for almost a full minute before snapping back to reality. I was about to return his text with an *'I love u'* of my own, but everyone around me stood up and began to cheer. I closed my phone and began screaming with the rest of my class.

Just after the commencement ended, Carolyn Shruggs, my only friend for the past eleven weeks, came over and gave me the most intense hug I'd ever received. Today her long dark hair was captured in a tight braid, but no matter the hairstyle, she reminded me of a young Nia Long, but every time I told her that, she'd shake her head.

"Don't compare me to her, girl! She is so much prettier than me!"

With her squeezing the life from my body, I hugged her back as fiercely as she had done to me and even though I had her by four inches and ten pounds, it still felt like she was trying to break my back.

Carolyn and I were the only female cadets in our class. Though she was the only one of a few black people that I actually knew, she was by far one of the most loyal and reliable people I'd ever met.

During academy training, I loved Carolyn like she was the sister I'd always wanted. Just like me, she'd gotten into civic duty despite outside influences, but even though she was so small that I thought holding a 9mm would break her wrists in half, she'd made her way through it. What she lacked in size, she made up for with sheer determination and guts. Nothing seemed to stop her.

"Charlie, you are white as a damn snowflake, but I'll tell you this. If we was in the hood, I wouldn't want anyone but you watching my back in a fight."

"I guess I'll take that as a compliment." I said, trying to laugh, but ultimately failing as I tried to breathe through her hug.

After letting go, she held my shoulders and looked up at me. "If you ever need anything, just let me know. You need a bed, I got you. Contacts? I got enough of those through family to start a hotline. You just be careful. I know you got an itchy trigger finger from being in Iraq, so just know that here, you have to ask questions before you shoot."

I burst out with laughter and after a few seconds, I forgot about everything that was bothering me. That's why I liked Carolyn. She had a way of instantly changing the way I thought, no matter how shitty I felt.

"Well, I gotta get home," she said after we finally stopped laughing. "I gotta let my hoodlum family know that I can legally put a foot in their asses if I need to."

Even though we were going to different precincts, mine in Katy, hers downtown, I knew I didn't want to lose touch with her. "You have my number. Call me anytime."

I looked around the bustling crowd to see if Sassia had come, but I didn't see her at all. When we got home, I was going to kill her. *She'd promised.*

My father ran up to me as quickly as he could and kissed me on the cheek. His dark hair was rapidly disappearing and slowly being replaced with the frost he'd always tried to avoid.

"I am so proud of my little girl. You've made an old man so very proud," he said and then kissed the other cheek as well. Even though he was a retired fire marshal, he was still regarded as a local hero for rescuing the mayor from his burning house about ten years back. Guess if you have to save somebody's ass, it might as well be an important government official. That or a baby will get you headlines any day.

Just when my younger brother was about to offer his congrats, we noticed Steven trying to get through the crowd. With his sandy blonde hair and six-foot frame, a complete contrast to everyone else in my family, he was hard to miss.

My older brother, Michael, nudged my shoulder and when I turned toward him, his piercing brown eyes focused on me. "You're not even married and you already took his last name? What, is D'Agostino not good enough for you anymore, Chuck? I mean sheesh, you're an Italian, and you couldn't find another Italian in the Navy? You shoulda stayed in Philly."

I threw a hard jab in his rib as Steve made his way in to our inner circle. He kissed me on the forehead before turning to my father and shaking his hand.

"It's nice to see you again, Mr. D'Agostino." He merely nodded at both my brothers, knowing how they felt about him, and returned his attention to me. "Well, *Mrs. Briggs,* that was an interesting change."

"It's less than a month until we're married. We've already filed for the marriage license, so I figured why not? I didn't want to go through the hassle of changing my name next month. You have no idea how much paperwork is involved with that."

He smiled at the same time my brothers simultaneously groaned.

"Did you get my text?" he asked, ignoring them.

"Just a few minutes ago, but as soon as I got it, everything got kind of crazy." I glanced around for a few seconds before asking. "Has Sassia talked to you? She said she was coming."

"She said she's feeling a little under the weather and she wasn't going to make it."

I shrugged it off, but I was still a little upset. We'd known each other a year, but it was only last week that I found out she was an escort. I felt like she was finally opening up to me, but with her not showing up, I guess I was wrong.

"I'm hungry!" My younger brother, Derek, shouted. "Let's go get us some grub!"

I looked at my fiancé. "Did you remember to bring me a change of clothes?"

"They're in the car."

I kissed my father and hugged my brothers as they left before us, promising them that I would be at the buffet. As we left the commencement, I thought about calling Sassia, but if she was sick, I'd have enough time to talk to her when I got home.

While Steve and I walked toward the car, I read the unhappy look on his face. "Say what you want to say, Steven. My father is heading to his car."

He frowned. "Why do you still want to do this? My mother wanted me to be a professional baseball player before she died, but you don't see me quitting to join a minor league team, Char."

"We've been through this a million times! Can't you just let it go? It's my life and my decision, and it's *final.*"

He pulled out his keys and remotely unlocked his silver Lexus. "So what happens if you don't come home one night? What the hell am I supposed to do then?"

"You're supposed to survive! I would if something happened to you! Why can't you just by happy for me? Is it so hard to support something I want to do?"

"Fine, your clothes are in the back."

Steven and I didn't utter a single word to each other as I changed into the red blouse, loose fitting denim pants, and white tennis shoes he'd brought for me. It felt funny wearing an ankle holster without my uniform, but I managed much to Steve's dismay. We rode in complete silence but when he pulled up to the ATM, I realized I didn't have my card.

"I'll have to go inside the bank," I said, hoping he'd say something in return. He didn't and soon pulled into an empty spot in front of the building. "I'll be back."

"I'm coming in, too."

I shrugged and we both entered the revolving door. Hoping to press my fiancé into speaking, I smiled and waved at the cute security guard. He was a young black guy, tall, bald with a well shaven goatee. He returned my smile and tipped his hat toward me, but instead of taking offense, Steve simply walked past me like we weren't together.

Steven Briggs was all about his male pride and when we were both in line for a teller I whispered, "So you're *that* mad?"

"Can we talk about this at home? I don't feel like getting into it right now."

I stood on the tips of my toes and kissed the back of his neck. Though the guard was nice to look at, I didn't want him leaving the bank thinking he had any competition.

He turned around and smiled and seemed about to say something when instead he forcefully pushed me down to the floor.

As I fell to my hands and knees wondering what the hell he was thinking, the familiar sounds of automatic gunfire rang out from behind us. Steve was almost on top of me when we hit the floor, his arms shielding my face. I looked behind me and watched as the handsome guard fell to the floor while holding his bloody left side. Two men with masks, armed with MP-5's, took the guard's revolver and came rushing toward us.

"Everybody in here needs to get the fuck down!" one of them shouted. "Don't do nothin' stupid and we'll be gone real soon!"

As one robber did a quick sweep of the building, the other one ran to the teller. "Just give us what's in front of you." Both had Mexican accents and as the gunman next to the teller leaned over, I saw a "Los Perdidos" tattoo on his forearm.

I immediately reached for the Beretta in my ankle holster but Steve grabbed my arm, stopping me. I could see the tears and fear in his eyes when he mouthed, "Don't do it."

"They already shot one person! I can't sit back and let him die!" I whispered. I looked over at the wounded guard; he was beginning to retch and grow pale. "He's *dying*, Steve!"

I ripped my hand from Steve's firm grip and when both bank robber's backs were turned, inched toward my gun. I had just made it when one of the robbers saw me moving.

"*What the fuck! She's gotta gun!*"

Everything seemed to slow down as I yelled, "Police!" I watched as the man with the teller began to turn toward me, but instead of aiming at him, I pulled my Beretta out and fired three shots at the man who'd yelled—all three shots hit him squarely in the chest.

I didn't have time to see him fall, but I heard the thud when he hit the floor. The other robber ran and fired shots randomly. When he saw me about to return fire, he picked a twenty year old, blonde woman up from the floor and used her as a body shield while still firing at me. I dove behind the deposit podium just as bullets tore through the wood, barely missing the top of my head and my left shoulder.

When the gunfire stopped, I peeked over the podium and saw the hostage at the entrance, but the robber was gone. People began running toward the man I'd shot, but when I saw he wasn't breathing, I kicked his gun away from him and ran over to the guard. He was barely breathing and I screamed for someone to call 9-1-1.

Reaching inside my pocket, I grabbed my phone, and quickly called dispatch. As I read off my newly assigned badge number, I screamed into the phone for them to get an ambulance to our location and rattled off as much of a description for the runaway robber as I could.

A man ran over and began to put pressure on the bullet wound. Dressed in a dark suit, he introduced himself as a physician and continued yelling at the guard to stay awake. Just then, time seemed to correct itself and everything began moving normally again. With the sound of an ambulance whining in the distance, I looked over at Steven. Still on the floor, he just shook his head and cried.

It was almost ten hours later, but I still felt the adrenaline coursing through my system. I'd been in hostile fire before, but I always had a unit to watch my back. Even though I was alone today, it felt damn good to be doing something positive. I had saved people and killed a bad guy. Score one for me.

"That's my girl! On her first day on the goddamn job, she thwarts a bank robbery, plugs a bad guy, and saves another cop's life!" Everyone was at my apartment and I'd never seen my father more proud of me than he was at that moment. He looked at my older brother. "What, you've been on the job six years and never even been in a firefight?"

My brother just shrugged before walking over and hugging me. "I'm just glad you're okay, Chuck. We didn't need to lose you too—so close to losing Mom and all."

I hugged my brother, but as I looked for Steven, my youngest brother pointed toward our bedroom.

"Look, guys, I think Steve and I need some time to talk and get through this."

"We understand," my father said jovially, and a few minutes later, everyone had left.

I plopped down on my couch and sighed. I was tired, drained, and stressed all at the same time. Since the shooting,

I'd had to give statements to not only HPD but to my superiors in Katy, listen to so much praise that my ears hurt, intentionally avoid nosy reporters, and deal with my jackass fiancé—who was ignoring me.

With our bedroom door closed, I thought about going in, but I didn't want another fight. Not right now. He hadn't said a single word to me since the bank robbery and the last thing I needed was an argument. I tried watching TV, hoping it would make me drowsy, but I was too wired to sleep. Wearing only Steve's basketball shorts and a sleeveless t-shirt, I grabbed my keys and walked out to my car.

As I revved my Charger several times, I was hoping that Steve would look out the window and wave for me to come back in, but the light remained off. I wanted to cry, but instead I pulled out of my parking spot, left the safety of my gated community, and headed north.

I was speeding on Barker-Cypress, running every yellow light and several red ones too before I finally slowed down. I was almost at Highway 290 before I pulled into a gas station. I parked in one of the open spots and pressed on the pedal so the engine roar would drown out my thoughts, but it didn't.

Why does he have to be like this? Why couldn't he understand that I was a soldier first? Why the hell was he the one crying when I was the one in the gunfight...? None of it made much sense to me. We had a serious case of role reversals going on. I felt sometimes like I was engaged to marry a pussy.

Before I could even finish the last question, I already knew the answer. I didn't want to see him hurt either, but that didn't give him the right to control my future.

For ten minutes, I just sat in the car as it idled. I didn't know what I was going to do about Steve, but this stress had to go and there was only one person I knew who could help.

Fifteen minutes later, I was banging on her door.

"Sassia! Open up!" I continued pounding against her door until she finally opened it. She looked angry as hell but I didn't pay her any attention as I walked past her into her cold, lifeless apartment.

I liked Sassia, but her apartment was the haven of sterility. She made stainless steel seem warm and cozy. Everything had a place, nothing was ever dirty, and the walls had no artwork, paintings, or pictures to break up the expanses of boring eggshell white. Other than her couch, her bedroom set was the only furniture she had. Her place needed a woman's touch, and on more than one occasion I'd chastised her for her lack of decorum.

"When are you going to add some color to these walls?" I asked.

"Never. I like the calmness that sterility brings." She quickly changed the subject. "Why are you here so late? Some of us *do* have to go to work in the morning."

"Where were you today? Steve said you were sick."

"Yeah, I was lying. Being around a bunch of trigger happy newbie cops isn't my idea of a good time."

I sat on her leather couch and threw my head back onto one of the pillows. "Where's the weed?"

"Why, officer, don't you need a search warrant?"

"C'mon, Sassy, cut the shit. It's been a long fucking day and I just want to smoke it away." After closing the door, she sat next to me and quickly reached inside of my shirt. "What the hell are you doing?"

She pulled her hand out after already having groped my breasts. "Just making sure you're not wearing a wire."

"How the hell am I supposed to have on a wire wearing this?" I asked pointing to my short shorts and sleeveless t-shirt. Her hand began to reach for my thigh when I grabbed it.

"I have to be sure."

"I'm still the same old Chuck, Sassy. You know that."

"That's true, but today, Charlie got herself a badge. People who get badges always try to make themselves look good in the first few days."

I guess she hadn't been watching the news.

"Look, I don't have a wire on and I'll prove it to you." I cleared my throat and began talking to my crotch. "I have been smoking weed with Sassia for about eight months now and I have occasionally brought weed to her apartment for us to smoke. I have both facilitated and participated in a felony and if I have a wire in my cooch, you guys can arrest us now. This is the truth and I swear it." I lifted my head up and when I saw her smiling, I smiled too.

"That was convincing. Do you always share such secrets with your vagina?"

"I have others."

"I'm still listening," she said while walking toward her bedroom.

"When I'm baked enough, I'll let you know." I'd stopped smoking so that I could enter the academy, but her weed stash was always some of the best I'd ever smoked.

Other than Carolyn, Sassia was the only friend I had in Texas. She was always so much fun to be around, plus she was one of the most beautiful women I'd ever met. I always told her she could be an actress, but she'd shrug it off and tell me that maybe she'd try it next lifetime.

In the year that we'd known each other, we didn't share many secrets, but when she told me she was an escort, I'd never been more shocked. It was the first time she had truly opened up to me and I began to feel like she really liked me.

Unlike her, I liked to share. I told her about family life in Philly, with my father and two brothers. We talked about my college years, the military, and most recently, Steven. When my mother passed, I was surprised to see Sassia there at the services, but her support was exactly what I needed and I loved her for that. Even though I told her a great deal, I was never fully truthful with her. I never told her how attracted I was to her, but somehow that never stopped her from trying to get in my pants. Still, that part of my life was gone. Steven was the man I was going to marry and if I could do four years of the Navy without indulging...

Well, that's not entirely true, but I could certainly resist the charms of Sassia, although at times it wasn't easy.

When she came back with a gallon bag, I'd already forgotten what I was stressing about. For an hour, we laughed and smoked. At some point she fixed a plate of snacks, and we ate and laughed some more. I wasn't supposed to, but I told her everything that had happened in the bank. As I told the story, she was so fixated on me that I began to grow a little self-conscious.

"Why are you staring at me like that?" I asked while trying not to cough.

"I don't know. Bravery is sexy to me." She inched closer to my face until her lips were almost on top of mine. Then, she exhaled her smoke and I slowly inhaled it.

She looked into my eyes and though I tried to look away, it was too late. Leaning over, she pressed her lips softly against mine, barely touching me. Whether I was high or mad, nothing seemed to matter, the rest of the world faded away, as I parted my lips to taste her tongue.

I loved the way our tongues wrestled, hers alternately soft and hard, sending bolts of electricity down my spine each time they touched. She quickly straddled me, reaching her hands under my shirt. I moaned loudly as her fingers softly traced the outlines of my breasts as we continued kissing.

It wasn't long before she pulled off my shirt and began to drag her tongue across my nipples. With each passing second, each one grew more erect as she took turns sucking on the tips.

"Oh God, Steven..." Even though Sassia hadn't stopped, I opened my eyes and realized where I was—what I was doing. I was betraying my oath to Steven. I reluctantly rolled Sassia to the side and pulled my shirt back over my head.

Without another word, I left a confused looking Sassia in her apartment and returned to the cold comfortless safety of the couch in my own.

Chapter 5: Satisfaction

Sassia

Damn.

I was horny and I was *so* close to finally getting her.

For the entire time we'd known each other, I'd wanted to sleep with Charlie, and why wouldn't I? She was extremely intelligent, ex-military, and about to be married. In other words, I liked that she was a challenge. Not only that, but she was beautiful—the spitting image of a young Alyssa Milano: beautiful brown hair down to her shoulders, perfectly round firm breasts, dark piercing eyes, and her lips were so pretty that I just wanted to suck on them—and I had. Plus, being in the military taught her how to take care of her body.

Even when she was an engineer who'd just left the Navy, I wanted to sleep with her. Yet at every attempt, she thwarted me. I didn't care for her reasoning, but I did know that she was the only person I'd ever met who'd rejected me—and I'd be damned if it didn't make me want her more. Now that she had a gun, a badge, and had actually shot someone—I wanted her so badly that I was still throbbing from our encounter last night.

Waking up this morning, I tried pressing my thighs together, pushing myself a little more during my workout, taking a cold shower and even jogged an extra mile, but nothing helped as thoughts from last night lingered. Re-entering my apartment, the faint smell of weed greeted me and the hotline began ringing.

Two jobs within a week? Usually the call came every few months, but if business was booming in this economy, who was I to judge?

I picked up the phone and let it beep a few times before I spoke. "What is it, CT?"

"Val, I've got a CFT for you. You'll be happy to hear that it pays well and it's in your neck of the woods."

Even though I'd planned on going into work today, a CFT would certainly help me think about something other than screwing Charlie. "Where is it?"

"It's in Phoenix."

I began pulling off my shirt, which I had just noticed was drenched in sweat. "Phoenix isn't that close. What's the background?"

"There's nothing major from what I see. Wife A wants Husband A to die in a deadly way...and, oh yeah, Husband A must not under any circumstances survive the, uh, encounter."

"You're a comic genius, CT. So what you're saying is that she wants him dead for no apparent reason other than that he should die."

"That's what it looks like."

I took off my jogging pants, rolled them into a ball, and threw them in the bathroom hamper. "I'll pass."

"What the fuck do you mean *'I'll pass'*? This is good money! Twenty-five thousand for a simple shoot-n-run, and you *pass*?"

"CT, I'm not about to kill someone who didn't do anything wrong." Including the three men in New Orleans, I'd dispatched a grand total of eight people. Each one of them deserved it and the world was a much better place because of it. I was a professional killer—that much I understood, but that didn't make me a sociopath. Or a fucking street hoodlum. I liked to think I had standards.

"You can't keep doing this shit, Val. People need for us to do a service and we do that service. You can't pick and choose who you want to off because of how well they treat people!"

"Well then, get someone else, CT! I mean, you brag about having dozens of us under your belt, so call one of them!" I'd never fought CT before, but I couldn't believe he was angry at me for turning down a job. It didn't feel right to me and a long time ago I learned that if a job wasn't right, don't do it.

Instinct trumps income. She had taught me that. It was one of the rules.

"It's about the principle, Val. Nice people die every day, but we don't get paid for them! You wonder why you get these shit jobs and not the six figure ones? *This* is the reason! You can't do this work and have a goddamn *conscience*! I swear to you that one day, it's gonna be the death of you."

"So that means you'll find someone else?" I asked pleasantly, trying to ease the tension, but he hung up on me without answering.

With CT mad and Charlie probably trying to avoid me, the only thing left for me to do today was to go to work. I was still on LZ's shit list, so her being mad made me a perfect three for three. Still, all that didn't matter. I didn't care who it was, but tonight, I was going to fuck someone's brains out...

...or not.

After putting on my biker suit and riding my baby, a month old, red with gold-trim Hayabusa, I pulled up to the front door of my job. From outside I could see everyone I knew huddled around the front desk.

I walked into the innocuous shop hidden amongst the larger outlet and retail stores not far from the Galleria. I strode under the flamboyant LZE sign, which was the only conspicuous part of the quaint shop, and walked into what could almost be mistaken as a legitimate massage parlor.

I looked over the shop and was instantly nostalgic. A couple of small palm trees rested in the corners nearest the door with a fabricated water fountain pouring into a small pool along the back wall. The bottom third of the walls were covered with an opal colored tile, while the top two-thirds were lined with Taijutsu symbols and bamboo-themed wallpaper. I even loved the aroma of scented candles, which permeated every inch of the room, a new touch since the last time I'd been here.

LZE was the abbreviation for Lady Zara's Escorts, the company that I had spent the last year working for. I greeted LJ's assistant, Anelle, a beautifully curvaceous dark-skinned sister who I'd grown to respect. Standing beside Anelle were Apple, DC, and Sabrina.

"So the rest of us ain't shit?" Apple said sarcastically while trying to suppress a smile. Her green eyes and caramel colored skin the obvious reason for her nickname.

I smiled. "Nope, but you will be once you get on my level."

"That's not what I hear," said DC. "Word around the counter is that you've been demoted. I hear that a certain Wilbur Tuttle is in your future."

They all erupted in laughter.

Wilbur Tuttle was an escort's worst nightmare: overweight, undersized, and always smelled like old salami. Not only that, he had the strangest fetishes—most of them concerning autoerotic asphyxiation. For a man with no neck, that was damn near deadly.

I left the front desk and marched through the door with the LZ in big, gold letters. "What the hell, LZ? How the fuck did I get stuck with '*Turtle*'?"

"You're still in my doghouse, Sassia. The other girls have taken your clients this week, and he's the only job available. If you want to get laid, paid and on my good side, you'll take care of Mr. *Tuttle*."

I had only been in her office a few minutes and I was already pissed. "If I take care of ...Tuttle, then you have to give me my whole commission."

She began to laugh and only then did she ever show her age. For a brief second, her crow's feet showed, but they disappeared as soon as she stopped laughing and merely smiled. Tall and slender, Lady Zara was a dark-skinned goddess and I often called her Iman's twin sister. Even now we all knew she could escort if she wanted, but she was all about her business and raking in the mountains of money I typically made her.

"You don't have a bargaining chip. Either you spend time with Mr. Wilbur Tuttle, or you don't get paid—at all."

"Fine," I conceded, "but if he asks me to watch him jack off while he hangs himself, I'm leaving."

She pinched her lips to keep from laughing. "I guess you're in luck tonight. He needs an escort to a masquerade ball."

I walked out of Lady Zara's office and past the ladies at the desk as they snickered. Phoenix was looking better by the minute.

I had just put on my helmet and mounted my motorcycle when I saw my manicurist, Thuy, following her boyfriend as he stormed out of the shop. They were about twenty feet in front of me and I watched as he headed toward his red Camaro, shouting something in Vietnamese. When she finally shouted something back, he turned and walked back toward her. Without warning, he grabbed her by her neck with both hands and forcefully rammed her against the glass window.

Even though he wasn't very tall, maybe a little taller than I was, he was thick and I could tell he was strong. I didn't see any gang affiliations tattooed on his arms and no one in the car, so I knew he was alone.

I jumped off my bike, hoping that someone would rescue her, but no one came.

Cowards.

They were all hiding inside of the shop and he continued to squeeze tighter against her neck. It pissed me off knowing that they were going to simply let him do it, but I'd learned a while back that no one ever wants to interfere unless someone's already dead. I thought about just shouting and making him stop, but I didn't want to. I wanted him to believe that no one cared.

It'll be easier if I just sneak up behind him.

As I began walking toward them, he threw her to the ground and headed back to his car. I quickly returned to my bike and tailed him as he pulled away. I didn't have to follow him very far; he pulled into a parking space in the same strip mall, not far from Thuy's shop.

I parked my bike in another empty space and as soon as he stepped out of the car, I accidentally bumped into him.

"Excuse me," I said, but he hadn't heard anything. Instead, he was paying attention to the breasts inside of my biker's jacket.

Gotcha, asshole.

"That's a nice jacket," he said. "I like a woman who knows how to wear leather *and* fills it out."

I smiled. "I like a man who knows how to admire a woman."

"Why don't I call you sometime? Then I can admire you for as long as you'd like."

I looked around the parking lot, which was full of people. "Why can't you just admire me now?" I pulled the zipper on my jacket down a little further, revealing the tops of my breasts, almost exposing my nipples.

He reached over to touch me but I knocked his hand inward. The surprised look on his face was short lived as I quickly punched him twice in the throat. As he fell to the ground, gasping for air and clutching his neck, I kicked him in the groin, putting everything I had into the toe of my boot.

As he held his neck with one hand and his nuts with the other, I went to work on his face. I punched him about a half dozen times. A couple walked by, looking in horror at what I was doing.

"This bastard tried to grope my breasts," I said to them. The man looked at my breasts and nodded while the woman, clearly understanding how I felt, placed her cell phone back in her purse and they walked away.

When I returned my attention to Thuy's boyfriend, he was curled into a ball. He wasn't such a big man now.

"If you ever put your hands on another woman again, I'll kill you," I said. When he didn't respond, I pulled out a small blade from the side of my boot and pressed it against his throat. He nodded and I knew we understood each other. "As soon as you finish shopping, I want you to go back and apologize to that woman and do something nice. Why don't you buy her some flowers and a new dress?"

He nodded and I turned to jump back onto my bike. Even when I pulled off, he was still lying in the parking lot, next to his car, clutching his throat.

God dammit, I loved rule three!

"Damn, that felt good." I was so invigorated by the beating I'd just given that I'd almost forgotten about what I had to do tonight. As the adrenaline rush followed, I thought about giving Mr. Tuttle a taste, but as I stopped to think, even I wasn't *that* horny.

I headed over to Thuy's shop where most of the women were still huddled and talking about what had just occurred. When Thuy saw me entering, she smiled. I wanted to return her smile, but I could still see the red marks his hands had left on her neck.

"It's good to see you," she chirped in her Vietnamese-American accent.

"Why do you let him do that to you, Thuy?"
"It was accident," she lied. She didn't know that I'd seen the whole thing. "He just always so stressed about work. He promises he won't ever do again."
You're damn right he won't. But I replied, "Maybe he won't."
I knew she didn't want to continue, so I changed the subject, letting her know I had a date tonight.
"So you want spa pedi and mani?"
"Like only you can do it."
For the next forty minutes, Thuy massaged my feet and worked on my pedicure, while two other ladies manicured my nails. When they were finished, they always made me smile. As always, I gave Thuy seventy-five even though the job was only priced on her board at thirty. She deserved it.
I left out of the shop just as Thuy's boyfriend was entering. He was still bruised from our encounter and recognizing who I was, he stumbled over the curb and fell to the ground. Making sure we understood each other one last time, I helped him pick up the flowers he'd bought for her.
After he disappeared into the shop, I knew it was time to get ready for my date.

"Introducing... Mr. Tuttle and guest."
The valet, who was wearing only boxers and was very well contoured, extended his hand and helped me out of the limo. As I ran my eyes across his frame, I smiled and licked my lips while 'Turtle' quickly scampered out the other side to greet me on the red carpet. Because of my broad smile and roaming eyes, 'Turtle' grabbed my hand and the smile on his fat face disappeared. Already six inches taller than he, with the additional four inches my heels provided, we strolled down the carpet looking like the odd couple.
Several of the men in suits who conversed along the walkway turned to stare at us, all of them gawking at my breasts through the sexy, low cut, white mini-dress I wore. I liked the fact that the butterfly mask concealed my identity, but LZ's diamonds around my neck and wrist highlighted the fact that most of them couldn't afford me. Just to put a cherry on top, I had clasped on a sparkling diamond anklet, leading their

eyes from my cleavage to my legs so that they could only dream about what lay between.

As I wrapped my arms inside 'Turtle's', at first glance it seemed like he was severely overdressed in his tuxedo. Other than the men in suits entering the mansion in front of us, every man wearing a mask outside of the house was parading flesh. With everyone's faces concealed, the only way I could distinguish who I'd been gawking at was by the color of their boxers, thongs, or in one case, a jock strap and cup. Still, no matter where I looked, it was all eye candy. This was certainly the kind of masquerade ball I could get into.

"Are you ready?" he asked nervously.

I looked at the balding white man and half-smiled, thankful for the fact that we both wore masks. "Sure," I said softly. "Let's do it."

While we walked along the carpet and into the mansion, his arm locked tightly against mine, I looked in awe at the host's spectacular home. The pillars flanking the front door were made of marble; the tiles decorating the foyer and inside the large oak doors were imported marble as well. I looked up and even though the room was barely lit, two large chandeliers made of crystal made the room glow. Hearing the sounds of splashing somewhere in front of me, I smiled as several women played in a water fountain where a replica of Michelangelo's David sprayed them with water from his elongated penis. No matter where I looked, from the exquisite paintings that decorated the cavernous room, to the eggshell colored, antique satin draperies—whoever owned this home loved beautiful things.

After a few steps inside the door, we were greeted by another mask, this one an extremely handsome, mahogany colored man.

"May I have your invitation, Mr. Tuttle?"

'Turtle' reached inside his jacket while I inhaled the scent of the delicious specimen before us. Smelling like musky baby oil, he was at least six and a half feet tall with abs that seem to ripple and bulge from his midsection—what I liked to call a 'party pack'. The kind of body that gets parties started and the kind I wouldn't mind putting my lips all over, either. I wanted so badly to touch them that I began to throb, but I closed my eyes and weakly exhaled. I opened my eyes and remembered that I wasn't here to indulge, I was here to escort.

As we walked away, I slowly bit down on one of my newly manicured nails. He saw me and smirked, both of us knowing that under different circumstances, I would've been his.

All around the mansion were some of the most impressive specimens of men I'd ever seen: white, black, Hispanic, and even a few Samoans, each walking with either a seductively dressed woman or a couple. Even the women were gorgeous, most of them practically nude and though they hung around much older men, everyone seemed to be having fun—well, everyone except me. I was stuck with the most unattractive man here and I'd wondered how he'd even gotten an invitation.

My questions were answered several minutes later when we went upstairs. There, 'Turtle' shook hands with a taller, older white man wearing a red satin robe. He was the only one I'd seen without a mask and someone I instantly recognized. With several beautiful women on each side of him, he remained seated on his sofa during the handshake, his eyes focused squarely on me.

"Tuttle, I almost didn't recognize you with that hideous mask. Glad to see you could make it, though."

"Of course I was going to be here, Derek. I always set up these little shindigs don't I? You bring the talent, I bring the money."

I finally understood that this masquerade party was a front. It was simply a high-class orgy. All the half-dressed people around the house were here to let businessmen indulge in their fantasies.

Mr. Tuttle continued talking to Derek Lander, a man who reportedly owned half the strip clubs and a few other sexually themed clubs in Houston, when suddenly Mr. Lander stood up. Even with my heels on, he was still taller than me, and as he approached us, I could see the lust in his eyes. Without warning, he took my hand and kissed it.

"Where did you find this *exquisite* piece?"

Tuttle smiled. "She's one of Zara's girls. Beautiful, isn't she?"

He turned towards Tuttle and seemed genuinely surprised. "I would've never let her go if I knew she had that kind of business sense. What's it been 10, 15 years?"

"Yes," Tuttle replied shyly, "she has a quaint little shop not far from the Galleria. Her collection is quite nice and Sassia here is certainly the crown jewel."

“So that heifer is still in business? I don't know why she keeps that shit-stand open, but..." He walked around me, smelling my neck, and when he returned to my eyes, I feigned a smirk. "I can certainly see why now. Shit, I remember not too long ago when *she* was the hottest piece of ass in Houston. Now look at her, recruiting the absolutely delicious ones.” Mr. Lander reached into his robe pocket and produced a card. “I know you're not making any *real* money there, so if Zara doesn’t treat you right, I most certainly will.”

I knew Derek Lander by reputation, and it wasn't a good one. No better than a pimp, he treated his girls like they were less than shit and regularly cheated them out of what they were owed. I smiled, but it wasn’t because I liked him. I smiled because it was my job.

“Sassia,” 'Turtle' began and then turned toward the other women, “and ladies, we have some business matters to take care of. All I ask is that you make our guests, the ones who are fully dressed, feel comfortable.”

“Ladies, that’s just a nice way of saying to refrain from fucking the help,” Mr. Lander blurted out. “There are a lot of rooms in this mansion and a lot of fantasies to be filled. Closed doors mean busy, open doors are invitations.”

As I walked downstairs, the idea of not fucking the help seemed almost like punishment. Several older men’s heads turned in my direction, but I didn’t feel like charity tonight. I needed someone with at least more stamina than they were willing to give.

After walking through several rooms, I sat down next to a man at the bar. He was handsome, caramel in complexion, and wore a grey Attolini suit. Drinking alone was never a good thing and even with his mask on I could see that he didn’t really want to be here.

“Is everything okay?” I asked.

“Look, I know why you’re here. Dre sent you, didn’t he? When you see him again, can you kindly tell him that I’m not into banging strippers?” he replied with an air of irritation. It was obvious that he'd been approached before, but he was too cute for me to leave him alone.

“I’m not a stripper.”

“Well then, I’m not into prostitutes, either.”

“You have me all wrong. I’m not into either one of those, um, professions. I’m here for what I thought was going to be a masquerade party.” I extended my hand. “I’m... ‘S’ and you are?”

“If your name is ‘S’, then my name is ‘Q’.” He turned to me, placed his glass of Patron on the bar, and sat back in his chair. After glancing at what I wore, he continued. “So, S, you’re telling me that a woman as beautiful as you just happened to be invited?”

“Well, I wasn’t exactly invited," I lied. "My friend, who’s an evil man-banging stripper and prostitute, invited me. Because my job takes me all around the country, I don’t have time for relationships. So, she thought that maybe a good fuck with a handsome, well off man would help me unwind.”

He laughed and I joined in. “Well then, I’m not your guy. The only reason I’m here is because I’m with a friend. This suit is his and I manage a delivery company. Sorry, but I think that kind of disqualifies me.”

I walked over to him and wrapped my arms around his back, allowing my hands to fall down to the bulge in his suit pants. He sharply inhaled and I softly brushed my lips against the back of his neck.

After feeling his erection rise to gigantic proportions, I knew he was definitely what I needed and I was certainly what he wanted. I kissed him from the bottom of his neck all the way up to the top of his nearly bald head.

“I won't tell, if *you* don't tell...”

We burst through the first available door and into a room staged like a dimly lit dungeon. I barely had time to notice, but candles were everywhere, and there wasn't a single bed in sight—only a table with stirrups and chains.

Panting heavily and kissing like two horny teenagers, he pulled down the sides of my mini dress, exposing my breasts as he pinned me against a wall with Velcro shackles.

After securing my hands above my head, he bit my neck, teasing it with his tongue as he fondled my nipples with his fingers.

"Yes," I whispered, as I felt his erection rubbing against me. As he began slowly moving downward, taking my mini dress down with him, he placed my breast into his mouth, circling my nipple with his tongue.

With my nipples now fully erect, he softly bit on them, sending bolts of lightning down my spine. "Harder...bite harder." Like the perfect student, he did exactly as I asked, biting the tips of my nipples with his front teeth and slowly pulling away from me. I could feel my toes curling in my high heels and my thighs were warm and wet with anticipation.

Reading my mind, Q went further down. Taking my dress completely off, he spread my legs in front of him and tasted me.

"Oh, my God," I whispered, trying to grab his head, but the Velcro was surprisingly strong. I pulled against the restraints, hoping that they would give so that I could touch my torturer, but they wouldn't. As he swirled his tongue around inside of me before bringing it out to tease my clit, I cried for mercy.

"Let me do you, baby," I pleaded.

"No," he said sternly. I could feel the echoes of his voice against my thighs.

The wetter I became, the deeper he pushed his tongue inside of me.

I needed this more than anything and the way my body responded to him, Q knew it, too. Moving my hips to the song his tongue played, I could feel the butterflies in my belly and I knew I was coming. "Damn," I said softly.

"You're going to come for me, aren't you?"

"Yes." He slapped my ass, but the stinging I felt made me gasp. "Then do it. Cum on my face," he demanded before he slapped my ass again, harder than before.

I loved it when a man talked shit. "If you want it, come and get it."

He placed my legs on his broad shoulders and with both hands palming my ass, he buried his face deeper inside my essence before rapidly flickering his tongue against my clit.

As my climax quickly approached, out of nowhere, Q began fiercely slapping my ass.

"Oh shit! Shit! Shit! Shit!" I came all over his face and chin, but with each slap, another wave of ecstasy followed.

"Fuck!"

Slap.

"Shit!"

Slap.

"Goddamn!"

Slap.

"I just had an orgasm!"

Slap.

“I can't—take this anymore!"

Slap.

He was relentless and I needed him to be. It had been so long since I'd had an orgasm this intense that I was beginning to think I'd never have one again, but here I was. I didn't know this man, but he had a tongue sent from heaven and the kinky streak that I needed tonight.

Wiping the cum from his chin, he stood up and released me from my bondage. My ass felt like it was on fire, but I didn't care. I immediately kissed him, tasting my essence on his lips as I licked his chin.

"My turn."

Already knowing how expensive his shirt was, I ripped it off him, tearing away several buttons, and callously threw it on the carpeted floor. Having a chance to finally look Q over, I was happy with what I saw. His bare, sculpted chest was much more beautiful than any delivery driver should ever have as I hungrily took his left nipple into my mouth.

Without warning, he began to reach for his mask, but I quickly stopped him before he could pull it away from his face.

“Keep it on. I like it like this.”

He smiled. “So you like your anonymity.”

"I do." I secured his hands in the Velcro bonds that he had placed mine in. "And they are here just in case you think about removing your mask again."

"Well then, S, the floor is yours...although I never suspected you of being shy."

I sucked on his bottom lip as I unlatched his pants. “Whoever said anything about being shy? I just like the mystique.” Continuing to unzip his pants, I slowly reached inside and pulled out his erection. When I had finally gotten all of it out, I caressed it and smiled.

Magnificent.

As it pulsated in my hand, I knew that I didn’t want anything that perfect to waste away between my fingers. I knelt down, slid him into my mouth and toward the back of my throat. A perfect fit.

I grabbed Q's hips and forced him deeper into my mouth. Pulling away, I began to suck on the tip as I ran my hand down his shaft. Without so much as a gasp, he looked at me curiously and seemingly mocked me through his mask.

"You don't like head?" I asked.

"I like pussy better."

"Me too."

"So why don't we get someone else?" he asked.

"I don't want to share."

"Seems selfish, especially on a night like tonight."

I unfastened his bonds, threw him on the only piece of furniture in the room—a bondage table, with stirrups. "So what."

He looked at the table, then at me. "Are these stirrups for me or you?"

This time I mocked him. "I never figured you for the *shy* type."

He smiled and sat on the table, placing his feet in the stirrups. After some minor adjustments, I was able to get the stirrups to lie flat and grabbed a condom out the bowl next to us. After putting the condom on, I mounted the table and slid my warmth down onto him.

"Shit," he whispered and though I hadn't let it escape my mouth, I felt the same. My previous orgasm coupled with how good he felt inside me had my body tingling again.

Magnificent.

I began slowly, never touching his body, only riding his cock. I was quickly wet all over again, the warmth returning and making him a little easier to manage. I cried out several times, curling my toes while he guided me up and down on his dick.

The way he controlled me—I needed this. Gasping several times, loving the way he felt inside of me as his body rocked against mine, we cursed each other with each powerful thrust.

"You got it, baby. You got it," he whispered as I leaned over, pressing my breasts against his flesh while continuing to ride him without breaking rhythm.

"Is the pussy good?" I asked, almost begging, needing to know that he enjoyed this as much as I did.

"The best," he moaned. "Keep doing it like that, S."

"Call me Sassia, daddy."

Shit.

I'd told him my name, but that didn't seem to matter. I was on the verge of coming again and I needed for him to call out my *name* when he was ready. Wrapping my arms under his shoulders, I looked into his eyes while I continued to rock—wanting to pull all of him inside of me as another orgasm approached. It'd been so long since I wanted to look someone in the eyes; I needed to feel like this again. Human.

Shivers ran down my spine and I rolled my head several times, trying to stave off the next orgasm, but as Q grabbed my ass and pulled me closer, while thrusting upward, I screamed in spite of myself.

As my body released another orgasm, I screamed so loudly that my voice echoed against the walls of our secret torture chamber. Q held me tightly; my body shivering as more warmth ran down his dick and onto our thighs.

"Did you come?" I asked, feeling like a newbie who didn't know the first thing about making a man cum.

"No."

As soon as he said it, I could feel the embarrassment washing over me. I was always in control, I *always* made my men come, but now I felt useless. Other then killing men, I was able satisfy them—easily, but this man was as stubborn as Boogie.

Boogie.

I quickly pushed that thought out of my mind before I took in a deep breath. "Why won't you cum for me?"

"The pussy is good, probably one of the top three, *Sassia...*" It stung as he said it. He was supposed to say my name as he came, but now he was just using it to prove how much power he had over me. "But..." he continued, "I just need to try something new."

"You need me to blindfold you, fuck you, and then set you on fire?" I asked jokingly.

"No," he replied smugly, "I need you to bend over."

"You want it in my ass?"

"You don't like ass sex?"

"Not with just any guy, *Q*. That's the kind of goodie you get when we've been together—for a few years."

“I understand.” He rolled me over and I thought we were going to go missionary when he stepped off the table. "It was nice meeting you."

I would've let him go, but my pride wouldn't allow it. He *had* to cum or else I was going to have to hunt him down.

"Okay," I conceded, "I'll do it." I grabbed his hand, slowly putting his middle finger in my mouth and sucking on it. His slumping erection quickly stood at attention again. I smiled as I turned over and got on all fours on the table, grabbing the lube that was next to the bowl of condoms. "Please use this."

It took a few moments for him to lube up, but it didn't take long for him to slide it inside. After a few strokes, I could already feel him fighting off his climax.

“Are you gonna cum for me?” I asked, placing both hands on the table and sliding my legs further apart.

“Don’t do that,” he breathlessly begged.

I heard him, but I wasn’t about to relinquish my control. I began to fondle my clit, sliding my fingers back far enough to feel his dick before bringing them back and playing with my clit again.

“Fuck,” he whispered. I felt his rhythm become more erratic. Bracing myself, I forced him to go deeper, pushing back as he pushed forward before I grabbed his arm and wrapped his hand around my throat. I continued playing with my clit until he clutched it so tightly that I could barely breathe.

He was almost there...and so was I. *Again.*

"Mmmm, Sassia—fuck!" he shouted and there it was. I could feel my clit swell and throb between my fingers as he cried out my name.

"Oh, shit!" I rubbed faster and as he pounded against me, achieving the apex of his orgasm, I came with him.

Magnificent.

Falling forward, he collapsed onto me and we slid onto the floor, breathless. Looking over at him and watching his chiseled form rise and fall with his breathing, only one thing went through my head.

“Q?”

“Yes,” he replied in a heavy pant.

“Have you ever thought about becoming a professional hitman?”

“A *what*?”

"Never mind, it was just something that I'd been reading about."

Too bad, he would've made a great Gideon.

Chapter 6: Sex....

...in the Champagne Room

St. Louis, 2 Years Ago

Sassia

"What is rule number one?" she shouted. As I pushed up, she placed the barrel of her favorite desert eagle behind my ear. "I swear that if you do not say this, I will kill you right now."

I'd been doing pushups all morning and already had more than a hundred under my belt, but there wasn't a single doubt in my head that she wouldn't hesitate to pull the trigger. Still, with her gun targeted at my head, I refused to show her my fear. In the two years since we'd met, I'd learned almost everything about her. The more she tried to maintain her anonymity, the more I needed to know and now I was paying the price for it.

With the first beads of sweat beginning to form on my head, I chose to focus on the task at hand—another push up. Previous experiences had taught me that answering before I finished the next twenty pushups assigned to me was an ass-kicking waiting to happen.

She shouted again. "Are you ignoring me?" She pulled the gun away from me and placed her foot squarely on my back. The extra weight caused a burning sensation in my shoulders that I hadn't felt in a while, but I refused to give in.

Once I finished the twenty, sweat was pouring down my face, but I answered anyway.

"No attachments—attachments make us weak and indecisive!"

She smiled and I could tell that she enjoyed torturing me. She knelt beside me and softly began sucking on my ear. "Give up, Val. You're asking too much. You want too much. You want to know too much," she whispered and as soon as my arms began to weaken, she immediately stood up. "What is rule two, Valentine?"

I started on my next set and with my arms already sore, I fiercely struggled with the following twenty. "Anonymity is the key to success."

My shoulders burned so badly that I dug my fingernails into my palm to keep the adrenaline coursing through my body. Still, my body remained taut and I was ready for my next bout of torture.

"And you do all this for my name?" She holstered her gun and sat on my back. "Tell me the other rules."

With her added weight bearing down on my weakened body, I shouted out the remaining four rules as quickly as I could. "Rule three: Defense is paramount to survival! Rule four: Prey is predictable, learn them to easily kill them! Rule five: Instinct trumps income! Rule six: Always have an out!"

After rule six, I collapsed.

"I wasn't finished yet. Ten more pushups with me on top of you and you would've known my name."

"Bullshit, Israel! You always add shit to the end so you don't have to tell me anything! You know what, I'll just call dispatch and find out!"

She was still on my back as I lay on the floor, but my heavy breathing brought us face to face. She stretched out next to me and kissed my nose. "Fine, but dispatch doesn't know everything."

"He can find out almost anything."

"Well then, I guess I'd rather let you hear it from me. From now on, call me Nava."

In the two years since she had saved me from New Orleans, I'd learned a lot about Nava, though no piece of information was more difficult to get than her real name. I'd called her Israel up until now because she never told me her name, only that she was Israeli. According to rule one, I really wasn't entitled. But after all we'd been through, I was tired of waiting for her to tell me. I was blindly following her, and I felt she owed me this much.

Everything had a price with Nava. To get anything from her, I had to earn it—and I did. For three straight days, I was forced to endure everything that she saw fit to put me through: gun training and knowledge, language and linguistics training, math, science, and of course, physical endurance.

Nava was only five years older than me, but she'd experienced more in that time than I ever had. The streets of New Orleans were like a war zone most of the time, but Nava was from a real war zone—Israel. She told me about the honor of being in the IDF, the Israeli Defense Force, but also the horrors of war. She was decorated for bravery several times, always competing against her three older brothers, but before her term ended, they all died. The oldest, Ethan, died in mortar fire. Her second brother, Isaiah, was killed in an ambush and the third, Aidan, was shot in friendly fire. With all of her family gone, she left Israel and used the only skills she knew to become a mercenary.

Now that she was in the States, she did contract killing.

I was still breathing heavily on the floor when she bent down and kissed my lips. "What was that for?"

"Seeing you work this hard makes me think things."

Since we'd met, I'd come to really respect Nava. Not only was she beautiful, but she was the most intelligent person I'd ever met. She spoke five different languages fluently, regularly used words I'd never heard, and could do math in her head more quickly than I could use a calculator.

We were also lovers. After being with Omar for all those years and working for him, I wasn't a stranger to being with women. In fact, I liked being with a woman more often than I liked being with a man. In my life, I learned that a woman could bring me to climax, while most men could only bring themselves to one.

She pulled my sports bra over my head, threw it aside, covering my right nipple with her warm mouth.

"I can't do this now, Israel, I need to shower! I stink!" I was so used to calling her Israel that even when I knew her name, she was still Israel to me.

She smiled and pulled her long black hair over her left shoulder. "I don't mind. This time..." Nava pulled down my shorts and slid her hand up my thigh...

Manhattan

Present Day

A young, voluptuous, blond girl tapped me on the back and awakened me from my daydream. "Valentine, that's you right?" I nodded slowly. "They just called your name. You're up next!"

The last three days had been hell, but even though I had less than seventy-two hours to make it back home, this job looked to be well worth it.

According to CT, I was here for Sergei Castarov—mid-40s, morbidly obese, and a dangerous Russian mobster. Sergei indulged in everything he could put his fat little fingers on: women, fast cars, and especially drugs. Had it not been for his father's name and the great lawyers continuously getting him out of a prison sentence on technicalities, Sergei would already have been dead.

With his father now barely clinging to life, my contract was for two murders. I had to kill Sergei, without making it look like murder; the older Castarov would then die of a broken heart—something I knew all too much about. Anything other than a natural death would result in citywide war, which meant my ass was on the line if it didn't go right. I had three days to do the job. It wasn't going to be easy, but it wasn't going to be cheap either.

The three day deadline wasn't a restriction of the hit. I had to be back in Houston in three days or LZ would fire my ass. With escorting as my only outlet for sex, I needed that job almost as much as I needed this one. Money and sex was the cocktail that kept me happy.

Doing this three-day job wasn't impossible, but it wouldn't allow me to follow all six rules perfectly. I had to improvise.

Oh well, I thought while walking toward the stage, *I like the challenge.*

The first day, I followed him by attaching a GPS tracker to his Bentley. Even with all his bodyguards, sneaking onto his Hampton estate was easier than I'd anticipated.

Cocky mobsters. Had this been another job, I would've blown everyone away and put a bullet in his head, but this wasn't and I couldn't. This job called for a bit more subtlety.

CT had already informed me about his strip club habit, but finding out how many he frequented was a nightmare. In the first twelve hours of his day, his driver and single bodyguard took him to six. I sat in my hotel room and charted his route through New York City, mapping out his favorite places to eat as well.

On day two, it was time to get a job. Because he'd spent the most time at a club called *The Double D's*, I figured that would be the best place to start.

The next afternoon, I put in my brown contact lenses and followed the directions to the club. The weather was still chilly as it had been during my visit three weeks ago, so this time I made sure to wear a sweater and jeans.

I found *The Double D's* on the outskirts of Harlem and was sorely disappointed at what I saw. The outside of the building was practically falling apart—pink paint was peeling away from the brick facade, the sign, consisting of over-lapping Ds, was only half-lit, and the few dried bushes around the building were in desperate need of water or mercy killing to release them from their limp limbo.

I entered through double doors covered with warping lath strips and peeling paint, and was greeted by an old man counting money from a tin cash box. His yellow smile widened as he saw me walk in.

"Are you looking for someone—perhaps you need a job?" he asked, rubbing his hands together excitedly.

"I'm not looking for anyone, but yes, I am looking for a job." I extended my hand. "I'm Rudy Moure."

He stepped from behind the counter, then circled me. "Why don't you come into the back room so that we can see how you dance?"

I hoped that I wasn't going to have to kill this pervert before I even got to Sergei, but as luck would have it, I was saved by his wife.

"I swear to God, Deni, if you touch that girl, I will cut your goddamn cock off!" She was as loud as she was skinny, shouting angrily as she stormed out into the front room. "Leave that poor girl alone!"

Her husband frowned and disappeared in the back as she extended her hand to me. "I'm Diamond and that creep there is Deni, my husband. We are the D's in Double D's. Most people think it's a bra size."

I shook her hand. "I'm very much taken, so you don't have to worry about me."

"You mean you like girls," she said casually. She certainly didn't sound like a New Yorker, not like her husband. She sounded Southern—almost like a guy I'd shot in Kentucky. Ah, the memories of that job . . .

I nodded shyly, back in the moment. "But I'm already in a relationship." She sized me up before allowing me to continue. "Mrs. Diamond, I had a job in the city and it fell through. I just need some quick money to pay off some of my bills so that I can get back home."

"And where's that?" she asked, eyeing me curiously.

I reached in my purse and pulled out a license.

"So you're from Gary, Indiana? You came from the Midwest all the way out here?"

"They're no decent jobs in the Midwest, especially in this climate," I lied. "I filled out an online application for an office here. They told me I had a job, but when I got here, they said they had to let me go. I spent every last dollar I had getting here and I just need some money to get back home."

"Well, we ain't no outreach center. Let me see whatcha' got."

I took off my sweater and blouse, revealing my frame. As soon as she saw my shape, she covered her gaping mouth with a liver-spotted hand. "Look at that flat stomach! And those arms, girlie! What did you do in Indiana before? Lift cows? And you got natural tits like that on that tiny frame?"

Deni rushed out from the back and stared at me. A trickle of drool formed at the corner of his mouth

"I just like to stay in shape. In Gary, you really have to know how to defend yourself these days."

I put my blouse back on and Diamond gave me a puzzled look. "Look, I'd hire you right now, but I don't think the other girls would take kindly to you."

I turned toward Deni and gave him the saddest, sexiest look I could muster.

He then turned to Diamond. "Look, we're hurting and with that body, she can bring people through the door! Dammit, Di, she's not gonna be here that damn long! The other girls will be just fine. If not, they can hit the goddamn road. It's not like they're putting us over the goddamned hump." After Diamond nodded, he turned toward me. "We don't need to see you dance right now, we'll start you off slow. Rudy, when can you start?"

"Tonight. I can start tonight."

I was pissed when Sergei didn't show up, but that night I cleared almost a thousand bucks with twenty-dollar lap dances. Of course, I had to give the D's their cut, but when they saw what I brought in they were so ecstatic that they cleared me to dance onstage.

That brought me to my third and final night. As the DJ announced my name, I stepped out on the small stage with my hair tied up, wearing thigh high boots, a leather mini-skirt, and a matching halter-top. After cleaning the pole, I focused on finding my target in the audience. With significantly more men than the previous night, it still wasn't hard to spot him sitting in a booth in the back. Seated to his right was his only bodyguard, who wore an all white linen suit and reminding me of the abominable snowman.

As the song began, I slowly untied my halter-top, letting it barely cover my breasts as it hung loosely around my neck. Onstage, I was a sex incarnate. I made love to the stage like it was the last man on Earth, drawing money from the wallets of every man near me. With the music blasting, I danced around the stage several times in my 6-inch heels, perching myself in front of random men in the front row near the stage. I kissed one man on his forehead, allowed another to put the tip of his tongue on my breast, but when I pulled down my thong and let one man softly blow on my clit while playing with myself, the crowd of drunken men went wild.

When my show was over, I needed help bringing all the money off the stage. After picking up the last few dollars, I stopped to refasten my halter-top when Sergei's bodyguard walked up to me.

"Mr. Castarov requests your presence in the VIP room."

He pointed in the direction of Sergei who waved at me. I waved back and after a quick stop at my locker, followed the bodyguard upstairs.

After opening the door marked 'private' for me, the bodyguard walked back downstairs and I was left alone with Sergei. The ambient light in the room was bright enough for me to see that he was clean-shaven; appearing much different from the wooly bearded picture that CT had sent me with the contract package. As I sized him up, I could see that he'd taken off both his suit jacket and his pants.

"You are very beautiful." His Russian accent was much lighter than I thought it would be, but still noticeable.

"Thank you," I said. I walked toward him and could see that there was a bottle of champagne waiting for me. Both glasses were filled, but it wasn't until I was closer that I realized it was Dom Pérignon Rosé on the table in front of him.

Only the best for his last night on Earth.

"You have done this before, no? Deni says that it is your first time, but no one is ever that good the first time." He patted his thigh, inviting me to sit on his lap.

With just his boxers on, I remained a few feet away from him and decided to start a conversation. "Mr. Castarov?" I asked, and when he nodded, I continued. "What is it that you want from me?"

He smiled while running his hand along his chin. "You like getting down to business! I like that! Why don't you start by giving Sergei a kiss?"

"No."

He frowned at my rejection. "Then give me the famous lap dance!"

"No." I began to walk away. "I don't take demands from you. If you want me, then show me how badly."

He reached into his jacket and pulled out a giant roll of money. The top bill was a hundred, but to make sure that the other ones weren't singles, I had him unroll them. They were all hundreds.

"I'm not a whore, Mr. Castarov. If you want something from me, then you ask for it."

He nodded and quickly changed to a softer tone. "Will you *please* dance for me?"

"Take off your shorts."

He moved quickly for such a big man, jumping up from the sofa and did as I instructed. As a reward, I took my top off and let it fall to the floor as I walked toward him. I grabbed a glass of champagne from the table before lifting my mini-skirt, showing him that I wasn't wearing anything underneath.

His eyes lit up and as his erection grew; I walked up and stood directly in front of him. Barely taller than me, I was able to grab both shoulders and push him down to kneel in front of my mini-skirt. I lifted my right leg and rested my boot on his shoulder as he stared at the sweetness between my legs.

I felt his overly excited panting breaths caressing my clit and as soon as the tablets dissolved completely in his glass, I returned my attention to Sergei. "Can you smell it?"

"No, Sergei cannot smell it," he whimpered.

"Get closer."

He brought his face closer and inhaled deeply. "It smells like fine strawberry vodka."

"You want to *taste* it, Sergei?"

"Yes," he whispered excitedly.

"Drink this." He pulled himself from under my skirt and I poured the tainted champagne down his throat. "Now you may eat it."

A lot could be said about how unattractive Sergei was, but as his tongue brushed against my outer lips, a shiver went down my spine. For several minutes, Sergei tasted me. His tongue was masterful as it slowly and carefully explored all of me, inside and out. He seemed in no hurry, using his fingers to spread me wide. As my knees began to buckle, I pulled him in closer—pressing my clitoris against his rough tongue.

"I like Sergei..." I whispered, but that didn't deter him from softly sucking on my clit. I reached over and grabbed the second glass, pouring it down my breasts. When it reached Sergei, he lapped it up, tickling me and finally bringing me toward climax.

"Is my flower ready to bloom?" he asked.

"Yes." I whispered hoarsely. I pressed against him, swirling my hips against the rotation of his tongue. I felt ready to explode.

I ran my fingers through his coarse hair, clutching handfuls of it as my orgasm tore through me. "Shit," I whispered, but as Sergei's pushed his tongue inside of me, I gasped.

When he was finished, Sergei quickly tried to stand up, but with my boot heel still pressed against his shoulder, I pushed him back down easily. He gave me a puzzled look, but I simply smiled. My essence was still on his face; I leaned over and slowly licked his lips.

"This is what Sergei likes," he said, sticking his tongue out. I sucked the tip of it before straddling him. "Sergei thinks he is in love."

I grew tired of him referring to himself in third person, but as I began to grind against his erection, he finally began to nod off.

"You okay, baby?" I whispered in his ear; already knowing what was happening to him.

"Sergei...is so...sleepy. Sergei...can't...can't move." His speech was beginning to slur which meant that the GHB I'd put in his glass was taking effect. I stood up and watched as he began to shake his head. I could see his eyes glazing over as he tried to focus on me, but instead ended up just gazing at the floor. He slapped himself several times and when that didn't seem to work, he balled up his fist and weakly hit his chest as he tried to stay awake. No matter how hard he hit himself, he was still beginning to lean over. I smiled at his efforts and he suddenly understood.

"You have...have *drugged*...Sergei?"

"Good bye, Sergei." I hadn't even finished saying his name when he stopped moving. He eyes were slightly open, but when I grabbed his arm, it was limp.

It was time to work.

I knew that I didn't have much time before his erection disappeared and my opportunity would be lost. I needed this to look like a heart attack and because of his size; no one would immediately question it.

I quickly stood up and pulled both the TB needle and the potassium chloride vial out from the pocket sewn inside my boot. After puncturing the top of the vial with the needle and drawing as much as it could take, I carefully inserted it along the vein on the underside of his penis. I'd learned from Nava that most coroners don't typically touch a man's penis unless they have to and because the needle was so small, I was sure that they wouldn't find the puncture mark.

I slowly injected the content from the vial into his body. When I finished, I pulled out an alcohol swab and proceeded to wipe down his mouth before pouring a little champagne down his throat. I cleaned up the room as well as I could and waited.

I remained next to him and felt his carotid artery until the pulsations stopped completely. Then, I put on my clothes and waited another two minutes before I took the eye drops out of my other boot. Lastly, I grabbed the champagne glasses and ran downstairs, grabbing the bodyguard, crying hysterically.

"What wrong?" the Russian man asked, slowly following me.

"Something's wrong!" I screamed. "He started clutching his chest and he won't wake up!"

The bodyguard ran up the stairs as fast as he could, screaming for someone to call 9-1-1. I placed the glasses on a table with several empty glasses already on it and walked upstairs to make sure that Sergei wasn't going to make a miracle recovery. After a few minutes of watching CPR, I knew he wasn't coming back.

In the ensuing chaos and hysteria, I snuck back downstairs, grabbed my book bag from the old locker, and crept into the D's empty office. I destroyed the copy of my license and quickly left the club. I thought about going back for all that money, but I didn't need it. This job had already paid me well enough.

Not wanting to run around the city half-naked, especially when it was still early in the evening. I found a gas station restroom and changed. From my backpack, I pulled out an oversized, blue sweat suit, a curly, auburn colored wig, and I took out my contacts. I quickly applied black makeup to my eye and used the eye drops from earlier to help with the tears. As I walked out of the bathroom, I pulled out a small, beige purse and shoved the makeup and eye drops into it. I kept my head down so that if anyone noticed me, it'd look like I had been on the wrong end of a beating.

Making sure that no one was watching, I called CT on the hotline, waiting for him to assure me of a secure line.

"I just finished cooking the ham."

"I didn't know you ate pork. Well, I guess once you've tasted pre-blackened black guy, everything else goes down pretty easily."

I knew he was referring to what I'd done with Antoine 'Rock Hound' Davis before burning him alive. "Cut the shit and quit the jealous routine, CT. I'm good at what I do and I can't help it that I'm sexy as hell. The way I see it, Antoine was at least cute. So you can say that I gave him a last meal." I stuck my hand out so that I could hail a cab.

"So what did you give Sergei?"

"He got a GHB cocktail with a potassium chaser. As long as they don't do an immediate autopsy, they probably won't find either one."

"He is pretty high profile. They may do one just because."

"He's a fat bastard, who had a heart attack and died in a strip club. That sounds pretty open and shut to me."

"You may play heartless, Val, but you're not. You're not like the reptilians that are practically running this country. You know they're systematically taking over the government so that they can enslave us. I have files right here..."

"What do the files say, CT?"

"It's nothing concrete, but Val, it's already happening and they've made their way all the way up to the presidency."

"Not that conspiracy shit again. I'm tired of hearing your 'the President is one of them' speeches," I moaned. Crazy bastard.

"I never said he was one of them, but no one around him is even human. All you have to do is look at the signs! The government is making us dependent on them so that they can get away with whatever they want! It's practically slavery, Val! When the revolution goes down, and it will, you're gonna be glad that I got you ready for this shit! I got my stockpile ready and I'm itchin' to kill some reptile bastards!"

I sighed, watching the ambulance as it sped past me and around the corner. Since it had turned the wrong way at the intersection, I knew that wasn't the one they had called for Sergei.

"You're a piece of work, you know that? Why do I even put up with you, CT?"

"There are three reasons why you do, Val. I keep you paid...very nicely, I might add. Secondly, because you're a kitten in life and a tiger in the sack, you need someone like me to remind you of how unbelievably sexy you are. And the last reason is that you secretly want me."

"You're right, CT. I do want you."

"Goddamit, I knew the truth would come out if I kept on you! Let's do this, Val. I will fuck you so hard I will blow your mind and your back out."

"Remember what I said about killing you afterward? I meant it. You sent me an Indiana license with the name, Rudy Moure? Were you trying to get me caught? What the hell type of shit is that? You know about the damn business!"

"We all can't have a sense of humor."

"I have a sense of humor," I said, as a cab finally pulled up. "I'll be laughing my ass off when I put a bullet in your ass."

"And on that note, the money should be in the account by the time you get home. If it's not, be worried. I'll call you if I have any updates, but stay clear of anyone who talks with a hiss."

I hung up the phone, hid my face, and instructed the driver to take me to the bus station. I had to get back home.

As I walked around the dingy and dimly lit bus station, I remembered why I hated them, especially the ones in New York. They were always filled with smelly homeless people sitting in all the available seats, overweight people who hadn't showered for days, crying babies, pretentious foreigners, and today there was a precocious little boy who sat next to me.

For the last half hour, Michael, the precocious child next to my tiny-ass seat, desperately tried to get my perspective on the war. I rolled my eyes several times, hoping he'd get the idea, but either he didn't understand or didn't care for my answer.

It wasn't until I finally asked him, "Where the hell is your mother?" that he gave up on bugging me and turned to an older white man on the other side of him and began peppering him with questions. *Obnoxious little fucker.*

The boy reminded me of why I never wanted kids, and not long after I'd gotten rid of him, my cell phone rang.

♫ *Chuck is calling.* ♫

It was my personal ringtone for Charlie. I recorded her sexy voice so I always knew when she was calling me. Answering on the second ring, I smiled knowing she was still awake. It meant she wanted to come over.

"Hello?"

"Where on earth are you? I was knocking on your door for ten minutes before I finally realized you weren't going to answer," she said.

"I'm at a bus station and I was really about to kill this little boy when you called. You probably saved his life." When I heard her sniffling, I knew why she'd called. "You and Steve are arguing again, huh?"

"When *aren't* we arguing? Today I received a commendation. I've been on the job less than a month and I received a goddamn commendation! I mean, he knew all this and he still didn't even show up! You don't know how much that hurt me, Sassy."

"You could've invited me. I would have been there ..."

"You don't like cops, remember?" She laughed, but I could hear the hurt in her voice and I found myself growing upset at Steve's callousness.

Rule 1.

I quickly shook off the feeling and changed the subject. "So, they finally gave you your gun back?"

"They gave me my service weapon the day after the robbery. I just had to go through a psych eval. I've shot and killed bad men before."

I've killed bad men. The phrase resonated within me for a few seconds after she said it. She really wasn't that different from me, even though we had two completely different lives. She got commendations for killing people; I got money. Out of the few people I knew, Charlie could understand me the best.

Perhaps if the circumstances were different...

But they weren't. She was still a cop and I wasn't. I knew I'd been growing a little too close to her and though I wanted to keep my distance, I still liked her.

Well, I'll keep my distance right after I sleep with her...

"So you shot a bad guy, they gave you an award, and then they examined you brain. Steve doesn't like that and now you're struggling to keep the peace with your fiancé. Is that about it?"

"You get right to the point, don't you? Anyway Sassy, I love my job, but I'm so damn stressed. Before we get married, which is practically next week, I'm starting to believe that Steve will ask me to choose between him and the job."

"So which will you choose?"

She grew silent. "I'd choose Steve."

I shook my head as Rule 1 flashed through my brain for the second time. I was disappointed to hear that she would choose someone over something she loved, but she wasn't me. "So why don't you quit now and save yourself the headache?"

"Why? He hasn't asked, so I'll be damned if I'll volunteer!"

Though still disappointed, I smiled. I wasn't used to the Charlie that gave in; I was used to the one who fought me and that's why I liked her so much.

Since Nava, I hadn't had a single friend. I kept to myself and avoided people like the plague. When Charlie moved in, she was relentless in her pursuit of making us friends. She knocked on my door at all times of the night and no matter how much I didn't give a damn about her life, she always managed to make me smile. It also helped that she was sexy as hell, and reminded me a lot of my former teacher.

"So why did you stop by? You wanted to get high again?"

"Yes! I needed to release some tension! Why did you leave me? Is it another *family emergency*? You know, as many emergencies as your family has, they should all be dead by now."

"You're one to talk! I don't even charge you for smoking my weed! To top that off, you're a cop who gets high, then gets a commendation for blasting away weed dealers! Talk about irony!" She laughed loudly and I suddenly felt like my day had a perfect ending.

"I miss you, Sassy. Come home."

"Why? So you can smoke out?"

"That's not why I called! I'm insulted!"

"So why *did* you call, Chuck?"

"I called so that we could smoke out—*together*! You're my partner in crime, my kindred spirit. I can't smoke without you. Smoking is an *us* thing—our time to bond."

We were kindred spirits, but we functioned on opposite sides of the law. I was paid to kill people and she was paid to keep them alive.

"Sure, we can smoke, but afterwards, I'd like to do some other kind of bonding."

"You're a predator, but you know I'm a one-man-type of woman. Just because you know a little about my past and Steve doesn't; that doesn't change a thing."

"I don't know why you stop yourself when you know you want to sleep with me. What Steve doesn't know won't hurt him. You never know, he may want to watch."

"Are you saying that you would let him join in?"

Now we were getting somewhere. "That depends. Do you want him there before or after I fuck your brains out?"

She laughed. "You never told me where your family emergency was at."

I took a few deep breaths, trying not to think of her climaxing—writhing around with her in my bed as Steve watched us.

"I'm in Mississippi."

"So you're on a job? Or have you forgotten that I already know what you do?"

"You're still a cop. My official answer is that I'm with family." Just as she was about to speak, the hotline rang. "Chuck, gotta go. I'll call you back."

"Be safe, Sassy," she shouted just before I hung up.

I picked up the hotline and remained silent as I waited for CT to say either run or that the money was in the account, but he said neither.

"You know that person you asked me to find?"

"Yes," I responded.

"I found him."

While CT continued to speak, the phone slowly drifted away from my ear. Fifteen minutes before my bus was supposed to leave, I went to the ticket booth and bought another ticket, this one to Memphis, Tennessee. It was there that I was going to find him.

After five long years, I was finally going to pay Boogie a little visit.

Chapter 7: Atonement

Memphis

Sassia

It was dark and raining when I arrived in Memphis. Perfect for my mood. Hardly anyone was inside the terminal and the clock on the wall alerted me that it was almost two in the morning.

Fuck!

I thought about catching a plane, but I hated airports and security guards. Because of the twenty-nine hour bus ride from New York and the additional fifteen it would take to get home, I had less than twenty-four hours to find Boogie.

I didn't want to kill him immediately, either. I wanted him to suffer for four days like I had—to experience everything that I'd gone through because of his betrayal. He'd left me to die and a quick bullet would ruin what I had planned for him. One day of anguish wasn't going to make what he did go away. When I realized how angry I was becoming, I unclenched my fists and walked outside.

Still in my sweat suit, I desperately needed a shower. I wanted nothing more than to get to a hotel room, but I had other things to worry about first.

The wind howled and rain hadn't slacked, but picked up velocity. I jumped into the first cab I saw. According to CT, Boogie's apartment was on the north side, but in Memphis, I was naked. Even though I hadn't planned on killing Boogie with a gun, I still needed to be prepared.

"There's a gun runner in the city named Hoops. He's not cheap, but if you need a throwaway piece, you can get something from him," CT had told me while I was still in NYC. "He stays in east Memphis and he's extremely cautious. When he asks for your Rudy Moure license, give it to him. When he scans it, he'll give you whatever you need."

I read the address aloud from a slip of paper, and the cabbie, an older Hispanic man, plugged it into his GPS. Without another word, he began following the turn-by-turn instructions. We rode on I-240 for about fifteen minutes before getting off on Poplar Avenue. Ten minutes later, we pulled up to a dimly lit, ranch style house that harkened back to the 1970s.

I gave the driver a fifty. "Wait here and I'll give you another fifty." The driver put the cab in park and I stepped out. After looking around, I realized it looked like the suburbs, but only because of the contrast with what the rest of the city looked like.

Because I learned never to go through the front door, I opted to go to the well-lit door on the side of the house. I opened the gate with the 'beware of dog' sign and knocked on the side door.

"What?" A loud, husky voice shouted from inside. I saw a man peeking out through the window and I waved.

The man quickly opened the door.

"Oh, shit," he said softly, "the entertainment is here." This man wasn't Hoops. Whoever he was, his hair was nappy and the grizzled beard with small pieces of lint didn't help his appearance either. I looked past his dirty t-shirt, down toward his pants, and saw that the bulge in his pants wasn't because he was happy to see me, it was a gun. I was in the right place.

I ran my finger along the underside of his chin. "I'm here to see Hoops."

The man stepped outside and shut the door behind him. He was bigger and taller than I'd thought. I also saw more of his face and noticed that his facial hair was masking a moonscape of craters on his skin. I didn't see a holster and I guessed that he was supposed to be the bodyguard.

"Fuck him, baby girl. It's just you and me. So, whatchu wanna do?"

I stepped a little closer to him. "Well, sexy, you know what I *really* wanna do?"

"What, baby?" he asked. "Let me know... shit. We can fuckin' do whatever."

"I wanna do this." I reached up and grabbed a handful of his hair. Before he had a chance to react, I quickly planted a flat palm against the side of his face. Releasing his hair and as he fell against the side of the house, I threw a flurry of quick forearm punches to his face. Dazed and slumping to the ground, I stepped over him and into the house.

Walking up the three stairs leading into the kitchen, I found Hoops sitting on a sofa in his living room. He was just as tall, but much more handsome than his guard. Hoops was sexy, with dark eyes you could get lost in, muscular arms, and his goatee was well-groomed. His light skin contrasting against the dark braided hair that overran his shoulders completed his "ghetto pretty boy" look. Only a few feet away from him sat several guns, his hands on the one he was cleaning. I was almost happy to see him, but once he saw me, he immediately reached for one of the guns on the table.

I ran over to him and just as he was pointing it at me, I knocked his gun away with my left hand and punched him in the throat with the right. Swiftly mounting him while he was still struggling to breathe, I was ready to hit him again, but I didn't.

I stood up as his bodyguard came rushing into the house. "I'm not here to rob you, Hoops. I need a goddamn gun!"

He leaned over and coughed. "What the fuck! Why didn't you just say so?" He put his hands up, halting his bodyguard from coming any closer to me.

I looked over at his bodyguard, who seemed to be pissed that I was still alive. "Because your man was trying to fuck me in the damn driveway and when I walk in, you're trying to shoot first and ask questions later, fucker!"

He was still clutching his throat when he extended his hand. I reached in my pocket and handed him my license. He slid it in a card reader and looked at me strangely. "I got an email saying that you was coming, chica. I don't know who the fuck sent it, but they already paid for whatever you were gonna need."

I almost smiled as I thought about CT. "I don't need much—maybe something small caliber with a suppressor."

"Beenie, it's good." He waved at his bodyguard who was still leering at me through clenched teeth. Hoops led me down a slim hallway toward the back of the house while he rubbed his throat. "Goddamn girl, you punch like a fucking champion. You ever thought about going for some golden gloves?"

"You ever thought about a better security system than just the big *dumbass*?"

"Guns are my security system. You just happened to have caught me at an inopportune time."

I rolled my eyes at his rhetoric. "Right."

With me behind him, he guided me into a room with automatic weapons hanging on all four walls. As I looked around in awe, he smiled and puffed out his massive chest proudly.

"Don't worry, these are all legal." He lifted up a rug in the middle of the floor, opened a trap door, and led me down into an underground chamber. In his makeshift basement were more guns than I'd ever seen in one place. "These guns—not so much."

I walked over to the wall that was studded with handguns and picked out a beautiful, gold Ruger Centerfire. "You got a suppressor for this one?"

"You want the matching color?"

"You have matching ammo, too?"

"Do I look like I sell pretty bullets?" he asked sarcastically.

"Well, you are a pretty man. I just had to be sure."

He smiled. "Anything else?"

"Yeah, I'll be bringing this back. Since you clean guns, I need you to take care of that for me and deliver it to me when you're finished."

"For as much as you paid for that tiny ass gun, I can have it delivered wherever you want."

"No, you don't understand. I want *you* to deliver it."

When I left his house, the cabby was still waiting on me. I told him the hotel I was staying at and we were off.

After a long, hot shower and a quick nap, I would be ready to find Boogie.

I slept until a little after noon. I didn't really intend to sleep so long, but after enduring such a long bus ride, sitting next to a redneck man who smelled like a slaughterhouse, I needed it. I'd taken a shower before I went to bed, but I still took another one as soon as I woke up.

I put on the pair of jeans and the top I'd worn to Double D's, slid on some matching heels, and put the lethal little Ruger in my beige Coach bag. After stopping to get some lunch at a rundown rib joint in Midtown, I rode another yellow cab to north Memphis to find Boogie. On the way, I thought about forgetting all the rules and just shooting him in his knees on sight.

Maybe I should miss all the vital organs and let him bleed to death, but as the thoughts of what he allowed to happen to me flooded my brain, I didn't want his demise to come so quickly. Each day I suffered was certainly worth forty-eight hours of suffering for him.

Focused so much on Boogie, it wasn't until the cab driver dropped me off about a block from where he stayed that I'd actually noticed how beautiful it was outside. With the sun high up in the sky, it was bright, the wind was cool, and it seemed like such a waste that I'd be spending it all indoors fucking over the man who'd left me to die.

I stepped out of the cab and walked around his block several times, hoping to catch a glimpse of him. All I saw were dilapidated brick buildings in desperate need of repair. None of the buildings were numbered so I was forced to look at each apartment individually. Several apartments had open doors where a few men would congregate and smoke, others had clotheslines with the pins still hanging, but no clothes. Some of the worst ones had no windows or doors, but I still saw people and furniture inside. Walking down the slim, cracked to shit sidewalk, there were broken bottles on both sides, reminding me of being back home in New Orleans.

Has it really gotten that bad, Boogie, or are you just hiding out in a shitty neighborhood?

A few men took notice of me, following me with their eyes as I looked at each apartment, but none of them said anything to me. When I finally made it to Boogie's apartment and still hadn't seen him, the anticipation became so overwhelming that I took a chance and knocked on his door. With the gun tucked into the waistband of my pants, I held my hands behind my back just in case, but he didn't answer. Instead, I was greeted by a young, fair-skinned girl with freckles across her nose. She came to the door with hardly any clothing on; a pair of tight cut-offs and a flimsy orange blouse. I smiled at her, but she looked barely old enough to be legal and I knew her type. With her blank stare, coupled with the redness of her eyes and the track marks on her skinny arms, I knew.

Damn junkies.

"Hello," I said jovially. "I'm from the rental office. Is Mr. Jackson in?"

"Naw, he's gone off," she said gruffly. "What the fuck y'all want, main?"

"Well, do you know when he'll be in, ma'am? We had a problem with his application and we'd just like to clear it up."

"I just told you he was gone, bitch. You don't listen? I don't know when he gon' be back. He get back whenever the hell he gets back. Damn." She slammed the door in my face.

I seriously thought about kicking the door in and beating her ass, but I bit my tongue and walked away. The last thing I needed was Boogie coming home to see his new girlfriend with her ass whipped. I *at least* wanted to surprise him.

As I walked away, I began balling up my fists in frustration. I knew I should've come last night.

"Initiative."

I rolled over and kissed him softly on the bottom lip. "I didn't hear what you said."

Sweat still clung to my body as I recuperated from the marathon session we'd just had. For the first time in the few months we'd been together, I had finally gotten Boogie to climax a second time. I loved when men challenged me and even more than that, I loved him. Unlike any other man, he had captured both my body and my heart.

I met Charles Jackson when Omar recruited him to be my driver. He was from New York, his accent gave that much away, but as much as he talked about the Bronx, Omar just gave him the nickname Boogie. Darker than any man I'd ever met; his low cut fade attached to his chinstrap beard, he was by far the sexiest. We didn't talk much at first, but even the first time we met, I knew I wanted him.

And I got him.

For months, we snuck around behind Omar's back, knowing that if he caught us together, we were dead. Living on the edge with Boogie was always exhilarating and the sex was just as intense. With all the men I'd been with throughout the years, not one of them could hold a candle to him—and he knew it.

He pushed away the covers and walked to the window. As the street light silhouetted his muscular contours and naked flesh, I contemplated attacking him again. Instead, I crept behind him as he looked out onto the dead street from his apartment window.

"I'm tired of being Omar's goddamn guppy, tired of just driving you around in that damn Caddy, Val. I came down here so I could make moves and be somebody. I want us to have a life together. I want us to be together. If we're gonna make this happen, we gotta break free of that goddamn Omar."

About six inches taller than me, I kissed him midway down his back, wrapped my hands around his waist and fondled his flaccid manhood. I liked that he had big dreams, but I wasn't sure I was ready to die for them.

"Look baby, Omar's grooming you. That's how he is. I've been around him for almost eight years and he took his time with me too. You just gotta be patient."

"Fuck being patient, Val. The best things come to those who make them..." He turned around and kissed me softly on my nose, "... and sooner or later, I'm gonna make this happen. Look, I plan on robbin' Omar before the month is out. As soon as I do it, I'm runnin'. Are you with me?"

I looked at him like he'd just gone mad. The last thing I needed now was him messing up something that was already so damn perfect.

"Are you fucking crazy? If we rob Omar, he'll find us. He's gonna find us and kill us, Boogie."

He laughed. "Look at this tat on my neck, Val," he said, pointing to the Valentine tattoo he usually kept hidden under his shirt. I'd asked, no begged, him not to do it, but Boogie wasn't like the rest of them. He didn't fear Omar and out of all the ways to rebel, he chose to do it with my name.

"I didn't do it for my health. Whatever I do, wherever I go, I want you with me. I love you. With all that money, we can see the world. There are places outside the NO where I can take you. Omar won't find us because he won't be able to catch up

to us. After a few years, he'll stop chasing and we would've already seen Paris, London, and all the expensive-ass cities on the other side of the world. Baby, are you with me?"

He made things sound so easy, plus the thought of being with him in cities around the world was just so damn tempting that I couldn't say no. "You promise to take me with you?"

"That's my word. I got you." He turned around and kissed me to seal the deal. "I love you."

"I love you, too," I whispered.

I awoke from my daydream after having waited six hours for Boogie. I had already strolled around the run-down neighborhood several additional times, but he never showed. With my time winding down, I used my phone to call a cab and with my last few hours, I decided to have some fun.

"Take me to Beale Street," I said to the cabbie, sliding into the backseat.

"You picked a good time to go down to Beale, main! Thurrs a lotta of things happenin' down thurr tonight. I was gon' go myself, but I gotta feed my kids. You got kids?"

"No," I said dryly, not interested in chatting.

"You want some?"

"No."

"You sexy as fuck though, main!" he persisted. "You single?"

"No," I lied, but it didn't matter what he asked, I was automatically going to say 'no'. With just a few sentences under his belt, I already knew I was ready to shoot this man in the face—and perhaps in the crotch. The Hispanic man from the night before had been quiet, but this guy was as obnoxious as they came. Even though he reminded me of some of the guys I'd met in St. Louis, he was still a perfect candidate to be a bullet catcher.

I looked for his license and found it mounted to his visor. "Look, Lawrence, let's not ruin this ride by conversing. You seem like a nice guy so please don't feel bad when I ask you to shut the hell up."

"Oh, I see. You must've caught yo' main out here messin' with these old hopped-up jump offs."

Instead of answering, I just faced the window and rolled my eyes.

Twenty minutes later, without, thank God, another word, he was pulling up to Beale Street. I'd heard that it was similar to Bourbon Street, but what I saw was nothing like New Orleans. It was barely festive, simply people walking from one end to the other and back. The street was maybe two blocks long and even with performers back-flipping down the street, there wasn't even a hint of Zydeco. This was pure vanilla shit, with no resemblance to my spicy hometown.

Disappointed, I walked into the first bar I saw and grabbed a Hurricane, which wasn't all that bad, before joining the rest of the tourists and pedestrians. I had walked half a block when I thought I spotted someone who reminded me of Boogie. Wearing boots, loose fitting jeans, and a muscle shirt, he even dressed like him. After staring for a few seconds longer, I walked across the street and began to follow the tall, dark-skinned man.

With the crowd slowing me down, I crossed back to the other side of the street where there was less traffic so I could see him better. Even though he was taller than most of the people walking down the street, I only needed to see one thing, and I did. As he turned his head away from me, talking to another man beside him, there was no mistaking the cursive 'tine' on his neck.

"Fuck me," I whispered, as I instantly knew the man walking down Beale Street was Charles Jackson. Checking to make sure that the Ruger was within easy reach, I dropped the Hurricane in the trash and walked faster. My heart pounded inside my chest and I almost began to hyperventilate as I thought about the last few years of my life. I knew CT was great at finding people, but after all the time Boogie had spent staying out of sight, I wasn't sure that I'd ever get this chance. A hundred feet separated us and as I began to close the gap, someone grabbed my arm. Shit.

"Hey, pretty girl, why you here all by yo' fine self?"

"Go fuck yourself."

Without even looking at the man who'd grabbed me, I ripped my arm from him and continued pursuit of my target. As he turned the corner, the man he was talking to and another man turned with him. He wasn't alone, but that didn't matter. I would kill the fourth brigade if I had to.

I arrived at the corner a few seconds after they turned and slowly peeked around. None of them were facing me but they were all laughing about something. Everything was falling into line—there wasn't any foot traffic, their backs were turned and the gun felt perfect as I wrapped my hand around it inside of my purse.

It was time for me to close the gap: sixty feet became forty, then thirty. I knew I had planned on torturing him, but I didn't care anymore. An execution was still an execution and no one deserved it more than that bastard. I wanted vengeance and if a bullet to his skull brought me that, I'd take it. Thirty feet turned to twenty and as the world around me seemed to move in slow motion, everything outside the range of Boogie and his boys became a blur. I slowly reached into my purse and began to pull out my gun.

This is it. It's finally happening. All those years ago and what he did to you...this debt will finally be paid.

The gold gleamed in the darkness and though I was upset that Boogie wouldn't know it was me, I finally had him.

♫ *Chuck is calling.* ♫

As the men turned around to see who was behind them, they all had guns in their hands. It was a goddamn ambush. I quickly fired one wild shot, causing them to scatter and made a quick right turn into a parking area.

Fuck!

I could've shot him long ago, but they were waiting for me. Somehow, they knew I was coming. I ran through the parking lot, ducking between cars as people began to flood the garage after hearing a gunshot. I put the gun away then looked around, but none of Boogie's men were following me. Never in my life had I wanted something so badly, but somehow, they'd seen me.

"How the hell could you be so careless?"

I grabbed the phone from my purse, but the call had already gone to voicemail. Not caring whose car it was, I punched the hood of the first nice Cadillac I saw.

I walked out the back of the parking garage but with the street flooded with police, I knew he was long gone.

"Fuck!" I shouted, this time kicking the driver's door of another car.

♫ *Chuck is calling.* ♫

This time I picked up the phone.

"What? Goddammit, Charlie! *What the fuck*?"

I didn't hear anything but whimpering on the other line. "Hello?"

"Sassy?" she asked, and now I could hear her crying. "They got him, Sassy!" she blurted out. "Those bastards fucking killed him!"

"Killed who?"

She was hysterical when she said it. "Please come home! They took Steve, Sassy. He's gone...because of me."

Chapter 8: Swan Song

One Hour Ago

Charlie

"You just don't get it! Some cops go through their whole damn careers and don't even get *one commendation!* I get one on my first day on the job and you can't even be there to support me!"

"I can't support you, Charlie? Is that what you think? When you were an engineer, I supported the hell out of you! We could've made a life for ourselves then! Now, you wanna be a goddamn super cop! How the hell am I supposed to support you when I always have to worry about you coming home?"

"This is what I do! This is who I am! I don't ask you not to be a tax attorney!"

"My clients aren't criminals and I don't keep three god-damn guns in the house either!" he shouted back, referring to my service gun, my carry 9mm, and the extra revolver I kept for safety.

With tears beginning to form and clouding my eyesight, I struggled to get the key into our apartment lock. Steve tried to pull me away from the door so that he could use his key, but I jerked away so that he couldn't touch me.

"That's fucking perfect! Blame this on me!" he shouted in the hallway.

We were both dressed up, Steve in a suit and tie; I was in a black cocktail dress that I'd bought specifically for this occasion. Tonight had begun with us reconciling, trying to get past the headaches of the past week, but that all ended when several people at the restaurant recognized me from the story in the newspaper. Some asked for autographs, a few even asked for a picture, but they all ignored Steven like he wasn't even there.

We were supposed to eat, the owner even offering to feed us for free, but Steve wasn't hearing any of it. Before we had a chance to eat, we left. My stomach, now growling with hunger, was making me even more irritable.

After jamming the key into the lock and turning as hard as I could, I finally opened the door and as I walked it, I broke the heel of my shoe.

"This is a great fucking ending to a great fucking night!" I hobbled to the kitchen to get some water before taking my heels off and throwing my keys on the counter.

"Why don't you ask your adoring fans to carry you next time?" he asked snidely.

Ignoring him, I walked to the bedroom and slammed the door. I began looking for my 'don't touch me tonight' sweat pants and my oversized 76ers t-shirt, but as soon as I found my pants, he walked in and stretched out across the bed.

I shrugged my shoulders. "Fine, I'll take the couch."

I had just let the dress fall to the bedroom floor and was walking out the bedroom with my pants and shirt when he reached over and grabbed me.

"What do you want now, Steve?"

He sounded tired, almost defeated when he spoke. "Charlie, I don't want to fight with you all the damn time about this. Can't we come to some kind of compromise?"

I sat down on the bed, my back still turned to him. "Fine, we can compromise when you tell me the truth."

"Not this shit again, Charlie. I told you that I had a client and while I was crunching all the numbers, I lost track of the time. What else do you want me to say? You want me to say that I missed it on purpose because I don't want you to be a cop?"

"Only if it's true."

"If I really wanted you to go back to being an engineer, I'd call your job and ask them to give you a drug test. I know about you and Sassia. Every time you get in the bed after you leave her apartment, you reek of pot. And don't try and bullshit me and tell me you don't get high over there."

I smirked as I thought about Sassy and I smoking and laughing our asses off. I stopped as I remembered her lips on mine.

"Are you smiling because I know or because you want to get high with her again?"

"Neither." I looked over my shoulder at my fiancé, wondering if he'd notice my cheeks turning pink. "So if you know all this, why not just tell? Hell, if you really want to screw me over, I could give you the division chief's phone number!"

"Because, Charlie," he slowly inhaled, "you would never forgive me. Believe it or not, I love you. I just want what's best for us. How could we ever start a family with guns in the house and me never knowing if you'll come home alive?"

"So, what's best for the both of us is me not being a cop? Is it best that I continue being an engineer as long as it makes *you* happy? How long am I supposed to be your version of happy, Steven? Maybe for the rest of our lives? And don't bring kids into this. This is between you and me."

He stood up and angrily pointed his finger at me. "I can't believe you! Everything is about you! Everything is always about you! I ask you not to do one goddamn thing—just one! You can't do the one damn thing I ask and I'm selfish? I asked you to leave the fucking bank robbers alone, but you couldn't listen to me, could you? It was about *you*! I'm about to be your damn husband and you didn't even listen to me when I asked you not to risk your fucking life! You're leveraging our future together because of that damn job!"

I had suppressed the tears from falling earlier, but now I couldn't manage to hold them back. "I do everything you ask, Steven! Everything! I left the military for you! I stopped taking birth control because you wanted a family! After only six months I accepted your goddamn engagement ring because you wanted me..."

Suddenly the room went silent and I realized what I'd just said.

Oh God.

The distraught look that he gave me let me know that he had heard every word loud and clear.

"You didn't want to get married to me?" he whispered. I could see the tears beginning to fall as he spoke. "All this planning and preparation and you didn't even want to be my wife?"

"It's not like that, Steven. I was just angry when I said that. Just listen to me." I stood up and went to hug him, but he pulled away from me.

"Don't touch me, Charlie. Don't fucking touch me."

"When you first asked, I wasn't sure. Things were moving so fast. You wanted a family, a house, and kids, but I had just come home from defending my country. Things were going so quickly, but I know for a fact that I'm ready now to be your wife," I pleaded.

As if he hadn't heard a thing I said, he just looked up at the ceiling. "It all makes perfect sense to me now. All the fighting and the hostility about your job was because you wanted an out all along. I just didn't want to see it."

I reached out to touch him again, but for the second time in a row, he withdrew from me. "Steven, I love you so very much and I want to be your wife. Your name is on my uniform for God's sake! I'll quit the damn job to prove it to you!"

When he finally stopped focusing on the ceiling, he began to look at me as if he didn't even know who I was. "I can't stay here right now. I need to get out."

He turned around and began walking to the door, but I grabbed him to make him stop. "Didn't you hear what I said? I said I'll quit!"

"Just don't touch me, Charlie. I can't breathe. I need some air." He yanked his suit jacket away from me and grabbed the keys off the counter. Without another word, he walked out the front door and slammed it behind him.

I threw myself on the couch, curled into a ball, and cried like the woman I tried so hard not to be.

Why couldn't he just understand that being a soldier wasn't who I was trying to be, but it was a part of who I was? Why did I have to tell him that I wasn't ready when he proposed?

I knew he was going to be upset when he returned and I thought about typing out my resignation before he came back. Hopefully that would show him how seriously I was committed to us. I put on the sweatpants that I'd been holding onto since we left the bedroom and threw the 76ers shirt over my head. Hoping to drown out the silence of an empty apartment, I turned on the radio and sat on the sofa.

Already tuned to the oldies station that Steve liked so much, I began listening to the words of *Yesterday* by the Beatles. As I listened to the words of the song, I almost felt as if Paul was singing specifically to me. When the song finished, I closed my eyes and thought about how on Earth I was going to make this up to Steve.

BOOM!!!

I opened my eyes and instinctively rolled to the ground. The apartment shook; it sounded like IED explosion. After getting up, I ran for my service pistol, but as I held the gun in my hands, I remembered where I was. I was in Katy, Texas and not in Afghanistan. I was home.

So why did it sound like a war zone outside?

Still, I knew what an explosion sounded like as I tucked the gun into my waist band. I cautiously walked to the front door. After opening it, I watched several people propel past me headed toward the parking lot.

"I'm a cop, what's going on?" I shouted.

A group of kids who were running by stopped and turned to look at me. A prepubescent blond boy wearing a Batman t-shirt answered excitedly, "There's a couple of cars on fire in the parking lot!"

I went back to my apartment, grabbed my badge, and clipped it to my shirt. Then I called dispatch to let them know about the fire before I ran outside to see what happened. When I made it to the parking lot, several dozen people were already there and the kids were right, some cars were on fire.

"Everyone get back!" I shouted. "I'm a cop!" Everyone took a few steps back with the exception of a little girl and her mother. The woman, barely out of her teen years, hugged the little girl as she cried profusely. I tapped the lady on the shoulder.

"Ma'am, you're going to have to back up."

She picked the little girl up and that's when I noticed she also had tears. "My daughter saw something she should never have seen, officer. She just watched a man die!"

"What happened?" I asked, hoping that they might've witnessed what had just transpired.

"She was just waving at this man, he waved back, and as soon as he got in his car, it just exploded." She covered her daughter's ears, leaned over close to me, and was barely audible when she whispered. "She watched as a man was burned alive in his car."

Suddenly my heart began to hurt and it was becoming increasingly harder to breathe. I closed my eyes and prayed, hoping that Steven was going to walk out of the crowd and tell me that he was okay. I needed any sign, him calling the apartment, sending a text, anything to let me know that he was okay. I opened my eyes and a tear fell as I knew that I had to ask the next question.

"What did this man look like?"

She continued to whisper. "He was tall, about six feet, blond hair, and he was getting in that Dodge over there."

She pointed to a red Dodge Charger that was in the middle of a four-car blaze. With sirens blaring in the background, I got as close as I could to the red Dodge and looked at the license plate. I covered my mouth when I knew there was no doubt that it was my car. Inside of the car, I could see the outline of a body still on fire. Inside of my car was Steve.

As the words of Yesterday ran through my head, I passed out.

When I came to, a firefighter was holding smelling salts over my nose while the rest put out the fire. Mists of water that sprayed from the hose helped to awaken me from what I'd hoped was a nightmare.

"Are you all right?" the firefighter asked. "You hit your head pretty hard on the pavement."

I nodded and he helped me up. I'd seen a lot of death in the military and never batted an eyelash—I was trained to keep a focused mind. Yet, as I looked at the hollowed shell of my car, everything came back to me and I threw up.

"Take your time, officer."

"I'm Officer...Charlie Briggs. That's my car with the body in it. Someone murdered...they murdered my fiancé."

"I know who you are, Officer Briggs. While you were out, we called in another unit when we saw the body in the car."

"How long have I been out?"

"Just a couple of minutes."

"Is there a perimeter set up? I need to make sure that I get to the witnesses as quick as possible."

"Look, Officer Briggs," he said, his massive hands pressing down on my shoulders, "everything is being taken care of and the both of us know that there's nothing you can do here. More importantly, cars don't just blow up. You need to get out of here, right now, and let us handle this!"

He motioned for another officer, a guy I recognized from the academy, to come get me. As the officer began to speak to me, everything seemed so surreal that I just focused on my car and couldn't hear a word he said. He just guided me back through the crowd and to my apartment building.

The firefighter was right, though. I wasn't even supposed to be anywhere near here, just like Steven wasn't supposed to be in my car. Whatever had caused my car to explode was meant for me, not him, and I wished to God that it had been me in the car. Death would be so much easier than the agony I was feeling.

Why was he in my car? Why didn't he take his truck?

I thought back to when he left the apartment. He was angry, so upset at what I'd just confessed, and somehow he had taken my keys instead of his.

Why did you do that, Steven? Why did you have to take my keys?

With my apartment door unlocked, the officer did a quick sweep before allowing me inside. Once the door was closed he asked, "Is there anyone you'd like to call or anywhere you'd like to go?"

"I just need to call my father."

I called my father, but when he didn't answer, I called my older brother and explained to him what had just occurred. I took several deep breaths, not allowing myself to cry. I needed to be strong. No more tears tonight.

"Chuck, are you okay? Look, I'll get Pops and we'll be on the first flight down there to come get you."

"No, Michael, stay there. I'm thinking someone set up a car bomb and whoever blew up my car was trying to get me. If you and Dad come down here or try to drag me back up there before they're caught, it might do more harm than good. I don't want you guys getting caught in the crossfire."

"I'm a goddamn cop, Sis. I know the risks, but down there by yourself is stupid. At least let me there..."

"No, Michael! Just listen to me! I will find the bastards who did this and they will go to jail for a very long time! I swear it! You and Dad just hold on and I'll let you know what's going on! I'll call everyday about this time to let you know I'm okay, but don't come down here now. Please."

He sighed. "Fine, but if you don't call every day, we're on the first flight down there."

I hung up with my brother and before I had a chance to thank the officer, there was a loud banging at my door.

"Who is it?" the officer shouted. In all the time we were in my apartment I hadn't looked at his name plate until now—Officer Reid.

"It's Carolyn Shruggs."

Officer Reid looked at me and opened the door after I nodded. As soon as the door opened, Carolyn rushed in and hugged me. "Are you okay, honey?"

"How did you get here so fast? You live on the other side of town."

"I overheard it on the scanner. I was on my way home from Katy Mall when I heard. I'm so... so sorry." As she began to cry, so did I, in spite of my vow not to.

When she finally let me go, she showed Officer Reid her badge, he left, and that's when the flurry of questions followed. "Where the hell was he going in your car, Charlie?"

"We'd just gotten into another argument about me being going back to being an engineer. He didn't want me to be a cop for the same damn reason that killed him."

"So, you suspect someone already? Who?"

"Who else would want to do it?" I stood up and began to walk around as I thought about the face of the bastard that escaped. "The only reason no one downstairs asked me if I had any idea is because we're all thinking the same damn things—Los Perdidos."

"I don't know, Charlie. A drive-by is one thing, but blowing up your car? That seems kind of big...especially for them."

I sat down next to Carolyn. "It can't be anyone but them. I put a couple of craters in one of their members and he dies, then I get a medal for doing it. It's gotta be them! I don't know anyone else! I haven't been in Houston that long to develop those kinds of enemies!"

"Were there any witnesses? Did you see anything?"

"A lady and her little daughter saw the whole thing. I saw them downstairs giving a statement. I was one of the last people there and when I saw what happened, I'm ashamed to say I fainted." Carolyn began rubbing my back and the last words that Steve and I spoke seemed to echo throughout the room.

"When you first asked, I wasn't sure. Things were moving so fast. You wanted a family, a house, and kids, but I had just come home from defending my country. Things were going so quickly, but I know for a fact that I'm ready now to be your wife."

"It all makes perfect sense to me now. All the fighting and the hostility about your job was because you wanted an out all along. I just didn't want to see it."

"Steven, I love you so very much and I want to be your wife. Your name is on my uniform for God's sake! I'll quit the damn job to prove it to you!"

"I can't stay here right now. I need to get out."

"Didn't you hear what I said? I said I'll quit!"

"Just don't touch me, Charlie. I can't breathe. I need some air."

"I can't believe that he's gone."

She held me so closely I thought she was going to collapse a lung. "You need to stay with us tonight."

"Thanks for the offer, Carolyn, but I really need to stay here—at least for the night. There are some things that I have to take care of first.

"Well then, I'll stay with you. I don't want you alone."

"Carolyn, you need to get home and take care of your family."

She glared at me as she tried to gauge what I was thinking. "You know they're already looking for the man who did this, Charlie. Downstairs all I heard was them throwing around the name from the guy in the bank, Juan Perez. They're thinking that maybe his brother, Carlos, is the one who did this."

"I know."

"So let them do their jobs, dammit." Perhaps it was because I hadn't responded but when she looked at me, she knew what I was thinking. "Don't do anything stupid, Charlie. They're gonna post some uniforms outside, you know that. If they were after you, they'd be stupid to do anything tonight."

"And since when are gang members the brightest people in the world?" I asked and Carolyn smiled. "Besides," I continued, "I have to call his mother and there's someone in the building who I can stay with."

She shook her head. "You got that soldiers' mentality. Don't let it bite you in the ass."

"I won't."

Someone knocked on the door and she stood up to answer it. "I'm serious, Charlie. This was a tragedy, but don't let it stop you from doing what you know is right. Let KPD do their job."

As she exited, another woman entered with a notepad in her hand. It was time for my statement.

"Can you hold on for a second?" I asked and she nodded. I walked to my bedroom and checked my phone. When I didn't see a message from Steve, the realization of him not coming home settled in. I wiped the tears away from the back of my hand and called Sassy.

She let the phone go to voicemail, but when I called again a few minutes later, she answered the phone with so much anger that I was caught off guard. "What? Goddammit, Charlie! *What the fuck?*"

I paused, thinking that I'd caught her in the middle of one of her jobs. I was ready to hang up when she spoke again, this time with a lot less frustration.

I couldn't hold back the tears as I spoke. "Sassy? They got him Sassy! Those bastards fucking killed him!"

"Killed who?" she asked.

"Please come home. They took Steve, Sassy. He's gone... because of me."

A little more than two hours later, I was curled up into a ball on the couch when a hard knock on my door startled me. I simply looked at the door and returned to the most comfortable position I'd been in all day. I was tired; tired of answering questions, tired of repeating the same story, tired of crying, and tired of being reminded that my fiancé was gone forever.

Even though they weren't from my precinct, every officer investigating had come upstairs to send me their condolences, but that wasn't enough. Deep inside, I knew that the officers were doing their job, but I wanted to be left alone. I wanted to think about what I was going to do to the man who had taken Steve away from me.

"Chuck, I know you're in there! *Open the door!*"

I jumped up from the couch and ran to the door. When I opened it, Sassia stood in the doorway, looking completely exhausted, with an apologetic look on her face. There were dark circles under her beautiful eyes. As soon as she stepped inside the doorway, I squeezed her as tightly as I used to squeeze my mother when I had a bad day. I tried to keep myself from crying, but it all came out in another flood of emotion. Sassia hugged me as intensely as I had hugged her, neither one of us saying a single word while we embraced.

For several minutes, we simple rocked as tears poured from my eyes. Taking her time, Sassia walked me over to the couch and we sat down.

"I see you're not holding up too well."

"All I wanna do is get the bastard who did this, Sassy. I want to find him first and when I do, I swear to God that I'm going to take my time taking his ass apart."

From out of nowhere, Sassia began laughing. Hearing her laugh when I'd confessed a pre-meditated murder not only caught me off-guard, but I quickly became defensive. "What the hell is so damn funny? Those damned Los Perdidos bastards ruined my life and it's funny to you?"

She covered her mouth but continued laughing. Usually when she laughed, it was contagious and we'd both laugh hysterically for no reason. Today wasn't going to be one of those days. From all the crying I'd done, my body was hurting too much to even smile. I threw a couch pillow at her, wishing she'd stop, but when she didn't, I stood up and left.

"So what, you're one of *them* now? Are you a killer, Charlie?" she shouted as I walked towards the bathroom. "You and your gang are gonna ride out and smoke those fools? Are you going to follow through with the whole eye-for-an-eye thing?"

"I'd be justified!" I shouted back. I continued into the bathroom, keeping my back to her.

"What comes after that—life in jail? And for what? You would waste your life for a piece of shit that didn't even have the courage to face you straight up?"

I grabbed hold of the bathroom door and squeezed it as hard as I could. "So what am I supposed to do? Sit around like a little lady and hope the bastard gets caught? That's not who I am!"

"Perhaps," she said softly, "but there are people out there who murder and there are people who believe in justice. You are justice, Chuck. Someone will find the person you're looking for and they'll deal with him, but I doubt that Steve would have wanted you to spend the rest of your life in prison. You survived, which means you should honor the memory of the man who died for you. Besides, cops in prison don't always fare too well."

Collapsing on the floor, I took several deep breaths to keep myself from hyperventilating. Sassy was right, but the nagging feeling in the back of my mind wouldn't let the man who killed my fiancé walk away free.

Sassia walked over from the couch and sat next to me on the hallway floor. "I've lost people too, and I promise you that whoever did this, will get theirs in the end." She kissed me on the forehead and I allowed my head to fall on her shoulder.

"Carlos Perez will get his. I'll see to that."

"That will come in time, Chuck. Right now, I'm focused on you."

"He's only been gone for a few hours, but I miss him so much."

"That doesn't go away. When my father died, I cried every day. The last day I cried is when my mother told me that we are all made up of memories, but not every memory will always be tangible."

I looked up at her as she looked at me. "You know that's the first time you ever spoke about your parents."

She shrugged. "Don't get too comfortable with that. I plan on dragging you around with tidbits of knowledge for a while."

For the first time today, I managed a smile.

"So," she continued, "I think we need to get out of this apartment—go somewhere where it's not a constant reminder of po-po."

She stood up and extended her hand to me, but I didn't reach for it. "I don't think I can go. They still need to come up here and finish. There's something that I might be forgetting or something that they might have missed..."

Loudly groaning, she interrupted me. "Look, Chuck, you can stay here and be miserable or you can go with me. Personally, I think they can survive without Your Highness, but who knows. They are *cops* after all."

"Hey, easy, I'm one of them."

"That's okay. I've already forgiven your mistakes." She extended her hand once more and this time I accepted, pulling myself off the floor and wiping away any leftover tears. "So are we going or what?"

"Where are we going?"

Sassia smiled mischievously. "You'll see when we get there, but you should put on a jacket. It gets cool on the road."

After putting on some loose fitting jeans and an old gray sweatshirt I met an impatiently awaiting Sassia in the living room. She took my hand and instinctively our fingers began to intertwine. A few moments later, we left the apartment and after dodging a few stray officers, snuck out the front of the apartment building. We walked toward her red sports bike, which seemed to glow in the dark.

"So we're riding your crotch rocket?" I asked.

"I prefer to think of it as a coochie scooter."

I smirked, but not long after I felt bad for almost laughing. As a self-induced punishment, I didn't utter another word.

When we made it to her motorcycle, I tried several times to straddle her passenger seat. Sassia smiled, but I was becoming more frustrated with each attempt. After finally making it on what I swore was my last attempt, Sassia softly kissed me on the cheek and I could feel my face becoming flushed.

She handed me her only helmet, started the bike, and sped off, passing by the small army of police that encircled the parking lot. Instead of looking, I closed my eyes, planted my face into her back, and held onto her tiny waist as tightly as I could.

A few miles later, we came to a stop and I finally took the helmet out of her back.

"Jesus, Chuck, I didn't think you were ever going to stop squeezing me! I know this isn't your first time on a bike," she screamed.

It was my first time, but that wasn't why I was squeezing her. I just needed to hold onto someone—to feel something tangible after my loss. I longed to be held and told that no matter how bad things would get, that everything would be all right. I wanted to have someone in my corner, to root me on when I went after that bastard that killed Steve. I looked up at Sassia and knew that she would never be all of those things, but at least I could hold her.

I nodded in response to her question.

"Well then, hold on tight, Charlie, because we're about to ride."

As soon as the light turned green, she was off again. Like a mad woman, she whisked past cars and weaved through traffic. If I hadn't been firmly gripping her top, I would've definitely yelled at her about speeding, but the adrenaline rush I felt at seeing the ground pass right under my feet was incredible. I felt alive but guilty.

It wasn't long before we were on the Highway 290. As we headed toward downtown, we began passing cars more frequently. Some were so close, almost begging to be touched, but I kept my arms around Sassia's waist. She sped down the freeway and as my loose hair tickled my neck from under the helmet, I looked around at the blurred buildings we passed. All the neon colors, shades of green, red, blue, and yellow meshed in a stream of lights. After seeing them for what seemed like the first time, I suddenly felt like everything was surreal and that what had happened would all fade away.

I lifted up the visor on my helmet. "Faster!" I screamed at the top of my lungs.

Without turning to look, we began going faster. I screamed into the night; my heart pounding at what seemed like a million beats per second, my flesh being burned by the night air, and my body yearning for another steep downhill thrill. The feeling of this type of freedom was amazing.

Still going at speeds I didn't dare care to see, I inched my fingers up inside Sassia's blouse and began feeling her breasts. I didn't know why, but if this was really a dream, it seemed like the right thing to do. Never taking her focus away from the road, she continued driving as I felt her braless nipples harden against the palms of my hands. Then just as quickly as the thought had come to me, I withdrew my hands and slid them back down to her waist. As I thought about what I'd just done, I felt sick to my stomach. This wasn't a dream. Steve's body wasn't even cold yet and I was already fondling our neighbor... my neighbor and friend.

Fifteen minutes later, we traversed a short dirt road, which led to a row of bikes next to a biker bar. With a delicious smell coming from the mobile Mexican restaurant on the other side of the parking lot, I realized that I hadn't really eaten much all day. When she cut the engine off, I took off my helmet and began walking toward the restaurant when Sassia sprinted past me. When I finally caught up to her, I learned something else about her. She was speaking in Spanish to the owner, a young, Hispanic guy. With all the gang tattoos sprawled over his arms, I guessed that he'd certainly seen his share of prisons.

"What did you say to him?"

She smiled. "Nothing important, but he's going to make us the best tamales you have ever tasted."

I didn't like that she ran past me and ordered when she didn't even know what I wanted, but I was so hungry that I didn't complain. While we waited for our food, she pointed at an empty bench next to the restaurant.

As soon as we sat down, I didn't have to wait long for the inevitable question. "So, I'm not complaining, but what made you do that?"

I shrugged. "I don't know—*grief*? For a second, things kind of felt surreal. It felt like Steve was at home and we were openly flirting all over again, but that won't happen again. I think the adrenaline rush from riding with you has passed."

"You need to stop all that moping."

"I don't mope," I retorted. "I'm grieving. How did you grieve when you lost your parents?"

"I already told you that I'm not going back there."

"See, you're still grieving and they've been gone for a while. How do you expect me not to grieve when it's only been hours you're still doing it after so long?"

She moved from the other side of the table and sat herself right next to me. "I got over the fact that my parents were gone a long time ago. They are dead, just like Steven, and no amount of complaining, grieving, or crying is going to change that. I get past it because I have to. Life goes on and as harsh as that seems, we're still alive! I've found my purpose in life, and maybe you need to find yours."

"Order up!" The man behind the counter yelled, unknowingly interrupting the tension that was building between us like static electricity.

Sassia stood up, stuck out her tongue at me, and went to get the food. I waited at the table and when she returned, she placed two tamales, both wrapped in aluminum foil, in front of me. As soon as she sat down, I slid my tamales to the middle of the table and asked something that had always been on my mind.

"You didn't even *like* Steve, did you?"

She raised a perfectly arched eyebrow, but still continued to peel the foil from her tamale.

I shook my head and looked around. "I don't even know why I called you. I thought maybe because you were always so lonely that you'd understand, but I was way off."

"I liked Steve."

The aroma from the tamales was getting to me, but I needed to know how Sassia really felt. "You only liked him because you wanted to get in my pants."

She smiled. "When you're right, you're right."

"How can you be so callous? I just lost my fiancé a few hours ago and you're talking like he was the worst mistake I ever made! We had something special, even if you were too self-absorbed to see it!" I pushed both tamales back toward her and folded my arms. "I'm ready to go home."

Sassia raised a finger, telling me to wait while trying to keep the contents of the hot tamale in her mouth. When she'd finally gotten it down, she spoke.

"Look, Charlie, I didn't like you either, but you were so damn persistent that you grew on me. Steve wasn't as persistent, so you can't fault me for not liking him as much as I like you. The fact that I even liked him a little speaks a lot about how much you've grown on me. Most of the men in my life are one of two types, those I can screw and those I won't. Steve wasn't the type of guy I'd screw, but if you wanted it, then I'd do it for you." She reached over and lightly patted me on the ass. "As long as I got some first."

I shook my head because I didn't realize how indifferent Sassia could be, but the truth was that I didn't know why I expected anything different from her. She was exactly the same person she'd always been and the only one I knew who could stand me right about now. Rather than continuing the conversation, I opted to just shut my mouth and think about how badly I wanted to punish the guy who had taken my Steve away.

Sassia chose to interrupt my thinking after only thirty seconds of silence. "So, you're still thinking about revenge, Chuck?"

"No," I lied.

"One thing about you, Charlie, you have to work on your lying. I would think that a girl with two brothers would at least learn how to lie, but your poker face sucks. I mean I can practically read exactly what's going on behind those pretty brown eyes of yours."

"The military taught me a lot of things, but being reactive instead of proactive wasn't one of them. I'm not going to sit around with my thumbs up my ass and wait for him to finish me off."

"First off, he doesn't have a chance in hell with that because the element of surprise is gone. Secondly, you're a cop, which means that every other idiot with a gun and badge is looking for him right now. The best thing for him to do is leave the city, hell, probably the country, if he doesn't want the death penalty or a bullet to the back of the head."

While Sassia spoke, I saw that she had already finished her tamales, but mine were still sitting in the foil on the wooden table. They smelled delicious and even though I continued to tell myself I wasn't hungry, my stomach thought otherwise. I slowly removed the foil and bit into the tamale. Whether it was because I hadn't eaten all day or because I was still in grief, it was the best thing I'd ever tasted. I rolled my eyes and hungrily took another bite.

With my mouth full, I tried asking Sassia what would make her think that he would leave town, but it came out muffled and I was accidentally spitting food at her. She laughed at my attempt to speak, but understood what I was asking.

"If everyone was after you, wouldn't you run too?"

"I'd stay and fight," I replied, finishing the first tamale. I wiped my mouth with my sleeve and then bit into the second one. "Only a coward runs."

"A coward who lives to run away lives to fight another day," she sang.

I wanted to respond, but my mouth was full of tamale. Instead, I shook my head to show my disapproval.

When she saw how hungrily I was tearing into the second tamale, she asked, "Have you eaten anything else today?" I shook my head at her, and this time, she lectured me. "Look, I know you've been through a lot today, but Chuck, you're gonna need your strength—especially if you're about to go into vigilante mode."

I finished up the tamale and licked each finger as it passed by my lips. When I looked down into the empty foil and didn't see tamale waiting for me, I stood up and instinctively began walking toward the stand. Sassia's hand grabbed my wrist and pulled me back down to the table.

Agitated, I asked why she'd stopped me.

"You need some real food. That bar behind us has some pretty good food. Why don't we go in there and wind down?"

I looked at the broken down building behind us and raised an eyebrow. It looked like every other run down biker bar I'd seen and from experience the food was certainly not anything for me to be happy about. I returned my attention to Sassia after a drunken man stumbled out from inside the stained glass doors and fell on his face. "You seriously want me to go in there?" I asked sarcastically.

"It's a lot better than you think."

"Not from what I see."

"Then stop looking through cop-eyes."

I almost smiled, but I wasn't ready yet. I glanced at Sassia and as she looked directly into my eyes, I knew that she was trying to get me to forget about today.

"You don't want food. You just want to get me drunk."

She feigned being offended before asking me, "Is that really such a bad idea?"

"No. In fact, it's probably the best idea I've heard today."

After stepping around the fat, drunken man still lying on the walkway outside the bar, I learned that I was right. The bar was almost exactly as I had pictured it. Instead of country music, 70's and 80's metal blared from the jukebox. Even though the bar wasn't full, the room was filled with smoke, most of it smelling like weed instead of cigarettes, which didn't bother me too much. It was also packed with bald or balding, heavily bearded men who wore either too much leather or too little denim. Most of them had excessively tattooed arms and even with the insignias plastered on the backs of their jackets, almost all of them looked too old to still be riding.

Several women also walked around, but most of them were half-naked and being ogled by the men. I had no idea why Sassia had even brought me here, but as I followed her, we found a table near the back corner of the room. I looked around and along with several Confederate flags that hung from the wooden walls and rafters, there were also a half dozen pool tables in desperate need of refurbishing.

"You like this place?"

"What can I say," she said with a shrug of her shoulders, "they make good food."

We had barely sat down when a huge, bald, black man wearing a checkered apron walked up to us and handed us menus. "Would you ladies like something to drink?" he bellowed.

Without looking at me, Sassia answered. "We'll need a couple margaritas and bring us a bottle of top shelf vodka."

For a few seconds, Sassia's eyes remained locked on his. It wasn't until I cleared my throat that he turned toward me and smiled. "Yes ma'am?"

"Do you like working here?" I looked up at the Confederate flag that hung directly above our table.

"I should," he replied nonchalantly. "I own this place."

"And you're okay with all of these flags?"

He laughed. "You liberal Yankees... these flags are for ambiance and the pretty faces are for lusting. Bikers love America, but Southern bikers love tits and their history, so I keep these rednecks happy as long as they keep me in business. You think they give a shit that my black ass runs this place as long as there's T.N.A. and the liquor's not watered down?"

I shrunk down in my chair and was too embarrassed to say another word.

Sassia just laughed. "What my friend is trying to say is that she doesn't like the taste of her foot, so bring us some burgers and fries to go with those margaritas."

After he nodded and walked away, I just covered my mouth with my hands. "I don't think I've ever been that embarrassed."

"Don't worry about it, Chuck. He's been a hardass ever since the first time I came here."

"How long have you been coming here?"

“This is my first time.”

"Then why the hell did you tell me that the food was good here?"

"Because there wasn't another way to get you in here! Besides, if the tamales are that damn good, it can't be all that bad here!" I didn’t want to smile, but Sassia had finally gotten it out of me. “See, now that’s the smile I want to see. Now that that’s done, we can get to some drinking.”

After about an hour, we had already had three margaritas each and the bottle of vodka was half gone, when I began laughing again. Sassia had finally opened up to me, telling me more about her parents and her job than I’d heard in the last year. I learned that she grew up in Mississippi and was an only child. She recalled how old she was when her father died in an oil refinery explosion and that forced her mother to clean houses. Eventually, she died too; succumbing to lung cancer and Sassia was raised by her aunt in Florida.

Still, I suspected there were things she kept hidden, but I openly told her about my family as well. “Well, you know my mother died a half a year ago because you were at the funeral. Damn breast cancer and that’s why I finally decided to become a cop. She wanted me to be part of the family legacy, like my father—the Philadelphia hero, and my older brother Mike. Like all Italians, my younger brother, Derek, was too stubborn to go into civil service. He rebelled and became a mechanic, I rebelled and became an engineer who was about to marry a Welsh yuppie. Neither of my brothers liked the idea, but my father only cared about me being happy.”

Now that we were trading secrets, I asked her a question that had long been on my mind. “So, Sassy, you’ve been an escort for about a year now, right?” She took a sip of her margarita and nodded. “So who was the best fuck you’ve had and did you do him again?”

Sassia began to chuckle and covered her mouth. She had her hand over her mouth so long that I began to think she wasn’t going to tell me until she sighed. “It wasn’t business related, so let me get that out of the way, copper.” I laughed hysterically as she began to recant her story. “I met him at a masquerade party and I was so goddamn horny that I was ready to burst. Anyway, I just thought he was some average guy that would help me get over the hump, but this guy—he was special. He was so nasty, but I couldn't get enough of that shit.

"So what did he do?" I asked a little more excitedly than I should have.

"Well," she began, "he ate pussy like a champion, choked me, fucked me, slapped me, violated me and only after he outlasted me, did he finally climax. Chuck, it's been a long time since a man made my toes curl and somehow, I'm going to find him again. Shit, while we were fucking, I thought about settling down with his ass."

"Why didn't you?"

"Partly because I never asked him his name, but mostly because I have too much going on in my life right now. Rule number one, no attachments. I don't need that headache right now, especially with what I do."

"So would you ever give it up? Would you ever give up escorting for the right person?"

She leaned across the table and was so close to me that I could taste her breath. "Are you putting in your application?"

I backed away before I answered. "Sorry, I haven't left my old job yet."

She sat back in her chair and smiled. "It's my turn, right?" I nodded, but I could already feel the effects of the alcohol beginning to make my head swim. "I've been avoiding talking about sex with you, but since you brought it up, who was your best?"

I sat back and thought for a minute on whether or not I should tell her. Even when Steven was alive, I hadn't trusted him enough to tell him that he wasn't the best—he wasn't even close. I finished off my fourth margarita and felt the burn as it worked its way down.

"My best was someone I'd met in the military... a superior officer named Captain Edwards."

Sassia smiled at me. "So she was *that* good?"

Shocked that she'd even guessed that it was a woman, I had to ask. "How did you even guess that?"

"Chuck, in the last year I've almost gotten into your pants seven times, I've counted. You already told me about kissing girls in high school! I mean damn, a straight woman would've stopped coming by, but not you. You know what that means? It means you've either been with a woman or you're not afraid to try a little muff diving. I know you prefer commitment first, which is why you never let me go all the way, but it's no big secret. Add to that the fact that you never said 'he' and it was obvious."

And there it was. In all the time I'd spent with Steve, he'd never come close to suspecting, but Sassy had me figured out before I even said a word. I knew I should've been grieving, but a great feeling of relief settled over me. It was as if the weight of hiding my secret had disappeared.

Sassia took hold of my hand and wrapped it inside of hers. "Tell me about Captain Edwards."

The warmth of her touch brought a flood of memories about my pre-Steven past. "Her name was Michelle and she was a highly decorated Navy Captain with eleven years of distinguished service. It began as innocent flirting, she would comment on how nice I smelled and I would blush. Then we'd occasionally go out, kind of on a date, but we just called it girls night out. On one of these co-called dates, we got really drunk and when she dropped me off at the base, she kissed me. One thing led to another and I found myself in her bedroom, sitting of her face and screaming like a damn banshee."

"She wasn't your first," Sassia interrupted.

I shook my head. "I did some stuff in college, mostly with my roommate. Michelle wasn't my first, but she was by far the best."

"What about Steve? Whenever I heard you two going at it, you were howling like a goddamn werewolf."

I smiled as I thought about Steve. "He was a good lay—the best man I'd ever been with. He even had a nice thick one, but he couldn't ever compete with Michelle...and I never wanted him to. I was fine with him being the best guy."

"So what happened with the captain?"

"Well, her husband found out we were sleeping together and threatened to out the both of us if we didn't end it. If the Navy found out that she was bi, then her career was over." I laughed, but I wasn't sure if it was because I enjoyed telling the story or because I was catching a buzz. I sipped on the cranberry juice and vodka before I realized that it was the former before I continued. "We still slept together. When he found out that we hadn't stopped, I retired before he had a chance to out her."

Sassia swallowed down two quick shots of vodka before she spoke again. “So, you were sleeping with Michelle while you were dating Steve. You're a cheating whore!”

“More or less, but it was at the very beginning of my relationship with Steve, so it doesn't count. Steve was just someone I was dating at the time, but after the whole thing in the military, he was there to support me.”

“And here I was thinking that you were a good Catholic girl. So, I have to curse Michelle for stopping me from getting in your pants.”

I laughed before finishing off my mixed drink. “Not really. You never had a chance.”

I didn’t know how we did it, but even with the both of us drunk, we made it back to the apartment building in one piece. After stumbling down the hall, we ended up laughing loudly in front of her apartment door.

“I had fun,” I said. “We need to do this more often.”

“You mean do this instead of getting high?”

“No, getting high is much safer than driving a motorcycle while knee-crawling drunk.”

We both giggled and as Sassia turned away from me and began opening the door to her place, I looked at my door just down the hall. The apartment that Steve and I had shared for the last year was the last place I wanted to be tonight. I really didn’t want to be alone in the bed we’d shared.

I wrapped my arms around Sassia’s waist and placed my head between her shoulder blades.

“What are you doing, Chuck? I gotta be at work in like,” she opened her door and looked at the digital display on her stove, “four hours.”

“Sassy,” I mumbled.

I could feel her rolling her eyes when she responded, “Yes?”

“Can I come in with you?”

She sighed heavily. “If you want the bed, you can have it.”

“Thank you.”

I peeled off the jeans and threw my sweatshirt onto the couch arm as Sassia went to look for a blanket. As much of an ass as she could be sometimes, I was glad that I had found her. I didn’t know anyone else who’d have been able to make me laugh after the tragedy that I’d been through today.

When she returned, I was down to my bra and panties. I was ready for her to attempt to seduce me or even feel me up, but when she threw the blanket at me and cut off the light as she left, I was a little confused. Trying not to dwell on it, I wrapped myself in the cover and attempted to get some sleep.

After about a half an hour of tossing, I picked up the blanket and tip-toed into Sassy's bedroom. I cracked the door a little wider and when I couldn't see anything, I whispered, "Are you awake?"

I waited for a response, but when she didn't speak, I knew she was sleep. Not wanting to be alone, I let my eyes adjust a little more before walking into her bedroom and lying down next to her. We were face to face and I found myself admiring at how peaceful she looked, even the darkness of the room. I smiled and turned away from her, content with not sleeping by myself.

Almost nodding off, I felt Sassy's arms creep around my waist as she slowly pressed her warm flesh against my body. Butterflies thrummed in my stomach and as she kissed the back of my neck, she whispered, "Good night."

I placed my hands on top of hers and quickly fell asleep.

Chapter 9: Small Concessions

Sassia

"CT, I need you to find someone for me."

"Are you on a motorcycle or something? I can barely hear you."

I'd dialed up CT's number on my cell when I was leaving the apartment, but by the time I finished reciting in all the required pass codes and waited for his security prompt, I had already jumped onto the freeway.

"Yeah, I'm riding to work. I still need you to find someone for me."

As the wind swept through my hair, all I could think about was Charlie's face between my thighs. I probably could have had her last night, but talking about her deceased fiancé put a downer on things—although talking about killing the man who'd done it brought the sex drive back online. Besides, I could hold off, since I guessed it wasn't going to be long before I was screwing her anyway.

I knew I was wrong for thinking about sex with her so soon after her fiancé had died, but the truth was I didn't give a shit about him. Steven was a nice enough guy, but he wasn't the type of guy who'd share. At first I saw him as an obstacle and now he wasn't. Chuck was officially single—end of story.

One thing that did bother me was how obsessed Charlie had become with the man whom she suspected of killing her fiancé. I didn't give a shit about him either, but if it meant getting into her pants, then I could certainly look into it.

“Fine," CT shouted, "but it’s the same price as before. Did you catch up to the last guy you were looking for?”

I thought about how Boogie had slipped through my fingers. I was so close to him that I could smell the musky scent he wore when he was grinding his body against mine. I had nearly ended his life, but somehow he'd seen me—knew I was coming. I could feel the rage pulsating through my body as I thought of how close I was to finally ridding the world of the one person who I thought would never betray me—the one person who knew my actual name.

"Hello, Val? Earth to Val, are you still with me?" CT yelled into my Bluetooth and I was finally brought back to reality. "Did you find the guy in Memphis?"

Rule number one, Sassia. Never deter from rule number one.

I softly exhaled and reminded myself of why I'd called. “Not yet, but I have his address. I’ll be paying a visit to him soon.”

“So who’s this new person you have me looking for?”

“His name is Ramon Gutierrez and he’s the leader of a gang called Los Perdidos. Find him.”

“Is he in Houston?"

"Yes, well, he was."

"Done.”

When I hung up with CT, my mind immediately shifted to Charlie. I didn’t know why the hell I’d left a cop asleep in my apartment, especially when I had three unregistered guns stashed around. I contemplated turning back around and kicking her out, but I didn’t really want to. She'd been through enough and even though I would never admit it to her, I liked having her spend the night—even if we hadn't actually slept together.

Dammit, Sassia, remember rule number one?

"Yes," I mumbled to myself, "but as soon as we have sex, I'm cutting her off."

I made it to work fifteen minutes before Lady Zara needed me there and for the first time in a while, I smiled at Anelle and the three gossip-mongers at the front desk. Without stopping to speak to any of them, I headed straight for LZ’s office. I walked through her closed office door and caught her in the middle of a shouting match.

"I swear to God, Lander, if you so much as wink at another one of my girls, I will nail your goddamn balls to the fuckin' wall! And you know I can!" She slammed her cell phone on the desk several times before brushing her hair back and turning her attention to me. "You're actually early? Are we turning over a new leaf or is everyone in your family alive today?"

Sitting down in the chair across from her desk, I maintained my smile. "You said I had a job today. I'm here because you said I had to be here if I wanted to get out of your doghouse."

"I hear that you followed through with Tuttle, not an easy feat. So, as a reward, you'll be having lunch with a new client. His name is Walter Sheppard and you'll be meeting him at the Granduca in his Resideza Imperatore suite." She closed her eyes and smiled. "God, I love the way that rolls off my tongue."

I stood up, heading for the door, when LZ cleared her throat and I knew what that meant.

"Sassia, he's a bit...eccentric. I don't have to remind you to be very *accommodating*, do I?"

"No."

I walked out of her office slightly more agitated than when I'd gone in. I knew I had a job, but I had hoped it was the dine-and-dash type. Ordinarily I would've jumped at the chance to turn another man out, but I just wasn't in the mood today. I had things to do and people to see, and because of LZ's new Mr. Piggybanks, I now had a room to see and someone to do. Whether or not I was ready for it was now irrelevant and everything that wasn't about my job had to be put on hold.

Walking past the ladies at the desk, I heard them whispering something about me being the boss's pet pussy. If I didn't need this as my day job, I would've already shot them all in the face—twice. Still with only a few hours to get ready until my date, I needed some time to prepare mentally.

With Charlie still in mourning at my apartment in Katy, I didn't want to ride back there. Instead, I jumped on my bike and headed to the warehouse district, toward 'El Segundo', the second of three additional apartments I had around the city.

Ten minutes later, I parked my bike next to the antiquated mechanic's shop-turned junkyard and walked into the seemingly demolition-ready building. There were five floors and an apartment on each floor, I didn't know any of my neighbors, nor did I care. Between the cement brick walls, metal doors, and added soundproofing, it made sense that these people didn't want to be bothered and neither did I.

From the outside, no one could discern this dull, gray building from either of the condemned ones lining the street, but inside, everything was as structurally sound as a new building. I pushed the four buttons on the cargo elevator and rode up to my loft. After unlocking my door, I walked in and headed directly to the closet.

I took off my biker jacket and the rest of my clothes, threw them onto the bed, one of only two pieces of furniture I owned. I've never been one for clutter or extraneous furnishings. Looking through my array of dresses and skirts, I opted to wear a sleeveless, red 'fuck me' dress that I had bought about three months ago and never worn.

I put it on and immediately fell in love again with the way the silk felt against my body. While it hugged my breasts, showing every contour of my large and luscious nipples, it dipped low in the back, exposing my curved lower back, and hung loosely around my waist, stopping just above mid-thigh. As it brushed against my legs, I thought of the mysterious Q dragging his hands against my thighs before ripping my dress and then I thought of Charlie doing the same.

Hard to choose the hottest image.

Feeling the heat generate between my legs as I thought about them satisfying me, I shuddered; realizing that I was getting wet and hadn't even left the apartment.

Damn.

I quickly stepped out of my damp panties and threw them into the hamper next to my bed. "Looks like I'm going to make a few people happy along the way."

I called a cab to pick me up and twenty minutes later, I grabbed my safe bag was on my way.

"Sassia, I presume?"

Smiling, I glanced at Mr. Sheppard who was certainly easy on my eyes. Wearing a golf shirt and khakis, he was easily eight inches taller than me. With a build that suggested he lifted weights, dark blue eyes that I could see my reflection in, and a rugged, once black beard that was graying nicely, I was quickly changing my mind about how my day would go.

Using his private entrance, I nodded and stepped into one of the most beautiful suites I'd ever seen. From the white marble floors to the embellished ceiling, the room was exquisitely decorated with hand-carved moldings, extravagant light fixtures, scenic oil paintings, and polished, antique furniture.

I was so enamored with the room that I was startled by the soft tap on my shoulder.

"Absolutely stunning."

"Yes, it is," I said, still admiring the room.

He kissed me on my exposed left shoulder. "I wasn't talking about the suite."

"Then you have good taste."

Still in the doorway, he wrapped his hands around my waist, inching up the dress as he nibbled on my neck and shoulder. From underneath his robe, I could feel his erection creeping up the inside of my thighs as my dress slowly moved upward.

"I want to be inside of you," he whispered, his voice raspy with desire, almost begging.

"And I want you to be." I really did.

I took a condom from out of my 'safe bag', which was still hanging from my shoulder. After opening it, I turned to face him, knelt down, and carefully slid it on. "Where do you want it, Daddy?"

"How nasty do you want me to be?"

"That depends. How nasty *can* you be?"

He pointed at the kitchen and more specifically, towards a circular, wooden dining table. With a devious smile, I headed for the table and after gauging its sturdiness, slowly leaned on top of it until my cheek touched the cool wooden exterior.

"Is this how you like it?"

Following behind me like a dog in heat, he grabbed a small tube of Astroglide and lubed himself before meeting me at the table.

I hiked my dress up just a little higher, perched my leg up on the kitchen table and welcomed him as he slowly slid into my ass. For the next several seconds all I could do was gasp, but as he pushed deeper, I relaxed and soon began to moan.

He grabbed hold of my waist, pulled himself closer to me, and in doing so, I began to feel every inch of him. For a man with such a thick dick, I'd prepared myself for intense ramming, but he was surprisingly gentle. The rhythmic sounds of him slapping against me reminded me of applause, and he didn't force himself inside me. With each plunge, I dug my nails deeper into the dark, wooden table—loving the way he took his time. My toes began to curl and the more I relaxed the more I liked the way he felt.

As my body succumbed to the pleasures of anal sex, I smiled. Typically I just tolerated sex with men. It was my job to, but after 'Q', Mr. Sheppard, and even Sergei, I was beginning to think I needed to relax and enjoy my job a little more.

It was a little past two in the afternoon when I left the luxury suite and called a cab back to 'El Segundo'. My ass was a little sore, that was expected, but all that really mattered was that he'd climaxed—another *very* satisfied customer.

I pulled my personal phone out of my 'safe bag' and turned it back on, hoping that CT had left me a message. When I saw four messages, I quickly dialed up the voicemail and listened intently.

The first three were from Chuck, telling me she was lonely and practically begging me to come home. Fearing that it was her who had also left the fourth message, I was ready to hit delete when a familiar voice took my breath away.

"Hello…Sassia, this is your old friend from St. Louis. You never call. I miss the times we shared…greatly. Call me soon and maybe we can meet up again."

As she read off her number to me, there was no mistaking that it was *her*. Her accent unforgettable, her voice as sexy as I'd ever heard. I clutched the phone as my body seemed to freeze in place. I suddenly felt like a child again, being called to the principal's office because I had done something wrong.

I waited until I had gotten back to El Segundo before I called. I nervously closed my eyes, took a deep breath, and pulled out the clean phone I'd gotten from CT. After a series of random beeps, I dialed the number and she picked up on the second ring.

"Are we secure?" she asked.

"Yes." I whispered even though I wasn't trying to.

"How are you, my *Valentine*?"

I used to love when she called me that. She would call me her Valentine right before she seduced me, but times had changed. I was my own woman now and I'd proved in the year that we'd been apart that I didn't need her; knowing that still didn't stop me from shaking.

I tried to sound as professional as possible. "I'm fine, *Israel.* How the fuck did you get my number?"

"So it's back to Israel now? And after you worked so hard to learn my actual name? That's hurts me, my Valentine."

"You still didn't tell me how you got my number and why the hell you're calling."

She laughed. "Straight to the point, I like that. I hope you don't mind me calling, I got your number from dispatch. It wasn't hard," she paused and laughed, "after all, he *is* just a *man.* Anyway, Valentine, I have a proposition for you—a little job if you will."

"Fuck you, Nava, I don't need your handouts. I don't need to prove shit to you."

She laughed in her most condescending manner, but I didn't see a damn thing funny. Nava and I hadn't left on the best of terms and how we parted left St. Louis PD tracking both our asses.

Nava was my teacher, my mentor. She'd taught me all about protecting myself, fighting, killing, and escaping, but it went deeper than that. Between our *survival lessons,* as she liked to call them, she educated me and taught me how to be a woman. It was because of her that I had so much pride and it was also because of her that I was so stubborn.

...and then there was the sex.

When we had sex, it was like the earth moved. Twice a week, after our survival lessons, she would bathe me, washing every part of my body. When she was finished, she would smell me and kiss me on my shoulder, which was her way of deeming that I was clean enough. Then, she would dry me off and massage me until every muscle in my body was so relaxed that I could barely move. By then I was always ready for her and she would taste me until I came—which never took long with her. Right after, the marathon of sex would begin.

Every time we made love, she was always the aggressor and we would follow the same ritual. At first I didn't mind, but as time went on, I wanted to show her that I could take charge. Hell, I wanted to try something different, but she wouldn't allow me to do anything. She always had to be in control.

As time went on, I slowly began to realize how much control she wanted. She didn't want an equal; she wanted a slave, even going so far as to tell me one night that I belonged to her. If I knew one thing that she hadn't taught me it was that I wasn't *anyone's* slave—not after what Omar had done to me. Being stubborn as I was, I disobeyed her and it cost me. The last time we spoke, we were both running away from the police and from the bullet-ridden house we'd shot up trying to kill each other.

"Are you still bitter about how things ended between us?"

“You don’t do social calls, Nava. What is it that you want?”

Damn, now I was beginning to talk like her.

“Word is that you’ve actually taken out a star by the name of Sergei Castarov. Even more amazing is that you’ve done it without a gun, in the middle of that house of degradation, and made it look like a heart attack. That is exquisite work, my dear. I taught you well.”

And there it was. Somehow she had taken credit for what I had done. To her, I was still her property. I had to swallow hard several times to keep the bile from rushing up my throat. “I pulled it off because I’m good. Is that all, or would you like to take credit for my birth, too?”

“I have a job that needs that kind of expertise. I need someone to die without making it look so obvious."

"Do it your damned self. You're the one who taught me everything I know, remember?"

"My Valentine is still as spicy as ever. I guess that’s why you took that Hispanic name and moved to Houston."

She knew.

"I did not call you to fight, Valentine. What happened between us was a little overboard. I loved you and you loved me too, but I will not be disrespected. You brought a *man* into my house—a house that sheltered you and protected you. To me, that is worse than disrespect, it is betrayal."

"You don't *own* me, Israel. That's what you just can't handle. You shot him in the fucking head, right in front of me, even when I told you it wasn't his fault! Don't ever fucking call this number again or I *will* find you!"

I hung up and collapsed on my bed. For the next few minutes, I listened to my heart race inside my chest and when I was sure that I'd calmed down, I called CT.

As soon as he picked up, I let him have an earful. "Why would you royally fuck me the way you did, CT?"

"What the hell are you talking about? Are you talking about *Nava*?" He sounded confused and even though he didn't know our history, he still knew to keep my shit quiet.

I began pacing around the empty apartment, trying to convince myself that CT was not going to be my next CFT. "Yes, goddammit, I'm talking about Nava! Why the fuck did you give her my number? What the hell is *wrong* with you?"

"Whoa, slow down there! Before you get all, 'I'm gonna gut you and spill gallons of your blood', she told me that you guys were old friends and that she wanted to get in contact with you! I just gave her your goddamn phone number! I didn't know it was that serious! What, is she trying to kill you or something?"

"You *do not* give out anything about me to anyone! Do you fucking understand?"

My heart was racing again and I stood up, pacing around the room. I'd managed to steer clear of Nava for a year and even without CT's help, she'd found me. Truth was, she was the best and if she wanted me dead, it would've already happened, but I needed to know why she'd called out of the blue.

"Sorry, Val, I get you," he said apologetically. "Look, because I fucked up, how about I give you this Ramon Gutierrez for free?"

"For a fuck up this big, you owe me five freebies."

"Three."

"Five."

"If I give you five freebies, can I at least get a kiss on the tip of my dick?"

"No."

"Okay, fine," he conceded, "for six freebies I get to suck on your toes?"

"No."

"Okay, you know what? Fuck it. Damn it all to hell because I'm tired of being your whipping boy! I ain't giving you shit and you don't give me shit! No Ramon Gutierrez for you and we just end this partnership now!"

I sighed. CT was so full of drama that I was almost tired of entertaining his bluffs, but I needed him. "Okay, for six freebies, I'll let you toss my salad."

"Ummm, I'll give you five and I get to smell the coochie."

"Deal."

"Okay, now that that's cleared up, the guy you're looking for, Gutierrez, is not your simple gang leader. Outside of running Los Perdidos, he's a major supplier of weed and illegals from our Mexican friends, but wait, that's not the fun part. He's paranoid as hell. He keeps at least four body guards around him at all times."

"Even when he's screwing?"

"Um, I said at *all* times, didn't I? Weren't you listening? This guy is certifiably insane. Known associates who have turned on him have often reappeared without their flesh. If there was ever a CFT for this guy, they'd have to blow up his houses—he has six. He also rarely goes anywhere twice."

"Does he have parents, children, or a woman in the states?" I asked, curious to see how the hell I was supposed to get close enough to this guy to ask questions.

"Nope, parents are deceased, no kids, and no steady woman. He's insulated himself pretty well. Bottom line, Val, unless you have the backing of the United States government, you're not going to even get close to him."

"Damn."

"May I ask why you're trying to get to this untouchable man?"

"No."

"What the fuck? I'm sticking my neck out while hacking these files and I can't even know why you have such a hard-on for this guy?"

"That's pretty much it."

He let out a sarcastic chuckle. "You're a goddamn piece of work. Perhaps you don't know how this goes, but Nava does. In order to get something, you gotta give something."

"This is a freebee, CT, I don't owe you shit," I replied defensively. I didn't know why I was trying so hard to keep Chuck's name from coming out of my mouth, but then I thought about CT finding out what she did and it seemed obvious.

"Fine, *Valentine*, perhaps it's time you got another handler. I won't risk the lives of the people I handle on some bullshit that they won't even tell me about."

CT's hyper drama twice in the same phone call? I knew that ordinarily CT would take a bullet for me before he gave me up, but I also knew when he was bluffing. He wouldn't leave me and we both knew it, but I still had to throw him a scrap. This time I was calling his bluff.

"Your loss."

"You would *really* do me like that?"

"I need to ask him a question about where to find one of his associates." I exhaled loudly and tried to sound defeated.

"See how easy that was? Now I can tell you about your boy's one vice. He loves to gamble on cockfighting."

Small concessions lead to great victories.

I smiled. "When and where?"

"That's all I have on him. If you want to find him, you'll have to find that out yourself."

"Any known associates other than his gang bangers?"

"Only three: Marco Portillo, Fernando Varejo, and Rafael Velasquez."

"Send their pictures to my phone."

"I can do that, but truthfully, I doubt you can break any one of them, Val. These files basically say that anyone who so much as talks about Gutierrez gets a skin-free makeover. If there are three people who are listed as his associates, they're not gonna give you squat on him."

I laughed. They hadn't met *me* yet.

I was a little disappointed when I learned the criminal underworld wasn't as clandestine as I had been led to believe. With one phone call to my weed supplier, I knew about every cockfight from Houston to El Paso.

Fortunately, luck was on my side. According to him, tonight there was going to be a huge fight on the north side of the city. As usual, I deflected several of his propositions before he finally gave up an address. Without thanking him, I hung up the phone and called Chuck.

She picked up on the first ring. "So, you *do* call?" The tone in her voice suggested that she was feeling a lot better than she had yesterday.

"You miss me yet?"

"I—I'm just not ready to go home. I don't want to be alone, you know?"

I knew exactly what she meant. When my mother died, the last thing I wanted was solitude. Still, I managed, and she would too—especially when I was doing all this for her.

"I still have some work to do..."

"Don't you mean some *people* to do?"

I intentionally ignored her snide remark. "I'll be home late. Why don't you get out the house and find something to do? Go for a run or find a low profile gym and get a good sweaty work out."

"I don't want to do anything. I just want to forget that yesterday ever happened. So what time can I expect you back home?"

"When I get there."

"So it's like that? I can't even *ask*?"

"And I love you, Boo, but if you want that privilege, you'll have to do more than just share my bed."

She sighed. "Why is it always about sex with you? Can't I just care about where you are and what happens to you?"

"Yes, you can, but the fact that you slept in my bed and didn't give up a piece means that I'm growing. If anything, you can at least give me that much."

"I give up. Fine, I'll get out of the house, but how am I supposed to lock the door?"

I swallowed hard. "There's a spare key in the top drawer of the kitchen cabinet."

I guess she sensed the hesitation in my voice. "Don't worry, I'll bring it back."

"And don't you dare makes copies, flatfoot."

"I wouldn't dream of it."

I hung up with Chuck and found myself smiling. I quickly shook the smirk from my face and decided it was time to get back to business. It was time for Chuck to have her justice.

Wearing a yellow Spanish top and blue jeans, I packed a small knapsack full of things I might need for the night and called a cab. When it picked me up twenty minutes later, I directed him downtown, which is where I needed to begin my quest.

As soon as the cabbie dropped me off, I noticed the swarms of people in red, headed toward the pro basketball arena.

Perfect.

Because I couldn't use my motorcycle, I needed a car and had come downtown to steal one. I was in luck because with a game going on; I was practically being handed the keys. Walking down each street several times to make sure that cops weren't on boost patrol, I popped the lock on a Caprice Classic that sat next to a meter. I didn't usually go for older cars, but the tinted windows and innocuous model were perfect. The car's team bumper sticker also told me no one would be looking for this vehicle until after the game.

After spending a few minutes hotwiring, I pulled out and carefully drove to North Houston. With a little less than three hours to do what I had to do, I didn't like being slow and cautious. Unfortunately, being prudent was the only option. Between the stolen car and the items I had in my bag, if I got pulled over, the shit was going to hit the fan.

Luckily, it didn't take long to make it to the cockfight from downtown. From outside and inside, the place looked like a normal bar, but when I told the bartender—an overweight Mexican man—what I came to see, he eyeballed me.

"*What's your name*?" he asked in Spanish.

"*Sassia.*" I replied in kind.

"You don't look like police."

"*I'm not.*"

"*Perhaps you can prove that to me*?"

"*Maybe I can.*"

I took his hand as he led me to the stockroom. As soon as the door closed behind me, he dropped his pants, revealing an average flaccid penis. "*Prove it.*"

I put my knapsack on the floor, quickly reached into it, pulled out a serrated hunting knife—I affectionately call it the tongue loosener—and shoved it into the underside of his nuts.

"Don't—fucking—try—me." I decided to speak in English so that there wasn't any misunderstanding. "My name is on the list and if you don't fucking check again and find it there, I'm going to cut your nuts off and before you have a chance to scream, I'll shove them down your fucking throat and make you choke on them. Do we understand each other?"

He sulked as he pulled his pants up and with a series of stomps against the floor, another man, this one skinny and dirty, poked his head out from behind a fake wall behind a wine rack.

"*Let her in,*" the fat one said.

The skinny one did as he was told and as soon as I entered, I could hear the crowds roaring in amusement.

With almost every man in the room stationed around one of the three pens, the same chants of death rang throughout the room. The smells of sweat, beer, blood, and chicken shit created a gag-worthy stench and I tried to breathe through my mouth.

"*Kill him! Kill him*!"

I made my way to the front of the pens just in time to see one rooster, covered in blood, collapse as the other continued to peck at it. By the time someone rushed in to stop the fight, the losing rooster was bleeding everywhere, including from one of its empty eye sockets, and was barely moving. The crowd roared with approval as the cock's owner stepped into the ring and held his champion rooster above his head.

Christ.

As the owner collected his money and the payouts were being divided, I walked away in utter disgust. These fucking people were dumber than the roosters. At least I didn't shoot anyone in the eye.

"Not yet anyway," I mumbled under my breath.

Someone should've stepped in sooner, but I also found it a little ironic that I could kill a man without any remorse, but when it came to a fighting three-piece meal, I couldn't stomach it.

I managed to keep my composure for forty-five more minutes, which is when both Ramon and Marco appeared. True to what CT had told me, Ramon brought along six heavily armed guards, while Marco was confined to the back of the pack.

I'd found my way in. *Never bring a chicken to a cockfight.*

Once Ramon arrived, everything seemed to move much faster. All three pens were consolidated into one huge one and suddenly four of the biggest roosters I'd ever seen were perched above the ring. The once rambunctious room was suddenly silenced as several curvaceous women in bikinis went around collecting bets. Not knowing what the hell I was doing, I put a hundred dollars on number three as one of the half-naked women winked at me, before they all returned to Ramon and sat in chairs next to him.

"*Begin*," he shouted and all four birds were let loose.

Not caring about the outcome and even less about the carnage, I focused my attention squarely on Marco. He wore a wife-beater, loose jeans, and a pair of new, white Nikes. He didn't appear old, maybe in his mid-thirties, but I noticed that his shaved head appeared to be his way of masking his balding and also there was a small soul patch of hair on his chin. The tattoos adorning his neck, arms and hands suggested that he'd been in prison several times, but the way he lagged behind Ramon and the bodyguards told me he was still not much more than a gopher.

Ramon was as fixated on the fight as anyone on the room, but I could see Marco had other things on his mind. Sensing that Marco was restless and would be leaving soon, I left the fight before it ended.

My hunch paid off.

I watched Marco leave the building and head to his car, and old, rusted out Trans-Am. The fucker was a walking stereotype and I would've laughed if I wasn't so focused on what I needed to do. A cloud of smoke appeared as he pulled off and I was soon in pursuit. I made sure to keep my distance, but after a twenty-minute drive, he pulled into the driveway of a one-story house.

I drove on past the house and parked the Caprice against a curb five blocks down. Even though I'd been wearing gloves, I still made sure that I hadn't left any traces of me behind as I cleaned out the car. I hopped over several fences, stopping in one backyard to change into a black sweat suit and skullcap, detailing which houses had guard dogs and which didn't in case I needed to make a quick getaway and retrace my route.

By the time I made it to the target's house, the lights that were on had been cut off and the only sounds I could hear came from a TV loudly broadcasting a Mexican game show. With his Trans-Am still in the driveway, that meant only one thing: sex.

I crept around to the side door and picked the lock; only a few steps in and I heard the sounds of a woman in ecstasy as the headboard banged against the wall.

"*Give it to me, papi! Give it to me*!" Her squeaky voice coupled with her Mexican accent made it hard for me not to smile, but I pinched my lips together and crept closer to the bedroom.

For several minutes, I let them go at it as I prepared for my interrogation. I placed a bandanna over my nose and mouth and pulled out both my Glock and the serrated hunting knife.

When I peeked into the room, they were going at it. He had her in doggy-style with her head buried in pillows near the headboard. I grimaced at his hairy ass as he plunged into her, but all that mattered to me was that their backs were to the door. They had made this too easy.

With his body harshly pounding against hers, I knew what was coming next. I quickly ran behind Marco, stuck the blade in his leg, and quickly put the Glock to his head.

"*Shit*," he screamed in Spanish and tried to look at the knife stuck to his thigh, but as I removed the safety, he returned his gaze to her back. "*Who... the fuck are you? What... do you want*?"

In Spanish, I told him what I wanted. "*Close your eyes and don't you even think about nuttin'! Don't you dare*!"

"*What's happening*?" the woman asked and as she pulled her head from the pillows, I could see that she was blindfolded.

Too easy. What kind of lame-assed criminals are these people?

As she moved to take off her blindfold, I punched her in the face. She fell back into the pillows, and I hit her on the back of the head with the butt of the gun. "*Don't fucking move, dumbass, or I will blow your boyfriend's brains all over your back*." Then I hit him on the top of the head with the gun butt. "*Put your head into her back*!"

Angrily, he did as he was told and she started crying.

"*Shut the fuck up*!" I screamed. "*Where is Carlos Perez*?"

"*I don't know who the fuck you're talking about, bitch.*"

I smiled because I was actually hoping he'd get tough enough to try me. Even with my knife already in his thigh, he was still a hardass. I would've admired him if I weren't already strapped for time. I pounded against the tongue loosener, burying it deeper into his muscular right thigh. When he tried to lurch back, I quickly shot him in his left ass cheek.

"Fuck you, you crazy bitch!" he shouted. *"Do you know who you are fucking with?"*

"I don't ask twice." I stood beside the bed and put the gun up to his girlfriend's head.

"Don't let her kill me, Marco!" she squealed.

"I don't give a fuck about her. You can kill me and I still won't tell your ass nothin'."

I put the gun in between his thighs, pinning one of his testicles against the barrel of my gun. *"You wanna try again?"* When I saw him beginning to waver, I began to twist the blade, which was already two inches deep in his thigh. *"This is your last chance! Where is Carlos Perez?"*

He suddenly screamed and I watched as tears began to fall. *"Dead! He's fucking dead!"*

"When?"

The tongue loosener had done its job, but I still kept my gun pinned to his balls.

"The robbery wasn't sanctioned! He wanted to be big and he fucked up! So they put him on the front lines right after the robbery! He's dead!"

He stopped short of saying that Ramon had anything to do with it, but I didn't want Ramon. I pulled the blade from his thigh, but kept the gun pointed squarely at him. There was a problem with this timeline. Marco said that Carlos had been killed on the front lines, which meant that he'd died during a gang war. If Carlos had been killed right after the robbery, then who in the hell put the bomb on Charlie's car? I needed more answers.

"Why are you bringing the fucking heat by blowing up cop cars?"

"Los Perdidos ain't after no fucking cop, but if I ever find out who you are, I am fucking going to rip you apart."

The girl chimed in. *"You're fucking dead, puta! You're dead!"*

Not liking the threats, I shot him in the right ass cheek and pulled the blade from his leg. Whether it was because of the blood loss or the pain, he passed out on top of the hysterical Latina.

What a pussy.

While she struggled to get out from under him, I punched her in the face a second time, this time with much more ferocity than the first.

"Don't ever threaten a woman of LRZ or the next time these bullets go in your fucking faces."

I knew that with bullets in both legs and a knife wound in his thigh, doctors were going to have to patch him up, which meant police would be involved. If he thought another rival gang did this, neither of them would speak to the police and instead, be planning revenge. I needed them quiet if I was going to find out who was really after Charlie.

With him unconscious and her writhing in pain, I made my exit. I spray painted LRZ on several of the walls, packed up my knapsack, and was ready to leave when I heard someone sneaking around outside.

I peeked through the window and saw Chuck walking beside the house with her weapon already drawn. She'd apparently heard the gunshots even though I'd hoped the TV was loud enough to mask them. She banged on the side door and when it came open; she extended her weapon and shouted, "*Police*!"

Damn.

As Charlie crept in, I unlocked the front door and burst out as quickly as I could. Even though I heard Charlie shouting, "Police!" behind me, I didn't dare look back. With my knapsack resting firmly against my back, I retraced my route from earlier, jumping over fence after fence, never deviating from the path.

With her in pursuit, running behind me like a goddamned track star, the last thing I needed to do was to get caught. She fired several warning shots, but with them missing my back by mere inches, I grew unsure if she was shooting to take me out. Instead of climbing fences, I decided hurdling them was a much better option.

"*Eleven...ten...nine...*" I was counting the steps that I had taken while trying to avoid the yards with dogs. "Now right in three...two...one..." I hurdled over the next fence as bullets whizzed past me, but this time they weren't nearly as close as before.

After jumping over one more fence I found myself staring down both sides of a deserted alley. I hadn't heard gunshots in about thirty seconds, but when I heard dogs to my left, barking angrily into the night, I knew she was trying to cut me off.

Fuck.

I doubled back, jumping over the same fences that I'd just finished hurdling in the hopes of losing her. I ran down Marco's street and hid next to a car. When the barking finally stopped, I thought about hotwiring a car, but if she was near, she'd hear it. Instead, I caught my breath and began walking further down the street when Marco's half-naked girlfriend ran out the house and saw me.

Barely twenty feet away from me, she pulled out a Colt .45 and began blasting in my direction, barely missing me and hitting a rearview mirror to my left.

"Shit!" I growled as I scrambled to hide in front of a brown Ford sedan. Now out of her line of sight, I pulled the Glock from my backpack, but as she continued firing while running toward me, Chuck tackled her.

I stood up and began to run, but this time Charlie saw where I was running and she was much closer.

"Police!" she shouted, but I wasn't about to stop. I leapt across the front lawn of the house nearest to me and ran as fast as I could. Once again hurdling fences, I could still hear Charlie's footsteps; she wasn't that far behind.

The burning in my lungs began to take effect as I continued my sprint. I'd learned to breathe in through my nose, but Charlie was too damn close and protocol was the last thing on my mind. In an instant, I'd forgotten almost everything I'd learned as I ran just to keep from getting caught. This time I couldn't count my steps, only react to them as I fell into several yards with dogs. Several times I slipped on dog shit and stumbled, but I couldn't stop.

When I finally made it back to the car, I opened the door and quickly slid in, happy that I had disabled the interior lights. Instead of starting the car, I closed the door and hid. Not fifteen seconds later, Charlie appeared, stopping right next to the car.

As she circled the car, I hid beneath the steering wheel, too afraid to move.

"Fuck!" I heard her shout as she continued running in the opposite direction she'd come from, away from the house. As I sat up looking around at the empty street, I couldn't help but laugh nervously. She'd almost gotten me...*almost.*

My heart beat wildly inside of my chest and as adrenaline pulsed through my body, the thought of Charlie chasing me was like a rush. I took a few seconds to gather myself, but when I went to turn the key, my hands were still shaking. I slowly inhaled, started the car and turned around, heading toward the main through street. I paused at the stop sign just in time to see her running behind the car, chasing shadows. Not realizing that I had been holding my breath the whole time she was near the car, I exhaled and quickly pulled onto the main street.

I ditched the Chevy in favor of an off duty cab. The old man took me back to the warehouse district where I sat the blade in the sink and filled it with bleach. Then I cleaned and dismantled the Glock, using a hammer to help destroy any evidence that it had ever been used.

After a change of clothes, I left the apartment and called CT. There was more going on here and I needed to know what.

As soon as he picked up, I spoke. “CT, I need to know if there’s an open CFT on anyone with the first name Charlie, last name either Briggs or D’Agostino.”

“I don’t see anything open on my network, but it may take some time to look on others. At this rate, you’ll use all of you favors up by the end of the week. I can’t wait for my up close and personal.”

“Fine, whatever, but I need that info ASAP. Something’s going down and I need to know what.”

He sighed. “Val, what the hell are you getting yourself into?”

“As soon as you know something, I’ll know something.”

By the time I hung up, I was standing next to my motorcycle. I jumped on my bike and made my way back to Katy, dropping small pieces of the Glock along stretches of Westheimer and I-10. Content that I had successfully disposed of all the evidence, I made my way back to the apartment and waited for Chuck. With all the excitement I’d had today, I was horny as hell and there was no way she was going to deny me tonight.

I would take it if I had to.

Chapter 10: Innocence

Charlie

When I returned to the gang banger's house, Marco was unconscious with his ass tooted in the air. His girlfriend, who was shooting wildly at the intruder until I tackled the gun away from her, was crying and wailing like she'd been shot too. I didn't see any blood though, just a swollen eye and a bruised cheek, but other than that, she was perfectly fine. Stupid, but fine.

I could've called it in then, but I still needed answers. I checked on Marco, but he was unconscious and bleeding from both ass cheeks, along with a gaping wound in his thigh. I returned to the living room where his girlfriend, who was bottomless, sat balling on the couch.

"Where is Carlos Perez?"

"Cojete tu solo!" she cried out.

She was telling me to 'go fuck myself' and my patience was waning.

"Where the fuck is Carlos Perez?" I shouted, this time grabbing her by the neck. Her indignant look told me she wasn't about to say a thing. With all the LRZ tags spray-painted around the room, I knew that she was either scared or plotting.

I walked in the room to find Marco still unconscious and ordinarily I would've quickly called for a bus and told someone where I was, but I needed to find the man who had stolen my life and Marco was the only shot I had. After searching the police database, the only one of Ramon Gutierrez's lieutenants that lived in the country was Marco. The only people who would know where Perez was hiding was going to be one of them and I needed that knowledge.

With gunshots in both cheeks and a deep knife wound on his thigh, I placed my gun right next to the wound in his leg. It was fresh and still oozing, so I knew it was going to be sensitive. When he awoke, he screamed like a bear and when he swung to attack me, I pulled away and showed him the Beretta I was carrying.

"I saved your life, you piece of shit! Where is Carlos—fucking–Perez!"

"¡Necesito ayuda! Estoy sangrando!

"I don't give a shit if you're bleeding, but I know sure as hell that you understand me. Where is Carlos Perez?"

He quieted his whimpering. "No sé."

He did know! I knew he did and he was keeping it from me! "Who shot you then? Can you tell me that?"

"No sé," he repeated.

"Don't give me that bullshit, Marco! Who the hell did this and where the fuck is Perez?"

The girlfriend began to cry louder and suddenly I understood why she'd been punched in the face. It all made sense. Whoever had run out of the house hadn't come here to kill Marco, they wanted information. Just like I did.

"Abogado." Seemingly out of breath, he asked for his lawyer before he passed out again. From all the screaming his girlfriend had done, his reply was barely audible; then I heard sirens in the background.

"*Fuck*!" Apparently even the people in this crappy neighborhood were sick of the gunfire and noise.

I stormed out of the house with more questions than I'd had when I got there, but when I walked through the front door, I took special notice of *LRZ* spray-painted on one of the walls. This had turned into something gang-related and I guessed that it was the reason Marco didn't dare speak. I was sure he hadn't seen the tags—not with the wounds he had, which meant that the intruder had told him who he was.

Marco knew who his attacker was, but they were plotting revenge and I'd run out of time. As an off-duty cop, I couldn't be found in that house after what had transpired tonight. I was already out of my jurisdiction and I had illegally discharged my weapon.

Who the hell had gotten to Marco and shut his mouth? What did LRZ have to do with all of this? Where the hell was Perez? Who had I been chasing?

When I'd made it to his house twenty minutes earlier, I'd heard gunshots. I wasn't sure at the time if it was the loud television, but I still pulled out my service weapon. With the door opened, I made it into the house and spotted Marco bleeding from his ass just as someone jetted out the front door.

I pursued whoever it was for several blocks, running as fast as I could to catch up, but they were fast. The way they leapt the fences and stayed away from the guard dogs meant that they knew the neighborhood and probably lived nearby. After a few blocks of chasing the perp who'd shot Marco, I'd backtracked, found them again. Had it not been for Marco's girlfriend firing a hand cannon and then me having to tackle her, I could've caught the LRZ thug who had done this and it would've all been over. As it was, I lost them again; he seemed to just disappear into the night.

Stepping into Steve's silver Lexus, I pulled away from the house with less information than I had before I went in. Marco was the only lead I had on Perez and with the apparent gang attack, now I was left with more questions.

Why the hell did LRZ want Marco quiet? Was there about to be a war between Los Perdidos and LRZ and I was inadvertently caught in the middle?

Without any answers, all I could think about was Carlos Perez and how he was the only one who knew all the answers. The sound of an ambulance rushing past me brought me back to reality as I found myself driving aimlessly around the south side of Houston.

After weaving my way through dark side streets and back to I-10, I thought about driving home, but didn't feel like being alone. With Sassia still working and the department forcing me out on bereavement leave, there was nothing for me to do at the apartment but wallow in misery. That wasn't my style. I stopped by a well known cop bar to have a few drinks and shoot the shit with some of the guys from work.

When I entered, everyone offered condolences, but several beers and dozens of gruesome cop jokes later we were all laughing. All the older cops talked about stupid criminals, lazy higher ups, or their dysfunctional lives; younger ones, myself included, reminisced about the academy. It felt so good to laugh that for an hour, I didn't think about how miserable the last week of my life had been. Once I felt my buzz kicking in, I saluted everyone goodnight and drove home.

I made it back to the apartment, but I sat in the car for a few minutes fondling Sassia's key. As I rubbed the key between my thumb and forefinger, I smiled. Sassia had actually let me into her life.

Was I going to let her into my pants? Intriguing thought.

I stepped out of the truck and slowly walked back to my apartment, waving at the uniforms that were still stationed in the parking lot. When I made it back to my apartment, I stared at Sassia's key for the second time.

"I'm sorry, but I don't want to be alone tonight," I whispered.

I took a couple of steps away from my door, moving toward Sassia's, and unlocked her door. As I slowly pushed the door open, I found Sassia straddling the arm of her couch, wearing a black satin negligee that hugged her form as the sweet smell of orchids permeated the room.

"Welcome back," she said softly.

Practically frozen in the doorway, she took my hand and guided me inside to the couch.

"What's all this for?"

She didn't answer, but stood behind me, wrapped her arms around my waist and licked the nape of my neck with the tip of her tongue.

I closed my eyes and shivered like a leaf in a windstorm.

You want to be touched. You need to be touched. Don't deny yourself this pleasure.

Allowing her to pull off my shirt, I softly exhaled as she drew my nipples into her mouth. Her tongue played in perfect circles, sending shivers rippling down my spine. I grabbed handfuls of her dark hair and pressed her face against my flesh, kissing the top of her head as she continued to tease my breasts with her tongue. She seemed to be in no hurry to move beyond my breasts; first one, then the other moving as if we had all the time in the world.

I need this.

As I seductively glanced at her and relaxed against the soft couch cushions, Sassia took control. She inflicted tiny nipping bites on the tips of my nipples, and then let her tongue trace a path over my belly and abdomen. With just her teeth, she pulled away my panties, pushed my knees apart, and tasted me. I spread my legs further wide open, feeling her tongue caress my clitoris. Suddenly there was nothing in the world but my clit and her tongue. I moaned softly, encouraging her, arching my back to take in more of her tongue.

With her tongue busy, I played with my breasts, pinching my nipples as she buried her face between my thighs.

"Yes...mmmm..."

With my nipples now erect and sensitive to touch, I left them alone and again ran my fingers through her hair. I wanted to taste her, to take her beautiful breasts into my mouth, but her focus was on me and she kept herself out of my reach. Each sway of her tongue sent bolts of lightning up my spine and as she dug her nails into my thighs, my grip on her hair tightened.

"You want me inside you?" she asked.

The involuntary, "Yes" that escaped my mouth surprised even me, but as my body arched to accommodate her, I knew what I wanted. We both knew. This night had been a long time coming.

As she slid upward toward me, again sliding her tongue over my belly and breasts, she parted my lips with her tongue and I sucked from her what she had tasted—me. With our tongues fighting for dominance and our mouths struggling for the next breath, I opened my eyes to see Sassia staring at me. I wanted to turn away, but her gaze was so intense that we remained fixated as our bodies fought for supremacy. I wrapped my legs around her waist and clung to her, desperate for more of what she had to offer.

I wanted to tell her that I loved the way I tasted in her mouth, tell her that the way her silk negligee brushed against my nipples made me want to scream her name, but I couldn't. I was suddenly gasping for breath when she slid her fingers deep inside of me.

"Oh...God," I whispered, but as she continued to suck on my bottom lip, all I could do was pant. Her fingers explored me, her thumb teased my swollen clit, and when my eyes began to roll, Sassia knew she had found my spot.

"Cum for me, Charlie," she whispered, her gaze still locked on me.

"No," I whispered back. "Not yet."

She rolled her fingers around, pushing upward; repeatedly massaging the only spot in my body that Steven could never seem to reach. My body began to spasm and once more, Sassia demanded that I cum for her. This time, I couldn't speak. I reached out and grabbed the back of her head, forcing her mouth against mine and as my body erupted, I screamed into her mouth, calling out her name and begging for mercy all at the same time.

"*I knew you'd cum for me...*"

I collapsed on her couch and watched as she took her fingers out of me and licked them. My body trembled as I watched her, fascinated, and when she was done, she gently licked around my lips before pushing her tongue deep inside of my mouth. I would've never done anything this nasty with anyone—ever, but the feelings of ecstasy and complete satisfaction in the pit of my stomach told me I liked it.

I opened my eyes the next morning feeling better than I had in the last few months. My body felt light and all the tension I had seemed to disappear.

"Good morning, St--."

Instantly, I remembered where I was and what I had done. My fiancé wasn't even buried yet and I had betrayed him by succumbing to temptation.

I pulled the covers over me as high as I could, but the tears wouldn't follow. I wouldn't let them. Now, more than ever, I needed to find out who had wanted me dead and why. It was back to business; no more fucking Sassia's tongue—for now anyway.

I spent almost fifteen minutes looking for every article of clothing that I had worn last night, while cursing both Sassia and myself.

"Didn't she know what I was going through? Didn't she *care*?" Even though I wanted to cuss her out, I was glad that Sassia had left; I didn't want her to see how angry and ashamed I was.

When I finally found my panties, I pulled my cell phone out of my pocket and saw that I had a message from my Lieutenant.

I dialed up the voicemail only to hear a terse, "We need to talk."

What the hell? Can I get more than an ominous message?

I called him back, hoping that they had made a break in the case, but when he didn't answer, I finished dressing, brushed my teeth, and quickly drove down to the station.

Making it to KPD in record time, I parked the car in a handicapped spot and ran through the flurry of first shift cops. Several of them glared at me while others shook their heads.

What the fuck was going on?

As I approached the glass door of Lt. Jameson's office, he was stroking his stark white beard, standing with Captain Hines and looking over my file.

"Briggs," he said in an unusually calm demeanor, "thanks for coming in. Close the door and sit down."

An uneasy feeling crept over me as the Captain, the younger and wider of the two, stood next to the Lt., both of them with looks of disappointment on their faces.

I closed the door and sat in the chair in front of the Lt.'s desk. "Did you find him? Did you find the man who murdered Steve instead of me?"

The Lieutenant sat down focusing his dark brown eyes on me while folding his wrinkled, white hands together. "What the *fuck* is wrong with you, Briggs? Are you trying to lose your goddamn job?" he asked solemnly.

"What do you mean?"

The wrinkled lines etched in his face all seemed to come together and form the most disgusting look I'd ever seen. "You know very well what I mean, dammit! Breaking and entering, assault in the form of torture, brandishing a firearm, leaving the scene of a crime… need I say more?"

"Lieutenant, I…"

"I'm not finished talking!" His voice bellowed loud enough for people outside his office to hear him. "A Mr. Marco Portillo filled out a statement last night and I'll just recap the good parts. He says that last night he was alone with his girlfriend when a female cop busted in, demanded to know something about Carlos Perez, stabbed him, shot him twice, punched her in the face several times, dug her gun into his hip when he didn't know a damn thing, and then left when she heard more cops coming! The neighbors say they saw a...let me see...ah, yes, a silver Lexus pull away from the house not long before HPD pulled up! Does that sound familiar?"

"I was there, yes, but I never shot him!"

"That doesn't matter, goddammit! I got the media all over this! They smell blood and there's nothing worse than a cop, one who just got a fucking commendation, going rogue! They are eating this shit up."

"What the Lieutenant is trying to say," interjected Captain Hines, "is that you could be in a shitload of trouble here. Whether those bullets were yours or not, at the very least you assaulted an injured man. You didn't call for backup and you left the scene of a crime. These are major offenses, Briggs. Now, I'm not ready to take the word of a known gangbanger over that of a newly decorated officer, but this has to be thoroughly investigated. We're waiting now for ballistics reports, and we need your service weapon."

"I was looking for my fiancé's killer and that banger knows something, Lieutenant! When I got to his house, it was already broken into and he was already shot! That son-of-a-bitch knows where the asshole is who tried to kill me! Doesn't that mean *anything*?" I screamed and though I tried to keep the tears from falling, they fell freely.

"You are not in the military, Briggs. We don't do military style justice here! You're not a goddamn vigilante! An officer of the law has protocols! You see him in danger, you call! As of now, you are suspended! Clean out your locker and turn in your badge and gun!"

When I stormed out of the office, I was sure that everyone had heard what went on, but no one came to my aid. Instead, I walked alone to my locker, grabbed my gun and shield, and marched back to the Lieutenant's office.

"Here!" I shouted, slamming them on his desk. "With that asshole still out there, at least I have my fucking fists to protect myself, right?"

The Captain walked over and stood in front of me. "Don't make me add insubordination to that already long list of potential charges. This is not something we *want* to do, Briggs, it's something we *have* to do. Effective immediately, you are on unpaid leave. And stay the hell away from this case. Let us handle it."

I wiped the tears from my reddened face and stormed out of the station. I was a clueless adulteress widow who was now jobless, all before my first fuckin' cup of coffee. There wasn't any way this morning could possibly get any worse.

Deciding against coffee altogether, for the next several hours, all I did was sip Chardonnay and rifle through photo albums of me and Steve. Seeing him smile reminded me of the happier times in our relationship, but in the weeks before he died, all we seemed to do was argue.

"You and that damned cop job! One day you're going to come home in some goddamn body bag! What am I supposed to do then?"

"It's what I want to do, Steven! Why can't you accept that?"

The worst part about it all was that he'd been right. I'd brought my job home with me and a body bag that was meant for me was served to him. Now the job I'd fought so hard for didn't even *want* my ass.

"If only I had some kind of lead, I could find that fucker and..."

And what? What would you do, Charlie? Would you kill him—end his miserable life? Then what? Like Sassia said, you're not a killer. Why continue to put yourself through this?

"Because had I died, he would've done it for me!"

Would he have? Were you really even a couple in the end?

My head collapsed into my hands and I cried until it hurt to breathe. I was tired of arguing with myself and tired of feeling so lost. I was a U.S. soldier and a cop and we didn't cry—we got things done. I wiped my face with the palms of my hands as tears began to fall onto the digital picture screen.

Without a scrap of evidence to lead me to Carlos Perez, I opted to finalize the funeral plans for Steve. With his adoptive parents deceased, I was the only family he'd had left.

I signed all the paperwork that I had been neglecting, but the truth was that even though we were about to be married, we'd never been further apart. We fought, we argued, and the sex was so scarce that I was beginning to think my pussy was going to shrivel up from underutilization. The night before I graduated, I had to attack him just to get laid.

I smiled as I thought about that night. If I hadn't taken what I wanted from Steve, I didn't have any doubt in my mind that I would've succumbed to Sassy that night when we smoked out together.

Sassy.

I knew almost nothing about her, except what she'd shared with me a few nights back. Still, I cared what she thought about me more than I probably should. Outside of Carol, she was the only other close friend I had. Most of my high school friends didn't believe in the military, my college peers were off making the world a better place, and the military camaraderie I thought I had disappeared when they heard about the lesbian affair. Now, with the academy days behind me, it wasn't easy getting to know people on the force. Even harder now that I was the ex-military, vigilante—badass, '*wannabe*'.

Pulling my hair into a bun and relaxing back into the sofa, I realized why I wouldn't let Sassia go when we'd first met. Why I didn't push her away or ignore her and let our relationship fade into neighborly obscurity. I needed someone around who wasn't me, or even like me, and she fit the role perfectly. Beautiful, mischievous, promiscuous, and mysterious were just a few of the traits that attracted me to her.

The way she touched me, kissed me last night, used her fingers and tongue to satisfy me, had the butterflies returning. Her touch was electric and I would never have imagined our paths would not only cross, but end in her bed...wrapped up in her sheets, smelling and tasting like each other.

Maybe when she comes home...

"*No*!" I shouted, while shaking the thoughts of us out of my head. Sitting alone in the apartment, I realized I was shouting at myself. I took a few deep breaths to calm down, wiping the lingering tears from my eyes, and concentrated on the task at hand.

"Burying Steven is my only focus. He deserves at least that much from me."

I thought about calling my father or speaking to my brothers, knowing that it may help ease the burden, but I opted not to. They meant well, but ultimately the request would be the same from them all.

"*Charlie, come back home.*"

I stood up and put the nearly empty bottle of Chardonnay back on the wine rack. Without any distractions and too much wine in my system, I cleared my mind as much as I could and returned to the paperwork. As I dotted the *I*'s and crossed the *T*s', I knew one thing: Until Steven was buried, I wouldn't allow myself to see Sassia.

Chapter 11: No Bad Deed...

Sassia

When I left Charlie curled up in my bed, she was dead to the world, a smile playing on her lips.

Don't you just love it when you leave them that way? Even though I was just thinking to myself, I still smiled and nodded as if someone else had said it.

I'd looked down at her lying on the bed and she'd looked so peaceful that I was tempted to kiss her, but I stopped myself. I liked Charlie, but I couldn't allow myself to *like* Charlie. She was cool to talk to, she took my fucking her last night like a champion, yet as much as I typically disliked being around other women, I wanted Charlie around.

"She's been working on you for a year now. You said as soon as you slept with her, she was gone, but look at you watching over her. You like her."

I whispered aloud as if someone was listening, when I was simply talking to myself.

So then, who exactly are you trying to convince, Sassia?

I snuck out of the bedroom and quickly showered. After brushing my teeth and calling the airline to make sure they had enough open seats, I threw on jeans, a t-shirt, and packed a small bag.

I *did* want to kiss Charlie good-bye, but if I kissed her and she woke up, then I'd have to concoct some story as to why I was leaving at five in the morning. There were things that I had to do and it was much better if she didn't know about them.

Usually I'd call a cab to pick me up, but with Chuck shacking up with me, I had to at least make it look like I'd gone to work. So, I hopped on my Hayabusa but before I started the engine, I called CT. He picked up, but as usual, it took him a while. I hated going through his endlessly annoying prompts, but I knew it was about safety for both of us.

"What took you so long?"

"And a good fucking morning to you too, Val. You know, I do sleep occasionally."

"So what's the news?"

"There is no *news*. I checked the local, national, and international wires—no one wants this Charlie dude dead. It could just be a local vendetta. Maybe a pissed off ex."

"Charlie is a woman," I said a little more curtly than I should have.

"Well, forgive me for not doing a background check. After you cussed me out the other day, I guessed that you wanted me to respect your privacy, but with all the goddamn attitude that I'm getting, I guess not."

"You haven't had your coffee yet, have you?"

"No, dammit, and I'm not finished ranting! Forgive me for thinking that Charlie is a man's name. Out of all the goddamn Charlie's in the world who happen to be men, please forgive me for making such a heinous mistake. Who is *she* to you anyway?"

"She's no one—just a neighbor with bad luck."

"And why do you care? Are you banging her—no wait, you'd have to kill her afterward. I'm guessing that you've made a little friend," he said in a condescending tone.

"Cut the crap, CT. Drink some coffee, wake the hell up, and keep your eyes on the wires and your ears open for street talk. There's something that's not right."

"And I ask again, Val. Who *exactly* is this woman to you?"

"She's just someone I know."

He paused and sighed. "You're fucking her, aren't you? Damn it! That's why you won't give me the time of day anymore. It used to be me and you—the dynamic duo. You wanted dick—*my* dick—back then, but now look at you! You went all the way gay. Why is it always the fine ones who go *super* gay on me?"

"I never wanted your dick, CT."

"That's what your mouth says, but I can't believe that you would leave all this sexy for another woman! You can chow down on carpet, but not man rug?"

I laughed before I lied. "CT, you and I have a working relationship, which means that you're not privy to my private life. Just so that your feelings don't get all messed up, we haven't fucked. But if we're all going super gay on you, maybe it's *you* that brings out the gay in us. Perhaps you've got the ability to turn straight women gay with just a few words? Or maybe it's the sight of your tiny little dick that does it."

"That shit isn't funny, Val."

"It is! And to think that there's a market for that! You could really be rich!"

"I don't need this. I'm going back to bed. At least I can bang you in my dreams—maybe even remind myself that I'll be sniffing you soon."

"And you wonder why I won't give you any. You're disgusting, CT. You're going to stay single for the rest of your life talking like that."

"I love you too, Val."

I started up the Hayabusa and made my way to Houston International. After parking in short term and locking up my bike, I made my way up to Continental's front counter. I smiled at the agent who gave me a faux smile in return. I handed her my license and credit card and she retreated behind the computer.

I looked up at all the cameras in the building and hated that I had to take this route. Usually, I would've taken the bus, but I needed to be back in Houston in time so Charlie wouldn't notice that I'd left town.

"And where are you heading today, Miss Thompson?" she politely asked.

"I need a round trip ticket to Memphis."

Again, she retreated behind her computer and I tried to drown out the incessant screams of the obnoxiously whiney infant behind me.

The next time the agent spoke, she was handing me my ticket. "Here you are...one round trip ticket for Amanda

Thompson from here to Memphis Tennessee. You have a window seat, your plane boards in seventy-five minutes, and I hope you enjoy your flight." I gave her the same fake smile she'd given me and walked away.

Yep, there was business to finish in Memphis.

After making my way through security and finally boarding the plane, I slid on my MP3 headphones and fell asleep to the sounds of Toni Braxton's *Makin' Me High.* Soon I was back in the lovely world of Charlie's pussy...

I wished the flight was longer, but ninety minutes was all the sleep I was going to get. With just my small bag in hand, I flagged down a cab and headed to the east side of Memphis.

When the cabby finally pulled up to Hoops' house, I noticed how much different it seemed during the day. It looked like shit at night, but during the day, it looked like Hurricane Hell had hit it. Along with the decayed wood beams that supported the porch, the siding was faded to the color of puke and the brick mortar was in desperate need of replacement. The worst part about it was that his house was in better shape than all the other houses on the street.

How the hell could a respected gun runner live like this?

I let myself in the gate and knocked on the side door.

"What?" A gruff voice shouted from inside. I knew it wasn't Hoops, so it had to be Beenie.

"Open the door, Beenie."

The curtain covering the glass moved enough for him to see who it was, but when he opened the door, he looked nothing like the man I'd seen just a few days earlier. His eyes were dark and swollen, his nose seemed a little misplaced, and his bottom lip had a split right down the middle.

I thought about not saying anything, but it was easier just to ask. "What the hell happened to you? You got caught messing with somebody's wife?"

"You did this shit, dammit. Yo' kung fu, judo shit fucked my face up. I would kill you right now for the shit you did, or at least fuck you up, but yo' boy Hoops asked me to step off. But I'll tell yo' bitch ass this one time—one goddamn time, watch yo' back."

I looked at his face and was almost sorry that I'd beaten him so mercilessly. "Don't worry, if you put a band-aid on all of that, it'll heal. It's just another one of life's funny lessons—never mess with a crazy woman."

He growled, then turned and walked up the stairs into the house. Right before we parted ways, I heard him mumble, "Whatever, kung-fu bitch. Yo' ass gon' be dead if you keep talkin' shit like that."

Stepping into the house behind him, I was greeted by a very enthusiastic Hoops. He didn't have the scars that I'd put on his friend, but I could definitely see the red marks I'd left around his light neck.

"I knew you'd be back. You can't resist me, huh?"

"I came for my guns. You never brought them." He circled me, smelling my hair as I stood in the kitchen. I didn't know why men liked doing that, but it didn't seem as important as what I'd come to do. "It's rosemary mint shampoo. It works wonders for my hair and maybe you can use some for your braids or to help Beenie with his stinky attitude."

He stopped moving and laughed. "I'll think about that, but you never gave me an address or a way to contact you. How am I supposed to bring the hardware when I don't even know where it's going?"

I wrote down the address to El Primero and handed it to him.

"Damn, can I get a number so that I can make sure you're home?"

"No."

"Well then why don't we just screw and get it out of the way?" His devilish smile was contagious, but I wasn't feeling him today. "You know you wanna do me."

"No."

"I thought there was something between us last time, but maybe it was just me. Can I get a blow job, then?"

Now I was agitated. "Look, Hoops, you're not a bad guy for me to know, but don't test me. I don't want your pretty face looking like Beenie's."

He looked over at Beenie sitting on the sofa and sulking. "I like it a little rough, but I really don't want you kickin' my ass like that. You whooped his ass something terrible."

“Fuck you, Hoops!” Hoops' supposed bodyguard shouted from the other room. "That ninjitsu heifer caught me off guard!"

“We can go another round if you like?" I shouted at Beenie.

"Fuck you! I don't hit women!"

I returned my attention to Hoops. "Now, can we get to my guns?”

I hadn’t planned on spending much time with Hoops, but when he brought out my gold Ruger, we were like old friends. I finally managed to drag myself away after almost an hour of gun talk and headed toward Boogie’s apartment.

It was just before noon when I arrived. I walked around the neighborhood, making sure that I could account for all escape routes before I walked up to his door. I wasn’t sure if he’d be home, but that didn’t matter. If the crazy woman from before answered, I was ready to kick in the door and wait for him to come home.

As soon as I walked up to his apartment, I knew there was something wrong. Looking through the blinds facing the street, all I saw was the generic beige carpeting and the sterile look of fresh paint on the walls. The crackhead bitch from hell was gone. No furniture, no stale cigarette smells emanating from the door. No Boogie.

Fuck!

I marched straight into the rental office, past the desk with the teenage dropout who was doing her nails, and into the rental manager’s private office. Catching the small, heavyset black man off guard, he quickly closed his laptop and shimmied up his pants.

“How can—can I help you?” he asked, stuttering. Apparently I had interrupted a nice porn session.

“There was a man living in apartment 209 a few days ago and now he’s gone! Where the hell did he go?”

“I’m sorry, ma’am, are you family?” he asked, still trying to fasten his pants over his tiny erection.

“I will be! That asshole got me pregnant and now he’s trying to run!”

He opened up a ledger and quickly ran his finger over the dates. “It says here that he had a family emergency and had to move back to Miami. And he... didn't leave a forwarding address. I'm sorry."

"Me too," I mumbled and left his office as quickly as I'd entered it. I didn't want to make a scene, but I knew that was the only way I was going to find out what I needed.

Damn it, I missed my chance!

I was so close to him that if I reached out, I could touch him. I'd practically had him in my sights, but I'd lost him in the crowd.

"Shit! I'm too damn close to let him get away now!"

Several of the natives walked by, practically taking my clothes off with their eyes, and so I began walking away from the property. I dialed up CT. I was lucky that he still owed me and I needed to find out if Boogie was still in the city. As soon as he picked up, I started quickly. "Charles Jackson, I need to know if he rented a hotel room or another apartment in..."

"Memphis," he said finishing off my sentence. "I already know where you are, Val. I flagged all of your ID's so that I could help you wherever you go."

I'd forgotten that he'd flagged all of the extra identities he provided for me. I would've flown as Sassia had I thought about it, but I didn't need the headache or the attention. "Sounds like you're stalking me."

"I am. Well, I'm stalking your luscious coochie but unfortunately, you happen to be attached."

"Anyway, can you do it?"

"Can I do what? Find Charles Jackson again? Yes. Will I do it? No! I won't do it because you're a goddamn fruitcake!"

"What the hell are you talking about, CT?"

"I decided to be nosy and got info on Charlie Briggs, Val. She's a fucking *cop*! You're getting played by a cop!"

"I knew she was a cop, CT!" I shouted into my phone. "I think someone's trying to kill her and I wanted to know if it was a pro! That's it!"

He grew quiet for a few seconds. "I see where this is going. Please tell me that you want to know if there's a contract so that you can take her out yourself."

"Fine, whatever, I just wanted to know if she had a CFT out on her."

"Sheesh, can I get a 'please'? I didn't see one, but that just means that either it's local or it's not profitable enough for any attention. But if she does have a CFT, kill her now so that we can collect."

I walked to the end of the street and spotted a strip mall about two blocks down. I began heading there to avoid all the whistles and cat-calls from the jobless men that permeated this section of the city. I pushed the phone close to my face as a couple of young girls walked by.

"I'm not going to kill her, CT."

His loud sigh was proof enough that he didn't need to know anything else. "Whatever, Val, but let me say this—messing around with a cop, finding out if she has a CFT, it doesn't look good."

"Whatever," I replied nonchalantly. "I'm a big girl, CT. I can handle big girl problems."

"Val, if she does have a local CFT and you're around her, they'll gun you down just as quickly as they would her. All I'm saying is that you promised me a sniff and I'm not into smelling dead cooch."

I'd just made it to the first store of the strip mall, a beauty shop, when a cab passed by. I tried to flag it down, but the driver didn't notice me and continued on past.

"Your concern for my well-being is extremely touching."

"Not really. I just wanted to suggest that you let me sniff it before you die. That way, I don't get caught in a random Harris County morgue like I'm some sort of sick pervert."

I began to suck on my teeth to let him know how bored I was becoming with this disturbing conversation. "So, about Charles Jackson?"

"So, this Jackson guy, you were supposed to end him a few days back. What happened?"

I heard him pecking at his keyboard. "Life happened. Something came up and he got away."

"It took me a year to find him the first time and I'm assuming that was by accident. I'm thinking some young, big-tittied, not too bright rental agent accidentally put his name in a computer and I found him. I don't want to sound like I don't give a shit, but that probably won't happen again. You know that, right?"

I didn't want to hear CT's opinions, just facts. "Just let me know if he's in the city."

"So why the hell did you fly to Memphis? I thought we had this talk about flying and cameras in an airplane terminal."

"Well," I sighed, "it was the fastest way to get here. I thought about calling him and letting him know that I was going to drive here. That way he could be here for me to kill, but at the last minute I decided that I wanted it to be a surprise."

"Sarcastic as ever, but you have a history with this guy. That history is making you careless. Each time you go through an airport, they track you by facial recognition and if you go through with different names, they flag you. One thing I don't need is my hitters getting flagged by the damn government."

"I'm sorry," I mumbled into the phone while trying to flag down another cab, "but you don't know this man. You don't know what I owe him. You've never been..." I stopped myself. CT didn't know everything about me and he certainly didn't need to know that. "Just find him."

"Look, I know all about your *bad guys deserve to die* kick. This is me you're talking to, but sloppy is sloppy. Besides, you already know how I feel about planes. Think about it. Before 9/11, major crashes happened at least a couple of times a year. Since the towers fell, the U.S. has only had one major crash and that was just two months afterward—before the new safety guidelines were enacted. One crash! So all of those crashes in the eighties and nineties meant that the government just let people die! Why did they allow it to happen? Well, I'll tell you. Population control. And also because fear is a great motivator. If you let people believe that crashes are a matter of chance, then they take a risk. If you let them think they're terrorists everywhere, then you can institute new safety protocols to systematically take away freedoms. Frickin' ingenious!"

I held the phone against my forehead just long enough to hear the end of his conspiratorial rant. "Are you done?"

"You don't believe me? I wish you could see some of the documents that I've seen after hacking into DOD. Your freaking mind would be blown if you knew about these genetic experiments, high profile assassinations that were deemed natural causes, the acceptable life loss, or ALL protocol and the mountains of files they have on the Reptilians."

"So have you found anything yet?"

"Yeah, it's all here!"

I shook my head. "I meant about Charles Jackson."

"How the hell am I supposed to have more stuff on a guy who knows how to disappear and has a common name like Jackson? Look, it may take a while. I'll call you if I do, but this whole Briggs cop thing, you should stay clear until it pans out."

"You mean I should let her die."

"I mean you should stay the hell away from her."

I quickly hung up the phone, not feeling CT's lecture. He didn't know Boogie and what he had done to me. He didn't even know Chuck... or how tasty she was.

And who is he to tell me to stay the hell away from someone? Several people had already tried and failed on that front.

After the third cab finally stopped to pick me up, I dropped off the gun back at Hoops' house. After a little bartering, he agreed to come to Houston, bringing all of the guns I wanted with him.

Taking the same cab downtown, I went shopping at the Victoria's Secret in Peabody Place. I bought a few suggestive teddies and some edible underwear that I knew I'd like to eat off Charlie.

An hour later, I was back on the plane waiting to get back home. It'd been a long time since I had butterflies in my stomach, but I couldn't wait to get back to see her.

I made it back to Houston a little before one in the afternoon. Not as upset as I thought I'd be for missing an opportunity to put a bullet in Boogie's head, I smiled as I walked out of the airport.

What the hell is wrong with me?

I pretended like I didn't know, but during the whole flight home, I reminisced about the things I'd done with Charlie. I actually missed her and no matter how hard I tried to shake the feeling, it wouldn't leave.

"You like her, so what? It's not the end of the world." I tried to convince myself, but it was more than that. Ever since I'd met Charlie, all I wanted to do was get in her pants—that was my *only* reason for being around her. Last night, I'd had her. To me, the chase was supposed to be over, but it wasn't. I liked having Charlie, with me and next to me when I woke up and no matter how much I wanted it to be otherwise, I knew that I was just lying to myself. The things we had done last night and the orgasms we shared reminded me of the sex with Nava, but she wasn't Nava. As I thought about all the conversations we had and all the smoking out we did, I actually laughed in front of a crowd, all of whom looked at me strangely.

What was wrong with me? I jumped on my bike and sped out of short-term parking, stopping only to pay my ticket. I was sure that the Beltway would be bumper to bumper around this time, but I took it anyway and found it much emptier than I'd anticipated.

I sped back to the apartment building, but just before I made it home, I took a detour to the north side and bought tamales for us.

When I finally made it back to the apartment building, I ran up the stairs two at a time, carrying my small bag, the naughty clothes I'd bought in Memphis, and the tamales. When I made it to my apartment door, my heart was beating much faster than it should have been. I took in a few deep breaths, but when I opened the door, I stepped into an empty apartment. I checked each room to make sure, but when I realized that she'd left, loneliness settled in.

She's a grown woman. Who said she had to stay here?

Hell, I *wanted* her to be here, waiting for me. I wanted the company, the endless flirting between us, but that wasn't possible now. She'd left.

Maybe I should have tied her up.

Tamales in hand, I quickly walked down the hall and knocked on her door.

"What?" she shouted.

"I have a special delivery for a Charlie D'Agostino," I chimed.

She didn't say anything for a few seconds, but when her peephole darkened, I knew she'd seen me. I gave her my best Vanna White smile before putting the tamales where she could see them.

"Leave them outside. I'll get them later." Her voice sounded husky, like someone who had just finished crying. She was clearly upset and I wanted to know why.

"C'mon, Chuck, open up the door. I bought you a present." I hoped she could smell the tamales.

"Sassia, just leave it at the door. I have a lot to do today."

“Opening up the damn door isn’t going to kill you! You’re speaking to me now.”

The sound of her scuffling against her wood floor let me know that she was walking away from the door and back into the apartment.

"Look, Chuck, I don't know if these mood swings you're having are because of me or because of your week. Just let me in so we can at least talk, dammit! I don’t want to share with the whole building."

After I leaned against the door, I could hear her as she began to walk back. I pushed myself away from her door as she barely cracked the door and the smell of liquor began to waft into the hallway. That coupled with her puffy, bloodshot eyes let me know that she’d been in her apartment pretty much since I’d left. She looked down at the tamales, then up at me.

“Are those for me?”

“They were.”

She began to close the door when I stuck my foot in to keep her from doing so. “What the hell else do you want from me, Sassy?”

“I want to know why you’re drinking. What’s wrong? Did I do something?”

“It’s nothing.”

“Then let me in so that we can talk.”

“No!” she said sharply. When she realized how harshly she’s spoken, she inhaled and spoke again, this time more softly. “Now just isn’t the time.”

“This is about last night isn’t it?” When she didn’t respond, I knew that it was. “Look, if you didn’t want it to happen, I understand, but don’t act like there wasn’t something there.”

Just then, a couple, a thick black woman and her slim male companion, opened their door and began to walk toward me. I turned to look at them, but before I had a chance, Chuck swung open the door and exhibited the full force of her rage.

“What do you know about *anything*, Sassia? You like being alone—that's all you ever talk about is how you like being *alone*! Since day fucking one, all you wanted to do is get into my pants! Now that you've finally fucked me, why don't you go back to being single? That's what you fucking wanted all along! I don't know what I was thinking! Letting you screw me before my fiancé was even cold in the ground. You’ve already gotten between my legs! You got what the fuck you wanted! Now leave me the fuck *alone*!"

I quickly removed my foot from the door as it came rushing toward me. As the door slammed and the echo resonated down the hall, several people opened up their doors to see what the noise was all about.

Great.

After hearing what I had done, several people simply shook their heads while I stood looking dumbfounded with a sack of warm tamales in my hand. The couple that had witnessed most of Chuck's rant walked on by me, with the heavy woman loudly clearing her throat and shaking her head, letting me know how much she disapproved.

The man with her began to eyeball me, but before they disappeared down the stairs, the woman condescendingly spoke. "Goddamn carpet munchers! Y'all should be ashamed of yourselves! The whole bunches of y'all need *Jesus*!"

The last time I'd felt this embarrassed was when my momma gifted me with a box of super absorbent maxi pads for my eleventh birthday. Throwing the tamales into her door, I screamed loud enough for everyone to hear.

"Don't you fucking blame me for this, Charlie! Don't blame me for this shit! You lived, he didn't! So don't you disrespect me because you can't live with the truth! Fuck you!"

I quickly walked back out to my bike and somehow the sky didn't seem as bright anymore. The excitement and anticipation I'd felt for seeing Chuck had fizzled like a wet Fourth of July firecracker.

What the hell was I thinking? I knew I shouldn't have gotten involved with her crazy ass! I should've just kept to my goddamn self and this shit would have never happened! Boogie would be fucking dead and my world would be fine!

I supposed that someone else would've cried, but I didn't. I wouldn't. I took in a deep breath and sped toward LZE. Might as well make some fucking money.

When I made it to work, Apple, DC, and Anelle were all crowded around the front desk, as usual. Did they *ever* fucking work? When DC saw me walk through the front door, she frowned.

"I heard you got Mr. Sheppard."

I thought about the man who'd attacked my ass. With all the drama at home lately, yesterday's rendezvous seemed much further away.

"LZ gave him to me. Why do *you* care?"

"I care because that was *my* commission, Sassia. I could've been good for a month on what he paid, but here you are, in here looking for more work. You know what? You're too damn greedy for your own good. If you need dick that bad, get married and leave this job to the young girls."

I didn't know if I had donned the look of someone who was about to kill her, but Anelle quickly jumped up and doused the flame.

"DC, this is a business and, girl, if you need money that bad then you should've gone to LZ. Yesterday wasn't Sassia's fault. Sheppard picked her and LZ made the final call."

"No, Anelle, stop covering for her! That bitch is always getting the good ones and we get left with the scraps! And she ain't all *that* fine, either!"

"DC, another word and you're gone!" LZ shouted as she stormed out of her office. "Maybe if you took your ass to the gym more often and stopped showing up so soft, you'd get more calls. Hell, if Sassia didn't turn away some of these calls, y'all bitches wouldn't have any damn jobs!"

LZ placed her arm around me and we walked to her office. Even though I knew her speech was made on my behalf, I knew it wouldn't gain me any extra popularity with Apple and DC.

Once we made it inside the oak doors, she closed us off from the rest of the building. After looking at me for a few seconds, she asked, "What happened?"

"I don't know. As soon as I got here, DC was jumping down my damn throat."

"That's not what I mean, Sassia. The confidence I usually see is gone. You look lost. What's going on?"

"There's nothing going on, LZ. I'm fine."

"Fine, you can lie to me all you want, but your eyes carry the burden of heartache."

I tried to laugh, but failed miserably and instead ended up coughing. "I just came here to see if there were any open jobs."

"Sit down." I sat in the chair next to her desk and as she stood over me, she slid me a thick, manila envelope. "How's that ass?"

When I opened the package, it was filled with my hundreds. I emptied the money on her desk and began to count it while I answered her question. "It's fine. He was a little bigger than I thought he'd be, but he was gentle."

"You don't need to count it, Sassia. Between Tuttle and Shepherd, that's a little more than sixteen thousand—the biggest commission I've ever given." As I looked at her in awe, she came around and began to massage my shoulders. "Look, I'm not dumb. You came here to work, fine, but you really came here to get someone out of your head."

"LZ, it's not heartbreak, it's not anything. I don't know what the hell..."

"Sassia," she said, cutting me off, "you would never tell me the truth if it was, but I see it in your face. I'm not about to put my best girl out there when you've got a lot already in your head. I need you focused and if that means giving you some time to yourself, I'm willing to do that."

"I don't need time. I need a fuckin' date."

She sat down in her leather chair. "This isn't debatable. I'm giving you the rest of the week off so that you can enjoy your money and so that these girls can actually make me some."

"But, LZ..."

She put up her hand and I knew that there wasn't anything I could say to dispute her. Disgusted, I walked out of her office, past the women and their disdainful stares, and straight to my bike. Perhaps it *was* time for me to get out of Houston—again.

"CT, is there anything on the board?"

I whisked past another car on 59 South, heading for El Primero and another secret apartment that I had, but hadn't been to in a while.

"If I gave you a job, how will you ever protect your *cop*?"

"She's a big girl. She can protect herself."

"Do I sense trouble in paradise?"

"There's no trouble, CT, and there's definitely no paradise. There will be for you if you keep asking, though."

"See, Val, that's why you need a man in your life. A man to help you through all these rough patches that life brings you.

You *need* me, girl! Why do you keep denying me? Don't you know I love you?"

"Funny. Do you have a job or not?"

"It's funny that you ask because I *do* have a job, but it's not your type. This individual hasn't done anything too awful—except they had a job that helped facilitate one of the greatest economic collapses in recent memory."

"So she's a stockbroker?"

"You caught that, huh?"

"It was a dead giveaway."

He cleared his throat. "She's a *banker*, but they're all evil anyway, right?"

"Where is she?"

"Chicago and it's not warm there. Shit, it's spring and it's still cold as hell, so pack something warm."

"Send me what I need."

"I'm sending the files to you now. You should be able to access them when you get off the phone. Oh, and no special requests this time—just a regular CFT."

"So what does a regular CFT entail?"

"It means you don't have to bang her brains out first."

"Jealous?"

"To my very core."

"I like the way you beg."

"Me too, especially if it gets me closer to getting some booty."

"You know the consequences. Is it worth dying for?"

"To be in the same bed as you? *Hell, yes!*"

I sighed before I hung up the phone with CT. He was relentless, but great at his craft. And not long after, I had everything I needed on my next target.

Chapter 12: Alone Time

Chicago, IL

Sassia

The chill of Chicago's night air smacked me across the face as the cold seemed to easily permeate the only sweater I'd brought. I grabbed my wheeled luggage immediately after the driver pulled it from under the bus and found myself a cab.

"Where do you wanna go?"

"I lost my ID on the way up here. I need a hotel that takes cash with no questions asked."

He sat back in his seat and thought for a few seconds. "You look like a nice lady, so why don't I take you to a Holiday Inn or something. I'm sure you could work somethin' out with the desk clerk."

"Look," I looked at the ID of the pale faced man in the driver's seat, "Phil, all I need is a place to stay the night that doesn't cost too much. Can you help me or not?"

"Sure, but most of the cash places is on the south side."

Perfect.

"Fine, take me there."

"Shit, lady, it's your funeral."

Nope, it's Lydia Thompson's funeral.

Burr Ridge, IL
3 Days Later

I awoke in the middle of the night, nauseous as hell, but still slightly euphoric.

Am I high? Drunk?

"Or both," I asked out loud as my head swam. I felt worse than the time when Chuck and I got drunk and smoked White Demon. For a few seconds, I didn't see anything. The room was almost pitch black, but as my eyes adjusted, I slowly raised my head to survey my surroundings. I didn't recognize much of anything as I looked down and saw a bald black man nestled comfortably between my thighs.

"Who the hell...? What the *hell*?"

After moving his head to the side and seeing that I wasn't wearing panties, I suspected what had been going on. Looking around, I saw expensive furniture littered with random people before I finally realized where I was. I was in someone's house...not sure whose, but I had a nagging feeling that there was something I was supposed to do.

Several times I tried to move, but both my legs and arms felt like lead weights. I thought about just sleeping it all off when small pieces of memory slowly came back to me.

I was in Chicago and I was here to party? I'm drunk and a little high, so that must be some of it. No, that's not it. I'm here to... I'm here to...?

I looked around the room once more to see if there was anyone I remembered, but the only face that seemed vaguely familiar was the man with his face plastered inside my thighs. I had one feeling about that guy and it wasn't good. *Shit! Why can't I remember?*

I closed my eyes and thought about the last few things that I could remember.

I came here on a bus. Check. CT gave me the name of the person I was supposed to... to kill.

Aha! It was coming back in pieces, but at least I was finally beginning to see through the fog in my head. I swung my leg up and over the head, stood up, wobbling a little, stepping over all the bodies that seemed to be passed out randomly on the floor. I remained focused on trying to remember everything.

CT had given me the names of some arms dealers...double check. The person I was supposed to kill was a woman—a black woman who had a blonde personal assistant following her around practically everywhere she went. The blonde...a black woman...was I supposed to shoot both of them?

And that's when it all came flooding back to me. I'd been in the city of Chicago the last few days hunting down prey: Lydia Thompson.

On my first day in town, I bought a Glock-22 from one of the arms dealers that CT had referred me to, but with the schedule that Lydia Thompson kept, shooting her was almost impossible. She rarely left the house other than to go to work and when she did work, a limousine service provided a bodyguard and a driver, who I suspected was a second bodyguard. While she was at home, her personal assistant, Lindsay, was with her practically everywhere and I even spied on them sleeping together when her husband left for his West Coast trip.

The truth was that I could've shot the both of them while they slept, but seeing them together, peacefully wrapped up in each other, reminded me of me and Charlie.

"Fucking *Charlie*," I mumbled under my breath while trying to get past the myriad of bodies strewn across the living room like a landscape of mannequins.

Even though Lindsay and Charlie looked nothing alike, I couldn't bring myself to kill her either. Besides, I didn't want any collateral damage; especially when Lindsay hadn't done anything other than choose the wrong person to work for. And screw.

Lydia lived in Burr Ridge, a suburb southwest of Chicago. I studied her subdivision several times, both at day and night, posing as a real estate agent who was new to the city. Since the area she stayed in was made up of athletes, most of them anxious to see what was under my short skirt, getting information about her and her husband proved to be extremely easy.

After only two days of spying, I knew everything I needed to know about Lydia. Born in the late 70's to a preacher and teacher, she was valedictorian of her high school graduating class, then came college and grad school. One of the youngest bankers to sit on the Chicago Stock Exchange, she sat on several boards, was married to a pro basketball player, and was the epitome of an overachiever. Everyone on the block knew about her and Lindsay, but they also knew about her one major flaw: parties. The type of party didn't matter—alcohol, drugs, orgies—she did them all in her home, but only while her husband was away. The most important thing about these parties—Lindsay wasn't invited.

"Keep what you do separate from who you are," I said as I walked up the steps, heading toward her bedroom. I admired Lydia for what she had achieved, but she was still just a paycheck.

On my third night in the city, I'd finally gotten the chance to meet her.

Earlier in the day, after knowing that her husband would be out of town and a party was inevitable, I decided to visit the Magnificent Mile and spoil myself. Buying a necklace and matching earrings from Cartier was just the beginning as I strolled through Armani, finally settling on an expensive piece with a v-neck and an open back. The search for shoes took me a while longer, but I finally settled on some Burberry heels with a matching purse. After all my shopping was done, I pampered myself at a local spa, opting for a hot stone message, a bikini wax that left me with a heart shaped patch, and finally a desperately needed manicure and pedicure. I was going to be the most pampered, well kept killer on the south side of Chicago... at least for today anyway.

I took a cab to the airport where I bribed a limo driver to meet me at my motel in a few hours. He began telling me about how he grew up on the south side, but as my boredom took over, I tipped him $500 to be there at seven and walked away before he finished.

He didn't disappoint, which was a good thing for him. At seven that evening, I received a call from the desk clerk; the limo was waiting. He didn't say a word as we made our way to Burr Ridge and when we pulled up in front of the house, I gave him another $200 to forget I ever existed.

I stepped out of the limo feeling like a movie star and with all the attention I received, I felt more powerful than I had in a long time. With the Glock tucked away safely in my designer purse, I stepped away from the limo and bumped into a man who introduced himself as Richard. Walking away from his Navy blue BMW 760Li, I didn't see a date and knew he was my ticket inside Lydia's house. He was tall, handsome, and built solid like an athlete, so I made sure he noticed me. I sheepishly smiled at him, he noticed, and we struck up a conversation.

"What's your name, *beautiful*?"

"Haley Tadd."

"Well, Haley, it's a pleasure to meet you. Is this your first party with Lydia?"

"Yes. I met her at a banker's conference in Las Vegas. We're not close or anything, just similar professions, and when I told her I was in the city, she invited me to come." I wondered if he would notice my play on words.

He didn't and he smiled as if he didn't care. "Did she tell you what kind of parties she throws?"

I cut my eye at him. "I'm from Sin City. No one can throw parties like we do."

He laughed and nodded his head. "Be careful what you say here. The Windy City might just blow you away."

I see he has a playful tongue as well...

I placed my hand just above my breasts and offered him my sophisticated laugh; not because it was funny, but because I needed him more fixated on my breasts than my face. He smiled and took my hand, never taking his eyes away from the breasts I'd practically thrown in his face.

Lydia's house was beautiful and she was a true socialite, but there wasn't anything here that I hadn't done or seen in Houston. I drank a few glasses of Dom Pérignon, smoked some white widow, and even did a few lines of coke on a dare. I was still lucid and had planned on taking Lydia out later on when I found myself waking up with Richard drooling between my legs.

Suddenly, the faint taste of salt on my tongue helped me realize what the hell had happened. I'd been drugged.

That goddamn Richard drugged me! Fucker.

I thought about shooting him in the face, but when I realized my purse was nowhere to be seen, I sluggishly walked back down the stairs, falling over bodies in the process, and went to look for it. I found my purse inside one of the downstairs toilets. After pulling out my ID and the Glock, I flushed the rest of it and went looking for Lydia.

Still feeling lightheaded, it took me a little longer to climb up the stairs than I'd wanted. I silently congratulated myself when I finally made it to the top, and went looking for the reason I'd come to Chicago.

When I found her, she was lying on the bed in her room. Sprawled across the bed, her hair covered most of her face and I checked the adjoining bathroom to make sure that no one would interrupt us. Sure that we were the only two people in her room, I grabbed a pillow and pushed it down over her face.

No fighting, no screaming; she didn't move a muscle.

With the Glock cocked and ready to fire, I pushed down harder on the pillow, but she still didn't struggle against me. Something was wrong. I pulled the pillow away from her face, brushed the hair away from her eyes, and saw that they were already fixated on the ceiling. I saw small traces of foam at the corners of her mouth.

A goddamn overdose! I went out and bought all this nice shit, bribed a limo driver, let a man drug me and probably molest me, all for a woman who would've died tonight anyway?

I sat down next to her on the bed and laughed. Life is just a fucking joke a minute. I flipped on the bedroom light and saw that her cocktail dress had been turned into a cummerbund, pulled up to just below her perfectly augmented breasts. She'd apparently had sex before she died—or after, but I didn't care. I just wanted to know why someone so rich would have so much damn bush. It looked like it hadn't seen a bikini wax in years, if ever.

"So, you had sex too?" I looked her over one more time before taking a picture and sending it to CT. "A few drinks, a little sex, and a lot of blow—hell if I can think of a better way to go."

I turned off the light and right before I left the house, I found Richard one last time. He was sprawled out on the floor like the rest of them, so I flipped him over and stomped him in the groin with my Burberry heel. He immediately woke up and curled into a little ball, gasping for air as I walked away.

I exited the house, thinking seriously about going back and shooting Richard for what he had done to me, but I'd spent too much time passed out. I could see the sun beginning to creep over the horizon, so instead I took his car.

I broke his window, hotwired the car and sped off into the night. I could've just taken his keys, but that wasn't nearly as much fun as stealing it.

I made it back to my motel before dawn, but not before borrowing some clean clothes from the arms dealer. After burning the dress in his kitchen sink and giving him back the unused gun, I ditched the car in a strip mall parking lot on the south side of the city—Richard would never see it again, at least not in one piece.

Two hours later, I was back on the bus and headed toward Houston.

I arrived in Houston a few minutes after noon and headed straight to El Primero. After taking a long, much needed shower, I saw that the personal phone I'd left behind had three voice messages. I thought about ignoring them, but when I saw that I'd had several missed calls from Chuck, I opted to listen to what she had to say.

"Sassy, this is Charlie. I am so, so sorry for what I said to you. I hope you can forgive me, but I know you probably won't and I don't blame you. If you get this message, call me."

I deleted that message and listened to the second one. *"I guess you're not calling back means that you don't forgive me so I'll just say this. The last few days we spent together were wonderful and that was the problem. Steve was killed because of me and here I was, enjoying myself and having sex with my best friend. It felt wrong on so many levels that I didn't want to think about it. You were right, though. I was mad because I was alive and he wasn't, but now that the funeral is all planned, I just want us to start over. Call me if you want to talk."*

I was more empathetic toward the second message than the first one, but I still wasn't going to call her. I already had too much vested in Chuck and I knew that it was just better for the both of us if I kept my distance. In time she'd move on, perhaps head back to Philly, but I wasn't going to allow myself to get dragged into her life anymore. CT was right. Me screwing Chuck—especially *Chuck the cop*, complicated things.

Still, even knowing all that, I listened to the third message. This time I could tell she was crying. *"Sassy, this will be my last message. Steve's funeral is on Sunday at 3 p.m. and I'd just appreciate it if you'd be there. He doesn't have any family, just me, and I'd appreciate your support one last time."*

I looked up at my clock and when I saw that it read 2:30, I deleted the message and hung up.

Chapter 13: The Removing of Veils

Charlie

"We found Carlos Perez. He's dead." The gruff voice from behind me said.

"When did you find him?"

"Last night. Apparently, he was shot and someone kindly set him on fire. Unfortunately, there weren't any witnesses. You didn't happen to know where he was, did you?"

It was nearing the end of Steven's memorial service and when I didn't think I had any tears left, I was ready to start again at the captain's suggestion that I had anything to do with Carlos Perez's death. I hadn't, but wished I had.

I looked over my shoulder just enough for him to see the fury in my eyes.

"I wish to God I had. I would've kept him alive to endure more."

He shrugged his shoulders and sat back. "Just had to be sure."

When the priest paused to grab his Bible, I turned and looked at the old man. "Is that why you're here? To ask me for my *alibi*?"

"No, I came for support, but I still had to ask."

Hearing that Carlos Perez had died was of little consolation as the priest recited Steven Briggs' eulogy. He said amen and the choir sang in the nearly empty Catholic cathedral, but I barely heard a word. I was in my own world—a world where Steve was alive because I had listened to him and hadn't stopped that robbery, where Carlos Perez was waiting for me to skin the flesh from his body, and where my best friend would've shown up to lend me support.

I glanced around the church, trying to smile at the few people who occupied the cavernous building, but I felt so alone. Only now did the realization of why Steven had clung to me so tightly resonate. He didn't have anyone else. No family, no friends; everyone who'd come today was here to support me.

When the choir finally finished and only pipe organ music filled the chamber, I approached the closed casket and wept over the handsome, kind man who I'd spent the last few years of my life loving.

The priest, a tall, young, sandy-haired man with wire-rimmed glasses quietly stood next to me for a few moments before he spoke. "All this guilt you're feeling, my dear, you must let it go."

"I can't. He gave his life for me."

"Christ gave his life for all of us, so that we may live. Do not grieve Steven's sacrifice—he is with his Father in a better place. The best way to show him that you appreciate his sacrifice is by living, not lamenting. "

I lifted my head, wiped the tears from my eyes, and nodded. In my heart, I knew he was right and still I felt more alone than I ever had. As the funeral ended and the pallbearers carried his body to the waiting hearse, I looked around again at the few people present.

Still, no Sassia.

I wiped the last of the tears away from my face. "I don't even know why I expected differently," I mumbled. "She got what she wanted."

A few people from my job were there, including my captain, but those who stayed to carry Steven to his burial site were all Carolyn's cousins and brothers. With only a handful of people heading toward the doors of the church, I silently prayed that my funeral wouldn't be this empty. *Who would show up when my time came*?

With Carolyn at my side from the beginning, squeezing my hand for support, I didn't know how to tell her how much I appreciated all that she'd done for me. She'd set up almost everything, including the program beautifully detailing his life, and helped me during the last few days when Sassy wasn't around. Still, with Sassia missing in action and God only knew where, I felt like my best friend had deserted me.

"Do you need me to drive?"

I shook my head. "No, I'll drive. I'll meet you there."

I watched her walk to her car before I unlocked the doors of the Lexus and stepped in.

"I'm sorry for your loss."

I jumped, not expecting anyone to be sitting next to me inside of my own car. Wearing a black dress that hugged her form and a dark veil that made her look like a ghost widow, she simply looked at me.

"Sassy, you scared the shit out of me!"

"The funeral was beautiful."

"Why didn't you come in?"

She shrugged. "I was late. The attention was supposed to be on Steven, not me."

"Why didn't you call and let me know you were coming?"

"I lost my phone."

"So how did you know about the funeral?"

"It was in the newspaper."

"So you didn't hear any of my messages?"

"No."

"How did you get in the car?"

"The doors were unlocked."

"No, they weren't. Are you going to talk to me or just give me one sentence responses?"

She paused. "What is there to say, Chuck? I was only around to get laid. Now that that's done, what else is there to say?"

"So you're saying that your sole purpose *wasn't* to get me in bed?"

"And you act like you didn't want me to. Let's quit the bullshit, Chuck. You wanted me to, so I did it. Maybe the timing was a little off, but I gave you what you wanted. Throwing it back in my face was a little unexpected, but now that I know where you stand, the shit won't happen again."

She turned and looked out the window. I half expected her to turn around and start laughing, but for the first time I'd actually gotten to Sassia. She was hurt—which meant that I *wasn't* just someone for her to bang.

I started the car and was the first in the meager convoy of three cars that began following the black hearse.

"Look, Sassy, I left messages apologizing about everything I said. That day was just bad, horribly bad, for me. I slept with my best friend, who just happens to be a woman I also smoke weed with, before I even buried my fiancé. Secondly, I was put on suspension from my job because some gang-banger accused me of tying him and his goddamn girlfriend up and shooting him in the ass—twice. And then finally, the autopsy confirmed that it was Steven in the car, like I didn't know that, and I was buried under a mountain of estate paperwork. It was a bad time..."

She continued looking out the window at the darkening sky. I reached over, squeezed her left hand, and when we came to a stop, softly kissed her palm.

"Can you forgive me?"

She sat perfectly still in the passenger seat, but she didn't say a word. Instead of forcing her to answer, I decided to just be happy that she had come.

The skies opened up and rain began to fall by the time we made it to the cemetery. *Perfect,* I thought. We drove along the winding dirt road to the gravesite, but when we stopped, it was raining too hard for anyone to get out of their cars. Carolyn's youngest brother, Julian, braved the rain and when I saw him coming, I unlocked the back door for him.

In the few seconds it took him to leave Carolyn's car and jump in my back seat, he was already soaked. He smiled at me, but not before eyeballing Sassy and extending his hand. "I'm Julian."

Sassy took his hand. "Sassia."

He turned his attention to me. "So, are we going to do this or what? The storm isn't going anywhere and they want to lower him in before the ground gets too bad."

"Does everyone have an umbrella?" I asked.

"There's not enough for all of us, but we're men," he said, still ogling Sassia.

Sassia smiled at him, "How old are you?"

He smiled back. "I'll be eighteen in a few weeks, but I know my way around a woman. Why don't you let me call you sometime so you can see how much of a man I am?"

"Maybe I will. I like them young, when you're still malleable. At your age, I can teach you a lot about how to please a woman," replied Sassia.

I rolled my eyes and intentionally reached between Sassia's legs to grab my umbrella. Neither of them seemed to notice as their eyes flirted and I stepped out of the truck.

Oh, my God, I am fucking jealous!

I knew and couldn't stop it, but even more importantly, I couldn't believe that I'd just pulled a stunt like that. As the rain poured from the sky, I looked at them inside the car and was kind of pissed that neither of them had noticed.

Thirty seconds later, Julian jumped out of the back seat and ran toward the other car. As soon as he was far enough away, Sassy stood next to me under her own black umbrella and said, "I never figured you for the jealous type."

"I was just getting my umbrella."

"You were marking your territory."

"I was trying to stay dry."

"You were trying not to get wet."

"How long are we going to do this?"

She smirked. "Long enough for you to suffer. Then after you suffer, you can admit that I'm right."

"Is this *really* the time?"

"It is if you *really* want to apologize."

"Can we do this after the funeral...please?" I pleaded, hoping that she'd at least give me that much time and when she nodded, I walked with the rest of the small group to the awaiting grave.

As if on cue, the rain began letting up as they lowered Steven into the ground. I hugged each of Carolyn's relatives, thanked them for their help, and stayed behind for a few moments longer to lay several roses on his casket. Both Sassy and Carolyn remained next to me as I wept and soon after, felt my knees begin to buckle. With the both of them there to support me, they helped me to my car.

"Thank you so much," I said to Carolyn, while trying to hold back the tears. I hugged her as fiercely as I could.

"You'd do it for me," she whispered. "The invitation for you to stay with me for a couple of days is still open."

“Thank you, but I think I’m going to head back home for a few days. I need time to just get away from all the craziness that’s happening to me.”

“Well, my door is always open for you.”

“I know.”

I finally released her, but not before both of us burst into tears yet again.

“You better come back!” she shouted as she stepped into her Honda Accord.

I nodded, unsure if what she was asking was even possible anymore. Turning, I saw Sassia waiting impatiently at the car.

"So, you're going *home*?" she asked as I opened the driver's side door.

"What else is there for me here? Steve's gone."

She slid in on the passenger's side and turned to face me, her veil still hiding most of her face. "What about Carolyn?"

"Will you please take that damn veil off? You look more like a widow than I do." She did as I asked and I almost smiled. Having her do something I asked was a rarity. "Look, Carolyn's a great friend, but I can't stay here just because of that. Houston is a great city, Sassia, but these last few weeks have definitely been a wakeup call."

I started the engine and pulled out of the parking lot onto the downtown streets.

"If there isn't anything here for you, what was with the jealous streak earlier?"

"It was just residual. Besides, you did that thing with Julian on purpose to *make* me jealous."

"I will neither confirm nor deny such a statement, but I will say how blatantly obvious it was that you were marking your territory. And that territory is between my legs. That much is clear."

"Fine, I was a little jealous. I tend to get that way when I've had sex with someone, so sue me" I tried to focus on driving through the city streets, but I couldn't and pulled over to park. "Sassy, how do you *really* feel about me?"

She sat back in her seat and folded her hands. "You're new pussy."

"Dammit, Sassy, can you be serious?" I asked. "I know you feel something or else you wouldn't be putting me through this."

"Like I said, new pussy, that's it." She said it so nonchalantly that I knew it'd been rehearsed.

"I thought what we had the other night meant something."

"It did mean something. It meant you went from untouchable to fuckable."

"Why are you always putting up some sort of front? The only way you can be this damn callous is if you heard the messages I left. Why don't you say something other than what you rehearsed?"

She turned toward me and glared. "Fucking is what I do, Chuck, in case you've forgotten, and I get paid well to do it. Just because I didn't charge you doesn't mean a thing. I was your Pretty Woman and you were my john—nothing else. If you want something else from me, call my goddamn job and schedule an appointment! That way you can pay for my services and should I choose to let it happen again, it'll be on your dime instead of mine."

"You're such a...a *bitch*! Now I'm sure that there isn't anything left for me here." I heard the coldness in her voice, but the caring in her eyes was unmistakable. The night when I had cursed her, she dropped the tamales at my door. She cared, but I knew she'd never tell me. "So *that's it*?" I asked.

"That's it," she replied, her arms folded across her chest.

Without another word, I started the car. Heading north, I didn't know where the hell I was going and only when I saw a 610-West sign in front of me did I even care. I wanted to make her confess, make her tell me something. I knew how I felt about her. It made me sick to my stomach when I yelled at her in the hallway and not even an hour later, I was ready to call and apologize, but she wouldn't answer my calls. She said she lost her phone, but I knew I'd hurt her and I wanted to make it all right. I guess I was too late. I apologized several times for what I'd said and I knew she heard the messages, but it was clear that whatever we had wasn't enough to make her speak to me.

"You're heading into fourth ward."

"Fuck you."

"You wanted me to say something, so I said it. I don't think this is where you want to be right about now."

"Whatever."

I didn't feel like hearing her shit, so I just continued to drive. After a few minutes of looking at the rows of single-family rundown shacks on both sides of the road, I knew why Sassy had warned me. Not wanting to admit that she was right, I pulled into the parking lot of a ramshackle convenient store and turned around.

For the next few minutes, the car was so silent that I turned the radio on just to hear someone's voice. Not long after, a dark blue Escalade, blaring reggaeton, pulled alongside us. In disgust, I rolled up my windows, glaring at a bald Mexican with tattoos all over his arms. When he saw how upset I was, he smiled and flailed his tongue at me.

I thought of flicking him off until I saw a picture of a king wearing a crown tatted on his neck. Instead, I stared at the light, wishing for it to turn green. When it did, I quickly drove to the next one, but it turned red before I could make it through. The same truck snuck up against mine, but this time, they were on Sassia's side and much closer than before.

"Hey, Ma," the passenger yelled, "how about we come to your place and fuck you and your friend's brains out?"

"How about this," Sassia shouted back, "we go to your place, but you maricones start fucking each other so we have something to watch when we get there?"

I quickly grabbed Sassia's hand and hissed, "What the hell are you doing, Sassia, *trying to get us killed?* Didn't you see those gang tats on their necks? It means they're Latin Kings!"

She pulled her hand away from mine and said, "So what?" before returning her attention to the men in the truck.

"I like the mouth on you, Mama! I can't wait to put it to some good use!"

Suddenly they turned down the music and a man leaned up from the backseat. He tapped the shoulder of the obnoxious passenger and then the driver. After shoving his black netbook in the face of the obnoxious passenger, they had a quick, animated conversation in Spanish.

Sassia grabbed my arm and looked at me like she'd just seen a ghost. "Chuck, we need to get the fuck out of here."

The light was still red and because the cross street was one-way, I couldn't make a right.

"The light's about to be green soon."

Without warning, Sassia unbuckled her seat belt and leapt across my legs, pushing the gas pedal down as she did. We quickly tore into the intersection and I took control of the wheel as we landed right in the path of an oncoming fuel tanker.

"Oh, shit!" I squealed and made a hard left. The driver in the truck blew his horn and with only a few feet to spare, the truck veered, barely missing the back of the Lexus as we shot through the intersection.

"That was close!" Sassia raised herself off my lap and I was ready to kill her.

I punched her as hard as I could in the arm.

"What the fuck? You almost got us killed, goddammit! What the hell were you thinking? You know what..."

The sound of my back window exploding followed by the appearance of two bullet holes in the front windshield cut my rant with Sassia short. I looked in my rearview mirror and saw that the Escalade was forty feet behind us and closing quickly. Instinctively, I pushed down as hard as I could on the gas pedal, bringing the Lexus engine roaring to life. The sound of gunfire behind us had my heart racing and I began to feel like I was back in Afghanistan.

"Why the hell are they shooting at us?" I screamed, barely keeping my head above the dashboard as I wildly drove through the narrow streets of the fourth ward. The sound of bullets hitting the back door made me anxious and all I could think about was what the Navy had taught me.

Small arms fire...9mm...coming from passengers side. Second weapon...submachine gun with suppressor...sounds like MP5K. Civilian vehicle... no additional armor...three total hostiles...

"I don't know!" Sassia yelled back, breaking my focus. "Don't you have a gun or something? We're like fish in a damn barrel now!" I pointed at the glove box and Sassia pulled out the only weapon I had, a Smith and Wesson 642.

"A goddamn pissy little revolver? What the hell am I supposed to do with this? *Throw* it at them?"

"I don't have time for your shit! Fire the damn thing!" I shouted as another bullet penetrated the windshield. "Do it now!"

The familiar sounds of bullets piercing the metal on my car made me wish that I had an up-armored Humvee instead of a luxury truck. A few bullets dinged against the driver's side door as I made another hard turn, almost taking out a tiny red Smart car as I raced around the corner.

Sassia peeked over her seat before closing one eye and firing a round through the hole where the back window had been. I wished that we could switch places, but I knew I couldn't stop. I prayed that she would at least slow them down, but as she focused and took her second shot, my military training began to take over. I swerved through traffic, making blind turns down residential streets. I didn't know what Sassia had done, but they were losing ground on us.

"Did you hit one?" I asked.

"I don't think so, but this .38 has more power than I thought it would!"

For a few seconds I didn't hear anything as I focused on getting the hell out of fourth ward. After I made two quick right turns in succession, the truck behind us was nowhere to be seen.

"Make a left here, Chuck! Good, now make another right here and a left at the next intersection."

"Make another right here and then another quick right!"

Without even realizing where she was taking us, I meticulously followed her instructions, swerving in front of oncoming cars and driving like a mad woman. Thirty seconds later, we pulled into a shopping plaza.

"Pull into a parking spot and get the hell out of the car."

I jumped out of the Lexus, glancing at all the dents where the bullets hadn't penetrated, but Sassia wasn't gawking with me. She grabbed my hand and we raced into a clothing store. After making a call on her cell, she pulled me into an empty dressing room and told me to stay there. She returned in a few minutes with new clothes for me.

"Put these on," she demanded.

"Why the hell were they shooting at us?" I whispered.

"They weren't shooting at us, they were shooting at *you*."

"How the hell do you know that? Maybe they just didn't like how you talked to them! I asked you to shut your fuckin' pie hole, but nooo—you had to fuckin' provoke them to shoot at us!"

Sassia grabbed me by the shoulders and pinned me against the wall. "They are after *you*, Charlie! I know that because I heard them speaking to each other in the car! They were asking each other if you were the person they saw on the goddamn screen! Now get changed!"

So the same people who killed Steve were after me again? Perez was dead, so who the hell was after me? Was there more family I had to deal with and if Perez was Los Perdidos, why the hell were the Latin Kings shooting at us when those two gangs couldn't stand each other?

As Sassia continued to throw clothes at me, I did what I was told. Ripping off what I'd worn to the funeral, I quickly put on the jeans, buttoned up the dark blue Henley, and put on the blonde wig she'd gotten for me, snatching it off a mannequin. I stepped out and saw she had changed as well. Her tight black dress had been replaced by blue jeans and a brick red, sleeveless top. She gave me the pair of tennis shoes she was holding and told me to hurry because there was a cab waiting outside.

I slid on the sneakers and as Sassia was pulling me through the store, I tried to gather my thoughts. "We really need to go to the police."

"Not *here* we don't."

She continued pulling me toward the door when we spotted the cab. Before opening the door, she looked around, spotted no gangbangers, and we ran to the car. As soon as we got in, Sassia told him an address that wasn't even close to where we stayed.

Now in the back of the cab, I repeated myself. "We need to go to the police!"

"Did you happen to notice the absence of cops during that little shootout?"

"So what are you saying, Sassia? Contrary to your warped beliefs, all cops aren't dirty!"

"Well that bit of knowledge makes me feel so peachy! Wake the fuck up, Chuck! All that time we spent running from the Escalade and no one came to fucking help! I don't call that coincidence! Some good citizen would have reported gunshots, not to mention your crazy driving. Maybe it's your world that's warped, Chuck!"

"That doesn't mean we shouldn't call."

"Let them find the truck. It has bullet holes in it, so it'll be reported soon enough. Right now, we need to get as far away from here as we can."

"And what makes you think you know what the hell is going on? Do you have some insight that I don't know about? I hope to God that you do because I'm about to go crazy!

Someone wants me dead, but I don't know who or why! What the hell do they want from me?"

"I don't know what they want, Charlie, but we need to get you out of here and someplace safe. Then we can figure it out."

"They're shooting at *me*, not you, Sassia! If you don't want to end up like Steven, then I suggest you get the hell away from me and let HPD take care of this." She exhaled loudly enough for me to know how agitated she was. "What do *you* have to be upset about?"

"I saved your ass out there! You gave me a pea-shooter and I managed to take out one of their tires! Can I get a 'thank you Sassia'? I mean, damn!"

"You understand Spanish. You didn't even bat an eye when those guys were shooting at us and then you just happen to hit a truck tire with two shots from a revolver. From a *moving* vehicle. Who the hell *are* you?"

She opened up the same little, black purse she'd had at the funeral and handed me my revolver. "This is yours," she said. "You might need it. As far as me speaking Spanish... Hello?? My name is Sassia Santinos and you don't think I speak Spanish? My job requires that I know my way around the city and I grew up in a neighborhood where there were shootings everyday and twice on weekends. Getting away is not rocket science, Chuck. Sometimes you just have to keep your cool and I learned a long time ago that the first rule of getting away is to change your appearance. My last boyfriend taught me that."

Without even allowing me to respond, she grabbed my head and pushed it down on her shoulder.

"What the fuck are you doing?" I mumbled.

"They're watching the freeway ramps."

I looked around and saw about a dozen Latin Kings, each with their own motorcycle on the on ramp to the freeway. I found myself involuntarily holding my breath until we passed through the row of men.

"Are we free?"

She shook her head. "Someone's after you, Charlie and they really want you. You can't go back home."

"My plane tickets to fly home are at the apartment and my flight leaves in a few hours! How the hell am I supposed to get out of the city now?"

"You don't. Chuck, first someone blows up your car and then the Latin Kings are after you? This shit is serious! Who the hell did you piss off?"

I shrugged my shoulders. Everything seemed surreal, a nightmare that I would eventually wake up from, but I knew that wasn't true. Someone wanted me dead and I had no idea why.

"How the hell am I supposed to know? My first day as a cop, I stop one goddamn robbery and then everything goes to shit after that! If I knew who was after me, then I would've stopped this a long time ago!"

Sassia sat back and closed her eyes as the driver jumped onto 59 South. "We can't go back to the apartment."

"Fine, just get me to a phone. I can call my father and he can find a way to get me out of here."

"I don't think these are random occurrences, Chuck. Someone wants you dead. I think that leaving Houston without finding out who it is means taking it with you to Philly. You'd be putting your family in danger."

"Shit!" She was right. "What the hell am I supposed to do now? Even more importantly, with Perez dead, how the hell am I supposed to find out who's after me."

The day had already started off bad and gotten considerably worse. I didn't want to believe that someone was after me, but I wasn't the type of person who believed in coincidences either. Los Perdidos, LRZ, and now the Latin Kings—someone was leaning hard on the Hispanic gangs to get to me.

We sat silent in the cab for what seemed like an eternity as I wondered what move I was going to make next. I didn't have a job and if I believed Sassia's theory, I didn't know who could be trusted. Truth was, if she hadn't saved me, I'd probably be dead. I looked over at her and it looked like she was almost as conflicted as I was.

She finally broke the silence a few minutes later blurting out, "You can stay with me."

"I thought you said we couldn't go back to the apartment?"

She smiled at me with the same confident, infectious smile that she had when I met her.

"With a job like mine, you have to learn to be...*flexible.*"

Chapter 14: Information and Ignorance

Sassia

We pulled in front of El Primero about ninety minutes after having escaped from downtown and *almost* certain death. I'd learned not to trust anyone and so I had the first cab drop us off at First Colony Mall. We took a second one to the apartment and I paid him just enough for him to be too pissed to remember who we were. As we stepped out the cab, I looked at Charlie, who was practically catatonic in the seat next to me. For a brief moment, I saw how vulnerable she was and even though I'd forgotten, Charlie was still a woman. I'd been shot at and seen enough death for ten people, but Charlie wasn't me. She was a woman who had lost and buried her fiancé, been shot at, almost blown up, and now she had no way to get back to her family—at least not with the price on her head. She was scared.

For ex-military she's too damn soft.

I smiled.

Well, she's no Nava—that's for sure.

I could smell the CFT put on her, but according to CT, none existed. There was a hit on her and even though I didn't want Chuck's death magnet near me, I wasn't going to turn my back and leave her to die.

As soon as the cab drove off, I turned to her. "We're here."

She looked at the luxury townhomes like she'd lost her best friend. "Where's *here*?"

"This is where we're going to keep you safe until we find out what's going on."

"I still don't understand why this is *your* problem?"

"This is my problem because whoever shot at you didn't care that I was in the car with you. The way I see it, we're both owed an explanation."

Instead of trying to pick her brain, I let her into the apartment and showed her around.

When I began to head back out the front door, she blurted out, "Where are you going?"

"I don't keep much food here. With all the excitement, you may not be hungry now, but when the adrenaline dies down, you will be."

"There's no phone in here! How am I supposed to reach my family and let them know I'm okay?"

"I'll get a phone for you while I'm out. In the mean time, why don't you just sit down, relax, and let me take care of you."

With a worried look still wrinkling her face, she sat uncomfortably on my sofa and turned on the TV. As soon as I was out of the building, I opened up my purse and pulled out the sat-com phone.

"What the fuck, CT! You told me you couldn't find a hit on Charlie Briggs!"

"Whoa, slow down there, Tits, there isn't one. At least not any hit for her on the wire."

"Then would you please tell that to the Latin Kings who just shot up her car. They trailed us all through downtown and North Houston after looking at a netbook with her freaking face on it! If that's not a CFT, I don't know what the fuck is!"

"So wait, you were in the car with the cop?"

"How is that even relevant?"

"What the hell, Val? I thought you were supposed to leave her alone!"

"I did leave her alone! Today was good-bye, but then some jerk-hole had to shoot up her damn car with me in it! If someone I trusted would've found out about the damn CFT, I wouldn't have gotten in the damn car in the first fucking place!"

"You're so full of shit, because I know you banged her! You talk so much shit, but you have a soft spot for the people you bang—except Rock Hound's crispy ass. You can fool yourself, but we both know you would've gotten in to save her ass!"

I pulled the phone away from my ear and rolled my eyes. I didn't know why I had to pull the phone away to do it, but it just seemed like the right thing to do when dealing with CT. "Can we not talk about this now?"

"I know you rolled your eyes."

"Are you watching me?"

"I know you! You know we're soul mates, but you just don't want to admit it. You want to know something though? You kill me. When it comes to having sex with me, you'd kill me! But you'd risk your ass to keep her alive..." He paused briefly and I could hear the gears in his brain grinding. "Val. Lovely, beautiful, intelligent, Val, where the fuck is she now?"

"I put her in El Primero."

"You put her where? You fucking took her to site A! That was some real 'genius at work' thinking! So what did you do with the guns that were already there? I mean, she is a cop! Having unregistered guns is still punishable by the electric—gas—lethal injection chamber in Texas, right?"

"It's not that serious, CT. My guns are hidden in a GSA class 5 safe, under the floorboards, which is hidden in my closet. If she can find it and then open it, we need to recruit her. Besides, it was the only place I could take her where I could keep the guns hidden!"

"Why would you hide her anyway, if there's an open CFT on her? That puts your ass right in the crosshairs! If whoever is looking for her finds her at *your* place, you're just as expendable as she is!"

I thought about throwing the phone away, but instead I just tightly clenched it in my fist. I took in a deep breath and walked several steps before I spoke again.

"CT, I've already been shot at today. Cursing me out is the last thing I need. Why don't you try helping?"

"No."

I closed my eyes and clenched my teeth. "What do you mean *no*?"

"I mean no, Val. You stepped in this shit and now you have to clean it up."

I knew this was nothing more than a shakedown. He wanted my goods in exchange for his services. I wanted to laugh, but I was too pissed that he'd rejected my request for help. Instead of offering, I decided to plead.

"C'mon, CT...*please*?"

"Begging's not gonna work, Val. You did this shit to yourself."

"You're such a fucking man, CT! You're still on the phone, so you must want something."

"You're right, I do want something."

I knew it! He was so predictable!

"You want pussy, right. Go ahead and be the man I know you are! Just jump in and disappoint me!"

"No, Val, I don't want pussy." He said, solemnly.

"Well then, what do you want?" I asked suspiciously.

"After this is all over, if you survive, I just want you to go on a date with me. A date that's separate from what we agreed to earlier."

It was so unlike him to ask for a date that I began to laugh. "A *date*? What is that, another euphemism for banging me?"

"You swear you'll kill me if you give me sex, so maybe I just want to sit down and have drinks—then we can get butt-ass naked, get nasty, and maybe you'll get to kill me if I don't put you to sleep first."

That was the CT I knew. "You're a piece of work, you know that?"

"Is it a deal?"

"Fine, I'll go on your date, but you'd better find out who tried to kill me today."

"I'll call back in a few hours."

I chuckled at CT's brashness and after hanging up the phone, I walked across the street and into the shopping plaza inside our subdivision. I bought some groceries so I could cook for Charlie and a disposable cell so she could call her family.

When I made it back to the apartment, Charlie was huddled in a corner of the sofa watching the Rockets play. I laid the groceries on my counter and put each one away before walking over to her. I could see that she was still reticent to speak, so I just ran my fingers through her hair several times and handed her the disposable. With a weak smile, she took the phone and immediately dialed her family.

Feeling good that I'd managed to make her smile, I left her alone and headed to my workout room. It had been almost a week since I'd been able to exercise, which was rare for me. I wanted to go all out until I passed out, but I decided against it, instead opting for a heavy run on the treadmill. After putting on extra sweats, I turned the treadmill up to its highest setting and ran, pounding the treads like a mad woman.

Who wants Charlie dead? Why do they want her dead? Why go under the radar instead of just putting out a contract?

For half an hour, the same three questions bounced through my head even as the sweat began pouring down my face. The more I thought about it, the more unsettled I became.

"What the hell am I missing?"

"Well, you could've gotten some beer..." She startled me, standing in the doorway at first and then walking towards me, "but since you didn't, I just wanted to thank you for the phone—and for keeping me alive."

"You would've done it for me."

"That's the thing, Sassy. You come off as this hard ass, but you always seem to go out of your way for me. Hell, even bringing me here when there's obviously a hit of some kind on me doesn't seem like something you'd do." I was still pushing myself on the treadmill when she walked over and turned it off. "Why are you doing this?"

I reached for the towel next to me and wiped my face off. "I like you. Should there be anything more?"

She stood next to me, which prevented me from stepping down. "Don't get all *Sassia* on me now. Leave *that* crazy bitch in the shot up Lexus. The woman I want to answer is the one who directed us out of the shootout, the one who disguised us on the sly, the one who pushed my head into her shoulder when she saw trouble, and then had an apartment that I didn't know about. The one who cares is the one I want answering."

Shit, CT was right. She was too smart for her own damn good.

"You want to know the truth?" She nodded and I stepped down so that we were almost face to face. "Fine, then I'll tell you. A few years ago, some crazy guy that I'd met didn't want me with anyone else. When he found out that I was in love, he had a hit put out on me. Long story short, he caught me, tortured me, and when he was about to kill me, someone rescued me. If someone hadn't stepped in then to save me, I'd be dead. All I'm doing is what someone did for me."

"Who was the guy?"

"It's not important."

"Who saved you?"

"The police."

"What happened to the guy?"

"He died during the raid."

What did they do to you?"

I wasn't sure if she was asking as Charlie or as a cop, but I didn't feel like telling her anymore than I already had. "What's with all the damn questions? It happened and I hate being reminded that it did. I moved on and I don't want to think about it anymore."

"Don't give me half the story, Sassy! Tell me everything that happened!"

"Why?"

"Because I care about you, Sassy, dammit! You think that you're the only one with problems? I really liked having a man who loved me! That man died for me and now the only person I think about is my next-door neighbor! I have all these fucking feelings and I don't know what to make of them! I just want her to open up and tell me something so I don't feel like this time I'm playing Steven and she's playing Charlie Briggs!" she shouted.

"Fine, you want to know everything? The man who put a hit on me was my boyfriend. See, he was this big time drug dealer and he didn't like being betrayed. I thought I loved him more than my own life, but I fell in love with his best friend. Well, the fucker found out and rather than kill me right away, he made an example of me—raped me for several days before he felt like I needed a bullet put in my head. Someone came in and saved my life the night he'd planned on killing me. You want to know why I'm helping you? It's because this is my chance for redemption!"

Hearing myself tell her what had happened felt like a massive weight that had been lifted off my shoulders. I hadn't ever told anyone that story and as Charlie looked at me awkwardly, I threw the towel on the treadmill and stormed out the room.

"Sassy, wait!"

I turned around and she was silent for a few seconds. Then she walked over and grabbed both my hands. "Aren't you afraid that he'll come back for you?" she asked.

"Not unless he comes back from the dead. I guess he met an even bigger asshole in prison who decided he wasn't worthy of breathing." I wanted to tell her about how Nava had saved me, how it was her who'd put the bullet in his head, but she was still on the other side of the law and I couldn't risk her knowing that much about my past.

"What happened to the man who you were in love with?"

I turned away from her and slowly inhaled, hoping she didn't see or hear my disgust. "He ran away, like they always do when trouble comes around."

"When...if I get back to work, maybe I can help you find him."

I shook my head. "Don't worry about it. I forgot about him a long time ago." I let go of her hands and pulled off my damp sweatshirt. "If it's okay with you, I don't feel like talking anymore about this."

She walked up behind me and tightly squeezed me. "I'm so glad that you shared all of that with me."

A part of me wanted to be glad as well, but if we were going to get out of this, I didn't need Charlie constantly on my brain.

Fortunately she read my mood. "Jump in the shower, I'm going to the kitchen to start some etoufee."

A few hours later we were enjoying shrimp etoufee, drinking Courvoisier, taking hits from my heart-shaped bong, and laughing like old friends. She told me things about her and Steve, while I told her some crazy things that had happened during my childhood. Chuck was genuine; there were no hidden agendas or motivations, which was something I really appreciated about her. Even if lingering thoughts of whether or not I should've brought her here had begun to surface, for the first time in years, I had someone to share things with.

I was ready to stay up all night when I noticed that Charlie's head had collapsed into one of the pillows. Without waking her, I put a blanket over her and kissed her forehead.

"Damn candy-ass G.I.'s can't even handle a little weed," I mumbled, but I was stumbling as well. I was on my way to the bedroom when the hotline rang. Not wanting to pick it up, I let it ring a few times before I finally gave in.

"What, CT?"

"You're gonna love me for this one, Val."

Unsure whether or not I was yelling into the phone, I asked him to stop talking while I snuck into my bedroom and closed the door. "So...what am I going to love you for?"

"Are you drunk?"

"High."

"You're a goddamn train wreck is what you are. Anyway, I've got good news and not so good news."

I closed my eyes and the world seemed to spin, but I laughed anyway.

"What's so funny?" CT asked.

"It's a girl thing. You wouldn't understand."

"Speaking of a girl thing, I sent some cleaners to your Katy apartment."

Cleaners were CT's way of making sure that nothing was left behind in case something happened to me—which didn't instill a great amount of faith. When cleaners were called in, it meant I wasn't supposed to go back.

"Don't let them touch my bike."

"Fine," he sighed. "Well, to get back to what I was saying, I found the netbook belonging to the Latin Kings who were following you."

Hearing that, I immediately tried to focus. "How the hell did you do that?"

"Well, you said that they were chasing you around downtown. So since Wi-Fi networks aren't all that secure, I hacked into several of them in downtown and north Houston. Since most people tend to stay in one location, I looked for an IP address that had used several Wi-Fi towers within the span of fifteen minutes and I came up with one computer."

"That's fucking genius. I swear, I could almost fuck you right now."

"Then we should set that up immediately."

"Key word being *almost.*"

"Anyway, I'm not finished. I hacked into your boy's netbook and found another IP address with the picture of your cop—one a great deal more flattering than the one I have. But check this out, the IP address that sent the pic doesn't exist anymore."

"What the hell does that mean?"

"IP addresses don't just disappear. Every computer has an IP address; it's like a signature, but one that is nearly impossible to clone because two IP addresses can't coexist. Anyway, whoever sent the pic doesn't want to be found."

"So as soon as someone sent her picture, they got rid of the evidence."

"Right," he said confidently, "and that's the bad news."

"So what's the good news?"

"Well, inside one of his folders, there's a timer attached to her picture."

"Why the hell is there a timer on her picture? What the hell is it counting down to?"

"That's the same thing I wondered, but the timer isn't counting down. It's counting up."

I rubbed my forehead, trying to flush out the haze surrounding me. "Why the hell does a timer count up and how is that good news?"

"On his computer, there's a base price for her. The base price is seventy-five thousand. For every twenty-four hours that she's alive, an additional ten thousand is added."

Suddenly my heart began to sink. "How many times has the timer turned over, CT?"

"Twelve, and in a few hours, it'll be thirteen."

"So in a few hours, her head is worth $205,000."

"You're goddamn right! This is the kind of payday we've both been waiting for! All you gotta do is plug that bitch and we're good! We can retire ..."

I sighed and began to pace around my bedroom. Now that I knew for sure that there was a CFT on her head, I wasn't about to kill the only friend I had. "I can't do that."

"What the fuck do you mean you *can't do that*? Val, at this price, every professional in the country is gonna be on your ass! I can't protect you from this! The longer you keep her alive, the greater the chance that they will find her and kill her. Then they'll kill you for hiding her or as collateral damage."

"Let them try."

"This is not the time to be all vigilante and shit. Most of these people will fuck you up, Val. You have no fucking idea!"

"Find out who put out this hit, CT. If you can't do that, find a way to stave off the pros for a couple of days."

"I'm not making any promises, but either you help me find out where the hell I'm supposed to be looking or you put a bullet in her ass yourself."

I hung up the phone and hid it in an old coat in my closet. The only thing I wanted less than Charlie's death, was to listen to CT goad me into putting a bullet in the back of her skull myself.

Chapter 15: Oh? No!

Charlie

When I awoke, I was covered with a quilt and the apartment was deathly silent.

"Sassy?" I managed to mumble. I wanted to speak more loudly, but the headache kept me from doing so. "Shit, I haven't slept through the hangover, yet."

I slowly slid off her couch and began to wander through each room. I didn't find Sassia, but one thing that I did notice was that this apartment was just as sterile as the one she kept in Katy. It was perfectly manicured, with nice furniture and well-stocked closets, not to mention a state of the art exercise room, but it was missing something. There was no *soul* here. It was aesthetically beautiful, but without a single picture of her or her family anywhere in the apartment, it was if this place had no life. There were no travel mementos, no collectibles; nothing personal.

Who the hell has two apartments and doesn't keep a single family picture in either one?

After snooping in her closets and drawers for some inkling to her past for several minutes longer, I still didn't find a thing and gave up. I thought about calling her to complain about her dysfunctional behavior, but instead I grabbed a grapefruit out of the refrigerator and decided to eat some breakfast.

I returned to her couch with a grapefruit half sprinkled with sugar, a glass of milk, and the same thoughts I'd had before I got wasted: *Who the hell would want me dead*? Since everything seemed to start when I interrupted the bank robbery, I grabbed a piece of printer paper from her exercise room and wrote down everything I knew:

Stopped Juan Perez and brother from robbing bank...Juan dead, Carlos revenge? Car bomb, but Los Perdidos has demolition expert? Los Perdidos lieutenant house vandalized by LRZ, he doesn't speak—possibly in on it together, but then Latin Kings make attempt. Were the Latin Kings the outside contractors to begin with? If they were, why did they need photo ID of me? Where's the connection?

For an hour, I wracked my brain trying to think of any connection between the three gangs and me, but I couldn't find one. Hell, I couldn't even find a connection linking the three gangs; they would never be caught dead working with one another. With my headache returning, I decided to rest it a little and see why Sassy had been gone for most of the morning.

She sounded almost cheerful after picking up on the first ring. "Yes, Chuck?"

"How did you know it was me?" I didn't even know how she knew this number when she'd just given the phone to me yesterday.

"I called myself while you were sleeping."

I looked over at the clock and saw that it was nearing two in the afternoon. "Why the hell did you let me sleep so long?"

"Yesterday was an unusual day. I didn't need you stressing and it allowed me to take care of some things without you worrying about where I was."

"And where *are* you?"

"I'm searching for clues, flatfoot."

"Cute. Searching for clues to what? To whoever it is that put a hit on me?"

"Yes. Something you don't know about me, because you're a cop—I deal with criminals, big wigs who owe me some favors. I have a tendency to collect those. Anyway, I found a few names and I'm looking into them."

"Sassy, what are you doing? You're going to make yourself a target and get yourself killed!"

"Chuck, don't worry about me. I've been around criminals a lot longer than you have. Look, I'll be okay. Don't leave, don't answer the door, and just stay out of sight."

"What, stay out of sight in your love nest? What if some really handsome guy comes knocking at the door?"

"Well, it's your life, but if it were me pretending to be you, I'd rock their world. But since you're *not* me, you should try as best you can and tell me about the details. Oh wait, you can't do that, you're still a cop. Just promise me that you won't arrest them."

"I can't arrest anyone anymore. I'm suspended, remember?"

"Damn, that's right. Awww, poor baby. Now you're jobless, homeless, and penniless? Guess that means you really shouldn't think about leaving the apartment."

"That sounds about right and I thank you for being so tactful with it all. I was sure you were going to add manless in there as well," I replied sarcastically.

"I thought about it, but while you're with me, I'll take care of you. You're like my family. Speaking of family, what did your father say to you last night? I noticed you guys had been talking for a while."

"I told him that someone was trying to kill me, but I was safe for the moment. Then he threatened to come down and hide me himself, but I couldn't let him put himself in danger."

"So he's still coming?"

"Not for two days. He said that's how long I have to find out who's after me. When my forty-eight hours are up, he's driving down here and taking me home under his wing. It's an Italian thing."

"I'd do the same if you were my daughter."

I quickly changed the subject. "Speaking of which, I noticed you don't have any pictures of your real family here either. Did they do something to you that was so awful?"

She was silent for a few seconds before speaking. "Look, Charlie, I'll be there as soon as I can. Don't make any unnecessary phone calls and try not to leave the apartment. Just so you know, I'm not going to let anyone follow me to you and I'll watch my back. 10-4, good buddy?"

I hated her corny police jargon almost as much as I hated letting her put herself in danger on my behalf, but nothing I was going to do on this end was going to stop her from being Sassy. "Fine, but if you get shot, I'm not coming to your funeral."

"It's a deal."

I hung up the phone feeling even more uneasy than I had before I called her. Not wanting her to be the only one working, I blocked out my number before calling Carolyn. It wasn't something I wanted to do, but it was the only way I knew how to protect her. When she picked up on the fourth ring, I quickly let her know it was me.

"Girl, they told me they found your truck riddled with bullet holes. Then I tried to call you and when you didn't pick up, I thought the worst. Are you okay?"

"Yes, but I'm going to need your help."

"I got you, girl. What is it you need?"

"Call my boss at KPD to let him know that I'm still alive. Let him know that I contacted you and because a contract has been put out on me, I'm in hiding. Next, the Latin Kings shot up my truck and if you need descriptions of the three men who shot at us, I'll be happy to give that to you, too. Finally, I need you to get any information about known assassins from each of the three major Mexican gangs. They seem to know me so it's only fair that I know them, too."

"Okay, I can do all that, but how am I supposed to get in contact with you?"

"I'll call you. There's a lot going on Carolyn and I have to be careful."

"Just be safe. I'll try to get everything ready for you by the end of the day."

I put the phone down and paced around the apartment, feeling a bit like a caged animal. With nothing to help me understand why I'd been targeted, I put on one of Sassy's sweat suits and began to jog on her treadmill. Maybe some exercise would get rid of the headache and replace it with some fresh ideas.

For more than an hour, all I could think about was getting more information and trying to stop whoever had destroyed my life. I was so wrapped up in thinking and jogging that I didn't hear anyone enter Sassia's apartment until the door closed. I quickly leapt off the treadmill and grabbed a weight bar.

"Chuck, where are you?"

I put down the weight bar and breathed a sigh of relief. "Back in the weight room."

When she appeared in the doorway, she was wearing a skin tight, red jumpsuit and matching boots with four-inch heels. "So that's what you wear to get information?"

"No, it's what I wear to get my bike, but I do have some info."

I turned off the treadmill and walked toward her, grabbing a white towel from the rack in front of her. "Well?"

"I still don't have any idea who is after you. The people I asked didn't know that, but they knew about your case. It seems that about 10 days ago, not long after you foiled your bank robbery, someone put a seventy-five thousand dollar hit on you."

"Is that all my life is worth?" I interrupted, "A measly seventy-five g's?"

"I don't know. Apparently. Ask me and I'll say what you have between your legs is worth that much by itself."

I wasn't sure whether it was the hour of jogging or hearing that sum of money, but my legs were ready to give out. I leaned against the same rack I'd just pulled the towel from and smiled in spite of myself.

"Thanks, I think. Why would someone do this to me? What the hell have I done to deserve all of this?"

"Well, now you know something. Whoever it is has the money to finance this."

"What I need to find out is who the hell is doing this and make them stop!" Storming past Sassia, I walked toward the front door.

"Where are you going, Chuck?"

"I need to go for a walk."

"You just got finished walking! Don't go outside and make yourself vulnerable! If you burn this place, I'm not sure where else we could go."

I turned around and grabbed the disposable phone from her couch. "So you *do* care?"

"I care about living. If they're looking for you and you come back here, you'll lead whoever it is back to the both of us."

"Don't be so damn dramatic. I know how to watch my back." I picked up the revolver I'd left on her coffee table the night before. "And I know how to take care of myself. I'll call if I something happens."

With my legs still feeling like jelly, I took my time walking down the stairs and as soon as I made it to the lobby, I called Carolyn again. The more she knew, the more she could help.

"Carolyn, I know it's soon, but I need to tell you something."

She immediately cut me off. "Not before I tell you what I found out first."

"Already? What is it?"

I could hear her exhale into the phone. "One of my brother's friends is Latin King, so I asked him if he knew anything about a hit on a cop. At first he was a little stubborn, but you won't believe what he told me." As I walked and listened, Carolyn recapped the whole story that had been told to her.

"Almost two weeks ago, a man named Guerrero gets a phone call. The person on the phone says that they want the LK's to kill a cop. Guerrero says they'll do it. They set up a plan to do it when they catch wind that Los Perdidos also gets a call to kill the same cop. Because of how crazy the contract is, a massive gang war goes down. There's a lot of collateral, including one Carlos Perez."

"*Holy shit.*"

"But wait—the story's not over. The Kings plant a bomb on the cop's car, but when the wrong person dies, they have to go underground. The two guys who failed are dealt with by Guerrero and everyone has to lay low. When Steve's funeral comes around, they pay off some cops to take a lunch break during your little shoot-out. When they miss you again, two of the three guys somehow stab themselves to death in the back and the third disappears. According to my source, whoever it is that set this up is tired of the amateur work and is about to bring in real pros to finish the job."

"Did they say why this mysterious person wants me dead?"

"All he knows is that you're doing something to interfere with their business."

"What, the damn bank robbery? It was two small-time guys! These guys weren't pros, just some local yahoos who didn't know what they hell they were doing!"

"You know how it is, Charlie. A couple of small-time guys use the revenue from bank robberies to get them some guns, drugs, and sneak a few people across the border, then they get big. The price on your head may just be a way of trying to maintain some sort of status quo."

"It's nice to know that me doing my job has cost me everything I ever cared about, and ironically gave me some sort of deluded status," I said.

"The shit sucks, I know, but LK won't let this one go and they're searching the city for you—now I know why. I wish I had more for you, but that's all I have right now."

"That's more information than I've gotten in the last two weeks. Have your inside man write a statement, get it to my chief, and I'll be calling you again later for updates."

"Already done...and, Charlie? Promise me that you'll just lay low until all this is over."

"They killed Steve and almost got to me. This is more than just personal, it's necessary."

"Then *please* be safe." She sounded desperate.

"I will."

With all the stress I was under, I needed something to help me relax. I left the stuffiness of the apartment building, leaving the outside door unlocked so that I could get back in, and walked around the adjacent apartment buildings surrounding Sassia's. The sun was high in the sky and it took a few minutes for me to adjust to the brightness, but once I had, everything seemed different. I felt like I was seeing everything clearly for the first time. Suddenly, I found myself missing home—missing the little plot we had in front of our house with its crooked, little sidewalk and a small patch of grass. Reminiscing about my mother and how she would always have brownies for us as we sat under my friend Ashley's maple tree, the only one with its roots still hidden underground nearly brought on another onslaught of tears.

As I thought about Ashley and the crazy things we used to do, like bribing boys with a kiss so that they would bring us candy from the corner store, an older Hispanic woman walked by with her poodle and then a carload of white teenagers drove by blasting rap from their car.

All of them were without a care in the world and I hated that my life had become so chaotic and purpose-driven. I had a rebellious streak, but for the most part, I had stopped doing things I liked and had replaced them with the things I had to do. Now that I knew that someone didn't value my life as much as I did, most of the things in my life that had once seemed important suddenly seemed like minor inconveniences.

If this is it for me, then I want to at least have enjoyed my last days.

Soon, I found myself chasing leaves as they carelessly blew in the wind and taking off my shoes so I could feel the grass between my toes. I sat against a large maple tree, closed my eyes, and listened to each breath, trying to remember how often I had done this with my friends on our old block in Philly.

Still smiling, I thought about my father and how often he used to save me from my mother when I did something wrong.

"C'mon, Susan, she's just a girl. Hell, she's really a tomboy. Don't act like you didn't do those things when you were young."

"Things are different, Michael. Boys now aren't as innocent as they used to be."

My father used to always tell me to stop and enjoy life, but I was always too busy trying to progress up through the Navy ranks and make my father proud of me—so busy in fact that I had just made it home before my mother passed away. Now wishing like hell that I'd had more time with her, I felt a few tears slip away, running down my face. It hadn't struck me 'til just then how much I missed my mommy.

I wanted to grieve more for the man I'd buried a little more than twenty-four hours ago, but the pain of losing him wasn't the same as it was in the days before his burial. I was angry at the world for having taken him, but now that I knew the person who had done this was out there and after me, vengeance had usurped grief. An eye for an eye...a life for a life...Catholic school had taught me that.

For almost an hour, I sat under the tree and when I had finished crying, I walked back up to Sassy's apartment and when I tried to open the door, I found it locked. Damn, I was going to catch hell for leaving it unlocked.

"What's the password?" she shouted from the other side.

"Open the damn door, Sassy! What if someone was after me?"

"If they were after you, they wouldn't kill you in plain sight. They'd wait for you in the apartment that you so thoughtfully left open for them! You make it so easy for them to kill us!"

I collapsed against the door. I was tired of yelling and if I was going to die, I just wanted to enjoy whatever time I had left. "Why do you have to be a goddamn hardass all the time? Your apartment is so damn bland and stuffy!"

She paused for a second before speaking and now I could hear her directly on the other side of the door. "How do I know that someone's not out there now and you led them here so that they could violate and kill both of us?"

"C'mon, Sassy, that doesn't even sound like something I'd do! I'd rather be violated alone than bring you into it."

"So you wouldn't sacrifice me to save your own skin?"

"Never!"

"That's the password."

She opened the door and had changed, wearing only a thin t-shirt. I paused for a second, mesmerized by her beauty. Her hazel eyes seemed to pierce through me, cutting through the façade that I put up for other people to see. As my heart skipped a beat, I knew that I had to tell her the truth about what I'd found out, but that would come later. I walked inside and after closing the door, I took her hand and guided her to the couch.

As she sat next to me, I leaned toward her, softly kissed her lips and slipped my fingers under her t-shirt. She gasped as I dragged my fingernails across her ribs and then gently cupped her breasts. They felt so good; soft yet firm, her large brown nipples rubbing against my palms. I let my head fall to her shoulder and for several minutes, I teased her nipples with my thumbs while sucking on her neck.

When her nipples were like marbles between my fingers, I whispered into her ear. "Take off your shirt."

Without a word, she did as I asked, leaning back on the couch and inviting me to take her body. For a brief second, I stared in awe at how perfect her form was. The musculature in her arms and six-pack put me to shame.

"Wow..." I whispered. *Who was this woman*?

She smiled and I kissed both breasts, wetting her erect nipples with my tongue before kissing her mouth once more.

This time when we kissed, our tongues fought, battling for supremacy as we invaded each other's mouths. She kept her eyes open as we kissed, watching me, unable to give me complete control.

I contemplated letting her take back the control, but I wanted this. If this was going to be the last time I made love to her, I deserved to be in control. As Sassy sat up and began to lay me down so she could get on top of me, I pulled away from her and shook my head.

"No."

She smiled then and closed her eyes as she laid down for me. Slowly opening and closing her bare muscular legs, she was taunting me—challenging me. I stood up, threw my clothes to the floor, and started at her feet. Taking each toe into my mouth, I listened to her gasp when I took them from my mouth and blew cold air on them. Goosebumps formed as I moved slowly up her legs, dragging my tongue along her shins, then her knees, and finally I pushed her legs wide so I could lick the insides of her thighs. I stopped for a moment to admire her pussy, one of the most beautiful I'd ever seen, though my experience wasn't vast. Her lush, dark bush had been sculpted into an almost heart shape, and that made me smile.

"What's so funny, flatfoot?" she asked, her voice husky as she rested her calves on my shoulders.

I looked up and could see her hardened nipples sitting atop perfectly sculpted breasts. I didn't answer her question, just turned my attention back to her pussy, noticing how wet she'd become. I couldn't wait any longer to taste her. Her body had invited me to return and so I slid my tongue inside her folds and tasted hungrily of her sweetness.

"Shit," she whispered, arching her back so that I could have more of her and I obliged. I pushed my tongue in further than I ever had, before bringing it back out to tease her swollen clitoris. Once my tongue touched her clit, she quickly grabbed my head, her fingers grasping handfuls of hair as she guided me up and down against her. I used my fingers to spread her wider, slipping them into her throbbing pink world.

With my head bobbing up and down and her essence slowly being fed to my tongue, she sat up just high enough so that she could watch me. I looked at her long enough to smile before I returned to my duties, teasing her clit then sucking hard on it, before heading back down to lap up any bonus essence.

Not long after, her hips began to pound against my tongue as her fingers began to dig deeper into my scalp.

"Are you coming?" I whispered.

"Yes," she quietly cried.

As she guided me and my tongue feverishly pushed against her clit, her legs tightened against the sides of my head.

"Fuck, it's coming."

She pushed me further down between her thighs, screaming my name. As she pressed against my head, I stuck my tongue inside of her, tasting her sweet cream as it flowed onto my tongue and into my mouth.

With her fingers still combing through my hair, she smiled. "Can I ask what *that* was for?"

"I just wanted to make you happy."

"That's not the truth, Chuck, and we both know it. You've always let me be the aggressor and you were content being passive and shy. Why the role change?"

I shrugged. "It's just that for the last hour or so I walked around outside and thought about my life. There were some things that I wanted to do that I may never get the chance, so I just wanted to be able to cross one of them off my list."

She stared at me for a few seconds before pushing me from between her legs."So you mean this whole eating me out thing was just you crossing shit off your *bucket list*?"

I leaned over, grabbed a towel, and wiped her creamy essence from my lips. "I knew you were gonna do this!"

"Do what? Get mad? What the fuck, Chuck? You went out there, made a bucket list, and now I'm supposed to be happy that you've resigned yourself to dying?"

"You say it like it's a bad thing. Your life isn't in danger. Your life hasn't been turned into shit in the last couple of weeks. Things don't always go like they're supposed to. Staying alive isn't a guarantee, Sassia!"

"I brought you here so that you could be safe, not so you could give me a goddamn suicide letter." She stood up and started to walk away when I jumped up and grabbed her wrist. "Let me go!"

She yanked her arm away so fiercely that I had to let go to keep her from dislocating my shoulder, but I wasn't about to give up. I tackled her and as we both fell onto the couch, I straddled her.

"I didn't do this so that you would be upset with me, Sassy. Dammit! Why can't you just understand what I'm going through?" She turned away from me, not looking me in the face. After a couple minutes of silence, I finally got off her. She quickly stood up and began walking toward her bedroom. "Why are you so mad?" I shouted.

"Because you don't trust me enough to keep you alive." she mumbled, without ever looking at me.

"I do trust you, but there's no perfect plan. How the hell can you guarantee something like that?"

"Because I can!"

After she slammed the door to her bedroom, I grabbed a pillow from the couch and cried. It was something I was getting too damned good at. My two talents: Eating pussy and crying.

Great.

The next morning I listened to Sassia's frenetic workout. For three hours, she ran, lifted weights, and practiced beating the shit out of her heavy bag. Thinking that she would beat on me if she heard me, I pretended to be asleep until I heard her walk into the bathroom.

Living with two brothers and being in the military had taught me a lot about people and that was that they were always less upset in the shower. Once I heard the shower start, I snuck into the bathroom and leaned against the sink.

"What?" she asked nonchalantly from behind the steamy glass door.

"I'm sorry."

"Is that all?"

She slid the door open and as the steam began to escape, I wasn't sure if it was all from the hot water or from her mood, but the look on her face was anything but pleasant. "C'mon, Sassy. You pretend to be so hard core, but we both know you're not. I made a mistake. How long are you going to punish me?"

"You don't get it, Chuck. I risked my life for you and you're already making plans to die. I never figured you to be the type to give up so easily, but I guess I was wrong." She slammed the door and I was forced to simply admire her silhouette. As I watched her hands sliding over her breasts, rubbing soap between her legs, I never wanted to be a bar of soap so bad in my life. The room was fragrant with the scent of summer-ripe strawberries.

What she said had stung, though, but that wasn't going to stop me from saying what I needed to say. "I'm not giving up, Sassy. What I did last night I wanted to do, but knowing that my life was in jeopardy just helped me gain the courage. If you want to think of what I did as me crossing off things on my bucket list, then fine, you can. Me, I like to think of it as fulfilling a fantasy."

She shook her head. "Whatever."

"Sassia, I just want you to know..." I wanted to tell her what Carolyn had told me about the Latin Kings, but I just didn't want to go down that road. At least not now.

"You want me to know what, Chuck?" she asked curiously.

"That if things were different, maybe you and I could have had something."

She sighed. "Stop getting so damn emotional on me. I'm going to do whatever I can to keep you alive."

"I know you will."

"Look, you probably smell like hell. You should...shower with me."

I quickly threw my clothes to the floor and stepped into the shower with her. With strawberry bodywash pouring down her body and disappearing into her nether regions, I bit on my lip, only for her to turn her back to me.

"You still mad?" I asked.

She handed me her loufa. "I missed a spot on my back. Can you get it for me?"

After scrubbing her back for a few minutes, she rinsed off and left me alone in the shower. I didn't mind, though. All the heavy breathing reminded me of last night and I knew that it was a sure sign that I was at the very least, near Forgiveness Road.

A few minutes later, I was drying off and left the warmth of the bathroom looking for Sassia. Still feeling a little anxious from last night, I wanted to finish what I'd started. When I found her, she was in the kitchen pouring herself a glass of orange juice. Still wearing the towel she'd left the bathroom in, there wasn't a doubt that she was still feeling a little anxious as well.

I began to approach her when a series of loud bangs at the front door interrupted us. My heart skipped a beat and Sassia hastily motioned me to get into the bedroom.

"Who is it?"

"It's Hoops, girl! You asked me to come give you. . ."

"I'm on my way!" she interrupted.

"Are you going to answer the door in a towel?" I asked, trying to whisper.

"I have a thong on!"

"Who the hell is *Hoops*?"

"He's someone that...that I've been dating. I have a date with him today that I forgot about!"

"Are you dating or are you screwing him?"

"Why?" She smiled seductively. "Are you jealous again?"

"Hurry up, girl!" Hoops interrupted. "I ain't got all damn day!"

She rolled her eyes and wearing only her towel, she casually walked to the door.

After realizing that it was someone Sassy knew, I breathed a sigh of relief, and then realized that I too, was still only wearing a towel. I turned toward the bedroom, but Sassy had already opened the door and the incredibly sexy man's attention was focused on me.

His perfect smile was indication enough that he wasn't someone Sassy was dating. "Damn, ladies, I didn't interrupt anything did I? If so, please don't let me stop you. I'll just watch quietly."

As he strolled through the door, I saw that his deep voice fit him perfectly. He was tall, light-skinned, and beneath his tight-fitting shirt, I could definitely see that his muscles were just as sexy as he was. With his neatly trimmed goatee and braided hair falling just past his broad shoulders, I caught myself staring until Sassy shouted at me.

"Earth to Katy PD? Don't you have some clothes to put on, chick?"

"Don't *you*?" I retorted.

He turned toward Sassia. "Hold the fuck up, Val. You got *5-0* in here?" He turned walk back out the door. "This shit is all messed up. I spent ten hours on the goddamn road trying to get here and you do me like this? Yo, I'm done."

"Who's *Val?*" I asked.

She grabbed Hoops' arm before turning to face me. "Val is my...my name for the people I *date.*" She turned back to Hoops and sighed. "Look, let me know where you're staying at and I'll come to you."

"I can't do that shit, man. Just being here with you is putting me at risk. I'm gone. Unless you two are gonna reward me with a show, I think I need to go."

He began again to walk out the door and I saw that same look on Sassy's face from last night reappearing.

"Hoops, is it? Look, I didn't mean to step in between whatever you and *Val* had planned, but just so you know, I'm not really a cop anymore." I sat down on the arm of the couch. "They suspended me for allegedly tying up some naked asshole and his girlfriend. Then I supposedly shot him in the ass...twice."

Hoops smiled as he turned around. "And you're not in jail?" he asked, seeming genuinely intrigued. "What caliber gun did you use? Was it just a flesh wound or did they have to dig to get the bullet out of his ass? Please, I'd like to hear more about your abuse of power. And just so you know that I'm not solely watching your breasts while you tell the story, I'll get it out the way now. You have a great rack."

I looked down, realizing that I was giving him a view he wasn't entitled to, and closed the gap in my towel.

Knowing the story already, Sassia smiled too, trying to cover her mouth as she did so.

"Does that matter? I'm not a cop and *Val* is my friend. If you two were going to have sex, even if it's for money, then I won't say a thing." Hoops gave me a confused look as he walked back into the apartment while Sassia, with her hand still covering her mouth, shook her head. "I know I'm new to this whole escort thing, but I'm trying to open up to some things that I've never had the opportunity to do before." I winked at Sassy. "In fact, maybe I'm the one who should watch."

Hoops came over and swung his arm around my waist. "Wow, I am so glad that you're honest and open with these things. You know, an escort *like Val* needs more friends like *you.*" Smiling at Sassia, he began to take off his shirt, revealing a chiseled chest and sculpted abs. "Whenever you're ready Val, I'll be in the bedroom."

Sassia shot him a nasty look and as she walked past me, she yanked my towel off.

"What was that for?" I asked.

"I'm going to need this," she mumbled.

"Well then, can I watch?"

"No," she replied before slamming the door. "You've gotten enough ideas for one day."

After getting a blue terrycloth robe for myself, I pressed my ear against Sassy's door. When I didn't hear anything but music, I cracked open the door to see Hoops' head bobbing up and down between Sassy's out-stretched thighs. She was apparently quite the tongue hound.

I watched him sway his head back and forth as if he enjoyed the taste of her and didn't want to stop. Through the crack of the door, I spied on them, watching his muscular back and bare ass, as he licked the same essence that I had. Her moans and arching back were familiar, and she had a solid grip on his braids, forcing his head hard against her pussy.

I closed my eyes and repeatedly whispered, "I'm not jealous," but I knew I was.

With the sounds of Anthony Hamilton permeating the room, I could feel my heart pounding, my clit throbbing, and feel my thighs dampening. With each breath becoming more labored than the last, I took a step away from the door.

Only a few feet away from the crack that I'd created, I still listened to the sounds of Sassy moaning and of Hoops asking her, demanding her to cum. Suddenly my stomach felt like it had been invaded by butterflies and with my clit yearning to be touched, I slid a finger in between my moistened thighs.

"Oh, God."

My clitoris was so swollen and sensitive that I was almost afraid to touch it, instead opting to slide my fingers inside of myself to stifle the moaning sounds I could feel growing in my throat. I returned to the crack in the door, hoping that watching them would quell the fire I was stoking. Instead, I watched as Hoops slid down his pants and Sassy brought his massive erection up to her face, engulfing him in her mouth. His back was still to me, and he was blocking her face.

With my fingers pushing deeper inside, I leaned against the doorjamb, and closed my eyes, trying not to watch them—trying not to scream, but when I opened my eyes, Hoops was watching me.

"Is there something I can help you with?"

I looked at his huge stiffened manhood then up at his face. "Oh, my God!" Mortified, I quickly stopped and stumbled away as I tried to close my robe. "I'm sorry, I . . ."

Sassy stood behind him, softly kissing his back, then she walked over and picked me up from the floor. "All that peeking in the door and we figured we'd better invite you to the party." I took her hand and she pulled me into her bedroom. Standing me next to an upholstered velvet chair, she removed my robe before sitting me down.

When I opened my mouth to speak, she put her hand over my lips. "I'll tell him what to do; you just shut up and enjoy whatever he does."

Then, she turned to him, whispering something into his ear that caused him to smile. Not long after, he was on his knees before me, sucking on my toes, one at a time. This was a delicious new experience for me. *Why have I never had this done before?*

While Hoops knelt in front of me, Sassy had gotten behind me, and was taking little nibbling bites on my neck, earlobes, and shoulders. Leaning forward, she cupped both of my breasts in her hands, gently kneading them, pressing my nipples with her strong thumbs. The fire between my legs had flamed into at least a four alarm.

"She's wet and ready. Taste her," Sassy demanded and Hoops did as he was told. His tongue worked its way up my shin, to the insides of my legs, and then he parted my thighs, planting kisses. He stopped for one agonizing moment to spread my legs wide, placing them over the arms of the chair. My inflamed pussy was exposed to the room's cool air, feeling strangely electric. I sank back against the chair, helpless, as Sassy's fingers teased my nipples and Hoops' bent forward and took my entire pussy into his mouth, sucking hard and plunging his tongue deep. He let go, then took only my swollen clit between his lips, and the fire raged. I could no longer control my hips, as they lifted and pushed upward to maintain contact with his face.

As Hoops began swirling his tongue around and around, Sassy nibbled on my neck, then pressed her tongue into my ear.

Oh, my god.

Suddenly Hoops stopped sucking on my clit, wrapped his massive arms around me, and placed me on the bed. Sassy's mouth was quickly on my breasts, licking and biting my nipples, and it was too much for me to bear. Hoops' face was back between my legs, his mouth covering my pussy, his tongue deep within me.

"I'm coming! Shit! I'm coming!" I wailed, but either they didn't hear me or didn't care. Hoops swirled his tongue around faster and Sassy held me close, sucking one breast, then the other. Even as I was coming, I knew that this was different. I felt like my body had begun to hollow out and suddenly a wave of pleasure engulfed me. I was having an orgasm, a tidal wave, unlike any I'd had before.

"Fuck! Fuck! Fuck! Fuck!" I dug my fingers into Hoops' hair as my body gyrated and contorted into positions that I had no control over. Nothing existed in the world but my pussy and I wanted more and more of that hot, wet tongue . . .

Almost a minute later, Hoops lifted his face from between my thighs; his goatee was covered in my explosive, massive orgasm.

"Now go put a condom on," Sassia instructed and as he walked away, then she turned to me. "It was good, right?"

Still breathing heavily, I gasped a deflated, "Yes."

"Still, I wanna see what he can do with that thing between his legs. She slapped me on the thigh. "Saddle up, cowboy; you're riding that thing next." Too exhausted to argue, I let Sassia pick me up and position me doggy style on the bed.

"I've ever taken that much," I managed to whisper. "He's not a small man."

"You're already good and wet, so just relax."

Hoops returned with his manhood almost fully covered and hungry with the look of lust. "Don't worry, white girl, I'll be gentle."

As he stood behind me, his hands gripping my hips, his reassurance didn't resolve any of the worry I already had. As he slowly pushed himself into me, I was still unsure whether or not I could take him, but I spread my knees apart a little more, relaxed, and welcomed him inside of me.

"Good girl," he said and when I felt like I couldn't take another inch, Sassia came out of nowhere and softly kissed me on the lips.

Hoops was by far the tightest fit I'd ever had. It took him a few minutes to work up steam, but as he slowly began to grind his body against my own, I was ready to explode again.

He wrapped his hands around my waist and each time he pulled our bodies together, I screamed in ecstasy.

"I feel your pussy tightening around me, baby, you about to cum for me?" he asked. And when I didn't answer, he slapped me on the ass—and I liked it. "I'm talking to you, so you betta answer my question."

I wanted to answer, but I was so busy screaming that I couldn't. Somehow the same hollow feeling, the same orgasm I'd had before was returning like a tsunami and I didn't want to miss it.

"You know what? I'm stopping." And he did!

Devastated that he'd stopped when I was on the cusp of another massive orgasm, I yelled, "What the *fuck*? Why did you stop?"

He was still inside of me when he once again slapped me hard on the ass. This time it hurt. "When I ask you a question, you better answer. I can make this pussy cum, right?" I looked over at Sassy who just shrugged as she played with herself, smiling as she enjoyed what he was putting me through. "She can't help you. The next time you're about to cum, I want you to scream out that Hoops is your daddy."

"Fuck you."

"Then I'm done here."

When I thought about the second orgasm that I was so close to, I knew I was going to hate myself, but I gave in. "Okay, I'll say it."

"Let me hear it, then."

"Hoops is my daddy," I whispered, allowing myself to relax again, feeling him stiffen up inside me.

Not wasting any time, he grabbed a hold of my waist and slowly brought me back down onto him. This time he didn't take his time, jamming every inch of himself inside of me and I loved it.

With each powerful thrust, the sounds of our bodies clapping against each other brought me closer to the orgasm I so wanted. He grabbed hold of my hair and pulled on it, pushing himself deep inside of me and I felt myself go numb. My body tightened around his manhood like a glove, with my breasts bouncing to our rhythm and my eyes rolling in pure ecstasy.

Shit, this is it.

"Hoops is my daddy," I screamed.

"Yeah, I like that shit. Say it again."

"Hoops is my daddy." I felt it and it was coming with a vengeance.

Deeper, faster, harder.

"Hoops is my daddy! Hoops is my daddy! Hoops is my daddy! Fuck! Hoops! *Fuckin daddy!*"

I loudly exhaled and he quickly flipped me over so that we were facing each other. After licking my nipples, he slid inside of me again and I could almost feel a climax on its way, but this time, he took something and stuffed if into my mouth.

"This time, no screaming."

He placed my legs outside his arms and began to pound me again. He was finally about to cum and I wouldn't be forced to endure trauma.

He took his time, teasing me with the tip of his penis before pushing himself all the way in. I was growing more excited as I watched him fight off his orgasm, but as I watched him, the smell—the taste of strawberries, the scent of Sassia began to invade all of my senses. With her seemingly next to me, I grew more aroused and even though she was across the bed, I could feel her inside of me. It was then that I noticed that Hoops had shoved her thong inside of my mouth.

I tried to push it out with my tongue, but the more I tasted her, the more aroused I became. With Hoops beginning to pop and Sassia's thong stuffed in my mouth, I dug my fingers into Hoops' back and released muffled screams through Sassia's satin red thong.

"Are you going to cum for her, baby?" Sassy asked, still playing with herself on the other end of the bed. "I want you to pull it out and cum on her."

Sashaying over to me, she perched her clit just above my mouth. Now I could smell her, taste her, feel her—"Oh, my God!" I screamed.

"Shit!" he shouted and as his body began to convulse, he pulled himself out of me, tore away the condom and came on my stomach.

His warmth spilled over my belly and even though I was eating out Sassia, I came as well. Sassia then moved back far enough so that Hoops could place his lingering erection inside of my mouth. With Sassia watching, I accepted him, removing all traces of leftover semen as he screamed out my name.

I could get used to this.

I awoke to the sounds of chirping coming from somewhere inside Sassia's closet. With the sun beginning to set, I stretched out in her bed as my body still tingled from my immersion into her world.

If it weren't so illegal, I could get used to living like this.

Smirking, all I could think of was Hoops inside of me while Sassy played the role of our dominatrix. Inhaling deeply and exhaling loudly, I managed to stave off the nasty fantasies that began to creep into my head.

"Sassy?"

I looked around her immaculate bedroom and it was only then did I hear the shower running. Rolling over toward the nightstand, I saw a small stack of cash. Leaning over, I picked off the small note on top. It read: 'For a job well done—Sassy.' I began to feel a little cheap, almost used, but with no job and no apartment of my own, I counted the money and figured no one would ever find out anyway.

"*Thirteen hundred for an hour's work?* Shit, I should've gotten into escorting when I was in college."

Even though Sassia had wiped away Hoops' explosion from my stomach, I still felt sticky. I found myself suddenly wishing that she would've awakened me so that we could shower together, but I wasn't going to press the issue. Instead, I spent the next few minutes thinking of how I'd crossed another 'to-do' off my list and how I'd wished that I'd crossed it off sooner.

Chirp. Chirp. Chirp. Chirp.

The same noise that woke me was now beginning to drive me crazy. I hadn't seen any alarm clock when I'd searched through the apartment before, but the ringing was so incessant that I needed to find it and stop it.

Opening the closet, I located a small satellite phone in one of the pockets of her pants. I looked at the bedroom door and heard the shower still running.

"Why the hell does Sassia need a satellite phone?" I whispered.

Chirp. Chirp. Chirp. Chirp.

Whoever was on the other end was desperately trying to get in touch with her and because the ring was so agonizingly irritating, I picked it up.

"Val," the voice said, "it's about time you fucking picked up! Look, I got bad news for ya, hun. I just sent out a couple dossiers on your cop friend. She's now got two real pros after her instead of just locals. I don't know who put this shit together, but they fucking know everything: her military history, who her family is and where they live, her cop job—which by the way she is suspended from and even all known associates—including one *Sassia Santinos*. They're after you, Val. I just sent one of the hitters her father's credit card info. He's going after Daddy to draw her ass out! It's time to stop fuckin' around. Look, either you put a bullet in this bitch's head or you've really fucked yourself! You hear me?"

I hung up the sat phone and the feeling that everything would turn out well was immediately replaced by dread. All along, Sassia was one of *them* and I didn't see it. I didn't want to.

It all seemed so obvious now: no lasting relationships, a spotty past, always disappearing, and of course, not a single picture of anyone in her family.

How could I have been so blind? I quickly realized that I'd been blinded by my own damn needs.

Searching around the room, I found my clothes and threw them on, hoping that she wouldn't walk out of the bathroom and catch me. Running into the living room, I grabbed the revolver, the blonde wig, and my phone, and then left the apartment as quietly as I could.

I ran down the street not stopping for several miles before I ducked into a busy café and searched the phone for a bug or a tracker. Once I was sure the phone was clean, I called my brother, Michael.

"Where's Dad?" I screamed.

"Whoa, Chucky, slow it down. What's going on?"

"Mike, I don't have time for bullshit! Look, you and Derek need to get the hell out of Philly. Find a girlfriend or somebody to stay with. Someone is trying to kill me and they're going after Dad!"

"Fuck me, are you fuckin' serious?"

"Get out of the damn house now and tell me where Dad is!"

"He just called about an hour ago. Said he was gonna stop at some motel in Beaumont I think, stay there for the night, and be in Houston tomorrow morning."

"I'm not bullshitting, Mike. Get out of the house, get out of Philly, and leave your credit cards behind! Pay cash for everything. Cards are too easy to trace."

After assuring me that he would follow through with everything I'd asked him to do, I called a cab and Carolyn not long after.

It seemed like an eternity before she picked up, even though it was only the second ring. When she answered, I was already hyperventilating, frantic, and the tears wouldn't stop. "I need—need you. She was one—she was one of them and after my dad..."

"Breathe, Charlie, breathe," she said. I inhaled a few times and when she heard me slow down she asked me what was going on.

"I answered a call to Sassy from some guy that she's in cahoots with, and with the people trying to kill me. He said that some hitters are going after my father."

"Oh, my God, have you tried reaching him?"

I began pacing in the alley behind the cafe, trying to think of what the hell I needed to do next. "If they have him already, then they would've called either me or my brothers. They don't have him, but I need to get him out of Beaumont as soon as I can."

"Beaumont? Why don't you call the police out that way?"

"Because if they do have him or are near him, they'll kill him."

"Well then, what do you need me to do?"

I gathered my thoughts and tried to think strategy. If the hitters didn't know I was coming yet, then I at least had the element of surprise. "All I need is a car, a Kevlar vest if you can spare yours, and two guns—one small caliber, the other has to be a shotgun. Can you do that for me?"

"You should call the cops, Charlie. You're not invincible. This is not just your fight!"

"I need to find out who sent them. If Beaumont PD is there and it becomes a firefight, I may never get a chance to find out who the person is that ruined my life. Not only that, but my father needs me; he and my brothers are the only family I have left. I need this Carolyn, even if I don't make it out, I'll die saving my family."

"Don't talk like that. You will make it out or else me and my brothers are gonna ride on whoever we have to."

I smiled. That was Carolyn and that's why I appreciated her so much. "Just don't get caught blastin' caps in fools."

"You're making this sound like goodbye." I could hear her voice cracking and knew she was ready to cry.

"Everything will work out. Just give me an hour to get there."

"Fine. Do you need me to come get you?"

"No, I'm gonna take a cab."

"All right. I'll have whatever you need by the time you get here."

"If you don't hear from me in a few hours, make sure to call HPD and Beaumont to let them know everything."

"I heard you the first damn time."

"And Carolyn...thank you."

"Just hurry up and get your ass over here so you can go save your father."

Sassia

After Chuck had fallen asleep, we spent almost an hour whispering; twenty minutes of it was his incessant pleading, the rest haggling over the price of the guns he'd brought. The kinky sex was a bonus for Hoops; one that he hadn't expected but I was sure as hell he enjoyed.

"Look here, that Gold Ruger you like so much is in the car. I drove ten hours for you—at least let me bring you the gun, poke you in the ass, and we can figure out the prices later."

What the hell was it with men and ass sex?

"Let me poke you in the ass too, and then we can see about dealing?"

"You're a comedian now?"

"Hoops, just bring me the Ruger, with a suppressor and we'll see about the rest."

A few minutes later, a soft rap at the door let me know that he had returned. "So here it is, polished and shit. Can I get some booty lovin' now?"

"How about this, Hoops? If you give me the rest of the guns you bought—for—let's say, price minus thirty percent, we can deal."

"How about *hell no*! I would shoot my own mother for that kind of deal." He perched himself against the doorway and directly in front of my face. "We had fun, Val, and your sleepy friend had some good tastin' pussy. I'd be willing to take maybe five percent off the total if you throw in five minutes of riding me. You got a phat cat, I found out that much when I was eatin' it. If it's as good as I think, I'll make it ten percent."

I smiled. "I know it's good, but too bad you won't." I began to close the door when he stuck his foot inside.

"Okay. Maybe we can work something out."

Having worked out the details of the guns he'd brought with him, I gave him the address of El Segundo and told him that I'd call him when I needed him there. Still pleading for another opportunity with me, I let him smell it again before he left. Not that I would've minded screwing his brains out, especially after the way he rocked Charlie's world, but he was a good runner and I didn't usually mix business with other business. I'd had to improvise quickly when Charlie got in the middle; turned out pretty damn good too.

"Just like strawberries," he said, kneeling down and putting his nose between my legs.

"I know," I retorted, snapping my thong back in place and stepping back.

"I brought you some primo shit, Val. I'd be tempted to walk away with half their worth if you just let me hit."

"You already got some pussy, Hoops, be *very* thankful for that. Besides, you've already spent the last ten minutes whacking at it, trying to get it back up. How much longer are you going to try—even when you know that I'm not giving you any."

"Shit, a brother can dream, right? Anyway, I ate it like a champ. And then I got down on your friend for you. Doesn't that grant me at least an opportunity to at least put the head in?" I shook my head and slammed the door.

"Damn, you evil! Let me at least taste it again!" He shouted through the closed door, but I had already locked it and walked away.

With Charlie completely exhausted, I took some money out of my own stash and laid it on the nightstand next to her. If I was going to keep the lie going that Hoops was a regular, then I had to give the appearance of such.

Twenty minutes later, I finished my shower. Having wiped off the sweat from the glass, I eyed myself in the mirror.

Damn, you look good.

It wasn't as if I needed constant reminding, but I do like telling myself from time to time, especially after thinking of how I'd gotten here.

Putting on the same towel I'd been wearing when Hoops arrived, I pushed open the door and went looking for something to wear. I was supposed to meet Hoops soon at El Segundo and I didn't like being late.

As soon as I walked into my bedroom, I saw the comforter in a mangled mess, but there wasn't a Charlie to be found anywhere in the room.

"Chuck!"

When no one answered, I looked for my phone and called her...no answer. I searched the apartment for her clothes and when I couldn't find them, I knew that she hadn't been taken, she'd simply left.

"Dammit, Chuck, why are you so fucking hard-headed? Fine by me if you want to kill yourself."

That wasn't the truth—I wasn't fine with it. I was actually worried. I smacked my cheeks several times as I thought about what Nava would say if she caught me breaking Rule 1.

No sooner than I had returned to my bedroom, CT called.

I reached into the closet and pulled out my phone. "Yeah, CT?"

"Where are you? Are you en route yet?"

I curiously glanced at the phone before placing it back to my ear. "En route where? The last time we spoke was when you asked me to collect the reward on Charlie."

CT loudly exhaled into the phone, his irritation on full display. "Val, I called you earlier to tell you that one of the hitters was on his way to get your cop friend's father. Were you fucking listening or was I just talking to myself?"

"I didn't..." Then, it hit me. Charlie must have answered his call while I was in the shower. "Fuck me!" I shouted as I began rushing through the apartment, looking for clothes to put on.

"We can do that later if you..."

"Shut up, CT! You and your big mouth have royally fucked me!"

"What the hell are you talking about?"

I threw a long sleeve, blue t-shirt over my head and fell onto my bed, yanking up my jeans. "I wasn't the person on the other end of that phone call! You told Charlie that the hitter was after her father! Why didn't you make sure it was me before you blurted that shit out? Jesus fucking Christ, what else did you say?"

"Well, I'm not the dumbass who gave a cop access to my fucking life, now am I? Don't try to shift the blame when I told you to kill her ass a long time ago! You're so goddamn hard-headed Val!"

"Shit!" I screamed, knowing he was right. I put on my sneakers and opened the lock to my safe. With Hoops too far in the opposite direction, I pulled out the Micro Eagle and shoved it into a small purse. "Look CT," I shouted into the phone, "I need to know everything you told her."

"I'll do one better. I record all of my conversations."

Why would a handler record his own conversations seemed like the right thing to ask, but I knew CT and it was all about covering his ass. Instead, I burst through my front door, grabbing my helmet on the way out and ran down the stairs to my bike before the recording came over the phone:

Val, it's about time you fucking picked up! Look, I got bad news for ya, hun. I just sent out a couple dossiers on your cop friend. She's now got two real pros after her instead of just local yahoos. I don't know who put this shit together, but they fucking know everything: her military history, who her family is and where they live, her cop job—which by the way she is suspended from—and even all known associates... including one Sassia Santinos. They're after you, Val. I just sent one of the hitters her father's credit card info. He's going after Daddy to draw her ass out! It's time to stop fuckin' around. Look, either you put a bullet in this bitch's head or you've really fucked yourself! You hear me?

"Did you hear it?"

"So, let me get this right, CT. You told her practically everything about her hitters and also that I should put a bullet in her head?"

He cleared his throat. "That about sums it up."

"Where's her father?"

"He's at a motel in Beaumont, the Roadside Inn. I'll send the address to your phone."

"The hitter after her father—what do I need to know about him?"

"It says here that he sometimes uses guns, but that he really prefers knives, up close and personal wet work."

"What about the other one?"

"His specialty is hand-to-hand, guns, and sometimes he uses poisons."

Jet fucking Li. Great. "It fucking figures."

I hung up the phone, and even though Charlie had a head start on me, I could get through traffic faster on my bike than she could in a car. After calling Hoops and letting him know to get a hotel for the night, I shoved the phone into my safe bag next to my gun, and hid them both in the satchel behind me.

I threw on my helmet, started the bike, and within minutes I was heading north on 59. Before long, I found myself going east on I-10, still wondering if I was going to make it on time. Charlie had a substantial lead on me and she didn't know pros like I knew them. This had all the signs of a set up and she was walking right into it.

"Why the hell did you answer my phone, Chuck?" Now, not only was she walking into a trap, but she knew too much and that was all because I broke Rule number *One.*

Dammit! Val, you really screwed up on this one.

Chapter 16: No Secrets

Charlie

With the exception of the vest, Carolyn had gotten me just about everything I needed.

It took more than an hour and a half to make it to Beaumont from Carolyn's house, but it took an additional thirty minutes to scout out the motel that my father had checked into. I found the Roadside Inn on a single lane secondary road, hidden amongst the tress on the outskirts of the small city. With the broken sign that only lit up only several letters in its name, it looked like something out of a horror movie. Between the motel and the convenience store down the street with bars on its windows, I wondered why on planet Earth my father chose this dump out of all the other respectable hotels that I'd passed.

While driving, I alternated between looking for a tail and thinking about what Sassia—or rather Val, really had planned for me. Was she trying to protect me or was she just driving up the price on my head? Who was she *really* and did I really know anything about the woman that I'd spent the last year with, not to mention fucked and now—fucked over by?

It curdled my stomach to think of what I would've done for her and ultimately, what she would have done to me. She was one of them—a killer—and there was no mistaking that.

Eventually, she would've sold me out; I didn't have a doubt in my mind about that either. Why else would the man on the phone tell her to put a bullet in my head? After I heard him say that, it all began to make sense. I always found it curious that a woman so beautiful had stayed single, especially in a city like Houston. I knew she said she was an escort, but even that didn't explain why no one ever came by. Then there were the constant trips to see family that she had no pictures of. For someone who saw family a couple of times a year, why wouldn't she have a single picture with any one of them?

I knew most of what I thought was simply speculation, but the more I thought about it, the more sense it made. Rubbing the side of the Colt Delta Elite on the seat next to me, I was glad that I had answered her phone. If she hadn't been in the shower, I wouldn't have even been here to save my father.

On the way to Beaumont, I wondered several times why my father hadn't called. I was sure that at least one of my brothers would call to let him know I was coming and when he didn't, I knew something was wrong. Knowing that, the last thing I needed was to call and then have my would-be assassin pick up and hear my voice. Instead, I spent the last thirty minutes replaying what I was going to do when I got there. Since the only entrance was through either the front door or the glass window of the motel room, I was at a disadvantage, but that wasn't going to stop me.

Making sure that I wouldn't be spotted, I adjusted the blonde wig and parked a half mile away, at the similarly rundown convenient store. More than anything, I wanted to bust into my father's room and let him know what was going on, but I'd been in the military too long. If I wasn't smart about how I planned this, both my father and I were going to end up on the front page of the Beaumont newspaper as unsolved murders.

"No, Charlie, you have to be smarter than that," I said, slowly inhaling to calm my nerves.

After finally gathering up enough nerve, I walked to the front desk of the motel. A dark-haired man was half-sleep behind the desk so I rang the bell.

"What?" he asked, startled. As he approached the desk, walking extremely slowly, he barely opened his eyes. "You need a room?"

He was only slightly taller than me, lanky, and his round white face was largely obscured by the same dark hair that was protruding from his unbuttoned shirt. When he finally made it to the desk, I could smell the stench of cigarettes and stale liquor.

"I'm here to see a man about a party."

The clerk smiled, already knowing what I was asking.

"We don't allow solicitations here, ma'am. Be on your way or I'll call the sheriff's office."

"It isn't that kind of a party. It's just a...a date."

I watched his eyes as they fixated on my breasts. He didn't even bother looking at my face when he replied. "Well, that changes everything. How can I get a date with someone like you?"

"Look in the yellow pages."

"Why so mean?" He sat back in his chair and gave me a crooked smile.

"Look, I just came here to meet an old guy by the name of Michael D'Agostino. If he ain't here, then just say so."

I turned around and began walking out when the clerk yelled, "Look, lady, we might not be a fancy hotel, but our people still want their privacy. This hotel does not condone women of the night either!"

I slid a fifty-dollar bill across the desk and when I saw his eyes get bigger, I knew he understood.

"Well now, I think I checked that fine gentleman into room 201."

"Don't spend it all in one place," I said, as I watched him stuff the fifty in his pants pocket.

I walked up the set of outside stairs next to the office and searched for my father's room. I didn't have to walk far before I found his door and knocked. When no one answered, I pulled out the Colt and gently turned the door handle. It was locked.

"Fuck!"

I thought about going back downstairs and asking the clerk to let me in, but I didn't have that much time. If the killer was on his way, I had to get my father out as soon as possible. I banged on the door one more time before opting to use the lock picking kit one of Carolyn's brothers had provided.

It took some fiddling around, but after a minute, the old lock popped open revealing a darkened standard motel room layout. I placed the kit back in my pocket and crouched as I slowly walked into the room.

Seeing a figure lying in the bed, I crept closer, I called out my dad's name, but when he didn't answer, I knew something wasn't right. I moved closer to the bed and saw that the figure was definitely my father and when I nudged his foot, he didn't budge.

Fuck.

I turned around to go for help when the sleepy-eyed desk clerk knocked the gun out of my hand. Then he lunged at me, a blade flashing in the dim light, stabbing me in the right shoulder.

"Goddammit!" I screamed, partly in fury at being jumped, partly in pain. It fucking hurt like hell.

I'd slowed most of his momentum and the knife hadn't gone as deeply as he'd hoped, but the entire right side of my body still felt like a bolt of lightning had run through it. With the knife still in my shoulder, I stumbled back, falling onto the bed and landing on my father's legs. Not missing a beat, the clerk jumped on top of me and tried to retrieve his knife to finish me off.

Using my left hand, I threw a hard palm strike to his jaw. It didn't have much force behind it but I hoped it was enough to stun him for a second. I caught a break though, hitting him in the throat instead.

He gasped as the lucky punch gave me enough time to push him off me and over the side of the bed. Still lying against my father's legs, I rolled over to the other side of the bed and fell onto the floor. Standing up as fast as I could, I pulled the blade from my arm. The pain was almost unbearable, but as fire engulfed my right side, I put the knife in my left and began looking for the clerk.

I spotted him crawling toward the door, going after the gun I'd dropped. Lunging at him, I tackled him and as we both fell into the shag carpet, I plunged the knife into his side.

"*Aaaaah*!" he screamed, spinning around, and as he swung his right arm backward, it caught me against the side of my face. A bright flash of light blinded me for a few seconds, but that few seconds was enough for him to mount me. "You fucking bitch!"

I could see the gun only a few feet away, but with him on top of me and one arm that wouldn't work for shit, I couldn't move. He punched me in the face and I heard my nose crack. He continued hitting me in the face and I could feel myself losing consciousness more with each strike.

"You...fucking...bitch! I'm...going...to...kill...you!" Never breaking rhythm, he screamed to punctuate each hit and as the world began to darken, I saw the knife still protruding from his side.

I grabbed the handle, pulled it out, eliciting a scream of pain from him. With him still on top of me and my vision blurred from his barrage of punches, I knew I only had one shot to live. With all the energy I could muster, I swung the knife at him, but I was too late. He had moved his arm back down in just enough time for the knife to pierce his arm instead of his lung. He howled like a banshee, but when he finished, he wrapped his hands tightly around my neck.

I had lost and it was going to cost me.

As my world began to fade, I suddenly no longer felt his hands around my throat. All I saw was the deranged and twisted grimace on my killer's face. Where had the sleepy desk clerk gone? I'd bought that one hook, line, and sinker.

I hadn't saved my father and I couldn't even protect myself.

I tried to scream, but the sound couldn't find a way out.

It won't be long now.

Feeling a single tear roll down my cheek, I knew I was not far from dying when a red hole suddenly appeared in the assassin's throat. His grip on my neck loosened and as a blank stare appeared in his eyes, he fell off to the side. With him now next to me, I instinctively gasped for a huge breath of air.

As his eyelashes fluttered, I could see that he wasn't dead, but a look of fear now replaced his rage. From out of nowhere, Sassia stood over us. Placing her leather boots between his face and mine, she leaned over, whispered something in his ear and then shot him three times in the chest and once in the face.

Pfft! Pfft! Pfft! Pfft!

I saw his body jerk after the first shot, but not with the rest. He was dead.

I closed my eyes, hoping that this was all a bad dream, but when I reopened them, the assassin was still next to me. His eyes were wide open but lifeless, and I knew who'd done it. I sat up as a pool of his blood stained the shaggy, brown carpet and made its way toward me. Instinctively, I touched my aching throat, massaging it gently. As I pulled my hand away I realized my left arm was covered in blood.

"What the fuck did you do?" I screamed, sounding like I had laryngitis.

Sassia was sitting on the bed, directly to my right and the strange tone of her voice startled me when she spoke.

"What did I do? I saved your ass."

I rose from the carpet to see that she was cleaning her gun, but it was still carelessly pointed at me. "Don't people say thank you anymore?"

I looked over at the man in the bed and the tears fell at will. He was dead and maybe if I had found out sooner, he would've still been alive. I wanted to call out to him, but as he stared off into the distance, I knew he couldn't see me or hear me. He was gone and it was all because I didn't save him. The bastard on the floor, the same one who had tried to kill me, but ended up with three holes in his chest, had killed my father. Even though he had nothing at all to do with any of this, he saw fit to make him a part of it.

I bit my lip and inhaled. I wished to God that I had pulled the trigger, but as I looked over my would-be assassin, I saw that the holes in his chest were focused on one area, his heart. I cut my eyes at Sassia while still holding my throat. "Didn't want him to get paid for something you worked so hard on?"

She didn't say a word, merely remained seated on the bed and looking at me as if she'd just saved me from an overanxious puppy. With her gun now sitting on her lap, I walked around her, grabbed my gun, and pulled the covers over my father. It was then that I saw what the assassin had done. His throat had been slit and he had bled out on the bed.

"*Get out!*" I screamed.

"I'm not the monster you think I am, Charlie. You've got it all wrong."

I pulled my gun out and aimed it at her head. "I said get the fuck out!"

Sassia put her gun down on the bed. "I'm not going to kill you, Charlie. I never was." She began walking toward me, but I backed up as far against the wall as I could. "We need to get out of here. You're still not safe. And you need some medical attention for that arm."

"You think I don't know that?" I asked, glancing at my father. "The man on *your* phone said there were two pros after me. He said that you should put a bullet in my head and save them the headache. I know about everything, Sassia... *Val*...whatever the fuck your name is! I know about how much my death is really worth to people like you. You said I was only worth $75,000, so why didn't you tell me that the price went up another ten thousand for each day I was alive! Why didn't you tell me that?"

"Would it have made you feel better if I did?"

"It's not about that, goddamit! I trusted you and you hid it from me! How the hell am I supposed to believe any of the shit coming out of your mouth now? Huh?"

The gun trembled in my hands. I didn't want to admit it, but I was scared. And I was a lousy shot with my left hand. Sassia had been one of them the whole time and once I thought could love her. Now, I couldn't even trust her.

"Chuck, I'm the best chance you have of escaping this mess." She sat back on the bed, next to her gun.

"Don't touch it!"

"Well then stop fucking pointing that gun at me."

"If you want me to put it down, tell me who you really are!"

"No. That will solve nothing. Just think about the fact that if I wanted you dead, you'd be dead."

I was so ready to pull the trigger that it hurt, I ached to kill her for her betrayal, but Sassia was right. She was one of them and she could help me escape this, but that was also the problem—*she was one of them.*

"Charlie, wake up!" Her shouting brought me back to reality. "Look, I get agitated when people are pointing guns at me. I'm not your enemy now, but you are making me one. Don't do that."

"So what, Sassia? You just put a bullet in that man's throat, and then you whisper something to him before you put four more rounds in him? What the hell was that about? Did you know him? Did he go behind your back and try to collect on his own?"

She laughed. "You've been reading too many spy novels, but if you put the gun down, I'll tell you almost everything you want to know."

As she stepped away from her gun, I rested the gun at my side, but still kept my finger on the trigger.

"Fine, tell me everything."

“No, I won't tell you everything, but I will tell you what I know."

"Who are you—really?"

She shrugged. "If you're asking if I'm one of *them,* then the answer is *no.* Yes, I've done some things that I'm not so proud of, but every person who I've visited, has always had it coming. Basically, they were bad people who the world could do without."

"Doesn't that make you a hitter, too? You kill people for profit."

"Semantics. I'm not a merc like the people who are after you."

"If you're not like them, what the hell did you whisper in his ear before you killed that man?" I asked, pointing the gun at the man on the floor.

She smiled. "I told him to never fuck with my friends."

"So you know him?"

"Nope, never seen him before in my life."

"How long have you known about the true price on my head?" I asked.

She lay down on the bed as if my dead father weren't even there. Her callousness made me want to shoot her—again, but with everything she was telling me, I was going to bury her anyway.

"Maybe a few days. The same day I found out about the initial price I also found out about the daily charge...which is why dispatch wanted me to put a bullet in your head. I make most of my money as an escort, but dispatch is the person who assigns contracts. The bigger the contract, the bigger his percentage. Since your contract is nearing two hundred and fifty thousand, it makes sense to him that I kill you."

"So, why haven't you done it? What are you waiting for? You’ve already gotten from me what you wanted. Why not finish the job?"

She remained quiet for about thirty seconds and when I was ready to ask again, she raised both her hands. "Because, Charlie, you mean a lot to me—maybe more than I've told you. For the longest time I have remained alone...on purpose, but then you came along. I can laugh with you, which is something I don't usually do." She slightly opened her mouth and I saw her wrestling with what she wanted to say next. "I really like you, Chuck, and you haven't done anything to deserve all this. I don't want you dead, which is why we need to get out of here."

I put the safety back on the gun and walked toward her, standing over her as she lay on the bed. "So why were you willing to let me go back to Philly without saying any of this?"

"After everything I just told you, you ask me that? Whether you're on the force or not, you're a cop, Chuck, and I'm the *opposite* of you. If you knew what I did before now, where would we be? I saved your ass more than once, but had I not been there, who would have saved you? Letting you go back home was the best thing for both of us Chuck."

I didn't sit down next to her, but I knew she was right. I needed her help every step of the way and now, more than ever. I just needed to know a few more things. "Who's after me? Who the hell let these people get to my dad?"

"I don't know, but I have a plan to end this tonight."

"So what do we do when this is over?"

"We go our separate ways. I save your life, I get you back to normalcy, and in return, you forget you ever knew me. I don't need a goody two-shoes cop fucking up my life, and you don't need a contract killer in yours."

I extended my hand. "Deal." I knew I'd just made a deal with the devil, but I didn't plan to keep my end of the bargain anyway.

"We have to move quickly," she said. "If we get caught here, we're both really fucked."

"What's your plan?"

"Half of it is already done. While you were passed out next to him, I took your picture. Since you look like someone really fucked you up," she said pointing to my swollen lip, bruised cheek, bloody arm, and broken nose, "I just needed a picture to send to dispatch."

"Why did you take pictures?"

She stood up from the bed and walked past me. There, she looked out the window and into what seemed like an urban forest of trees. "So that the people who put the contract on you will think you're dead. That way, the second hitter is called off and when they want to see your body—which they will, we can find out who caused all this."

I walked past her and said a silent prayer over my father's body. My brothers were going to hate me for this. He was gone, I knew that, but every time I looked at him, I remembered how badly I had failed him. He didn't deserve this. I'd seen death so many times before I'd stopped counting. I always figured that I had somehow grown immune, but after the deaths of both Steven and now my father, I knew how different death was when it hit home.

"I want this finished tonight. How long do we wait until they want to meet up?"

"I don't know," she said, still looking out the window.

"Where are we supposed to meet? You usually do these things, right? So where do they like to meet?"

She turned around and looked at me. "Still playing the cop?" she asked, sarcastically. Sassia walked behind me and stroked my hair. "We'll find out who did this and I swear to you, they will pay," she whispered.

I felt little reassurance, but I had lost too much for it to mean anything. All along, I had been best friends with someone who killed people for a living. What the hell was I doing wrong to deserve this life? Why was this happening to me?

I turned to Sassia. The pain in her eyes as she looked at my father was unmistakable and though I wanted to believe it, I knew she was simply playing her part. She had lied to me—had *always* lied to me, but it wasn't just the lying. She was one of them and I couldn't forgive that. Friend or not, she *had* to go down with the rest of them.

"So now what?"

"Now we get the hell up out of here."

I tucked my gun in my waistband, took the assassin's knife and the sheath on the side of his leg. I quickly put the blade inside of its cover, tucked it inside my pants and we stepped out of the hotel into the star-filled night. She quickly ushered me down the steps before asking me for the keys to my car.

"Where's your bike?" I asked.

"I hid it." She looked at my stab wound. "Besides, people might see your wound and ask questions. We need your car."

I pointed in the direction of the convenience store. "It's parked over there. I didn't want the man who killed my father to see me."

As we began walking down the dirt road, the first minute was filled with silence. With thoughts of my father overwhelming me, it wasn't until Sassia spoke up that I realized we were already at my car.

"I'm going to get some supplies from the store, so you stay here."

I sat in the car, alone and in pain, wondering if I'd see the sun rise again. According to Sassia, she'd take care of everything, but that meant trusting her and that wasn't something I could afford to do anymore. I had to stay close to her if I was going to bust her and the people who started all this.

When she returned, she had alcohol, gauze and some Vaseline. After dressing my stab wound, I knew that she'd been trained as a medic somewhere.

"Who taught you how to do this?"

"My mother was a nurse."

"I don't like the plan. I get to pretend I'm dead while you go after the person who killed my father and my fiancé?"

"That sounds about right."

"No, it doesn't. You need a better plan."

She opened my door and I gave her the keys before she started the car. "You *still* think I'm one of them, don't you?"

"You *are* one of them. Just because you only kill bad people doesn't change the fact that you're a murderer."

"And this coming from a war vet?"

"What I did was for my *country*! My job was the protection of America and its citizens, so you could do what with your freedom? Go and kill bad people? Don't lecture me about morality!"

"You've killed people just like I have, Chuck. The only difference is, you kill bad people because the government says it's okay. That way, they can make their money. I kill bad people because someone else says it's okay, that way I can make mine!"

"What the hell happened to you to make you like this?"

"Life," she mumbled.

I grabbed a spare shirt from the backseat and pressed it against my wound. After a few agonizingly deep breaths, I turned to face Sassia. "Well then, Sassia, or should I call you Val, maybe instead of being so cryptic, you can tell me a little more about you. I'm tired of the lies. Tell me something to make me believe you're on my side!"

"What's the point?" she grumbled.

"Humor me!" I shouted as she pulled out of the parking spot and back onto the road.

For the next few minutes, the only sound in the car was that of the roaring engine. I glared at her, wanting to know the truth about who she really was, but she didn't even turn in my direction. It wasn't until she turned onto the I-10 feeder that she even glanced at me.

"His name was Omar," she blurted out. Instead of asking who the hell Omar was, I just listened. "Omar found me when I was young, after my parents had died, and he raised me like I was his little sister. He watched over me, took care of me, and if anyone even looked at me funny, he whipped their ass for me.

"Eventually Omar fell in love with me, but because I wasn't sure what love was, I felt obligated to stay with him. He whored me out until I met a man named Charles."

She smiled, but only briefly, before continuing her story.

"When I met Charles, I realized what love was and I even plotted to help him rob Omar. Omar found out and on the night Charles and I were supposed to disappear, Charles left without me. Omar didn't like being betrayed—so instead of killing me quickly, he chained me to a bed, injected me with something to keep me barely lucid, and his boys repeatedly and brutally raped and tortured me."

I watched as her jaw tightened and as she began clenching the steering wheel. I thought about saying something, but I didn't want to break her trance. She was finally telling me her story, or one she'd made up, and after all I had gone through, I felt like she owed me some version of the truth about who she was. I peeked at the knife wound to see if it had stopped bleeding, but as she began speaking again, I simply pressed harder and hoped that I wouldn't have to become my own field medic and stitch myself up.

"For three whole days, I was raped so many times that I lost count. They beat me, sodomized me, urinated on me—to them I was just a whore begging for death. I begged each one of them to stop, pleaded for mercy, but not one of them listened. One of them even told me that mercy was for the weak—that voice I could never forget. To them, I was going to die anyway, so why not get a piece of the ass that Omar always bragged about? Since I was drugged for most of them,

I don't even remember how many men there were, but on that third day—when I was supposed to die—it wasn't a cop that saved me. It was a killer who saved me.

"After seeing what they had done to me, she offered me a chance for retribution, more or less. She told me that either I could kill some of the men who had done this to me, or I could die with the rest of them. To me, there wasn't an easier decision. Each of them were bound and in cold blood, I shot three of the men who'd violated me—all of them in their dicks. Two of them crawled around for a few minutes before I finally put them out of their misery, but the last one—the one who told me mercy was for the weak—I let him suffer. I put bullets into his kneecaps next, then his hands. Ten minutes later, he was still alive, so I unloaded the rest of the clip into his chest, his heart to be more specific.

"You wanted to know why I had the look of a killer, that's why. I killed three men and I don't feel a damn bit guilty. The man I shot back in that hotel room, it was either him or you, Charlie. Now you know everything. Satisfied? I'm not one of them, but I'll be damned if I let something like what Omar did happen to me again!"

Hearing her explanation made me feel a little guilty about labeling her. "I'm sorry if I called you one of them. It's just that I needed to know why you're so mysterious, so guarded. If that had happened to me, I don't know what I'd have done, but why didn't you go to the police after it all happened?"

She shrugged her shoulders. "I would have, but the woman who saved me also took me under her wing. She became the new person who watched my back and it took me a while to realize that all I had done was trade Omar in for a different model. She always held what I'd done over my head, so I just kept things to myself. You're the second person I've ever told."

"Who was the first?"

"The guy you spoke to on the phone."

"And he is..." I asked, hoping to get her to tell me more.

"He's dispatch."

I felt a little uneasy that she was talking to a man who facilitates killing, but she *had* saved me more than once: the funeral, hiding me in her apartment, and now at the motel.

"So why become an escort after what Omar and his crew did to you?"

She laughed at the question. "You act like I know how to do something else. The only thing I was ever any good at was banging guys' brains out. I never went to school after I turned thirteen and I don't have any useful skills. Everything you know about me I learned from the woman who killed my last boyfriend! Shit, Charlie, the only thing I know how to do on my own, the only thing I was ever good at, was fucking!"

"So let me get your plan straight. This guy on the phone, the one who said you should kill me..."

"And also the man who told me where you were so that I could save you," she interrupted.

"...Yeah, that too. So the man who *saved* me, you sent the pictures of me being dead to him. Now it's his job to get the pictures out to all the other people who want to kill me so I don't have to worry about my family, right?"

"Right," she answered quickly.

"But what about the hit money? How are you going to get that?"

"For something that big, they're going to want to see you dead for themselves. No one is going to send that kind of money without physical proof—so I'm going to have to go meet them."

"*We're* going to have to go meet them."

As her eyebrows furrowed, I could see the look of disgust on her face. "Look, Charlie, the point is to keep you safe. How the hell am I supposed to do that if you're with me to meet the person who wants you dead?"

"How the hell are you supposed to provide proof if I'm not there?"

"I'm still working on figuring that one out!"

Sassia

We fought the whole way home as we thought up and discarded several dozen plans. I wasn't sure if the one we partially agreed on would keep her alive, or me for that matter, but as soon as we pulled up to El Primero, the sat phone rang. We had run out of time.

"Yeah," I answered.

"This is Val, right? I don't want to give up any additional information by accident."

I eyed Charlie, hoping she'd get out of the car, but when she didn't, the only choice I had was step outside.

"Yeah, CT, it's me. What's the word?"

"Well, let me be the first to congratulate you on a job well done! It's not often that I get a payday like this, but you made it happen. I mean, it takes a lot of balls to plug a friend, but you, you're fucking ruthless and I love that shit—even though it doesn't bode well for our date, I'll take my chances."

"She's not dead. She's in the car with me."

"Dammit, *Val...*"

"Stop your bitching and get to the point."

He cleared his throat. "Well, I put the pictures out to every underground outlet I could and only a few minutes ago I got a message. It says that they're already in Houston and they want to meet up in the warehouse district in two hours."

"How do you know it's them and not someone trying to get at me for taking their hit?"

"Because, they sent me an IP address with the note and the GPS co-ordinates where they want to meet. Then, when I tried to trace it, the IP address disappeared. It's them."

"Send everything to my phone."

"So let me ask you something. If she's still alive, where did all the blood come from?"

"It came from the first hitter. She passed out in his blood and I took a picture of it."

"So she killed the hitter? Damn, maybe we should recruit her!" he said, jovially. "Maybe she'll let me get in her pants, not make me beg like a dumbass, horny teenager."

"She didn't, I did." I whispered into the phone. "So relax and quit the fantasizing."

"She saw you kill the hitter?" He was quiet for a few seconds and I could already hear the gears in his brains working overtime. I knew what he was thinking, but I still didn't want him to say it. "Val, what does she know?"

I sighed. "Not that much."

"Stop fucking with me, Val. What did you tell her?"

I bit my lip and spoke softly into the phone. "She knows... a lot. She had a gun in my face, so I had to tell her something."

"You told her about me?"

"Not so much about you...mostly about what you do."

"Fuck me!" he shouted. "You told her too much, Val. You fucking told her too much! *She is a cop*! What, you think she's just going to let you walk away from this and the both of you live happy, normal lives? It doesn't work that way, and you know it! A cop is a cop, first, second, and last."

"You don't know that!" I argued. "She's not even a cop anymore. She's suspended."

"I don't give a fuck! I don't! We both know that it's too far gone now and you know what has to be done. Sheesh, Val, out of all the people in the world, you ally yourself with a cop! I knew this shit was bad from the beginning and now you've gotta kill a cop."

"If I kill her, they'll never stop looking for me."

"I can hide you til the shit blows over."

"CT..." The last thing in the world I wanted to do was kill Chuck. I knew she wouldn't let me walk away, but the worst I wanted to do was put a bullet in her leg and escape. Now that I had told her about how things work, there was only one possible outcome and CT knew it. She had to die.

"I know you *like* her," he whispered, "but she can't walk away from this. Part of this job requires anonymity and you screwed that up by befriending a cop. She dies, Val, and we both knew that from the minute you told her anything."

I took a deep breath and looked at the figure who was checking her bandages in the car. "I'll take care of it."

"You'll have to. If you don't, then you're rogue. Once you're rogue, I'll be sending everyone I have after you."

In all the time I'd known CT, I had never heard him more serious. "I said it's done."

"Don't die. You still owe me a date."

I hung up with CT and walked back to the car. "We have two hours to get this plan together."

Just pulling up to the dark, half-constructed building, we'd barely made it on time while trying to come up with something worth risking our lives for. I'd assumed we would have more time, but whoever put the hit on Charlie had been in town the whole time and that had significantly cut into our time to prepare.

Even though I hadn't been to this small office building before, I knew the area. The first few floors had been constructed, but when the recession hit they put the rest of it on hold. To make matters worse, it was only a few miles from El Segundo. I was pissed knowing that whoever this was had possibly been down the street from me the whole time.

"I can't breathe," Charlie announced, now starting to fidget around, trying to find a more comfortable position to be in.

"We follow the damn plan!" I hissed, barely moving my lips. If someone was watching us, I couldn't let them see me talking to myself.

She stopped moving and I stayed in the car for a few minutes before a series of five construction floodlights lit up the car and illuminated a pathway to the building.

Showtime.

After finally meeting up with Hoops to get some extra clips for my gun, I found myself wishing that I had gotten something bigger. The gold Ruger stayed in my hand while I hid the Micro Eagle along with a few spare clips inside the waistband of my jeans as I stepped out the car. Opening the back door, I slid the body bag out and let it drop as gently as I could to the ground.

"Is this going to work?" Charlie whispered and I could hear the anxiety in her voice.

"Shhhh. It *has* to."

As soon as I pulled the black bag out of the car with my one free hand, the light bathing the car went out and I was forced to drag it to the building.

"Damn, you're heavier than I thought you'd be," I grumbled, but after almost making it past the third light, a semiautomatic burst rang out, each shot hitting the body bag I was dragging.

Fuck.

I quickly dropped the body bag and ran back to the car. I hid on the passenger's side and pointed my gun up at the second floor window where the shots were coming from, but it was already too late. Whoever had shot at me had disappeared. When the third light began to blink, I remained behind the car and pulled out Charlie's phone. I thought about calling CT so that he could get a satellite over me, but that would take too much time.

I put the phone away and listened for any movement near me, but no more shots came. The third floodlight went from blinking to rapidly flashing.

"Someone is telling me to move." I mumbled, so with my gun still pointed towards the building, I cautiously walked toward the bloodied body bag. I squatted over the bag and saw several holes in it, each one in what would be the chest. Whoever had shot at me wasn't aiming for me—just making sure that the person in the bag was as dead as promised. The shooter wasn't dumb and obviously not prone to missing. All of a sudden I was hit with a wave of nausea.

I grabbed the top of the bag and moved toward the steps. With the body thumping against each stair, I finally made it into the small office building to see a series of arrows laid out on the tiled, white floor.

Without any lights yet installed, once inside I could barely see ten feet in front of me, but I could see that the taggers had gotten to this building. Spray painted names of gangs, mostly Los Perdidos, were on the walls along with some of the cities wards and streets. I continued through without stopping.

For the building to be so lively with the fluorescent colors of spray paint, it was as quiet as a tomb. The body bag was now leaking blood, growing heavier and beginning to stick to the tiled floor. I gripped the end a little tighter and with barely any light inside the building, the only choice I had was to continue my path along the arrows.

"One, two, three, four, right...six, seven, eight, nine, ten, eleven, left..." I hadn't counted my steps in forever, but it broke the silence and helped me to focus. If I was going to get out the same way I came in, knowing how to get back to the front was crucial.

Rule six.

After counting out nearly fifty and mapping more lefts than rights, I finally made it to the end of the arrows. At the final arrow were stairs leading down to what I assumed was the basement and the end of me dragging this damned body bag. I reached for the only light switch I saw, but when I flipped it up, nothing happed. I flicked it a couple more times and when I was ready to give up, the light finally came on.

Dammit.

Someone was fucking with me and I didn't like it. The floodlights, the shots, the arrows, and now this—someone was letting me know that they had all the control and I had none. The sick feeling I'd had earlier returned.

"Just focus on the job, Val. Do what you were trained to do. If shit goes south, you can handle it. After today...you start over."

I sighed and dragged the body down the stairs, each thump reminding me of what I had gone through as I pulled the body down the stairs. At the bottom of the stairs was a small boiler room, but on the other side of the room, a bright light shone under a closed door.

"This is it."

I almost wished that Charlie was here for me to talk to. I quietly said a prayer for her, then myself, just like my mother had taught me before she died. Seeing Charlie pray over her father reminded me that maybe there was a God and maybe he hadn't given up on me. Once I said amen, I dragged the body to the other side of the boiler room and opened the door.

With the ceiling panels missing, I could see all of the falling insulation and all of the wires leading to the middle of the room. I followed a few of the wires past the cubicles and wheeled office chairs throughout the room, where I found three servers sitting atop a table and what looked like a homemade EMP sitting beside them.

"What the hell?" I asked as I looked around at the setup. I dropped the bag; my hands bloody from its contents, and went over to the EMP.

So this is how they did it. This is how you send an untraceable email.

"If you're wondering if that's how I sent the emails to LRZ and the Latin Kings, then yes it is." A voice spoke from behind me, reminding me of why I was here in the first place. I knew that voice.

I turned around to see a T.A.R. 21 pointed directly at my head.

"So it was *you* this whole time?"

2 hours earlier...

Charlie

As we pulled up to the apartment building we'd spent the last few days in, Sassia stepped out of the car and began talking on the phone. For the few minutes she was gone, I was overwhelmed at the thoughts of confronting the person who'd set this all up. Images of Steven and then my father flashed through my head and only when my fingernails dug into my palms did I realize what I was doing. I unclenched my hands and thought about all the things I would do when we met face to face.

Are you going to kill them?

"Yes," I answered with more intensity than I'd ever had. Whoever had done this to me would die and there wasn't a doubt in my mind that it was going to be by my hands.

So what about Sassia? Are you going to renege on your deal?

As I looked over at her and watched her argue on the phone with the person I suspected was her dispatcher, I knew I owed her my life and the truth was that if she weren't an assassin, I could love her. But she was still a killer. She would always be. I was a cop, she was a crook, and my primary directive was to protect and serve the public from just such people. Bringing her down would stop her from murdering someone else—maybe someone who didn't deserve it, either.

"Yes."

How will you do it?

I had known Sassia for more than a year and there wasn't any way I was going to get her to go to jail. If worse came to worse, I'd shoot her if I had to. In the back if it was necessary.

When Sassia returned to the car, the stressed look on her face let me know that we didn't have nearly the time we thought we were going to have.

"Two hours is all the time we have to put this shit together."

"Where are we supposed to meet?"

Sassia looked at me and shook her head. "I'll tell you when we get there, Charlie."

"You don't trust me."

She paused. "I just think it's better if you don't know. The last thing I need after this is all over is police surrounding me. I'm sure you understand," she added sarcastically.

"Fine then, *Val*, but we only have two hours. So we're going to have to move faster than we planned. We can at least start by getting a newspaper." She started the engine but said nothing more.

We didn't have far to drive from her apartment; only a few blocks. We bought a couple of newspapers and walked back to the car. After a few minutes of searching the obituaries, we found exactly what we were looking for.

"Here we go. Perfect. A lady named Sheryl Lee, age 26..." Sassia began eyeballing me as I looked over the picture the deceased's family had provided the newspaper, "...yeah, she looks kinda like you, too."

"What does it matter what she looks like if she's gonna be in a body bag?"

"The more she looks like you, the better chance we'll walk away. Remember, Chuck, for the kind of money that's on your head, no one's just going to accept my word. Since poor Sheryl died yesterday, they'll probably still have the bag with her in it at the morgue. If not, we may not have enough time to get this thing going."

"Then let's get out of here and find Sheryl."

Half an hour later, we were in southeast Houston, rolling up the long driveway to Knight's Funeral Home. I was surprised that the gate wasn't locked, but that didn't seem important. All I cared about was getting Sheryl Lee's body and getting the hell out of here.

As I stepped out of the car, I could feel the stiffness settling in my shoulder, but the bleeding had finally stopped. Even though the front entrance was barely lit, Sassia quickly ran around to the back door. Under the bright white light, she began picking the lock as I stood over her.

"Why the hell don't we go through the front?"

"No one makes deliveries to the front door. If I pick that lock, the alarm will go off!" she whispered loudly.

"How are we supposed to pick the lock?" I asked.

"Cut the shit, Chuck. You have a lock picking kit in your back pocket. I saw it in the hotel room. Don't get all cop-like on me now."

I reluctantly handed her the kit that Carolyn had given me and not long after, we heard the familiar click of an unlocked door. I was officially committing a B & E, but with all the other crimes I'd committed tonight, including leaving a murder scene, this seemed minor.

When the door opened, Sassia returned the lock picks, looked at me and I found myself inadvertently holding my breath as she pushed the door open. After a few seconds of waiting, no alarm went off and I slowly exhaled. With just under eighty minutes left, we snuck through the funeral home and found Sheryl in the cooler, still in her body bag.

"Fucking awesome!" Sassia whispered.

"What the hell is so great about stealing a dead body?"

Sassia opened up the body bag, then took the killer's knife from out of my pants and unsheathed it. After cutting Sheryl from her shoulder to her elbow, a small teardrop of blood came out. "They haven't embalmed her yet! When she thaws, she'll still have blood in her system which means she can do a better job passing off as you."

Sassia returned the knife to me and zipped up the body bag.

"Thanks for the physiology lesson, but can we get the hell out of here? This place makes my skin crawl."

Without much effort, we carried the body to the car and threw Sheryl into the back seat for the final ride of her life.

We'd spent less than ten minutes sneaking in and nabbing Sheryl and I was happy that we had finally caught a break. "What now?"

"Now, we need to get some guns."

We didn't drive back to Sassia's second apartment; instead we drove to the warehouse district. After pulling up to a warehouse that had been converted into lofts, Sassia's phone rang.

"Yeah," she said and eyeballed me suspiciously before stepping out of the car.

By the way she looked at me, I knew it was the man she called 'Dispatch'. I thought about eavesdropping, but I didn't want her knowing that I hadn't planned to honor our deal. She was probably thinking of ways to dispose of my body afterwards, but I couldn't think about that now. I had to focus on staying alive and taking all of them down.

Not long after Sassia returned, Hoops appeared from behind a car. Winking at me, I began to get out of the car when Sassia asked me to stay back.

"Why do you want me to sit in the car? I do have the right to defend myself or am I supposed to go to this mysterious place without weapons, too?"

"You're really getting on my last nerve, Chuck. You are still KPD, suspended or not. If Hoops is going to help us, he needs to make sure that we're all on the same side...at least for now."

"What is that supposed to mean?"

"Tomorrow, you're a cop. Tonight, we shut this thing down. Whatever it takes, right?"

"Whatever it takes," I replied. I was in agreement with our doing what was necessary, but I still folded my arms to let her know how displeased I was. She stepped out the car without another word, not seeming to give a shit that I was displeased. Following Hoops, he led Sassia into the building and they disappeared from sight.

I quickly pulled out the cell phone and called Carolyn. She picked up on the first ring and before she had a chance to say anything, I cut her off. "Carolyn, don't talk, just listen, because I don't know how much time I have. My father is dead, the assassin killed him and almost got me, but they're both in a motel room off South Boudoin Rd. in Beaumont. Find out anything you can about a man with the nickname CT, another man named Omar, and a man named Charles—cross-reference them with a woman named Val and a bloody shout-out anywhere in the country. But first alert HPD about something going down somewhere in Houston. We're meeting up with the people who are trying to kill me."

"Where is it happening?"

"I wish I knew, but keep it on high alert. When this is all done, I hope to have two professional hitters in custody."

But probably just one.

When I saw Sassia returning to the car, I spoke faster. "Let HPD know something big is going down right now in the warehouse district and if something happens to me, find out anything you can about how those names connect." I quickly hung up and rested my head against the window pretending to be tired.

Sassia knocked on my window and waved for me to come out. When I stepped out of the car, she lead me toward a Caprice sedan and opened the trunk. Inside were about a dozen guns, some were legal, most of them weren't, but they all appeared in perfect condition.

As I looked over each gun, Sassia began to tap her feet. "Look, Charlie, I hope things go well, but if they don't, you're going to have to look out for yourself. If you're going to be watching my back, I'm going to need you to carry something you're comfortable with."

I shook my head. "Sassia, these are automatic weapons. Even if things do work out, if we get caught with these, we'll end up in federal prison."

"Well then, take something legal." She picked up a Desert Eagle in one hand, aimed it off into the distance before nodding and picking up a USP in the other. These are legal, right?"

I grabbed the USP from her, an M9, and an ankle holster, along with several additional clips. "Yes."

"The next time you call Carolyn," Sassia said as she looked at me, "make sure to tell her that you didn't grab the fully automatic weapons. We wouldn't want you to end up in deep shit with ATF, right?"

I offered her a sneer and continued checking out the guns. I suspected that she'd been watching me, but I wasn't about to back down. "If things don't go like they're supposed to go, it makes sense to have backup."

"I am your backup."

"So what happens if you get shot first, *Val*?" I yelled.

"Then you're my backup!" she fired back.

"Ladies, ladies," Hoops said in a calm voice, "let's not start the shootout early."

I turned away from Sassia and focused on making sure my gun was going to work.

Not wasting much time, Hoops was at my back, sniffing my hair and pressing his manhood against me. *He must walk around with a hard* on, I thought. Then I remembered what had happened earlier and though I was disgusted that I had let an arms dealer eat me out and fuck me, I was still slightly turned on. Opting to focus on the next hour of my life rather than indulge his fantasies, I stepped away from him.

"So it's going to be like that?" he asked.

"You thought otherwise?"

He stepped closer to me. "That's a lot of hardware for someone so...soft," he whispered, touching my breast.

"An arms dealer is telling me *I* have too much hardware?" I laughed at the irony.

"I'm offended. After everything we've shared today, you think of me as something as unrepentant as an arms dealer?"

"Cut the bullshit, Hoops. These are guns, some of them illegal, and you're selling them out of the trunk of a car. If you're not an arms dealer, what are you then?"

"I transport rare arms and antiquities to important clientele."

"So you're a gunrunner."

"Personally, I wouldn't say it with as much disdain, but I guess that would sum it up."

I didn't respond, but I glanced over at Sassia, whose wide smile was enough of an indication that she'd sent him my way.

"I don't know if you knew this, love, but you still smell like me." Hoops said, squeezing my ass.

I turned and pointed the USP at his face and he immediately backed up. With everything that had gone on since our encounter, I hadn't had time to wash his cologne or his scent off. I was almost embarrassed that he'd noticed, withdrawing the gun and putting it back at my side. Killing Hoops wasn't as important as avenging my father's death. Besides, he was way too pretty to just shoot.

Still not getting my hint, he followed me and gingerly rested his chin on my left shoulder. "I don't usually say this to white girls, hell—I don't usually say this at all, but your pussy was good…real good. Perhaps when all this madness ceases, I can help nurse you back to health. I've been told I have a healing tongue."

"I'm almost flattered," I said flatly. "If you're so concerned about how great the pussy is and nursing it back to health, why don't you help us out with more than guns? Why don't you go in there with us?"

"I'm a lover, not a fighter," he whispered into my ear.

"Sounds like a coward to me," I said smugly. "Perhaps you're more of a pussy than a pussy eater."

"Knock it off, you two and get ass on your own time, Hoops," Sassia said, cutting in. "Right now we have shit to do."

Hoops still kept his chin on my shoulder, but it wasn't soft anymore. He was slowly digging his chin into my neck. "Just so that there isn't any misunderstanding, Val tells me that everything here stays between us. I'm inclined to believe her, but just in case, I need assurances."

He walked around to the back door and pulled out several pieces of paper. "This is a confidentiality agreement. I need your signature."

"Are you fucking *serious*?" I laughed. "This shit would never hold up in court. Gunrunning is still a federal crime!"

"Whether it holds up or not is irrelevant. All that matters is that if I go down, we *all* go down."

"Get that fucking piece of paper out of my face," I yelled and turned toward Sassia. "Did you sign this?"

"Yup," she answered without even taking her eyes away from the gold Ruger she was fondling.

I snatched the paper from him as he shoved a pen in my face. With this, I knew that there wasn't any way to bring down Hoops without me going down as well, but because I hadn't planned on it, I signed it. He was pretty smart, I had to give him that. Smart and pretty; seemed like a lot of that was going around.

As soon as I finished, Hoops handed me a small silver package. "A peace offering," he said.

My eyes lit up as I recognized that it was a wound packing kit, along with two suppressors—one for the M9, the other for the USP. He then tossed Sassia two pairs of gloves. I quickly ripped open the package, took off the bloodied sweatshirt, and went to work sealing the knife wound in my shoulder. After wrapping my shoulder in gauze, I felt like I had almost completely repaired the wound.

"Can we go now?" Sassia asked, impatiently tossing me an extra shirt.

Hoops watched me closely as I put on the new shirt. After getting an eyeful of my boobs, he closed the trunk of the Caprice Classic and asked me if there was anything else I needed. I shook my head no and after he drove off, Sassia looked at me.

"You ready?"

I gripped the M9 in my hand before placing in into my ankle holster. "Do I have a choice?"

We dragged the body from the trunk and Sassia shot three bullets into Sheryl. Two in her skull and the last one into her heart. I didn't know what the significance of the last shot was, especially with two already in her head, but now was the time I had to trust that Sassia knew what she was doing.

Both of us put on gloves and with a little effort got the body back into the bag and into the back seat. As soon as we finished, out of nowhere, Sassia hugged me and I found myself hugging her back, breasts pushing against breasts. I hated that I had to do things this way, but after tonight, this would be the end of all of this...one way or the other.

We made so many turns that I began to think Sassia was deliberately trying to confuse me, but after fifteen minutes of driving, we finally stopped.

"I can't breathe," I shouted. It was dark as hell in the trunk and for the whole ride, all I saw were random images of my father: his throat slit, lying in a pool of his own blood and standing over him laughing, was the hired killer who had been after me. I tried to move around, get the images out of my head, but the walls of the trunk still felt like they were closing in.

"We follow the damn plan!" she shouted back.

She didn't know what I was going through back here and it began to piss me off at how callously she shoved me in here. *Why couldn't I ride in the backseat and let the damn cadaver sit in the trunk?*

I could smell Sheryl through the seat and it made me nauseous. Several times I gagged, almost vomited with her smell and my father's images combining to make it seem like I was next to him, but I forced myself to remain focused.

"Is this going to work?" I was so anxious now that we were here that my voice began to crack as my body shook with a mixture of excitement, anticipation, uncertainty, and fear.

"It has to," Sassia said and stepped out of the car.

I listened intently as she pulled the body out of the car, grumbling as she did. As soon as the door closed, I began to count.

"No matter what happens, stay in the car for five minutes."

"What if something happens before then?" I asked.

"No matter what happens, do not open the trunk for five minutes. They may shoot off a few rounds to let me know they're serious, but whoever this is will want proof and they're not going to shoot me until they have it."

"What makes you so sure they won't shoot you and look for themselves?"

"Because, that's not what I'd do. I know one thing about the business and it's that you don't kill the person who filled the contract. If they did, it'd be the last thing they'd ever do."

I was glad that she was so sure, but I wasn't. As soon as I got to sixty, several shots rang out and I was ready to push the trunk open, but Sassia had already planned for this. My job was to follow through with what she had asked me to do. I continued to count and when I got to three hundred, I pushed down the back seat, carefully maneuvered my way into the car and snuck out of the passenger's side back door.

We were at a construction site that was unfamiliar to me. I saw a series of floodlights, but they were powering down and the faint glow they provided wasn't enough to see the building. I pressed myself alongside the car, grabbed the M9 out of its holster, screwed on the silencer, and did the same for the USP. I then surveyed the area as best as I could, but being too far from the street to get an address, I had to use the downtown cityscape to see we were just north of it. We were still in the warehouse district and the fifteen minutes of driving was meant to throw me off.

Silly girl, didn't you think I'd recognize downtown?

I reached for my phone, but it wasn't anywhere on me. I quickly checked the ground around the car, then inside the car and trunk when I realized that Sassia had taken it. The hug we shared wasn't meant to be emotional, it was so she could grab my phone. She'd gotten it because I'd practically given it to her.

"Fuck me!" I whispered.

With my phone gone, I returned my attention to the building. I did a quick sweep with the M9 before slowly walking toward the entrance. I passed a small pool of blood, which by the sheer amount I knew wasn't Sassia's, and followed the trail of blood up the stairs. Peeking around the inside, I did another quick sweep to make sure there weren't any guards or cameras before I snuck into the dark building.

Without a single light to help guide me, I looked down the long hallway in both directions before I could make out the blood-stained arrows on the floor.

"Better than bread crumbs," I muttered.

As my eyes adjusted to the darkness, I took notice of all the vandalism. Spray-painted walls, broken glass, and the unmistakable smell of urine permeated the entire floor. While trying to hold my breath, I carefully followed the arrows down a series of hallways until they took me to a set of steps. I quietly prayed that these steps wouldn't creak or groan with the slightest pressure like the ones at my parent's house, before I stuck a single foot out to test it.

No creak. I crept cautiously down the series of steps and into a boiler room that hadn't yet been completed. Fiberglass hung from the ceiling and random pipes decorated the floor, but as soon as I made it to the door on the other side of the room, I heard two voices. As I peeked into the room, it was pristine and looked nearly finished, a complete contrast to the rest of the building. Several cubicle walls were obstructing my view of Sassia and the person she was speaking to. I immediately recognized Sassia's voice, but the other wasn't familiar at all. It was female and with her hard Middle Eastern accent, I could barely make out what she was saying.

Did something happen in the Middle East that brought this back on me?

I crept into the room and hid behind several of the cubicle panels in front of the doorway as I tried to hear what they were saying. I stopped when I heard the sound of heels walking across the floor, barely twenty feet in front of me. Still hiding behind panels, I crouched down on the floor and began to crawl closer when I finally began hearing what they were saying.

"You betrayed me, Valentine. The last time you betrayed me...with a *man* no less, we both know what happened to him. Men are supposed to be used as our instruments, not as equals. We use them and then they are useless and must be discarded. You make them equals and they take everything, like they took my family and your body!"

She walked around the room a few times, coming within a few feet of where I was hiding, before she stopped in front of Sassia and began speaking again.

"This time, you have insulted and disrespected me more than I could ever have imagined! You submit yourself to these...these men with your whore job, but I can forgive you for that—because I love you. Yet instead of just ending the treachery there, you do the unthinkable. You give up everything I taught you for a fucking... cop... whore!"

"I don't belong to you, Israel. Whatever I do with my life is up to me. I like men. We almost killed each other once already because of one! What the hell made you think I would ever want to have anything to do with you? You're just too damn pathetic to move on and find someone else."

The loudest slap I'd ever heard jarred me. It felt like it had happened right next to me even though I was sure they were still at least twenty feet away.

"I should've known that you were never going to be anything other than a whore! You were a whore when I found you and you whore now for a living! You undermine everything I taught you by screwing around with a cop whore!"

"She wasn't a whore," Sassia said defiantly.

"I don't care! She was a cop, Valentine! Did you think that this little story was going to have a happy ending? Did you think that you would have a *relationship* with a *cop*? How stupid can you be?" When Sassia didn't answer, I heard the Middle-Eastern woman's heels angrily smash against the floor as she headed toward Sassia. "Did she know who you really were before she died? Did you tell her that you were a killer—no different from the useless men I sent for her family?"

"I am different."

"You are no *different*, Valentine. When the contract became rich enough, you turned off your deluded moral compass and killed your so-called best friend. I knew it was only a matter of time before you did. When will you learn that you will never have friends and you will never find anyone who accepts you like me? In your heart you know that, but you just needed incentive to help remind you."

"I didn't kill her for the money. I shot her because she was already dying and as long as she was alive, her family wasn't safe. She asked me to do it because I had already told her what I did. She died knowing who I was. When you're dying in a ditch somewhere because someone better than you killed you, who will ever know that you existed? Your brothers are dead and you chase a woman who doesn't give a shit about you! Who will care when *you* die, Nava?"

The woman laughed, but a burning sensation in the pit of my stomach was growing.

Everything that had happened the last few weeks wasn't about me at all? It was something that Sassia...Valentine had brought to my front door?

I did everything I could to hold back the tears and the rage. Going in with my vision blurred and filled with fury was going to get me killed, but I didn't care anymore. I took several deep breaths and remained hidden.

"Your twisted sense of altruism has failed you, my Valentine." She walked away from Valentine and unzipped the body bag. "This is who you are! This is who you've always been! Ever since that night I saved you from Omar....the night you shot those men in cold blood, I saw the fire in your eye! You are a natural murderer—a killer! You're no different from me!"

"Those men deserved it! They raped me! They sodomized me! They took what they wanted and didn't give a damn about mercy! Those are the people I kill! I'm *nothing* like you! You destroyed her life for petty jealousy! None of this had anything to do with her yet you brought Charlie in as a pawn because you were too scared to face me yourself!"

"*You* brought her into this, not me!"

"Give me my goddamn money and get the fuck out of my way, Nava!"

"She was a whore!" The woman shouted so loudly that even I jumped back. "A whore who went back and forth between you and her husband-to-be and you allowed it! Have I not taught you better? Have I not taught you to respect yourself better than how you were brought up?" she asked indignantly.

"You don't fucking control me! I left St. Louis because you were no different than Omar! That's always been your problem. You think you own me, but you don't, dammit!" I heard Sassia cock her gun and I gritted my teeth. It wouldn't be long now.

"I *do* own you!" the other voice shouted. "You would be nothing without me! I saved your life and that means you owe me your fucking life!"

"I don't owe you shit! You weren't shit to me then and you're not shit to me now! Give me my fucking money and let me go!"

I heard the sound of heels walking quickly across the floor before the sound of a second loud slap echoed throughout the room. "Don't you ever talk to me like that again! I taught you better! You are lucky that I don't just kill you now and be done with you!"

I heard Valentine chuckle after the woman had slapped her, and wondered if she had gone completely crazy. Was she trying to get herself killed? It served her right if she was.

The woman fired off her weapon, a semi-automatic, and after the echo of gunfire died down, the room was almost silent with the exception of an electronic buzz.

"Put down your weapon, now!" It took several seconds before I heard the thud of a gun against the floor. "Still defiant. You know that I can kill you right now and no one would know. No one would ever care," she maliciously added. "You don't even exist, Valentine. This electromagnetic pulse bomb behind me would erase every indication I was here and all the police would be left with is your dead body. I could do that with just a flick of a button."

Valentine laughed again, but this time without as much condescension as before. "But you won't, Nava. If you do, every hitter this side of the Mississippi will be all over your ass. Where could you go, especially with CT tracking you down? Besides, you won't kill me. For some insane reason, you're still carrying a torch. You still want to fuck me."

This time Nava laughed. "You know, this would have been so much easier had she died in the car explosion. Her fiancé was just an unfortunate casualty, but you know the penalty for breaking the rules, Valentine. You should know them because at one time you lived by them...breathed them... loved them. When you fucked your whore, I could see you getting soft, so I had to do what I thought was necessary. You were going to bring us all down if you kept fucking her." She paused for a second before continuing. "Out of all the people to fuck, you chose a cop. Why? You knew that being with her had doomed her, yet you still carried on like no repercussions were coming. By protecting her, you had forgotten your loyalties and I could kill you without reprisal for that alone."

The room began to turn hazy and my blood began to boil all over again. As callously as someone would throw out a bag of trash, this woman I had never met had put a hit on me and my family. Thinking I was dead, she pissed over everything I had ever loved. *Yes, this woman will pay with her life...so will Valentine.* I knew it and there was no going back from here.

After some pecking at a keyboard, Valentine asked, "So, you finally sent the money?"

"I did get a little overzealous by shooting her a few more times, but I wasn't sure if I could trust the hitter. When I saw it was you, all was forgiven."

"Don't ever call me again, Nava. I don't want to see you or hear your voice. All this bullshit over petty jealousy."

"Not jealousy, but preservation! Have you forgotten the rules I taught you? I could not have my star pupil dating a cop! I did this for us! I did this so that you would understand how much I love you!"

"Did you hear me, Nava? I said don't ever contact me again. You're fucking sick and you need help."

Val began to walk away and I peeked around the corner just in time to see Nava rush Valentine. With her back turned, Nava tackled her to the ground and pointed a TAR directly at Valentine's head while grabbing a handful of her hair.

What is rule one, Valentine?" she asked, but when Sassia didn't answer, she softly pulled on the trigger. "I *will* kill you."

Pinned to the ground and wincing in pain, Valentine didn't see me. With Nava sitting on top of her, she didn't see me either and I slowly crept closer, staying behind the cubicle walls as I approached them.

Reciting rules like a child in school, Valentine did as Nava demanded. "No attachments—attachments make us weak and indecisive.

"You were weak and now that this cop is dead," she kicked the body bag, "you can again be strong! Rule two!" she shouted.

"Anonymity is the—key to success."

"Your anonymity was compromised the minute your military cop-friend entered your life. In doing so, you made her expendable. Three!"

"Defense is paramount to survival."

"Four!"

"Prey is predictable; learn them to easily kill them."

"Five!"

"Instinct trumps income."

"*The final rule!*"

"Always have an out!"

"And don't you ever forget any of those again!" As she stood up, she slammed Valentine's head against the floor. When Val lifted her head, a streak of blood was streaming down from her nose.

As I watched Valentine get on her knees and reach for her Ruger, I knew what she was about to do. She was about to kill the woman who had done this to me.

No fucking way. I'll kill you both if I have to, but this Nava-Israel bitch is fucking mine!

Kneeling in front of Nava as she smiled sadistically, I saw Nava cocking her TAR and all I could think about were my father and Steven. They had died for nothing more than simple jealousy. *Fucking jealous bitch!*

As the tears began to well in my eyes, I thought about letting her kill Sassia, or rather Valentine, before I killed her. This whole thing, everything that I'd been through wasn't because I had done anything wrong, but simply because I had known—almost loved—the woman everyone but me called Valentine. I grabbed both of my guns and made sure the both of them were ready to fire. If I was about to die, I would die like a soldier and I didn't care who I hit.

I quickly jumped up from behind the cubicle even though I was practically running around the corner, everything seemed to move in slow motion when I yelled, "*Police!*" and began to fire.

Sassia

"*Police!*"

Charlie suddenly rushed from around the corner, but Nava had already begun walking away from me. As Charlie began wildly firing, I noticed the deranged look on her face. She had heard everything. She knew that I was the cause of all of this—that I had brought this all to her doorstep.

I wanted to ask her for forgiveness, let her know how sorry I was for screwing up her life, but when one of her guns slowly began to aim at me, I knew she didn't want an apology, she wanted vengeance. As she fixed her aim on me, I quickly pulled my Micro from behind my back. We both fired off shots, and then a loud explosion came from behind me. I felt

Charlie's bullet sting my arm just as an invisible shock wave threw me across the room into complete darkness.

Nava had set off the EMP.

When I came to, the darkness was so absolute I couldn't even see my own hands. I had a massive headache and my arm was burning, but I was obviously still alive. If not, Hell had a long way to go before meeting expectations. Unsure how much time had passed, I pushed what felt like paneling off me and began to slide across the floor in the direction I hoped was the door. I didn't know how, but I'd held onto my Ruger, though I had lost the Micro.

"Damn!" I was about to stand up when a silenced gunshot brushed past my face and I quickly dropped to my belly. Focusing the Ruger on the area of the room where I suspected the shot had come from, I fired two silenced shots in return. Rolling over, I moved just in time for a volley to miss me, then listened as two more suppressed shots from across the room randomly aimed at each other.

Shit! We all had silencers.

I thought about firing in those directions, but after the last series of shots that just missed me, it seemed wise not to give up my position. As my eyes began to adjust, I inched across the floor, trying to make as little sound as possible while searching for the exit.

After finding a set of upright panels, I began moving slowly by them when one of them fell on top of me.

Pfft! Pfft! Pfft! Pfft!

Shots came from what seemed like every corner of the room. I stayed under the panel until the shooting stopped before I tried to move again. Without a chance in hell of seeing any of the shooters, I closed my eyes and instead focused on the sound of anyone breathing. I didn't hear a thing in the room except for the faint ticking of a clock.

No lights, but a ticking clock? A secondary bomb?

With my eyes closed, I remembered the EMP that Nava had sitting on the table next to the servers. I figured it was there to erase data, not thinking that it would be part of her rule six, but I was wrong. The ticking clock meant that whatever Nava had planned wasn't over yet.

I knew Nava, which meant there wasn't a lot of time before the clock stopped ticking and we'd all be dead.

Maybe if I...

I shot once into the darkness at the position I'd last heard shots coming from, while holding onto the paneling as a shield. I saw a small muzzle flash about thirty feet in front of me and aimed a little lower.

"Goddammit!" Charlie screamed and suddenly a flurry of shots came from ten feet to my right. *Nava.*

I shot twice and though the flurry of shots stopped, nothing at all was said.

I sucked in as little air as I could so that I could listen for anyone moving. Then out of nowhere, Nava began to speak as if she were out of breath.

"I take it... by the silence... that we're all out of ammo." Charlie shot in the direction of the voice and Nava shot back once. "I guess I...was...wrong, but...it doesn't matter now. A rib...punctured...my lung in the...explosion. Shot twice...in the side..."

"You deserve to choke on your own blood. Karma is a fucking bitch, ain't it?" Charlie shouted, not a shred of mercy in her voice.

"You didn't...you didn't kill her after all..."

"No. Why the hell is the clock ticking, Nava?" I asked and a flurry of bullets came from Charlie's direction.

"What the fuck, Charlie? What are you doing?"

When she didn't respond, I knew that it wasn't by accident.

"Rule...rule 6, Val. Building rigged to explode. No evidence...no evidence left behind." I could hear the wheezing in Nava's voice, she *was* choking on her own blood. I didn't care. Sending several shots in her direction, I heard her cry aloud as another one of my bullets hit her.

"Fuck...you...Val! We'll...all...die here together! The EMP...was just the first. The bomb in...the building...goes off...fifteen...minutes...after...EMP. Gotta...love...rule six."

For almost a minute, not another shot was heard throughout the room, but as Nava's wheezing grew worse, I knew her death was inevitable. That wasn't what worried me. For the whole time, I hadn't heard Charlie and I was slowly crawling around the room trying to find my way out of this deathtrap.

Then I heard Nava scream.

"Uh...uh...uh..." The sounds of her being stabbed to death were unmistakable and it was all happening barely ten feet from me. I slowly scooted away and took aim, but as I shot into the dark, the stabbing continued.

I slid further away, hoping that Charlie stayed focused on Nava, but the stabbing stopped and Nava's cries along with it.

It was just me and Charlie. I knew that it'd happen, just not like this. *How sadistically poetic*, I thought.

"Chuck, there's a bomb in here. I want us to walk out alive, but I swear to God I'll kill you if I have to." When she still didn't respond, I backtracked where I'd come from, knowing she would follow my voice. When I didn't hear anyone moving, I spoke again, this time from the other side of the room. "Say something, goddamit!"

Charlie ignored my pleas. I quickly moved from under the panels and quietly began working my way toward Nava. If anyone was heading in the direction out of here, it was going to be her. With no time to be discrete, I sat on all fours as I began making my way toward where I'd last heard Nava being stabbed to death and drowning on her own blood.

I suddenly found myself in a pool of what I suspected was blood. I tried to take my time and move through it, unsure whether it was Sheryl's or Nava's, but as I bumped into a body, I froze. I slid closer to the body and felt its warmth. It was Nava. My ex-lover and mentor. My Angel of Vengeance. I felt along the contours of her face for the last time, my fingers becoming saturated in her blood. I held my breath, feeling for a pulse to confirm the inevitable. The gaping holes in her flesh could only mean one thing: Charlie had gone mad with the assassin's knife, literally ripping her apart.

I stood up and had barely taken a step when Charlie shot at me, hitting me in my shoulder and knocking me back onto the floor. As I fell, I rolled away.

"What the fuck is wrong with you, Charlie?" I asked, nursing the same arm I was hit in earlier. "If we don't get out of here, we're both fucking dead! I know Nava! She wasn't kidding about another bomb."

She answered with a flurry of semi-automatic shots to where I'd just been. She'd found the TAR. I wanted to talk some sense into her, but there wasn't any time left. I rolled over on the floor, wincing as I bumped into one of the room's corners with the shoulder she'd shot.

I fired several Ruger shots toward Charlie's last position, but when she fired from almost next to me, I ducked and without realizing it right away, I landed on what felt like my Micro Eagle.

'Bout time I finally got some fucking luck.

I crept, inching against the wall, for what seemed like an eternity as I thought about the ticking bomb and how much time we had left. The clock resonated in my ears almost as loudly as my own heartbeat. The bullet in my arm burned more intensely than the flesh wound I'd received earlier, and I was no doubt bleeding from both.

Where the fuck was she?

I continued to slide against the wall until I reached a doorway. Since I had only seen one doorway when I entered, I knew this was the way out. I slid against the doorjamb, but the door was closed.

Fuck!

As soon as I opened the door, I knew that Charlie would know where I was, but I didn't care. A shot in the back was better than being blown to shit any day. I grabbed the door handle, and a rash of bullets flew through the composite wood door, peppering me with splinters.

There was no mistaking where Charlie was now so I fired several Ruger shots into the direction of the TAR.

The loud thud on the floor where Charlie dropped her gun was barely five feet away. Not hearing her move, I fired several Micro shots in the direction of the thud before turning and opening the door. I quickly opened the door and a pain I'd never felt before pierced my back. Charlie had stabbed me.

I'd stepped right into her trap...and she'd stepped right into mine. Some pair we were.

Charlie

The two bullets, one in my thigh, the other piercing my abdomen, hurt like hell, but I'd managed to hold onto my guns. I'd lost most of my clips in the EMP explosion, but now that I had a chance for vengeance, I wasn't about to give that up—even if it meant I had to die, too.

My gloves were covered in Nava's blood from what I'd done to her. With every piercing of her flesh, her body screamed for more and I listened to it. I stabbed her for Steven, for my father, and for myself. The pain from where her assassin had stabbed me burned like a pain I'd never felt before, but I still continued pushing the blade into her—allowing her last few moments on Earth to be filled with the same agony I felt. I knew Valentine was shooting at me, but I didn't care. I needed to do this almost as much as it needed to be done.

Now, it's her turn.

I listened as Valentine made her way toward the door, the one I'd already found and closed. I entertained the thought of her really being worried about me, but I knew better. She was the one who'd done this to me and fucked up my life. She was the reason Steven had been blown to shit, she was the reason my father had choked on his own blood, and she would be the person who paid for both their lives. With Nava's admission of a bomb and the knife I'd taken from my father's killer, it seemed like poetic justice. It had to be, because it couldn't have been planned more perfectly.

I heard Valentine fumbling over the dividers and followed her in her journey across the room. She tried to backtrack several times, telling me about the bomb that Nava had placed, but none of that mattered now. It was just us. She'd gotten lucky a few times and hot-shot me, but I was alive, which meant that I was destined to live.

It wasn't long before I could almost feel Valentine's heated breath just under me, begging me for forgiveness, but there wasn't any to be found. After missing her so many times with that piece of shit semi-automatic, I quickly took the knife out and stabbed her wherever it would go.

I got her in her back!

As soon as she fell over, she rolled and kicked me in the abdomen where I was already bleeding like a stuck pig. Unprepared, I wretched and let go of the knife.

"Who did you think you were fucking with, Charlie?" she whispered.

A bright flash of pain alerted me that she'd kicked me in the face. *She knew where I was the whole time? No, that was a lucky kick.*

I began to swing wildly, hoping I'd catch her, but a punch across my left cheek sent me to the ground. As soon as I was on the ground, Valentine mounted me and assaulted me with a series of punches.

Left, right, right, right, right...

I blocked the next right and punched her in the throat. With her slightly stunned, I punched her in her abdomen and quickly rolled on top of her. Without any weapons, I elbowed her in the chest and went to work on her head. I felt my fists connect against the side of her head as I threw wild punches.

More ferociously then I'd ever thrown punches before in my life, I swung at Valentine. Putting her forearms up, she blocked a few, but she couldn't stop them all.

"I'm...going...to...fucking...kill...you!" With every wild punch, I told her about her predetermined death. I was finally breaking her guard when from out of nowhere, a knife pierced my side and my body suddenly froze. I loudly exhaled several times, trying to get my body to move, but I couldn't. I reached for Valentine, trying to grab her neck but my fingers began to lose feeling and I was slowly falling to the side.

"Not when I'm so close," I whispered. I reached out one more time, but the hardest punch I'd ever felt came across my face. I felt my lip crack and begin to bleed even before I hit the floor.

"Fuck you, Chuck," she said maliciously as she retook control.

For what seemed like an eternity, Valentine worked me over and there wasn't a damn thing I could do about it. My nose was already broken from what my father's assassin had done and I could feel my jaw giving way. Soon my already puffy eyes were so swollen that I couldn't see the slight silhouette of Valentine's punches coming anymore.

So this was how I was going to die? So close to vengeance? A bright light appeared in the darkness and suddenly it was gone.

"What happened?" I asked when suddenly I felt a bullet penetrating my left shoulder, then grazing my right.

"I'm doing whatever it takes."

"I thought you were my friend." I said weakly.

"You thought wrong, Chuck. Trying to kill me negated whatever you *thought* we were."

I didn't hear the gun go off, but I did feel the third and fourth bullets rip through my abdomen. The pain was excruciating, but only for a moment as the darkness took over. Trembling from pain and probably bleeding to death, I just wanted one last ounce of energy to wrap my hands around the neck of that damned *Valentine.*

Chapter 17: See you...later

"And on this day, we celebrate a hero. A hero who put her life on the line from day one. From foiling bank robbers, to bringing down international hitmen, our very own Super Cop has gone above and beyond in the line of duty. So today, we award Officer Charlie Briggs, the Medal of Valor—our highest honor."

A thunderous swell of applause greeted me as I appeared from behind the curtain. I'd just gotten in from Philly, dealing with the fallout of what had happened to my father. No one knew the whole story and I wasn't about to tell them either, but because of my role in my father's death, my eldest brother, Michael, still refused to talk to me. Derek, my younger brother, was happy I was still alive, especially with all that had happened. He even offered to come live with me in Houston, but I couldn't let him do that. At least not right now.

I didn't know how I'd survived all the bullets, knives and explosions, but what hurt the most was that I wasn't able to attend my father's funeral. After two months of intensive physical therapy, I went home to visit his grave and prayed that he forgave me...for not saving him and for the things I'd done in his and Steven's names.

I wheeled myself across the stage and my chief smiled like he'd just hit the lottery. Both he and the mayor shook my hand, and then stood next to me for photo ops before handing me my framed medal. If only they knew. I was ready to kill and die that day, but as it happened, I was given another chance.

As the applause waned, they handed me a microphone, but as I declined to speak, the sea of blue in front of me all began to chant, "Speech!"

Laughing, I took the microphone to another wondrous round of applause. This time, when the clapping finally died down, I spoke, even though the wounds in my belly, side, and arm still screamed with the effort.

"Being an officer of the law isn't just what we do, it's who we are. Part of the job requires sacrifice, but what I did is not any different from what any one of you heroes would have done in the same shoes. I guess this award is really for all you guys who do exactly what's required because you get no recognition. Never forget that law begins and ends with us. This is for you, Dad. I love you and miss you."'

Tears began to fall as Carolyn walked on stage and wheeled me off. For several minutes, I heard chants of "Briggs," but after shaking so many hands before I'd even gotten the award, I was dead tired and ready to go back to the hospital for another dose of morphine.

"Carolyn, you don't have to push me. I can walk."

"The physical therapist said that you shouldn't strain yourself," she replied. “You almost died, Charlie.”

“You keep reminding me of that, but I didn’t. I’m still here so I guess that means I have things left to do.”

“Call it what you want, Snowflake,” she said in her admonishing tone, “but you won’t be taking care of anything while I’m around.”

"He also said for you not to baby me."

For the last three months, I'd been recovering and ever since I'd left the hospital a month ago to go back home, Carolyn called almost every day to remind me of what I needed and to reiterate her offer for me to move in with her. Because she had been there when they brought me in and spent almost all of her free time by my bed, I felt like it was the least I could do. Besides, after everything that had gone down, I didn't want to live alone right away anyhow.

She was wheeling me to my car when my cell phone rang. After looking at the phone's screen, I knew the number from somewhere, but I couldn't remember from where.

"Hello?"

"That was a beautiful ceremony. It was so touching that it almost made me wish that I was up there on stage with you."

I knew that the number was familiar. It was the phone Sassia had given to me and subsequently stolen from me on the night...

I raised my hand, letting Carolyn know that I wanted to stop.

"Hey, Carolyn, I need to take this." She frowned, but understood what I meant. She slowly walked into the crowd of officers, turning around a few times to make sure that I didn't sneak away. When she was finally out of sight, I returned the phone to my ear.

"You thought you killed me, but I wasn't quite ready to die yet," I said, speaking to a ghost.

"You're just a little tougher than I thought. After all that crying you did, I figured you to be soft." She paused briefly before continuing. " I wish things hadn't ended the way they did. You would've made a great sidekick."

"A sidekick? Right. Why would I want to be anywhere near you? Everything that happened you brought on yourself. Then to make matters worse, you brought it on me and my family! You wish things were different, but it's because of you that I'm in this goddamn wheelchair in the first place!"

"Better than a body bag, right?"

"You have some fucking nerve calling me Sas—Valentine, " I whispered into the phone. The last thing I needed was anyone knowing who I was talking to, especially after the story that I'd concocted that had me taking out Nava Aliza Stahl, a professional assassin and suspected terrorist, alone.

"So, is that how you're going to talk to the person that saved your life?"

"Person? You're a ghost. You don't even exist. And saved *me*?" I asked incredulously. "It was because of you that I was in this shit in the first place! If it weren't for you, Steven and I would be married and enjoying our lives together! My father would still be alive instead of in a coffin! How exactly did you save me?"

"You're so damn melodramatic. You don't remember the secondary explosion because you were dying when I dragged you out the building. Shit, I just made it out when the whole fucking building imploded. It was me who called the cops. I called the paramedics. I'm the person who kept you alive until they came."

"No thanks to you for that one, too! You shot me a bunch of fucking times, stabbed me, and then left me for dead! How the hell is that saving me?"

"Can't you just be glad you're alive?"

"You called for a goddamn 'thank you'? If that's what you wanted to say, you just wasted your time. As soon as I'm able to get up and walk around, I'm going to be all over you like flies on hot shit. Believe that."

"I don't think you've ever threatened before. I like it!" She said enthusiastically. "Anyway, I didn't call for that, Chuck. I wanted to make peace that night, but you were so wrapped up in your holy crusade against me that you gave me no choice. You called Carolyn and asked her to bring in the police. You stabbed Nava to death and then you came after me! Even through all that, I still rescued you from the imploding building? Who do you think can tell the police the real story about why you don't deserve that medal? Not to mention that non-disclosure agreement you signed with Hoops. To my knowledge, pre-meditated murder is still punishable by the electric chair in Texas—even for cops."

I wheeled down the ramp to a backstage holding area and out of the line of prying ears. "You signed it too. If you do that, we're both screwed."

"Do I look stupid? No, Charlie, it was just you. I'm a professional hitter—why do I need to sign some shit like that?"

She was right and had played me the whole time. I'd let my heart and my clit rule my brain for too long. I would've laughed at how stupid I'd been if I weren't so pissed. "So what, you rescued me. It still doesn't make up for what you took from me! It was because of you that both Steven and my father are dead."

"So you keep saying. Why haven't you told your buddies about me? Why the secrecy? Are you going to try again to kill me, Chuck?"

"All I'll say is watch your back, Valentine. If it comes down to us again, I guarantee you won't be walking away—at least not without handcuffs. Don't think I'm not already on it. I've found two of your shell businesses from the apartments you rented: Kelli R. Ltd and Rudy Moure Inc. Cute, Valentine, real fucking cute."

"Whatever do you mean?" she asked facetiously.

"You know what the hell I'm talking about, Killer Ltd and Murder You Inc. You just made anagrams for your shell corporations." She laughed and I wheeled myself back onstage to see if I could find her, but all I saw was a crowd of blue; officers laughing, hugging, and talking. I slid back behind the curtain because if I knew Valentine, she'd already come and gone and finding her in the crowd would have been impossible. As I stood up and paced around, unable to sit still any longer, I slowly swept the crowd. Passing officers smiled, waved, and congratulated me as I did so, but I continued speaking. "If you really wanted me dead, then you would've shot me three times in the heart, once in the head. That is your signature, right? For a woman with the name Valentine, it's not that original. Even your name, Sassia Santinos, is an anagram and I figured that one out, too."

"Well aren't you the smart one. Smart and pretty; seems like there's a lot of that going around."

"So what do I call you? Valentine? Sassia Santinos? Or..."

"You should really stop walking around. You know better. The doctor said for you to take it easy."

"So you *are* here."

"I can neither confirm nor deny that information."

I stopped and sat down in an empty folding chair. My body was still weak from all the physical therapy I'd had. "Why don't you stop playing games and show yourself. We can end this right now."

"Know this, Charlie. I have eyes everywhere. Besides, you're still on the sidelines and it wouldn't be nearly as satisfying if I didn't get you at your best."

"Are you still going by the name Sassia Santinos?"

"Of course not. I can't make it that easy for you."

"With a name like Sassia Santinos, you were telling me who you were all along...*Sassia.* Your real identity was there the whole time and I didn't see it. I guess I didn't want to. And to think I was ready to love you at one time."

"You're too sentimental, Chuck. It was... what it was. I told you that already. We were friends and we fucked. There was nothing more to it than that."

"Look, this is just us girls talking. Why don't you try telling me the truth at least once? I know you have that much of a conscience or you wouldn't have saved me, if you actually did."

She laughed. "Oh, Chuckie. The truth was that I'd wanted to get away from this life for some time and I figured if I ever did, it'd be for someone like you. I'd settle down, get a regular job, go on a strictly pussy diet, but I guess that isn't possible anymore. Now, I have someone to find. When I find the man who helped make me the woman I am, I'll be coming for you next. Get well, I'll be seeing you soon."

"I *will* find you, Valentine. Trust me on that."

"Charlie," she said solemnly, "if you come after me again, all bets are off. You will die and this time, I'll make sure the job is done right."

"Is that a threat?" I stopped in front of the double doors leading outside.

"It's a certainty."

I exhaled, knowing that I needed to choose my next few words wisely. "You know where to find me. Try and stop me from finding you."

"It's your move."

Before she hung up, I could hear her speaking with a man whose voice I recognized, and I had no doubt it was done for my benefit.

"I'm so glad we've finally met. I didn't think you were ever going to keep up your end of the bargain."

"I'm a woman of my word, but if you want to screw, you know my price."

"Yeah, yeah, death and gloom, but I'll gladly pay it. Shit, ten times over, and maybe some family members. I still get to smell it too, right?"

She laughed. "So what do I call you when you're not working?" she asked.

"Call me CT. I like it when you say it. Add two letters in between and you spell my favorite body part, rhymes with shit and hit." He laughed. "Now, what do I call you these days?"

"You already know my name, CT. It's Valentine."

Then the line went dead.

A Word from the Author: D.V.Hent

Hello,

For all of you who read the first book, I want to guarantee you that this is also not a B.O.A.T.S book. I've heard so many people say that my first book read like a memoir that I want to assure you that my stories are works of fiction! For those of you who haven't read the blog on naughtyinkpress.com, I'm basically saying that this novel isn't based on a true story—so don't ask!

If you're reading this, then it means you've finished Valentine and I am currently awaiting your review. If you feel a need to tell me how great my book was, then thanks, I am *greatly* appreciative. With this being only my second book, though, I know there are areas where I can grow and become as good as the greats, so I typically prefer brutal honesty than a pat on the back.

Don't get me wrong, most everyone likes to be bathed in admiration, but I don't ever want to settle and give you a product unworthy of the best possible work I can do. Sometimes, I even go above and beyond to make things harder on myself because writing seems to come so naturally. To me, it's so much fun that I figure that it couldn't possibly be this easy to craft a good book and that's where you come in. Your purchase, your praise and your promotion of what I do not only humbles me, but invigorates me to continue writing. So in essence, I don't write for profit, I write because you all motivate me to.

Because I don't want this to be a drawn out love letter, I'll keep this brief. It was Beverly Sills who said: **You may be disappointed if you fail, but you are**

doomed if you don't try. And it was EJD who got me into writing by reminding me that even though our time on Earth is limited, the stories we tell are eternal. This particular story, *Valentine*, was probably one of the most rewarding experiences I've ever had. Had I not written this book, I would've been heartbroken if someone else had written it down and prospered from it. It was so much fun that I even left a few bread crumbs throughout the book so you might understand how I enjoy brain teasers: Kelli R. (killer) and Rudy Moure (murder you). Also the true meaning of Sassia Santinos is in here as well and if you haven't gotten it yet, try taking the first letter from each chapter as a way to help. See, I told you writing is fun.

~***D.V. Hent***

Reviews for If You Don't Tell

How far would you go to find that elusive person for your fantasy? How close?

The debut erotic novel from D.V. Hent is nothing less than an amazing ride through the lives of three individuals. Set in Houston, TX, the characters and their antics will have you smiling, laughing and gasping at their situations concerning life, friendships and taboo revelations about African American sexuality.

... Raw and real, ***If You Don't Tell*** *is a bold new addition to the world of erotic fiction. An eye-opening read from a fresh new literary voice on the rise." – Apex Reviews*

"Stay tuned; this is a hot, steamy read that is full of surprises. I recommend ***If You Don't Tell*** *to readers of all genres."*
-APOOO Book Reviews

LaVergne, TN USA
25 September 2010
198441LV00002B/5/P

9 780984 250813